STARBREED

The Biography of Aquina

Samantha Askeborn

Order this book online at www.trafford.com
or email orders@trafford.com

Most Trafford titles are also available at major online book retailers.

Printed in the United States of America.

ISBN: 978-1-4669-7269-8 (sc)
ISBN: 978-1-4669-7268-1 (e)

Trafford rev. 05/16/2013

www.trafford.com

North America & international
toll-free: 1 888 232 4444 (USA & Canada)
phone: 250 383 6864 • fax: 812 355 4082

INT.

. . . . a being to another being, a specie to another specie, must be accepted. Too deny the alliance is to invite negativity. Refusing disturbs a delicate balance as old as time itself. Same members of a specie possess the strengths of union and alliance to a higher degree than others.

There are those who say fate is responsible for the mysteries of the affinity, and some say it is God. But who is to say what is . . . . and what isn't. And who is to say . . . . they are not one in the same.

Whatever the specie and regardless of star system, strata of evolution and intelligence . . . . the affinity remains fluid and alive.

And perhaps once during an entire age will come one without peer, elevated . . . . abilities enriched in the manner . . . . a student of the mysteries.

CHAP. 1

Arbus Ceti . . . a fringe system on the tucon frontier . . . the empire had all but forgotten, being of little strategic worth. From "Ceti" one usually went into the empire, the hub of which was over seventy parsecs, or out to the spiral rim; a desolate unexplored region offering meager worth to an organized civilization.

Usually only the lone or rogue trader looking for gems came to the few surviving outposts such as Ceti-2; more than not frequented by desperate people, outlaws, raiders, barbarians and other more base primitives. Essentially a place no-one would normally visit by choice. The closest trading area with any burgeoning civilization exceeded a parsec in distance, heading into the empire.

Ceti-2 is not a large planet nor hospitable, though home to a nomadic fragmented people. Harassed and subjugated by raiders, they on occasion ambushed their foe; but, at best the Ceti had only brief periods of uneasy peace.

A semi arid planet displaying few places with meager pools/ponds of precious water and stunted vegetation. Most buildings are of light brown with blue streaks, or an off rust color, consisting of a crude but substantial adobe material smoothly faced. Those with scarce wood usually used as struts for doors, are the homes of established miners. Dwellings ideally suited against the abundant sand storms, violent winds, to much sun, and a scarity of rain. Frequented by hellish storms being the norm rather than the unusual, made for a truly hellish place.

Ceti are a people uniquely suited to their planet, with thick crusty outer layering, and rather large feet, as none were over five feet in height. They are bi-ped with two arms, reaching to within inches from their knees (or 18 inches from the ground), and hands incorporating four digits equipped with short claw-like nails. Facial features are even, perhaps impish as the head is normal and proportional to the body. But the eyes are small reddish brown or black. The ears extended just slightly over the top of the head with the customary contour on the back side, except in addition there is another "flap" in front, which could and often did close over the ear at will. An excellent natural method for preventing injury during any of the sometimes violent sand storms.

The more "settled" of the people are amost all miners. Adept at digging, a select few cultivated the lapidary art of cutting and polishing the planet's only natural resource other than heat, precious and semi-precious stones. Settlements of any size where trading was conducted, had its collection of crude rudiment oblong buildings and "field", whereupon adventurous traders could land and conduct business.

Ceti's because of constantly paying tribute, are perpetually poor leading to gross deficiencies, and no organized spaceport. In existence . . . only occasionally an old rag-tag field leading to alleyways and streets covered with an inch or more of fine granular sand. The crude adobe structures, octagon in shape, housed no regular records, thereby making futile any inquiry as to who came and went, and with what. Only some of the more established miners kept a few "notes", and only for controlling prices; and depending on the trader involved varied quotes would be used. This manipulation of price and the quality of stones offered, was the only edge or method of control they could exert. Raider groups had tried but found it unusally difficult to break this monopolistic practice of the ceti's.

Although clannish by nature, the ceti's are astute traders, excellent gem and exotic metalsmiths, knowing full well the value of their polished gems and rough stones. These stones are in-turn either sold outright or used to barter/trade for other goods on some other culture outpost or trading post.

CHAP. 2

Their approach was equatorial as Ceti-2 filled the screen, with sensors and scanners on maximum . . . . constantly alert. Within visual distance they confirmed scanner report of one small ship on the makeshift field, situated close to the settlement. As the trader, owned by the Tywr noble family, began settling rolling clouds of sand and dirt billowed up caught by winds accelerated by an approaching sand storm. Senior and owner of the modest ship, Roak secured ship's power and reduced to minimum settings all main systems; but kept auxiliaries on full power, necessary precautions considering the locale. He viewed this as prudent and not unreasonable precautions in an area frequented by raiders and pirates.

While busy with the ship Roak dutifully reminded Aor'y about the quickly approaching sand storm. She nodded and began taking out hoods, full shields and some other articles, all necessary items to combat the insidious sand. As she was separating the items, "is it your wish to trade only or buy?" "Possibly both Aor'y. I'll know better after they present what it is they wish to exchange. Primarily I think we should look for the pale yellow or red stones." "Okay, but, I think the green are much prettier and sell better." Aor'y remarked thoughtfully.

Standing just beyond the closed air lock inner door, Aor'y began putting on the hood and face plate; but stopped when Roak spoke. "Aor'y, watch yourself. While in this settlement we will be in the open and vulnerable. We cannot risk being surprised by raiders." Roak remarked, tired and rubbing his thick 17 inch neck.

Only a short stout neck, Roak is quite well proportioned for his average height of six feet eight inches. Barrel chested with a thick waist supported by two muscular legs, serviced two well formed arms and hands each with five digits. From the top of the large high forehead ran the spine ridge comb. It began rather small on the otherwise symmetrical head, with its well groomed crop of black hair, and became more pronounced as it came down lower. In the vicinity of the shoulders, this ridge gained in height until reaching its maximum of 2 to 2.5 inches along mid back. From that point it decreased again until hardly noticeable at the base of the spine. On some tucanan males the ridge was not only higher, but more pronounced, but covered with fine hair along the top. It is also a sensitive area; in that, it would move as a result of high or rampant emotion.

His bearing is not only that of an aristocrat, but, as Aor'y noticed on many occasions, also that of a military officer. It showed in Roak's speech, sometimes the way he moved, mannerisms, and reactions to abnormal situations. A kind of precise correctness about him . . . a neatness not only on the personal side, but actions as well. Only his seeming insatiable lust for adventure worried her, as it did now.

In keeping with normal physical differences of gender, Aor'y's spine ridge is smaller and more delicate in appearance than Roak's. Actually an inch and-a-half smaller, but . . . the comb is as fine as spun silk, and one of her primary errogenous zones. At five feet 8 inches . . . . 2 inches below the average for tucanan women, it is the only area in which her physical attributes might be considered flawed. And this is be her own admission, for she is sensitive about her height. An issue Roak found amusing. He felt she was anything but flawed, stressing points such as the delicate nose, ears, the ample rust colored hair highlighted with black tendrils; and would go on at length about the generous mouth with perfect lips. Too emphasis, Roak would often with an expression of total seriousness, delicately brush her lips with his own . . . and slowly with great care, move with a slow senuous touching first one lip, then both.

Once past that point, Roak began referring to the chin, neck, and shoulders. Her skin a medium tan is in contrast to the male's more burnished color with no other body hair. Roak often pointed to the well proportioned figure whenever she slipped into her mood. And Aor'y would often smirk and point out how males in general were gifted in "areas of substantial erotic interest to women." Which was true enough.

For instance, all tucanan males have inordinantly long tongues, and correspondingly large male organ. Roak however could touch the bridge of his nose with tongue fully extended; and his maleness is fairly prodigious in keeping with normal males. It on more than one occasion caused him some indelicate moments.

Each finished donning their hood and face plate, gloves, and with a nod Roak pushed the exterior door release. Confronted by swirls of dust and sand, he and Aor'y quickly stepped onto the ramp keying the door secure behind him. Both walked warily into the settlement, ruts and gouges in the street from heavy wagons and wind-blown sand retarded their progress to little more than a snail's pace. While in the street each kept a hand close to their side-arms, and caught themselves almost constantly looking sideways, and behind them . . . . alert for possible ambush.

"Psssst . . . here, this oasis. As arranged our contact will meet us here." Roak said in a low voice as he pulled on Aor'y's sleeve. With a side long glance in both directions, especially from whence they came, he entered followed by his attractive partner. Odors of liquor, adobe, unwashed bodies and uneaten food assailed their noses. Roak was better prepared than Aor'y who felt her stomach lurch. With left hand over her nose, she still coughed trying hard not to cause undo attention. Roak closed his nose using only his mouth to breathe and still found it difficult.

While walking to a table, disturbing the ever present dusting of sand on the floor, Roak attempted too nonchalantly look around, but stopped when he bumped into a table. The light was poor and dingy, many seated at the bar looked up and grumbled, annoyed shaken from their drug or liquor induced stupors. Seated, he signaled their order, Roak appeared to rest and relax, Aor'y followed his lead, but is uneasy . . . . feeling the short hairs standing on the small ridge of her neck. The oasis was not the name of the place, but an indication of its type of business. And by the countenance of the clientele, Roak knew his suspicions were well founded. It is precisely these situations . . . . he sat with his back to the gritty wall, right hand resting on his blaster, and ate-n-drank with his left.

A native studied them carefully from several tables away, herself wary and suspicious. Purchasing a disgusting local liquor, she gradually moved across the dim smoke filled room toward them, introduced herself and sat in the one vacant chair. In low muted tones, speaking imperialese, they discussed the types of stones, and W'er told what the ceti miner wanted for an outright sale or trade. The price was high, Roak could meet it, but meant not being able to make any other purchase. After some moments he assented, and the ceti contact motioned for them to follow. Slowly, and what Roak hoped would be taken for nonchalance, they exited the oasis and began walking leaning slightly forward against the wind.

The storm grew steadily worse, swirling sand around them until they could barely see their guide. It not only obscured vision but bit and scratched exposed skin, getting under the face plates, scarves into the hair especially worrysome to Aor'y because of her long tresses. Both started cursing the sand, but neither could be heard above the relentless howl of the wind.

Progress was slow, agonizingly slow until the diminutive ceti turned and was bumped into by the two traders. Roak caught their guide before she fell and barely saw the object pointed too by the little ceti. Side stepping over several ruts, they quickly covered the few intervening paces . . . stopping before a stout looking door. Turning the diminutive ceti motioned for them to enter . . . expressing the urgency to get off the street. Roak smiled under his face plate, pulled his blaster pushing it into about mid back of the short guide. He motioned for their trembling guide to enter first. The dwelling was not large, Roak estimated eight to eight and-a-half yards square divided by half walls and curtains. Pleasantly surprised at the lack of odors, such as they encountered at the oasis; in fact only a bare hint of the normal ceti odor lingered intermingled with fragrant oils. He and Aor'y enjoyed the fresh wood scent as they shook off loose sand following the example of their guide.

Two cetis inside, one mid-age female and one equally old male jumped up startled at sight of the blaster held so menacingly as if they would be reduced to atoms any second. The male squeaked, "is this the way honorable traders deal?" "No old one, but we do not intend to be ambushed either." The ceti nodded, "caution is admirable, but my self needs not this excitement."

"We came here to deal old one." Roak said. "Yes, yes too bargain that is why I live still. Yes, yes, bargain we shall." Said the old ceti happily. Still smiling the mid aged male added two stools to the well worn table. They seated themselves as the old woman brought what Roak swore was a full liter bottle and several crude mugs. Smiling broadly and with much ceremony the old man poured a liberal amount in each mug. Lifting his mug the old one saluted Roak bowed to Aor'y and drank. As custom, Roak went to drink when his nose easily detected the familiar aroma of hard beitra. "Beitra?" Roak remarked. "Only Roak such as tucon noble." "Thank you old one," and drank, savoring the liquor even though it bit savagely as it cascaded down his throat. Aor'y looked questioningly at the ceti.

"Raiders killed, beaten many by Roak . . . . yes, yes . . . . killed many, saved cetis much," laughed the old man. Within seconds of excusing himself the ceti returned with a palm size bag. Afterwards the bargaining began in ernest. Hour after hour, back and forth they haggled. "Alright old one, I will pay your price." Roak sighed. Just as Roak began sealing the bag . . . . "for Roak, friend of ceti." The old one held out to Roak an index fingernail size jewel exquisitely cut and polished. Its fire red brilliance, like a small star casting its beauty . . . . adding color to the light given off by the lamp above, and to one side of the table.

Roak silently clasped left forearm with the ceti . . . . a gesture-salute among solemn friends, comrade-at-arms. With the exchange consummated, the traders bid goodby to the ceti family preparing to depart with a considerable worth in stones.

Excercising caution, Roak opened the door just enough to see out, but this proved futile. Even with his goggles under the face plate the storm and wind blown sand proved too much. Opening the door, leaning half in and half out, Roak peered around the corner and up the street; but still wasn't able to detect anything out of the ordinary. He motioned to Aor'y, a salute to the cetis, and they are out the door. Stepping into the street each had a hand close to their sidearm. While trying to sidestep the worst swirls of sand, they, are watchful for spies and attack. The spies were usually members of or paid informants hired by raiders. The very fact their return to the ship was uneventful only made Roak more uneasy.

A spirited walk up the inclined ramp, keyed the outer airlock door, and then quickly inside. He and Aor'y leaned against cold bulkheads, and relaxed for a moment looking at each other. With a smile of relief each began undressing in an attempt to discharge by blower and suction as much of the sand as possible. Each stripped completely, and put on a clean one-piece coverall obtained from a recessed locker. Only then did Roak key the inner door so both could enter the ship. But

Roak had that "prickly feeling," and knew an attack would come. He didn't know from where or when, and it knawed at him. With the ship's main systems on maximum, sensors and scanners on full . . . . the small ship lifted off.

Organized raiders were usually few, operating with one sometimes two small heavily armed vessels. Roak knew if a fight ensued they would have trouble. "Aach!" He exclaimed, and said more or less to himself . . . . "If only one ship attacked . . . (loud sigh) the much needed repairs were put off once to often.

Problem . . . . their one and only set of guns was not reliable all the time. Roak and his attractive partner arced away from Ceti-2, and set course for a neighboring system one and-a-half parsec away. Afterwards he took the precaution of hiding the stones . . . in a secret hideaway located deep in the bowels of the ship. Without them, the stones would always remain safe. It was the only comforting thought he had. "Keep scanning Aor'y (contraction for Aor'tiaws), I feel them." Roak said, rubbing the back of his neck. "They are there waiting for us." He muttered.

Feeling nervous and with an edge to his voice, he decided to warm up their one set of guns. "Aor'y, I'll be aft warming the gun." "Okay partner," replied Aor'y, tight lipped. Roak put his left hand on her shoulder and gently squeezed then turned walking quickly aft.

While she plotted their position for a quick change in course . . . . attack came from underneath. The raider was obviously familiar wih the type of ship they attacked, for they did so away from the only gun position, and hit fast and hard.

As Aor'y manuevered the ship, Roak operated the gun with mixed success. She valiantly tried to maneuver so as to keep their gun on the incoming raider; but was not successful enough to avoid being hit. Her first penalty struck them just behind Roak's seat almost causing him to loose control of the gun. However, Roak did succeed in scoring two hits; but, it didn't stop the raider from delivering a crippling blow to the small trader.

Listing badly, sparks flying, and burned debris everywhere, Aor'y handled it as best as was possible. Roak stayed by the gun expecting the raider to come in for the kill. Almost as if by cue their attacker angled toward them slowly, itself badly damaged. Roak waited, then suddenly firing a rapid burst in a tight pattern . . . . scored. Hopelessly crippled, the raider drifted aimlessly away under no apparent control. They themselves crippled . . . . "It is a bad thing to happen now." Roak said, after Aor'y appraised him of the damages forward. "Indeed." Roak muttered. "I am surprised we still have atmosphere."

Although a limited amount of energy flowed to the gun, the main controls and most of the fuel, and main engines were damaged or out-an-out destroyed. And both of them realized that with little or no maneuvering power, they would continue to drift unchecked.

Making his way forward, climbing over debris and conduit hanging loose and aimlessly, Roak was not surprised to see the control console section almost as badly damaged as the rest of the ship. It seemed wherever he looked there were burned out panels, equipment and conduit short circuiting. With a sigh of resignation, he quickly dumped the electrical load to stand-by, and pulled at pasic material, tamped out small flickering flames with gloves, and cleared hanging pasic conduit, and other like material. Having stopped the little fires,

Roak began clearing and stacking in the ejection hold as much debris and garbage as he could jam into it.

With the passage of several dirty frustrated hours piling garbage, suddenly the realization . . . . he hadn't seen Aor'y for some hours. She laid half under the main console valiantly micro welding and reconnecting or bridging systems in an effort to regain some measure of control. Turning the corner, Roak walked into the control compartment surveying pieces and sections of equipment littering the deck. And noticed laying on the deck, half under the main control console, a pair of very shapely legs. Noticing Roak, she squirmed out from under the panel. "Roak." Aor'y's face smudged with soot and grime. She leaned on the chair while still sitting on the deck, tired . . . . "I don't think this piece of junk will move again." "It is in poor shape, . . . but, we have little choice in the matter. We must get moving again. I expect another attack at any time." Roak said.

But the attack he expected didn't materialize. Indeed they "saw nor heard" from any other ship. For the next several days, ship's time, while the near crippled ship drifted, feverish activity was taking place. They bridged and reconnected the main controls directly to the engines. Every spare part or bit of conduit was used, spare boards, bio chips and parts from unsympathetic controls were made to fit and ultimately function.

Totally exhausted laying side-by-side in control, when nothing more could be done without outside help . . . . they allowed themselves much needed food and sleep.

Awakening, each visited the small bio compartment and after food decided to try minimal thrusters and see if they could maneuver. Roak arranged the circuits. The ship began to vibrate akin to shaking off unwanted sleep, but they had thrust. Collectively they let out their breaths not realizing they were holding them. Roak and Aor'y hugged each other for several seconds . . . . and parted smiling. He nudged the controls and the instruments instantly began reporting faster acceleration. "That's enough . . . . ohhh," sighing, feeling the k not in his stomach loosen as he backed down the controls saving precious fuel; but the ship was moving. "We're up to sub-1, now almost . . . . 2, its about time. Hmmmm some speed . . . but to where?" Roak asked.

All they could detect of the many hundred stars was about five or six that had evolved planetary systems amidst the black void; and looked at one-another knowing the spiral rim wasn't that far beyond. They attempted to determine their relative position with only limited success. His best guess . . . . they are located amidst the rim systems; but, which one or set he had no idea.

He assumed there was nothing but uninhabited, uncharted systems and if any had life . . . he blinked, they wouldn't want to encounter it; especially not in their present circumstances. They immediately began to ration everything including fuel, food, liquor . . . everything. In short, all consumables and would continue until a suitable landing site could be found.

Velocity remained constant until two days later, ship's time. During her morning watch, Aor'y noted a marked increase in their velocity. Using the scanners at minimum power, she picked up a system directly within their trajectory. Roak knew as did Aor'y, they must find a place to land within this system. If not . . . . the alternative was not at all pleasant. Passing and scanning each planet proved fruitless. Leaving those outer planets behind, there remained only four. It was obvious only one planet would support them, although the small cool reddish one would also suffice. Still the larger had an abundance of water, higher gravity, which of course they could easily handle.

Using precious fuel the course was substantially altered to intersect with their target's orbit. With a sure deft touch born of countless similar maneuvers, Roak achieved and stabilized an orbit at approximately 80 miles, and occasionally much lower to enable accurate scanning and sensor sweeps using absolutely minimal power. Successive orbits yielded up an immense quantity of information to their one functioning C'pter brain. Although not constructed for the recent "load" requirements, the tiny C'pter was nevertheless behaving well. Absorbing all necessary information, i.e. position, landing sites, ship condition, lack of supplies and all related information had been correlated, the optimum answers were forthcoming.

Amongst the eagerly awaited answers, a complete picture of the planet such as age, mass composition, climatic conditions, orbit equal to 30 plus . . . . times faster than homeworld, revolution equal to 7 times plus . . . . than homeworld, and a race terribly primitive. Wearing animal skins and use of rudimentary tools, and loose types of tribal authority. The news was not promising, and nature of the information suggested an equatorial orbit for planet fall. More economical than a polar orbit as Roak wished to use the planet's own rotational speed, approximately sixteen hundred feet per, to excellent advantage.

Roak and Aor'y sat back and waited for the orbit to intersect the corridor, that optimum angle of approach allowing the least amount of vibration and consumable fuel so as to achieve an economical and safe landing. Each had quickly prepared the areas of the ship still intact for a possible rough planet fall.

The proposed site gradually brightened with planetary dawn, and final preparations and computations were completed. Secured in their seats, they marveled at the immense size of the oceans; and using a large spiral . . . . angled down close enough to notice crude vessels floating near land masses. Roak turned and caught Aor'y's attention, "hold on its time to pay for the ride." Taking manual control he altered their spiral and angle of attack, and began the proper glide path . . . for a gradual elliptical approach; thereby offering the best hope of picking the ideal landing site out of the list of possibles.

"There Aor'y pointed, we'll make for that open flat area toward the end of this land mass." "Looks good, and reasonably clear of obstacles to me Roak . . . . lets do it." Aor'y smiled, trying to look confident. During the final portion of their approach, both could easily distinguish and began cataloging the coordinates of the primitive villages, some possibly trading or fishing huts and great expanses of forest. One thing struck each of them . . . . the extreme primitive wildness of the planet. And being inordinately careful, Roak maneuvered the ship lower; but because of the dense atmosphere, and the over-all poor condition of the ship . . . the buffeting, vibration and jolting made for a very uncomfortable ride. The ship already almost wrecked was never designed for the type of landing it was now called upon to make.

The landing, far from Roak's typically flawless maneuvers was a bone crunching affair, and in so doing consumed most of their remaining fuel. Shaken and wobbly, they each made their way out of the control area taking sections, varied areas and shutting down all ship's systems, in an effort to conserve what power was left for future needs. It was then they felt the additional gravity, and for some moments found it difficult. With slow small tentative movements, he began slowly, gradually one foot and then the other. Gradually he is able to check over the ship carefully anxious to prevent fires or explosion.

CHAP. 3

Relieved the initial check-out went so smoothly, Roak agreed with Aor'y, a small refreshment would be a welcome break from their grimy work. It helped sooth his sore muscles and numb some of his tension. With Aor'y . . . . much the same, and helped her submerge growing anxieties and fears. The word marooned kept rebounding through her mind, turning already nervous stomach muscles into a knot, she fought hard against the rising tide of panic and subconsciously looked to Roak for strength. Having been in difficult positions before, Roak is better prepared psychologically, and knew instinctively . . . Aor'y needed him to be strong. As he sipped the liquor, and looked at her . . . and again felt the familiar glow, a warm protective feeling he nurtured from their very first meeting, strangely, Roak could and did think of worse predicaments . . . fates . . . than marooned with Aor'y. In fact, the more he thought about it . . . . the more pleasant the situation appeared.

Looking at her again . . . with a small smile, . . . "you must realize . . . we aren't going to leave this place unless we become very lucky." She nodded. "I know . . . . we're marooned, unless we can repair most of this," waving her hand indicating the ship as a whole. Then indicated the most critical of the damaged equipment . . . . then looked up at Roak shaking his head, no. "No, ... it'll take better than we to repair this ship. And . . . . I'm not so sure its even worth fixing."

"Aor'y?" "yes Roak." Her voice and its inflection, her eyes and body language spoke, and indicated many things to him. When he spoke, in addition to the smile . . . . his nose flared just a trifle. An unmistakeable signal to Aor'y, who filed it away in her mind for use later. "You did a fine job with the bio-lectrics. Can you rig a pulsar signal?" "I think so . . . . but, it will never be strong enough to reach the empire. We are . . . . oh I don't know how many parsecs from even the most distantly traveled trading lanes." "But, a steady pulsar signal is our best hope." Roak insisted. "It may require years, and almost certainly be detected by one of the outposts . . . ." "Possibly, though the gravitational forces and radiation are terrible out here. I feel sure the signal will be reflected." Aor'y countered. "As it is I can barely walk." She said plaintively. "We'll become acclimated to this planet soon." And standing he half turned. "It isn't as difficult as it seems, and we don't have many choices." Roak said solemnly.

The first day each went about self-appointed tasks, in an effort to do everything possible to make the ship more liveable, warm and confortable. This meant getting rid of all large debris, wrecked equipment, trying to repair existing non-functioning circuits and trying to pull down loose conduit, and or tying it and mono-form material out of the way.

With all large debris finally outside, in a fair size pile, and the ship reasonably clean, Roak carried the last big piece of debris outside and looked around. Trying to make sure no primitives were about, he pulled his side-arm blaster, a hand-held weapon seven inches in length, grayish in color, and equipped with a variable energy discharge control, from its holster, and proceeded with short bursts to reduce the large pile to a small tiny mound of molten slag. Unfortunately his simple act had profound consequences . . . . as it did not go unnoticed.

A small scrawny waif perhaps ten or eleven watched from behind the bowel of a large oak. Terribly hungry, well beyond the point of undernourishment, she was overcome by fear and terror. She stayed in the refuge by the dense undergrowth, not daring to crawl away.

When the great fire in the sky roared over her village, it was the last straw for the elders. She had been born under a full moon, a very bad sign for an already heavily superstitious people, and other occurences coupled with this recent happening the elders cast her out to starve and die. Her only clothes, a thin shift was no protection from cold nights, as the spring was still young. Nor did she possess any weapons to either hunt or by which to protect herself. Thin and emaciated with bare arms and legs, she is covered head to toe in soot and dirt. Hair caked and soaked, and snarled chewing on grass an such, she usually huddled under ground level branches of pine and fir for shelter.

It was a new and unexpected morning as she had prayed to her deity for release the previous night. Feeling much weaker and barely able to crawl, she felt sure death would come that night. But it didn't . . . . and she cried . . . . a pitiful wail of torment. Laying on her back the sobbing gradually tapered off, and after a time . . . . tear filled eyes, dried. A blur at first, her vision soon cleared . . . it was at that precious moment she saw the small clusters of large black berries. Blinking several times did not make them disappear, but continued to hang just out of reach. Slow, agonizingly slow she began to sit up . . . pausing to rest . . . . finally she reached a sitting position. And with head gently b umping numerous clusters, closed her eyes, giving thanks to a deity who she thought existed only inside her pounding heart. With a whimper . . . she began eating . . . soon gulping, swallowing as fast as she could. After some minutes she began to slow down a little as juice ran out from the corners of her mouth. Desperate not to loose any, she licked her hands repeatedly after cupping them around her mouth and chin. As the plump berries burst forth their sweet tangy juice, try as she might . . . . it still ran out of her mouth down over the chin to drip onto the dirty shift. Gorging herself to the point of holding the little distended belly, the waif laid down where she was and slept like the dead.

She awakened and sitting up . . . ate slowly but heartedly. And as before overate to the point of being sleepy, and laid down again to rest. While for the waif it is morning of the second day . . . only a half hour, or so, passed for Roak and Aor'y. Roak continued to pile small debris while Aor'y cleaned and salvaged what she could of their living areas. For both it is frustrating and time consuming.

Her superstitious nature, Roak appeared as a "God" when he burned the pile of garbage. Not so much the act, although it was unusual, but the manner in which he did it . . . a bolt of energy from his hand. Cold and hunger were all but forgotten as she crept slowly closer, through dense undergrowth until only about thirty feet separated them. Fearing discovery, she dared only an occasional glimpse. Awe and wonderment washed over her as she watched wide-eyed. While the pile was unattended and being ever watchful, lest the god discover her, she crept repeatedly to the slag and warmed herself.

Gathering all functional weapons on board to the living quarters, Aor'y sat down with Roak and proceeded to separate each weapon for its usefulness in their situation. All of the swords and daggers were kept, adding to his blaster, Roak inserted a formidable dagger with the black metal grip, into his boot. Then added a medium length sword to his belt, lowered the blaster on his hip and resecured the holster to his pant fastener.

Roak stayed and watched. He enjoyed looking at her and had several times caught himself staring. All of this was causing predictable reactions both voluntary and involuntary. Half turning with her back to him, she calmly changed the girdle like shorts for the blue-green pair. Standing erect, she adjusted the belt at the top. It is virtually transparent and with very high leg openings, which allowed the maximum of movement. Slipping out of the only other garment, Aor'y held the black tunic, folded it, and put it carefully away. With exception of the scanty girdle and belt she is nude; but, felt perfectly at ease as they are . . . . after-all . . . . crew members together. Still, a slight impish tongue wet full lips and Aor'y observed Roak under very long sultry lashes, as she stretched before reaching for the blue-green form tunic. She slid into it, with certainly more movements than was required, and ran both hands over the material framing her figure, molding itself to her form. Closing the touch fasteners, she was almost ready.

Roak's spine comb moved, eyes began to glaze, and his knees and thighs hurt from flexing muscles imperceptibly . . . . all typical reactions. His mind reasserted itself, for to loose control now . . . . meant respect lost. He knew instantly this formidable female would be his coupling mate. In the fashion and custom of her world such meant the male must best her in the phase of combat of her choice. He glanced at her and felt a wee unsure of himself, then dismissed the feeling . . . . but still?

Aor'y however, always desired Roak. Differences in their social and family station, and stature, caused her to believe the wish unobtainable. Now with the present situation all that had changed. She realized Roak could be hers, and his desire for her . . . . she had already seen. That glow of power, she felt it throughout her senses . . . it was so sweet.

She is no longer hurrying, but continued at a normal pace dressing herself. Intending not to wear the matching slacks, instead settled for knee high boots, dark blue in color. Aor'y liked the effect, and knew Roak would appreciate her appearance all the more. Aor'y then gathered up her array of weapons. First to be attached to the belt is a long thin dagger, and a miniscule palm anti-grav hidden and half held easily between the breasts. Her regular side-arm is attached to its belt fastener on the right hip, and with two anti-grav devices and the universal translator, she is ready.

Exiting the compartment she noticed Roak also carried two of the small anti-gravs and the translator; and she smiled inwardly, he still stared. She stood very close to him and said sweetly . . . "Are you prepared?" He felt like showing her . . . just how prepared his body is . . . . but thought better of it, and answered, "yes." It is the way he said yes, and the eyes, told more. Her pulse quickened a trifle.

Turning to the exit hatch, he walked down the ramp as Aor'y followed close behind with an impish grin. The issue of weapons and their priority behind them, the remainder in storage, the ship's gun still serviceable, all contributed to putting Roak much more at ease. And the only other problem area, the bio-compartment had been repaired. Roak reassured Aor'y, it was her chief annoyance, the compartment would continue as long as the generator continued to function. And both would continue longer than either or both the traders would live.

Roak and Aor'y turned their attention to the immediate encampment, with the idea to fortify their position. With her help to steady them, and Roak using a small anti-grav unit, then started cutting a white-gray stone using his blaster. Transporting the huge stones proved awkward. Assembly of the cut stones into a wall was only slightly more difficult.

It was not to be as high on the ravine side only half again Roak's stature; however, the balance of the perimeter was to be easily twice his height and more. Sighting across the top course of blocks . . . he saw the clearance would be close but manageable. Enabling the finished enclosure to just clear the top of the small ship. During their brief work periods, Aor'y noticed prints around the slag pile and made a mental note for later recall.

Of course with the blocks transported and maneuvered in a virtual weightless condition, it did not require to many hours, ship's time, to complete their initial labor. Locking-in the last few remaining stones . . . it is finished. Both stood admiring their work and thinking about the one main entrance, and the one disguised exit. But however strong the wall, they still relied upon the ship for shelter and source of sustenance.

It is this situation and the continued necessity to leave the ship and hunt, gather food, and the priority of visiting the vast ocean sighted earlier . . . . that brought on problems.

Locking and securing the ramp made for all practical considerations the ship secure. Placing the huge entrance stones on a pedestal hinge, so as not to waste power of the anti-gravs, made the final touch. Standing outside, the perimeter did impart a solid feeling of security which was satistying. Roak felt more calm . . . large wooded hills close on two sides, ravine on the third, and a good downward sloping field on the fourth. Their immediate task completed they could now investigate the immediate area around them. Above all, Roak and Aor'y realized they must be secretive about their excursions. The native primitives would not understand them, their clothes, weapons, ship, tools or anything else about them.

Information gathered during the initial orbits provided the initial basis for scheduling excursion, work and other endeavors. One day, ship's time, for Roak and Aor'y was equivalent to more than seven and-a-half days planetary time. And having gotten accustomed to the gravity, air, the heat, moving about became much more pleasureable. Awakening with planetary dawn and feeling inpatient, Roak decided they should prepare and launch their investigation. Starting out after resetting the door, the duo walked casually in the direction of the ocean. Aor'y looking . . . and touching gently admired plants and flowers, carefully cataloging everything she saw using the portable C'pter. Already the day was quickly fading, and finding a clearing they sat down, talking in low muted tones until it became light again. "I find it difficult accustoming myself to the frequent changes of light to dark." "It does offer problems, but is in itself not unattractive, we can rest a brief period before we rotate back into the star's rays, again." He and Aor'y listened to the animals, looked at the strange stars and longed for home. As they watched the horizon rapidly lighten, unfamiliar stars faded only to reappear again. With dawn far enough advanced, Aor'y and Roak continued on their way. Several times they encountered parts of the trail overgrown, and paused to cut and slash their way through. And while Roak did most of the cutting, Aor'y busied herself analyzing plant samples.

During their third rest period, Roak observed a small area of light not far away, and decided this was an ideal opportunity to glimpse the natives without being seen. With Aor'y close behind they crossed the flat scrub covered intervening ground quickly, and obtained an excellent vantage point from the top of a nearby knoll. They witnessed a scene both fascinating and horrible. Roak slipped on his gunner's lenses and was pleasantly surprised. He could see many times better through the gloom. Both watched as several natives riding four-legged beasts were attacking and killing helpless villagers.

Aor'y shook her head with frustration and anger. "Roak we must do something." "Yes, I know." He replied, and quickly pulled his side-arm from its special holster. Taking careful aim, he killed five of the six riders almost instantly. The beasts in a terrified frenzy bolted from the village, running headlong wild-eyed for the forest. The villagers surrounded the last rider, but Roak burned him instantly in a brilliant flash of energy. Terrified the villagers prostrated themselves from fear wailing plaintively, not daring to look up for some time.

Realizing their opportunity, Aor'y and Roak quietly slipped away. Retracing their initial steps back the way they'd come, then altered their course for the ocean. While resting during the dark intervals, they discussed at length the attack on the village and the probable consequences of their intervention.

The elder of the village sensing the danger was past started shouting, helping the wounded, and the others followed his example.

There was no further contact until two rest periods later. While walking back from a large inlet carrying a sizeable container of fish, along a different route than taken earlier, they heard screaming. Running a short distance through the trees, Aor'y arrived first. A native child was desparately trying to climb out of the reach of a large salivating carnivore. Quickly reaching for her blaster, she was successful in burning down the beast with the first bolt of energy. The child did not show any inclination to leave her perch; but, kept looking at the spot where only seconds ago stood a mad killing beast. Aor'y stared walking slowly to the clearing saying . . . "We should see if she is all right." "Go ahead," Roak said. "I'll stay here in case of trouble."

Wearing the tiny belt translator, she was able to understand almost all of what the native girl child said. The inflection of fear plainly evident in everything she said, intermixed with wonder. When Aor'y spoke the translator operated in reverse, after absorbing the characteristics of the native language, the translator worked in near perfect fashion.

Standing still, with feet well apart her striking highlighted hair billowing out from the breeze accenting the green-blue shades of her work uniform, Aor'y could not fathom why the child would not come down from her perch. A trifle impatient,

Aor'y ordered the girl to come to her. Some minutes lapsed before the little native showed any inclination to move up or down. Finally after some seconds with much trepidation the child slowly descended. Immediately, she knelt and then prostrated herself on the ground. She told her, . . . "go little one, I will not harm you." The girl slowly stood up keeping tiny hands over her eyes and backed away bowing, and suddenly . . . . she turned and ran. Aor'y stood and watched the dirty emaciated child run away, and mentally noted to set out food for the poor creature.

She considered the possible danger involved, but something had to be done, and Aor'y was determined she would try to save this . . . . her little primitive. Roak walked up holstering his blaster and said, "such strange behavior." "Well . . . . they are terribly primitive." Aor'y countered. "We probably appear very frightening and strange to them." Roak nodded.

Upon their return, while Roak was busy with duties within the ship, Aor'y quickly prepared some of the local food. Warming it she placed the container in a convenient location. Looking around . . . . was not unduly concerned to neither see or hear the little creature. Nonchalantly she turned and walked back to the door, closed it . . . re-entering the ship. Sitting in the pilot's seat, she waved a control. Images coalesced upon a small screen, showing an area some thirty yards square in which sat the small container. A wisp of vapor curled up from the container, and Aor'y smiled envisioning the aromas spreading. Before leaving the controls, she set it for automatic monitoring.

For each of the next three dark periods, she set out the same container filled with warmed food and smiled each time it was emptied.

Roak observing this while he worked tried to understand Aor'y's need. He knew it to be potentially dangerous, but said nothing partly because of her need, and his ever increasing desire for her. He watched Aor'y more each day. His eyes followed the senuous movements, the lithness and strength of her body, and natural scent, which seemed to capture and enslave his senses. With will power he forced patience refusing to succumb, telling himself there would be time aplenty after the important and necessary work was completed. In the same instant came the realization . . . . there would be offspring. Eyes misted, spinal ridge moved and he dreamed of the pain of winning in combat with Aor'y, and exquisite pleasure of her submission and his conquest. With a loud sigh he shook his head, rubbed sore eyes, and returned to work.

CHAP. 4

The next few days, ship's time, were uneventful. With exception of Aor'y feeding the native, both traders as yet had no face-to-face contact with he natives as a whole. Both mutually agreed to always have on their person minimum two small anti-grav units in case of need. Roak felt it only smart to be as totally equipped and prepared as was possible in light of previous happenings.

However, the third day while walking their now accustomed path, noting the beautiful surroundings, sounds of furious activity drew them to a sizeable clearing where the natives worked feverishly cutting down some of the giant plants. "Roak? Do you see the primitive tools?" "I see them . . . . but we should not interfere." He said, trying to sound firm. While talking one of the "plants" fell over on the closest native. Though not seriously injured, it firmly pinned him in place. And Aor'y not really sure of a plan, stepped out from concealment walking boldly out into the small clearing. The more astonished primitives prostrated themselves on the ground. Many of those running stopped at the clearing's edge to watch . . . . their curiousity dispelling initial fright.

She bid them to rise and give an account of their work. Not really understanding the stupidity, Aor'y decided to deal with the situation herself. Reaching into her tunic, she palmed the mini anti-grav, estimated the plant's mass and attached the grav "unseen" to her wrist, so that its plate touched the plant. While her wrist kept the two touching it would operate effectively. She wrapped her left arm as far around the fallen plant as was possible. Flicking the stud with her nail, she felt the weight nullify, and gently stood balancing the plant . . . . guiding it with her right hand.

A simple technical feat for the traders, but one of "God-like" proportion to the natives. Aor'y and Roak did not until later realize this fact, and by then . . . . it was much to late. Roak was clearly worried, but followed at a discreet distance. She nonchalantly turned at a slight angle, pulled her side-arm blaster, made sure it is on minimal, and neatly cut almost a dozen of the huge plants letting them fall where they may. Turning she returned the blaster to her holster, and continued along the native path toward their village. One of the natives must have raced ahead to find the little girl. She had made peace with the village elders after he'd been told of her survival. When from urging by the elder, she told of being rescued and fed by the gods, a tentative reinstatement had been ordered by the elders. It was conditional . . . . she had to present proof. Now very healthy looking, she was in the center prostrated on the messy ground.

Aor'y smiled inwardly, and dropped the plant out of the way with a loud heavy thump-thud. Straightening, she decided to satisfy her curiosity about the village. Looking at the little waif, maternal feelings once thought dead stirred deep within her being. Aor'y acknowledged the child. "Stand little one and show me your village." With apprehension the girl stood bowing, squeaked and with a sweeping gesture . . . "my unworthy village."

Surprised and repulsed by what she was seeing, Aor'y could not help looking disgusted by the conditions of the village. The squalor, filth and stench was almost unbearable, and was in some places. Stench in places was enough to overpower a person, but held her hand over nose and mouth.

Most of the small village consisted of tiny huts with dirt floors and lean-toos covered with thatch-like material, and open cooking areas with fish drying in the warm daylight. Garbage laid almost everywhere sometimes covered with dirty or wet straw. Trampled open areas were worse, with offal laying stagnant and animals of varied species lived inside and outside the huts. Only one hut was larger than the others, and Aor'y correctly guessed the dwelling was of the elders or a similar person. She noticed many types of small odd animals scurrying about as she walked, obviously domesticated for they remained within the village.

She continued the casual inspection, looking this way and that, only the small native girl moved close. Villagers clothed in skins and a coarse type of crude cloth kept a wide respectful area around her. Watching fertively and gesturing, chattering excitedly in their guttural language, the villagers formed a loose circle around Aor'y, and the little former outcast.

Moving parallel with Aor'y, Roak remained keeping a watchful eye all around the area, ready for any eventuality. The little girl explained . . . she was an orphan of this village. It only required minutes and the waif revealed everything about her history and problems with the villagers . . . gesticulating at many individuals. She indicated to the waif an understanding of her situation, and assured her the villagers would amend their treatment. After seeing all she felt there was to see, Aor'y said she was going back to the clearing, and the waif dutifully informed the villagers. They shrank back as Aor'y returned to the site of the accident. Just at the fringe of giant plants, she plainly saw the old man was standing and going from plant-to-plant wondering at the fallen logs. Talking excitedly to two other villagers, the old man was gathering support to plead with the goddess for help, to move the logs to the village.

The translator was able to decipher virtually all the conversation, voice inflection and understanding the importance with regard to their form of address for her. Aor'y with mixed feelings kept silent except for a small sigh. She was well aware Roak heard and saw everything, and now realized his words of caution should have been heeded. But there was nothing she could do now except play out her role, return the waif to her village, and depart as suddenly as she had appeared.

Aor'y strode into the clearing, villagers on both sides paying close attention as the orphan walked forward trying to show confidence. "Stop!" . . . . Exclaimed Aor'y with authority. Speaking to the waif, she grasped the child firmly by the shoulder, the anti-grav lodged against the little body and pressed the tiny stud . . . . the child's weight nullified. Aor'y raised the weightless body even with her face, while the villagers all prostrating themselves . . . . and shook with fear. Abject fear filled the child as she heard . . . "Henceforth your name is Val'py, meaning . . . female child who behaves as a warrior, and that is how I shall call you."

"Now continue . . . . Val'py." Aor'y said setting the child down gently, resetting the anti-grav. Val'py backed up several paces then prostrated herself, beaming with a large smile. Regaining her feet she turned and told the villagers to stand. And began talking to the elders, they in turn tried to make her understand the needs of the village. Aor'y did nothing to stop her, occasionally smiling when Val'py attempted to relay colored information, which Aor'y already had learned by the previous exchange during the conversation.

In no time, little Val'py gained substantial importance letting it be known . . . . only she could speak with the goddess.

Darkness came quickly and while the villagers and Val'py were absent, Aor'y and Roak talked at length. With a resolve to reduce their contacts with the natives, Roak aided Aor'y in cutting to length all fallen plants as the principle elder needed, and transporting them all to the same spot where the first one still lay. All the pieces were cut and stacked neatly, Roak smiled at Aor'y and whispered they should leave.

The following day, ship's time, Aor'y encountered little Val'py picking wild berries, and gently made it clear she could indeed understand all that was being said, and kept Val'py's secret so she would be re-established in her village with position and respect. Thereafter, Val'py dared not lie, and gave truthful and candid accounts of happenings within the village, and her own involvement was faithfully detailed.

Changing directions and using alternative pathways during their periodic excursions for food, did little to assuage the daily routine. Although using caution, glimpses and encounters with the natives did occur, but handled effectively by Roak.

Still these occurences were becoming troublesome, and Roak more than Aor'y worried because evidence pointed to natives coming progressively closer.

Days and entire star months came and went, ship's time, during which the planet underwent many seasonal changes. Aor'y and Roak limited their excursions and therefore saw less and less of the villagers. Only Val'py did they usually see, and then only from a distance. It was disturbing for as their "time" crept ever so slowly, Val'py and her people aged quickly. The villagers and Val'py, when those encounters happened saw Aor'y and Roak, and could not understand their not ageing, which only increased the awe and esteem by which the villagers held them.

As the schism in time increased, encounters with the natives became still fewer, and it was with descendants of the original villagers . . . . when they did occur. Their mere presence and appearance, all contributed to implanting them in the minds and hearts of the natives. Inevitably they were weaved into the superstition and mythology of the local tribes and villagers as god and goddess, especially in light of their not ageing. And though the approach of their ship was seen by tribes for thousands of square miles, each heralded it in their own fashion.

Time lengthened and more attention was paid to their living quarters and general comfort. Closeness and the increasing belief of not being rescued caused affection and related feelings long submerged . . . . smoldering to emerge and began to burn hot.

At the outset, the possibility of rescue was not a good one, but actually living the reality of it was most difficult. Roak having most of the duties to perform was less filled with resignation because Aor'y filled his thoughts. Aor'tiaws facing reality wih no . . . . or only a meager chance-hope of rescue was most of the time thinking of Roak. She realized under normal circumstances those of aristocratic families never allowed or permitted their members to arrange a marriage (or joining) contract with those not of their "station". However, these were far from normal circumstances, and knew she will join with Roak, soon.

CHAP. 5

Her thoughts travelled, and recalled the time of their first meeting. For Aor'tiaws . . . a trader was not an unsuitable occupation, born on the second planet of the Tucon star system. Two members of her joint family already held guild membership, and active papers; thereby making it possible for her own family members to sponsor her for guildship. This being one of only two ways a citizen might apply.

It was three years of intense instruction, piloting, navigation, ship mechanics, ship propulsion systems, life support requirements and planetary customs, and the like, before she would be awarded a subordinate trader's status and papers. Although normally most women did not seek to be traders, because of the arduous physical and mental training, and the very nature of the guild business. But Aor'y thrilled in the hardships, dangers during flight maneuvers, and won respect from many of the hardened male members, and admiration from the few women. She accomplished her assigned training tasks well enough, and hardened herself both physically and mentally to the point even the instructors took notice. Only when this level of performance had been repeated year after year, ... did she come to be noticed by senior guild members.

Normally a person having just completed guild training would be given sub-trader status and credentials, but because of Aor'y's competence, her guild training was recognized and rewarded. Senior guild members bestowed status one full level above that . . . . to associate. Three years and clear sponsorship stood between her and a full trader's status and certificate-plick.

Those required years were long and arduous, but she learned. Sponsorship did occur, and Aor'y was awarded, in a quiet and dignified ceremony, full status and ticket. Now . . . . she is able to contract with a guild, business enterprise, local or planetary government anywhere within the empire. There was also the chance to go free . . . . be an independent trader. Quietly in a moment of reflection, the ceremony concluded, she decided . . . . she will be a free trader. And because of the prevailing unrest throughout the empire, Aor'y wished to "crew" with another free trader. But however she tried, she could not find an established trader willing to accept her, or had a vacancy she might fill.

Acting upon information secured by one of her family, she began frequenting "establishments" and "clubs", whose clientele were mostly free traders . . . . independents. She kept going to these clubs, and as she sat sipping soft beitra and listening to music, and the flow of conversation . . . . almost always the name Roak came up. "Oh . . . Roak did this, or

Roak did that." Aor'y overheard stories of bravery, or perhaps bravado, feats of daring . . . out running a raider saving an excellent prize, and there were many others. Some of the "talk" was critical, but most was clearly admiration, while some of the men were obviously jealous. In all of it, good or bad, there is always respect.

After a time wherever Aor'y had waited and asked about Roak, she had left cryptic messages. Hoping this elusive Roak to contact her at this very club in which she was now sitting, and enjoying the music. More than an hour had already slipped by as she sat slowly sipping soft beitra, a soft version . . . about 90 proof variety. It was her second goblet, and absorbed in thoughts of the recent past, and the effect induced by the near hypnotic notes of music contributed to a slight euphoric mood. She blamed the beitra for her mood, and especially for not noticing his entrance.

Slightly startled, she turned after hearing, . . . "Roak, here, I've been waiting . . . ." What she saw definitely brought a quickening to her blood, and ideas, no clear plan, but plenty of ideas. Aor'y noted a full tucanan male with an unmistakeable air of power and authority. A strong solidly built person dressed in black tunic with metal-weave arm coverings, soldiers brown leg and lower torso coverings, arm and waist weapons belt with a long dagger finished off with black metal calf length boots.

He approached several friends and while quietly talking not sitting down yet, looked up . . . . saw Aor'y and gave the trader's nod of recognition. Aor'y licked a full lower lip and instantly wanted him. Roak didn't stay with his friends long explaining . . . it is business. When he did finally approach her little table and stopped . . . she stood offering her hand. He clasped her hand warmly, and she his, Roak . . . . "Greetings trader Aor'tiaws." "Greetings to you trader Roak." Aor'y replied. "The owner is an associate of mine and indicated you have looked for me." Roak explained. "Yes, I have." Aor'y replied.

"Business or charter?" Roak asked, openly appraising her. "Both." Aor'y replied. Roak looked at her raising a brow quizzically. "I shall explain."

Aor'y went into necessary details explaining her predicament, pausing only long enough to order more drinks, and then continued her narrative. "So, I am in hope you may suggest something or someone who is looking for a partner." "Interesting." Roak replied. "You have your papers?" "Of course." Aor'y replied, taking out her folded i.d. folder from the inside tunic pocket, and handed it to Roak. Seconds ticked by. He finished his drink, and Aor'y immediately signaled for two more. Roak finished his inspection, and returned the folder to her without so much as a smile. Drinking deeply from his goblet and sat for well over a minute staring at Aor'y. She had mixed feelings but quelled them, knowing he was thinking, and would speak when ready.

Finally . . . . "I find you acceptable Aor'tiaws. If you agree . . . . I will accept you as a partner." Roak stated, but this time with a warm smile. She swallowed once . . . . "I accept." "Good." Roak replied. They stood and clasped arms in the traditional manner, clasping each left forearm with the other. As they released their hands those around them, mostly traders of one status, or another, offered good speed and drank to them. During the next few drinks each, Roak and Aor'y exchanged the customary information both personal and professional. A customary formality when crewing.

While Roak was ordering various foods, Aor'y thought how pleased she was the young trader accepted her as a partner, and intrigued that an aristocrat should choose such a life. She continued to listen to the talk about Roak, fascinated wanting to learn everything possible about her partner. Some of the talk was exciting while occasionally it is sordid and repulsive. Even that was exciting to her in a way that was embarrassing. Most of what she heard answered the obvious questions, still she wanted to learn more.

Aor'y knew Roak's status, she had seen the family birthmark making him a "Tywr", and knew he would not reveal much about himself.

CHAP. 6

Several days lapsed, consumed by first priority items. Equipment repaired and arranged so as to sustain themselves and insure their protection and survival was of immediate concern. Following their difficult planet fall, and the necessary equipment repaired . . . inventory had been taken. Much of the navigator's console had to be dismantled and cannibalized, as well as other equipment; plus the almost sole use of a ship's generator. She expended considerable time and effort assembling e-chips, d.I-chips and lesser components required for a pulse signal generator system. It was long hot, sweaty, dirty and frustrating.

When completed she reiterated about her skepticism concerning the ability of the signal to carry the distance. The C'pter filled the main forward screen with star systems from their present position back . . . . across dozens upon dozens of parsecs to the home system. It was depressing news. There were so many obstacles, not to mention conflicting gravitational fields from stars, clouds and asteroid concentrations. Both sat numb, staring at the screen.

Mechanically her thoughts centered on the pulsar, she prepared food, rather assembled it from the processor, and opened a small bottle of soft beitra. The meal was largely spent discussing the signal's probable chance of successfully reaching the empire, through the "maze" provided by the C'pter. This period of discussion long after both food and most of the beitra had been consumed. But little had been added . . . . only the same persistent hope of rescue. Tired and ragged both laid down to rest and were asleep almost instantly.

Immediately after their wake-up period, and had refreshed themselves, attention was drawn to to the navigator's area now occupied by the pulsar signal equipment. Once aligned, Aor'y looked at Roak . . . . who nodded, the signal was switched to generator mode and initiated.

Crossing planetary orbits of the system they are currently in, and on into the void . . . the pulsar moved on its errand. It crossed intervening open areas, rebounded from fields, reflected, but it kept moving closer. System by system, inexorably forward further seeking the empire's outposts. Most of it was warped by gravitational forces, and other galactic anomalies. So much so that as much as thirty-three years (ship's time) had slipped away from the marooned two-some.

It was when they had started the third year, and no sign of rescue was heard, Roak decided they should enter "sleep mode" to conserve themselves for as long as possible. Aor'y agreed. All that could be expected had been done and more. And sufficient food was on hand, satisfactorily preserved to ensure their longevity.

Roak went through all checks and computations with the equipment, and felt everything was working perfectly. He so arranged the controls to wake him each seven year period. Just prior to entering the chambers, Roak constructed over their compound an artificial roof, comprised of layers of low energy forming a dense opaque structural field. This guaranteed their continued protection and peace-of-mind while in sleep mode.

Both entered their chambers and started the equipment, exchanged promises of joining when next they awake. Expressing words of affection both drifted off to sleep. While time sped by them, Aor'y and Roak slept untouched, unscathed each dreaming of each other, and different scenes of exotic beautiful worlds.

Immediately after their first awakening, and needed preparations stood together ready. Aor'y felt nervous, and Roak . . . . he found it difficult to concentrate because of his elation. He set-in the recording log to receive their names, rank and profession, followed by family and individual status if ranked amongst the nobility. Reciting his family and status, Aor'y sucked in her breath, for by birth Roak is a duke. Her head swam with the realization and possibilities. Aor'y thought of their children . . . her children will be nobility, well positioned in empire society.

Squeezing his hand, she looked up at Roak through misting eyes with admiration and much affection. By recorded ceremony they are joined, and enjoyed each other repeatedly. Their "combat" instead of held prior to the joining came after, and though weaponless, but no less intense and enthusiastic. Only sore muscles resulted, but the physical activity and release of emotion was a welcomed glorious respite.

They allowed themselves three days, ship's time, whereupon Aor'y and Roak re-entered their individual chambers, and once again enjoyed secure sleep. Each of the three subsequent awakenings were largely repetitious of the first, with exception of the ceremony and physical combat. Strenuous excercises were performed, but with almost artistic flair, affection, care and enjoyment. And as before returned to the sleep chambers, each thinking about the other.

During their fifth sleep period, the pulsar signal found its target destination, a far and lonely outpost set out on the frontier of the empire. A small outflung trading post intercepted the low energy signal, an old style pulsar barely readable. After some seconds listening to it repeat, the operator recorded and treated it to special analysis. Barely decipherable data derived from the many varied types of tests revealed the probable type of generator, wave type code, density and other characteristics important only to technics. But it was a signature of sorts, and could therefore be interpreted and understood.

With the advent of new sub-eith-tic communications, years earlier all outmoded equipment had been removed. The outpost's operater instinctive questions were mostly answered, and discarding other possibilities, was identified as originating from passe' equipment outdated approximately 33 plus years ago. And the signal was thought to originate somewhere perilously close to the galactic rim.

After the N-pter and E-pter analyzed the available data, point of origin was fixed. The signal definitely originated thirty-three years and odd star months ago, dangerously close to the rim; and in seconds the E-pter ejected a coding plick indicating the location with star system co-ordinates. Two operators took the plick and quickly plotted, checked and rechecked their findings. All data and findings were then subject to a limited debate, because no-one wished to be in any way responsible for submitting incorrect or incomplete information to the area station. That station in turn would immediately analyze the findings of the outpost, and relay the information and all related data to the system office; and so on until it is received by guild headquarters on Tucana.

Excitement began running high. Reasoning no system known in that quadrant, and three parsec wide area, had progressed to the extent necessary to have developed the complex technology and equipment with which to initiate a pulsar. Those present listened .... it repeated the same message. Slowly eliminating other alternatives .... the conclusion .... ? It had to originate from the lost trader. No other explanation fitted the facts as well, and a long pent-up sigh went out from the several guild officers present. The senior operator/technic on duty related the news with all available data, and other subsequent information to the next post. Closer and closer to the hub of the empire, travelling from system station to system station until reaching and received by Untey-3.

CHAP. 7

Old and disused the military base with its unused and antiquated equipment in mechanical disarray, staffed by mostly a civilian contingent operating and maintaining the communications equipment relayed the news and data, et-cetera to trader guild headquarters. And simultaneously to the old military headquarters complex within the capital on homeworld, Tucana.

Trader guild council headquarters received the news and accompanying data from the comm. technic's, and most current business stopped completely. High atop the main building complex a hastily arranged meeting was to begin. Council leader stood. "Please." Assembled seniors quieted. "Fellow guild seniors. I have the pleasure of announcing the interception of an old style pulsar distress signal, confirmed to be that of our lost brethren." Announced the leader. Motioning for silence over the roar of approval . . . . "One of our frontier outposts intercepted the signal. It is particularly fitting our own people should receive their signal-message. Notify spa-inf. representatives, present them with all general data, so all may celebrate with us." The leader said.

As the news spread traders did indeed celebrate, with formidable numbers offering support for an immediate rescue. All data had been quickly relayed from communications section to the ranking officer on duty, and by the time it was shown to the senior officer on duty . . . . the whole of military headquarters complex was buzzing with the story.

Although the feeling was subdued, in keeping with habit and tradition within the headquarters complex, the rejoicing and celebrating was no less intense in their own fashion. There was convened a special meeting of the "circle", group of senior most admirals. Only purpose being to discuss ramifications of the recent message concerning the discovery of a distress signal from the lost traders. Concern centered on whether they could or not equip a rescue mission with a reasonable chance of success. By mutual agreement they felt such a mission could be launched with an excellent probability for success, depending on raider activity in the intervening area.

Now that the location of the traders had been firmly established, concerns were raised because so much time had elapsed . . . they would not find them alive. Many shared the opinion and concerns, but it did not effect the majority who zealousy advocated for a rescue mission.

Without disturbing those ships currently used for protection and patrol, there were still several small ships available. Although fallen to age-old disuse, the military hierarchy maintained confidence in the space-worthy integrity of the ships enough to assign them for a lengthy mission. Knowing they would be called upon to provide at least one ship, orders were issued to maintenance areas, outfitters and other departments the admirals thought necessary. Maintenance was expected to prepare several ships in case more than one was required for space; and making them presentable for service. Aside from totally replacing all the communications equipment in favor of the newly developed apparatus, outfitters inspected and if warranted . . . replaced all guns, and such other equipment as that department deemed appropriate.

New activity is evident and those senior officers thought it high time they flexed a little muscle. Most of the duty was routine, except when patrols "saw action." True, they had lost ships to the raiders, but it couldn't be helped. Emperor Solc'Hatr refused to help the military's call for ships and crews. He had severly cut their number of ships, and reduced the number of personnel to dangerously low levels. All the resources normally going to the military was instead fattening the tens of thousands of unnecessary and useless politicos empire wide. Making matters worse, the practice of paying off for trade routes was a concept some questionable nobles used. The corrupt emperor even had gone so far as to pay-off more organized raiders not to attack the empire's trade routes and ships.

Regardless of the reasons or causes, raiders still accounted for most of the losses sustained throughout the trading lanes. However . . . undisclosed to the general citizenry was the number of military ships missing each year. A number increasing geometrically to frightening proportions. These and other factors added fuel to the already growing discontent, and unrest spreading much like a virus throughout the empire. Because of this, there occurred more than one meeting between top level council members of important guilds, and some senior admirals in the military were also to appear. Up to the present various actions-plans had been and even now were being implemented. But as yet there was no actual break or open insurrection.

Spies in the employ of the palace often reported meetings and other such activities as they thought noteworthy. And many people, sometimes influential people would be detained for questioning. And almost always these people were "detained forceably." Not only were most detained, but imprisoned without even so much as a hearing. Unless the person or persons belonged to the nobility there existed virtually no chance of them being ever released.

Many of the emperor's ministers and confidants looked upon it as a much needed and welcomed diversion . . . . this rescue mission. It began occupying people's attention and caused citizens to look at other concerns, other problems, other than the emperor;s failings.

Senior officers in charge of overseeing preparations such as provisioning the ship, insisted only volunteers be accepted for consideration. Once the service-wide call was issued, the problem was not gathering volunteers on the contrary, it was weeding through the rapidly increasing numbers in an effort not only to reduce the number, but finding the most qualified in the disciplines necessary. Indeed it proved much more difficult for the selection board than had been originally anticipated. With no way of knowing the conditions to be encountered, nor if indeed they would find the survivors alive, every effort was employed to include a varied and wide array of equipment aboard the ship, in an attempt to cover all contingences possible, and several not thought to be possible.

The senior officers mutually decided to insure the maximum amount of experience, and expertise in the crew. And followed thru with a tight plan organized and executed as those during the "pre-Hatr dynasty" era.

Aged, grossly overweight, intoxicated most of the time, Emperor Solc' Hatr, (last of his line), listened to his highly corrupt advisors and agreed to the blessed diversion represented by the rescue mission. Two young but seasoned officers exited the imposing, multi-level and sprawling palace, doing little to mask their disgust. If it were not a necessary formality neither of them would have bothered. Grumbling, one recalled the emperor wailing . . . "But so few military types are available with any real experience." The officer dangerously close to loosing his composure would have been executed immediately. Only the swift action of his companion stopping him and speaking urgently to him prevented a disasterous confrontation.

At the outset all senior circle officers present concurred, only four crew. They did not enjoy refusing qualified people eager for the assignment. But by the following day the selection committee had made the appointments official.

Supposedly the basic reasons for only a crew of four was the lack of area for crew and survivors alike, plus supplies. One reason was not explained to the citizenry, but reflected upon the expressions, and in the eyes of the admirals within "the circle".

Much had not been explained . . . . with the large probability of attack, and capture, or destruction, they could not risk anymore qualified people. Overall the number of such people in uniform was already dangerously . . . almost critically short. And none of the circle wanted to entertain the thought of loosing both ship and crew.

All available data was given to each of the crew during the intense briefing during, the balance of the selection day, and the next. Fully prepared, the ship was provisioned with half again more food rations, bio-mals and the like, plus personal equipment of all kinds. For one to look inside, it would be difficult to find space for the necessary crew members. Each volunteer is outfitted with, what some thought to be, extraneous garments of several types. When nothing else could be packed inside . . . . it was time.

A final briefing was given to the crew prior to departure in an effort to prepare them for what they could fairly expect to encounter. Chief and foremost of these problems covered was the raiders. What to expect, and about when, and where they could fairly expect trouble.

CHAP. 8

The ship, the crew is to use . . . while old was not quite that of the slightly larger ships of the empire. In truth it more resembled a large armed scout rather than an actual cruiser. And while the final briefing was in progress the ship received another quick once-over by outfitters, and all was as it should be. With anticipation the crew assembled at the old field headquarters building on Untey-3, one of three moons orbiting "homeworld"; each possessing atmosphere and population. Here they received all final instructions, and prepared to disembark upon the long journey to the galactic rim.

The crew comprised of two males and two females . . . was thus balanced; however valuable military disciplines far outweighed any other consideration. First three crew-members, while solid military skills had other skills much prized on such a mission, only one of which was survival techniques. The fourth crew member, a female, is the physician, or more accurately termed bio-physico technic, equipped to handle virtually any conceivable emergency.

Other than making and discarding contingency plans, and attempting to approximate the area of probable attack from raiders, the initial portion of their journey proved uneventful. As physician . . . one of her multiple tasks was to note anxiety levels of the crew including herself. The closer they came to the proximity of Arbus-Ceti, the higher the levels of anxiety became. She countered this problem by the issue of "liquor" on each off-duty period. It is soft beitra, something to divert attention while hopefully reducing stress. Off duty breaks helped, but pent-up tension was still dangerously high. Duties were assigned and certain crew members had gun positions in accordance with the ability of each person. The officer appointed as senior, and therefore "captain" was called upon to double as pilot and gunner, while the physician saw to the communications console.

Once within the general area of space known as Ceti, crew's routine changed drastically. Outwardly calm they prepared for the inevitable attack everyone believed was sure to come. Two crew members occupied gun positions, and warmed them as a precautionary measure. Those particular guns required an operater, and were found on the sides of the ship. Located in the stern, the underside and the bow, just underside of the operations deck, where robot gun positions and were controlled by C-pter or controlled individually by the pilot. When brought up to temperature, each one in turn is test fired to insure proper functioning.

From that point on . . . as they began penetrating the ceti system only one gunner was absent from their position at any one time. As the physician looked on, she thought maybe a prayer . . . . but, didn't instead she was distracted by light signals and instruments. Ship's chronometer device kept recording "their time" as they progressed on through the inky blackness of space. Piloting an elliptical course, the captain reasoned, at their last "session" by such a course, he hoped to avoid an attack because of being off the more frequently travelled routes.

Hours passed and increased stress and psychological pressure was again becoming palpable. The captain's plan to skirt around most of the system proved to no avail, as the attack came quickly, and ruthlessly. Scanners and sensors initially picked-up two small ships approaching them very fast from two different directions. As the alarm sounded, and the off duty gunner scrambled into her harness, robot guns and directional were shifted into automatic are put into automatic mode.

The battle was joined. Gunners tracked each target of opportunity valiantly, while the pilot attempted a designer's nightmare of gyrations, and collective maneuvers hoping to end the attack swiftly. Whereupon one raider, the slower of the two, absorbed two hits crippling the ship. Damage clearly was enough to force it out of the battle. During and after this exchange, the second raider inflicted three hits. While not proving fatal, another words the ship did not break-up, or disintegrate, life support was seriously damaged, and the main drive systems reduced to a hopeless pile of debris.

Although wounded the port-side gunner inflicted one serious hit, and the starboard gunner scored another crippling hit, when the raider passed underneath. Coincided with a medium hit by the robot gun mounted just there, covering such contingency. Though none proved fatal, they sufficiently knocked out the engines and weapons batteries, because virtually no radiation showed on the short range scanners, leaving it to drift helplessly.

Resulting damage on the rescue ship is extensive with rubble scattered almost everywhere, hanging plastiform and radiation leakage. Main engines were useless junk, the auxiliaries still in fair operating condition were used in place of the main drive . . . propelling them away from the battle area at reduced velocity.

Most of the fuel was intact, and with foresight and thought the captain, and intelligent planning would at least see them through to the survivors, and hopefully to a base for repairs. Dealing with repairing damage, and clearing debris kept their hands occupied while the physician cared for the one male gunner suffering from a fatal dose of gamma radiation. The female gunner who was similarly effected, although not to the same degree, was able to still function, and help . . .

Less than six hours later, ship's time, the male gunner died of radiation exposure. Three silent crew members prayed for their comrade, and consigned his body to deep space. Looking on . . . the female gunner wept a little . . . . knowing soon she will be next.

Most important of the critically damaged equipment . . . . the life support system. Everyone realized the odds against them and worked constantly to keep the one system of paramount necessity to them functioning as long as possible. At the close of that day, while replacing a faulty bio-valve, the female gunner collapsed, and was made as comfortable as possible by the physician. Now down to two active crew, the captain was forced to rely upon newly repaired circuit modules, and the navigational trackers to keep them homing on the signal. Once satisfied they were indeed tracking properly, he confirmed the course settings, activated all short and long range scanners, and switched over to automatic. This afforded him freedom to help the physician, and work on damaged equipment. Largely though he paid attention to the life support apparatus.

Navigational bio-deck is, despite problems with other related systems, still functioning well enough to guide the ship avoiding obstacles and returning to follow the signal. Although considerably slower the ship, and its worn crew continued their journey ever closer to the rim, knowing . . . questioning for how long their own existence would prevail.

Two and-a-half parsecs away from the small yellow star, the female gunner succumbed to radiation poisoning and died. Momentarily the physician was overcome . . . it was just too much, and she began to weep openly. She had been so confident her friend would rally, but it was not to be.

Calming herself and together with the pilot, actually doing most of it, she prepared the body. Now, it is only the two of them, and solemnly they carried their friend's body to the cargo and ejection hatch. The pilot tried, but could not read the customary words, and trying to force his throat to cooperate attempted to improvise. She couldn't say anything, but touched her friend's body . . . to say farewell. With a slight audible whoosh of gas . . . . the body container rocketed from the ship consigned to deep space.

Taking charge of his emotions, Coss'ar helped the physician to sit. Pouring a liberal amount of beitra into two goblets, handed one to the woman telling her to drink. The ship seemed cold, forbidding . . . no longer a warm vibrant thing, but a machine . . . . he blinked several times. It felt much the same to the physician who looked here-n-there, no joy in the once sparkling eyes. She had never really thought of death, a discontinueance. But now . . . she realized it was quite possible, maybe probable. They sipped and talked slowly sometimes painfully as Coss'ar looked on seeing, hearing her fear. Sitting close together for several hours talking sometimes in whispers, they finished the beitra, and agreed to return to their necessary tasks. Tidying up the ship and trying to clean as much battle debris away as possible consumed the balance of that day.

Within a half parsec of one star, and within almost a full parsec of another, the pilot determined their position, and checked over the signal data from the navigational deck plotting a course toward the small yellow star. It was proven the signal originated from one of its satellites. But they would need to be almost within the system before ascertaining which one is their target. Exitement and anticipation . . . . the journey was almost at an end.

CHAP. 9

The star's planetary system was almost totally equatorial, while their approach is polar, which extended an advantage of picking up the signal not only clearly, but quickly without guesswork or unnecessary course corrections. Coss'ar plotted and entered a course deviation for the third planet . . . . the clear origin of the signal. They intercepted the third planet's orbit by using a large elliptoid intersection, fairly putting them well within a respectable orbit of medium height.

Coss'ar didn't feel it a particularly difficult maneuver, a little tricky perhaps, but not what he would call necessarily difficult, . . . a small puff of air expelled in silent thanks to the universe. Of major concern was not so much pinpointing the traders, but the continued functioning of their badly damaged life support.

Instantly . . . the elliptical approach of the rescue ship registered on the sensor instruments within the marooned ship, aborting the continued restful sleep enjoyed by Roak and Aor'y. Gradually the gasses were reversed, and metabolic rates slowly increased as required nutrients are added to their bodies. After a little over an hour later both were awake smiling at one-another with ever increasing anticipation. Both listened to the pleasant trilling notes announcing an incoming ship.

He was beginning his first orbit, that Coss'ar decided to hold their position with full sensors scanning the planet's surface pinpointing the exact locus of the traders. And wished all he had to do was enter the atmosphere, land, and pick-up survivors . . . and depart as quickly as possible. But he didn't think it was going to be quite that easy. Forced to consider the condition of his ship, and what remained for a crew, plus the survivors waiting for rescue, Coss'ar shook his head knowing there were to many variables. With no hope of solving them easily himself, he decided to forget his impulsiveness, curb his initial desires and do as he was trained.

Not quite three-quarters into the first orbit, sensors discovered and locked-on to the exact locus of the survivors. He altered the orbit doing everything he was ever taught so as to minimize the strain . . . . and started the approach slowing systematically. Gingerly easing the ship down proved to no avail. The accumulated strain of the battle, and entering a dense atmosphere proved terminal for the life-support system. Thus all further maneuvers and flight must be achieved on stored unmixed, unprocessed atmosphere. A similar elliptical approach was used, and a soft planet-fall was made only a few yards from the first vessel's position.

Coss'ar and the physician faced less than a second of indecision and joined the marooned traders, that even then were anxiously waiting outside the main hatch. Pleasentries were short lived, exchanged information, and the bleak status-quo hadn't substantially changed. Coss'ar and the physician described the battle, and what transpired afterward in meticulous detail. Roak and Aor'y's reactions, once they had grasped the implications and understood the situation as it then existed, were of course entirely predictable.

They faced the would-be-rescuer itself joining the marooned people seeking rescue. It definitely was not the cheerful, happy occasion Roak and Aor'y had anticipated. Joining Coss'ar, Aor'y and Roak sat in the compound, despondent, just sitting no conversation. Dien'Labr (or just Dien as Coss'ar called her) thought, saw, knew what would elleviate some of the depression. She returned quickly with a medium size yid container, sat it down next to everyone and began passing out litre bottles of beitra . . . . hard beitra and goblets. Dien urged everyone to drink until they had their fill.

Soon it began having the effect Dien hoped for, as she kept filling goblets, and drank a good deal of the beitra herself. Coss'ar was looking at Dien and motioned her over to him. She smiled impishly and sauntered over filled his goblet, filled hers and listened as he whispered things reflected in the wanton look on her aquiline face. Stealing a glance over at Aor'y and Roak already in each other's arms, Dien sat on Coss'ar's lap and shivered.

She loved his touch, as he rhythmically massaged her back, and slight ridge comb. Dien opened the first fasteners of her tunic, and said . . . "Coss'ar, I want . . . ." He probably only half heard her, already undoing the last of the fasteners. Opening her tunic he snaked out his long flat tongue. Her entire right breast felt his warm wet touch, while she scratched and bit at his neck and shoulder whispering for him to take her into their ship, and finish what he'd started. Coss'ar regained his feet and easily carried Dien who clutched several full bottles in her hands. Dien waved to Roak already carrying a half nude Aor'y into the other ship. It proved to be several hours before any of them re-appeared within the compound. And it was Coss'ar who appeared first. Seeing Roak, Coss'ar asked . . . . "Roak, how could it be still evening when so many hours, ship's time, have passed?"

"Coss'ar my friend, (with a broad smile), while we four were enjoying ourselves the planet has done three complete revolutions." Roak replied. "Three?" Coss'ar croaked, throat dry and trying to think through the beitra induced cloud. "I vaguely remember your explanation, but experiencing it first hand is startling." Coss'ar said looking up and around at the moonless night. "Yes it is, Aor'y and I had a difficult time at first, but managed." Roak replied. After enjoying a rather large meal, all four relaxed sipping from goblets of soft beitra. They began trying to re-analyze their situation from every angle. The military ship's life support was effectively destroyed. With the similar unit in the first ship also useless, and dismantled . . . the units from each ship proved fruitless, as enough modules in proper functioning order were not available . . . . to assemble one complete functioning unit.

Coss'ar asked, more or less thinking out loud . . . "If there was a method, and did Roak investigate it, of compressing enough atmosphere to make a trip back to the closest base?" "It is simply a matter of being to far away." Roak answered. Aor'y and I are now in the thirty-fourth year sixth star month marooned here; and prior to activating our sleep mode systems, we tried everything that was possible in order to leave." Roak explained in a matter of fact voice.

Though not as bad as the previous evening, it was still a disconsolate withdrawn group of four that ate together, and talked that night. When planetary dawn arrived all four entered the rescue ship continuing their conversation. In general dialogue was kept minimal discussing any possible options they may have overlooked earlier. Possibly the only bright ray shining out of the gloom . . . was the rescue ship itself, and what it collectively represented to the group. Aside from providing additional shelter, protection, additional guns, substantial quantity of auxiliary power; it represented additional food stuffs and stores plus other provisions. The ship's compliment of tools, a multitude of various garments, hand weapons and all manner of survival equipment was re-itemized, and partially divided.

Dien interjected and listed verbally the extensive bio-deck equipment with B-D'pters with the best array of instruments and supplies, plus herself . . . . a fully trained technician. When the tentative inventory was complete, the future didn't appear quite so bleak.

Roak and Coss'ar stated they wished sleep, and decided after some hours, ship's time, rest they will begin extending the compound, and the energy envelope surrounding the exposed roof area. Aor'y looked at Dien, and smiled conspiratorily, walking in with Roak, while Dien followed Coss'ar . . . neither will sleep very much . . . .

Upon awakening and a brief period refreshing themselves, the four gathered together in the compound, and decided how they would alter the area. Roak and Coss'ar dismantled the short-end wall now inbetween the ships and moved the blocks aside. The new ship was moved up against the first . . . thereby more than doubling their effective living space. Of course with the other ship up in its new position, the large stone blocks were not sufficient to enclose the larger perimeter. Because the new ship standing a full measure taller than the smaller trading ship, they found nearly twice the number of blocks were now required.

With all four using blasters and anti-gravs the necessary number of blocks were cut and transported to the compound. Rest periods taken during the evening-dark intervals enabled them to utilize the available daylight to best advantage. Almost five hours, ship's time, were used cutting and transporting the material.

Spending the next rest period eating with some soft beitra left little time for discussion before planetary dawn once again began to shine. And during the next several hours . . . the wall was extended well beyond the ships lengthwise, turn right angles across then turn to enclose the front and return to the door's corner stone. Once the height is correct, Roak re-activated the force field, which effectively sealed the top and all sides guaranteeing their safety.

The compound finished, the group arranged a small banquet of sorts, when Dien left them for several moments. After a-half hour the three started glancing around for her, and in seconds Dien came out of the larger ship carrying once again a large yid storage container. "What I didn't tell you before . . . well I wanted it to be a pleasant diversion. Just before leaving on this mission, I had stored a large quantity of beitra in the large hold," Dien confessed grinning. Putting down the container gently, she began passing around two bottles to everyone. And that evening, and well into the planetary day, first night period, they toasted the universe (their deity), the star's, the emperor, the empire, themselves, and each other, and every item they could think of; and well into the second and third night periods.

CHAP. 10

At some point, even Coss'ar doesn't exactly recall, it is however recorded within the ship's C'pter, during the attack by the two raiders on the small rescue ship . . . . Coss'ar was able to quickly dispatch one report detailing the attack, and its aftermath. He included the extent of damage sustained, crew losses and injuries and their intention to con tinue the mission. Once the equipment situation had stabilized and systems had been repaired, as much as could be . . . . the last message relayed by outpost to post:

> "They consigned to deep space two of their comrades, and because of resulting equipment failures was not able to return."

Scant weeks passed and the last message was received and finally, after inspection, relayed to Untey-3. This particular occasion the message was sent only one place . . . . military headquarters, where those who knew were sworn to secrecy.

A hurried meeting convened, the admirals already had the deciphered message in front of their places on the table. Discussion centered around the crew and equipment loss, just when their personnel drain was becoming dangerous. Raider activity had, in certain areas of the empire escalated making the need for reinforcements necessary. Thereby affecting a steady drain upon reserves already well below the emergency level. The damage estimate under study; one ship and four expert crew lost. It affected the old guard at the headquarters shaking their confidence, and forcing some to re-assess their ever increasing . . . tenuous position.

The first and foremost problem was available equipment, and trained personnel. Military's position is one of few ships and still fewer officers with hard experience to crew them. Worse, the threat posed by the varied factions of raiders was increasing to alarming proportions, becoming a formidable threat to most of the fringe areas of the empire. After much deliberation the admirals adjourned the meeting assigning the officer in charge of protocol, the unpleasant task of informing the palace. Communications officer was summoned and given a copy of the message to be sent to the council of the traders.

Reluctantly an officer, one of junior rank, was dispatched to the palace with a report explaining the admiral's decision. Once past the outer guards and corrupt secretaries, the officer made his way through the mass of hangers-on, corrupt officials of far flung star systems, corrupt under assistant ministers until he caught the eye of the assistant minister for military affairs. He in turn handled the matter of handing the message to the minister, who waited for an opening with the emperor. In moments . . . it was put into the grubby hands of the old monarch; who upon reading the message . . . . waved it off with his hand agreeing to its contents.

However, when the implications of the message was felt, as it certainly would by the emperor . . . . there did manifest upon the wrinkled puffy face . . . a distinct look of fear. Fear the empire should hold him ultimately responsible for reducing the ability of the military to such a low point, as to hamper it from being able to mount a more effective rescue mission. The young officer exited the palace in a decidedly better spirits than he arrived.

Before the officer regained the old lobby within the large collection of monoliths known as military headquarters, the message was already being heard by the tucanan system. Within hours the majority of systems throughout the empire would have heard the news. Most if not all citizens throughout that massive area hearing it first, were dismayed. In most cases that feeling gave way to almost open hostility toward the emperor, especially among the remnants of the military. When pressed for details . . . the military spokespeople only gave out the known facts. That in itself was inflammatory enough to put the people dangerously close to revolt.

When confirmation came the spies notified the outlaw leaders of raider groups the news, happenings and probable resulting outcome. Raiders were vexing, chafing to strike in numbers. Some of the leaders were more willing to wait and bide their time . . . . unlike others, and it was those others who undertook raids, and attacks on imperial ships sometimes to their undoing. However, that didn't stop them from striking, pillaging, burning and sacking trading outposts, and centers plus ground targets on relatively defenseless planets.

Two spies from the empire's military had been discovered, and fed to newly captured tuni-gors (a cat larger in size, but similar in countenance to that of a sabor-tooth from the early dawn of terran mammals).

As time passed the number of raiders increased steadily, but the number of ships grew more slowly. Ships were old, and always expensive. Old ships underwent extensive renovation, and the placement of additional gun emplacements. This was the normal sequence for ships bought or stolen/hijacked by the raiders. Unfortunatly for the empire's military, raider leaders knew fairly well the strength of the empire's remaining fleet units; that is the operational units, but there are still some old near outdated ships kept deep underground nearly forgotten . . . .

CHAP. 11

Once . . . during the beginning of the empire, eons ago, the fleet had been a formidable force to be reckoned with . . . . now, only a faint shadow of its former self. During the entire reign of many emperors, ship manufacturing facilities had been left virtually dormant, and the supportive industries on which the industry depended, many orbiting docks, only skeleton crews are on board . . . . unused. Truly an incredibly large complex industry laid almost totally bereft, allowed to wither.

Estimating the rate of ship conversion, the raiders believed it was only a matter of time, and there will be enough crewed ships, arms, and their organization tight enough, to mount a serious challenge to the remains of the old guard. Thus forever eliminating them as a force within the empire. Hence the fall of the monarchy, this being the path of their rationale.

With the passage of another year, a further message was received, and immediately it was priority. Knowing it originated from the ill-fated rescue ship.

"Two more have died from indigenous life forms, the pilot Coss'ar and the trader Aor'tiaws. Time dilation they observed, for each of their years, the planet number-3, and its uninhabited satellite, cycled around their star more than thirty-three times. The only ones alive were the trader Roak, and the bio-technician."

Again another meeting convened, and all present agreed . . . . if there is to be another rescue attempt, it must be well planned, done in secret, and soon. But it was not to be, for the emperor firmly rejected any such proposal. Each year the military slipped further and further in effective readiness as the empire moved slowly toward civil war. It continued for nine more years and three star months, and at the end of that time a fateful meeting took place. Every senior officer belonging to the "circle" was present, and discussed the subject of a military overthrow of the emperor.

CHAP. 12

As a small child, little more than a toddler, she played in the compound or outside the high stone walls of her parent's home. Massive monolithic walls to her, but the main door always yielded to her touch. Although sometimes unnerved by its size, she accepted it as a matter of course after her "aunt" explained how it moved.

Aquina knew her parents were gone from her . . . . and yet not fully departed. Because her aunt Dien told and repeated stories about each of them, so she came to know of them, and thereby held a fragment of each warm in her heart. These pleasant periods were cleverly weaved into and throughout Aquina's informal academic and personal training. Although the larger of the two sections of the house was closed to her, she found plenty in-an-around the smaller section to pique her interest. And although Dien cautioned Aquina, certain areas of the house, it seemed the youngster was always getting into something. As a child, her inquisitiveness was virtually all consuming, unbridled, and many a time Dien admonished the child, getting into places and touching things that were forbidden to her.

It wasn't long before Dien realized the child was not being prankish or deliberately testing Dien's authority, but simply little Aquina's insatiable curiosity. Virtually every day presented a deluge of questions. True, many were simple childish inquiries, but when the questions began becoming more pointed, meaningful and complex . . . . it was then Dien began Aquina's formal education. And was not unsurprised to discover an academic potential, and appetite equal to her curiosity.

The child's mind was like a sponge, and unlike some cases where such a thing discontinues with some children, Aquina's continued, ... voraciously soaking up Dien's instruction. It seemed to Dien, Aquina turned to academia because of lack of others . . . . children of her approximate same age, but wasn't sure. Partly because of the reason, and the child's birth . . . . quite often during Aquina's toddler and small child years, this period Dien would catch herself staring at her. Watching for what . . . . she really didn't know. But something, an indication, anything to bolster and confirm or deny her suspicions.

Dien recalled as if it as only yesterday. A while after Aor'y's death, Roak met and later joined with a descendant of Val'py. The resemblance to her long dead ancestor was remarkable, and from the same town, though now a more bustling little community. Though the native population finished a bloody series of conflicts that same year, planetary time, he and Asta were joined.

To Asta, Dien is Roak's cousin and life continued at the new status-quo for only a brief time. It seemed as though almost immediately Asta was pregnant. And to Dien, who felt the whole thing was unnecessary, it was to short a period, and had questioned several precepts; but then remembered the time and biological differences.

The birth itself, coming only a star month after discovering the pregnancy, was uneventful until the last stages when unexpected hemmorraging occurred. Working frantically Dien did everything she could to stop the massive bleeding, but to no avail. Only minutes after giving birth Asta died. Controlling herself, Dien carefully cleaned the body and draped it with a white and gold coverlet, and exited the cabin. All this had taken place in the larger ship. Their fallen comrades are held in stasis within special containers tucked away in the cargo hold.

Dien cleaned and dried the infant, covered her and went to see Roak waiting patiently in the lounge. Talking to Roak, who accepted the situation remarkably well, she introduced him to his infant daughter. All together she remembered not being out of the other compartment more than a tiny fraction of time. Yet . . . . when she returned to Asta's body . . . . only the rich coverlet was in evidence. She knew in her heart and soul . . . Asta was dead, yet the body was not to be found. Immediately telling Roak, he sucked in his breath handing the infant to Dien went into the other compartment and searched . . . . but found nothing except the coverlet. Dien remembered him saying . . . "Only the great ancient one could spirit the body away without our instruments detecting a presence. We must watch Aquina closely, and give her every opportunity." "Is that the name you've chosen?" Roak looked at Dien. "I had not thought of it, but yes that name was on my tongue, ready . . . ." He stopped eyes widened a little, and looked down at the infant. "Perhaps . . . . only . . . ." His voice trailed off replaced by a large smile.

Dien entered into her journal the time and date, and a total account of the disappearance of Asta's body, and all the other related facts.

So, from the onset, when Roak lay stricken from a poisonous bite from one of the lower-order life forms, she watched and waited. From infancy, Dien fed Aquina supplemental nutrients and medication.

Dien was jared back to the present. Aquina was repeating a question about a proposed excursion. She ascented, and while the child held her jacket and hat, Dien slipped on her special facial mask. A dab here and a dab of color there and she was ready, and seconds later keying the large stone outer door secure, ventured forth toward the fringe of "their large forest."

As they walked, Dien adjusted her side-arm watching little Aquina smelling flowers, looking at butterflies, and running her hands gently through the flowers and plants. Multi-colored insects flittered about "her" while small rodents scampered up and down the large "plants". Some chattered others squeaked, while still others with long ears and twitching noses hopped in the child's direction.

Sitting down the child is making little noises at the rodents and other little animals, and with a sigh Dien sat on a stone about three yards away alert for the unexpected. But soon Dien too was caught by the happy moment, as she watched little Aquina laughing and making little sounds at the animals. They came closer and closer until many were within her reach. She didn't attempt to touch, but held her hands out open pointing with a finger, and all the while Dien watched, observing.

This behavior of the animals was anything but normal, and remembered. Dien thought she would make no decisions without more evidence. She knew small animals often responded to a child's innocence, she'd seen it many times, so this episode thus far didn't prove or disprove her suspicions. Glancing at her wrist instrument cluster . . . they could only stay a few more minutes. A slight rustling of underbrush caught Dien's attention, and looked to the left to see a dangerous apparition. She instantly realized it is real, too real. Estimating fourty plus kilos it is grayish brown in color with a long snout, large fangs, and well formed head and pointed ears. It stood perhaps a yard tall on four legs sporting a medium length bushy tail. Once clear of the brush it stood quietly with ears up and forward sniffing the air.

Slowly Dien pulled the blaster quietly from the holster, and just as it came free . . . she rested it in her lap . . . . there came a loud throaty growl from very close behind her back. She sat deathly quiet knowing instinctively the animal would kill her if she moved.

Little Aquina looked up at that instant, and what transpired almost caused Dien to forget about the carnivore still emitting deep guttural growls behind her. The child extended her diminutive left hand to the forest carnivore, and as she did, began talking softly in a language that rocked Dien to the core.

Not since she was little more than Aquina's age, when all tucanan and empire youth receive their formal temple training, had she heard that language. And Dien . . . . then it was from old plicks, because at that time there remained only a tiny few priestesses who could haltingly speak the awesome language handed down from the temple. Dien listened as the dear child repeated herself. She sat dumbfounded as the fluid sounds rolled from the child much like soft music.

First one, then two tears as she saw the big animal slowly walk to Aquina, its rail wagging from side-to-side as its demeaner became softer. It stopped and sat on its haunches and first the left paw, and then the right paw going up and down until it found her little hand. She still sat on the ground, but couldn't hold the paw because of its size, and weight, and continued to hold out her hand. A second . . . . another, and the animal leaned a little . . . . its long pink tongue came out and a small sound like a "whoooof." All this while the small little rodents and others were on her other side playing with her right hand. Finally the large animal laid on its stomach, and crept up to the child, who . . . . made sounds as if to kiss, and the left hand stroked and petted gently. The head swung to one side and barked, and out of the surrounding brush and undergrowth emerged nine other beasts. With exception of coloring and some size variations they are all quite similar.

The first animal was obviously the leader, and as the pack appeared the animal rested his head on the child's thigh obviously content to share the affection. Some sat but the majority walked, layed down, while others crept slowly to Aquina's side. She petted and talked to all of them in turn and cooed, and other sounds, to the other smaller animals on her right side.

For Dien it is the culmination of many years. A long time of wondering, questioning, and frustration not knowing. Well . . . . she knew now.

Calming herself, Dien tried to think how best to handle this extroadinary child. It wasn't until the next day Dien realized . . . .

it wasn't little Aquina who had to be handled differently, but herself . . . . she must change.

Meanwhile the carnivores began leaving as well as most of the little rodents scampering off chattering wildly. This Dien realized was their chance to leave unhampered by the animals. And walking back Dien knew they both had entered into a new phase of their lives.

It was fortunate they lived in the outland region, more than just rural, it is an idyllic existence. For the natives the whole entire area was taboo, off limits. The one native village, from which Val'py came, was right on the fringe of the forbidden area. For anyone, and any native traveler who asked . . . . it is a "magical" or "mystical" place. Especially shunned when poaching natives, after venturing into the forest, were never heard from nor seen again.

CHAP. 13

For Dien and the child, the time passed quickly. And all the while Aquina was growing, animals of varying species congregated around the compound. During those years while she progressed admirably in her studies . . . . animals benefited as well.

In the forest laws of nature prevailed normally, but entering the overgrown and scrub covered medium-sized field, surrounding the compound on three immediate sides and hills, the laws changed. Hunter and hunted sat, some lived, came and went in very close proximity to one-another. Wildcat and lynx came from the high hills, and mountains and sat with the hare, hawk settled close to the pidgeon, and quail. The forest carnivores sat with the deer and elk, and there was always the scores of rodents and other animals.

And the others came, the injured, sick and sometimes females about to give birth, throughout, Dien tried to keep a faithful account even though there were so many of them.

She witnessed and instructed Aquina in her own art as a bio-technician, or physician. And on more than one occasion, though no sound was heard, Aquina would suddenly leave the compound only to return later with a bird . . . . wing injured or sick, or a forest carnivore with wounds inflicted by another. She helped to deliver dozens upon dozens of liters from all kinds of animals large and small. An animal never cried out in pain after she began treating and talking-singing to them.

Very early-on, Aquina began singing and humming to the animals and realized by altering several notes, she could put them to sleep. An instance, during any of her forays to stock her "bags", usually a veriety of berries in one and herbs and spices in the others, she was never alone. Animals and descendents of animals all knew her by sight, scent and by voice.

During these excursions now approaching that of a young teen woman, she wore blue, green tights or white with a glossy metal belt. Always wearing a sword, Dien's insistence and by her instruction, Aquina became very proficient, more for utility use rather than defense. A hilt and grip of gold the blade is as if chromed the shine was so remarkable. Using the blade, she'd open a thicket exposing unseen berries and herbs, or to expose roots and the like.

Sometimes, she ventured to within a short distance of the native village, where she picked nuts and other goodies. And as usual she sang songs of her own making in that special language, vibrant and lilting to the animals around her. And more than once the breeze carried her voice over the village, and beyond. It was a stimulating, prideful thing to the villagers and immediate countryside . . . . the mythus was close-by.

One bright morning several brave young men quickly ran along the main path and after a short walk slowed, and covered the remaining few hundred feet crouched . . . . then crawled on their stomachs to a point some thirty yards from where Aquina sat. They had crossed the boundary between the village and the "forest", and were fearful; but the music . . . . the enchanting voice held them as if they'd been tied and dragged to the spot.

Aquina sang sitting on a log wearing blue shimmering tights, and a transclucent white blouse billowing sleeves, and a gold belt. Her hair flowed about her caught by the breeze, shiny blond hair with red highlights. Surrounded by a variety of animals, she continued to sing and occasionally stand with arms out-stretched and slowly turn about dancing around them.

Totally entranced and hopelessly infatuated the three watched as the vision slowly picked up a gleaming sword, and gulped frequently as she petted and kissed the carnivores. They watched as she picked up three large sacks with no apparent effort, and begin walking further into the forest followed by the animals.

The screeching cry from a hawk-like bird caused them to look up just as it flew overhead straight for the vision of loveliness. Aquina emulated the sound, and the bird swooped down landing on a branch next to her. A few words and the bird hopped over landing gently on her shoulder. That was it. All three young men crawled quickly back, crouching and soon bolted . . . . running as fast as they could. Not stopping until they'd passed the boundary . . . . slowed to a walk talking excitedly. Reaching the village they quickly told what they had witnessed and heard.

Each quickly looked around at pottery and clay paints for the colors she wore. Finally one pulled out a pot with the color blue and went on describing the blouse. The villagers listened excited while the three young men, faces still showing awe described the hair and figure of the goddess. Several girls stood frightened as the three young men pushed and tugged at their bodies trying to show what the goddess looks like. All three men told identical stories, and the elders saw . . . . obvious wonder and infatuation.

As time progressed and the seasons changed those colors were seen and adopted by not only the village, but the entire countryside.

The planet experienced changes as well. Dien knew much of what was happening. One set of sensors and scanners had been positioned well concealed on the crest of the nearest hill.

Between her rapidly progressing level of study and the effort, and with time, the animals caused her to overlook the passage of years. During this period, Dien began physical training and dispensed with any further formal academic training. For during Aquina's life Dien carefully omitted any knowledge of her true identity. Her education was kept on a general basis except for the bio-physico, or physician aspect.

Hardly without notice because of her schedule, she began blossoming into a beautiful woman. She gained in height, a few kilos of weight and her light tan skin took on a slight, a hint of a burnished color complimenting the light color of her hair. And her figure continued to fill out adding dimension and fullness to an already stateuesque body. Even Dien remarked about some of the changes, especially when making or letting out tunics, and working on blouses because of her over ample bosom, and slacks because of larger hips. Aquina could accurately be termed, "a tall leggy blonde." Her longgg waves of blonde hair is highlighted with stark red streaks. A model's face featuring high cheekbones and a creamy, flawless complexion . . . . a model's face and innocent teenager's face . . . . but for the body. Tall and statuesque at 5'10" and a 39"D bosom, about 25" waist, and 36" hips, plus long senuous thighs and calves.

To some degree Aquina's attitudes had changed and psychologically became more stable and well rounded, purposeful and aggressive. She developed a flair for painting and design expressed by hundreds of sketches depicting her forest friends. And she related to things differently now . . . . no longer through the eyes of a child, but that of a young woman. It changed and colored her perspective of many things.

One of these things . . . . her ability with all living things had not changed except to deepen, and intensify. With her coming of age the power, her aura of fundamental power increased geometrically. And with it the beginning of a sense of calm and self-assuredness . . . a partial awareness of latent strengths not yet developed or fully recognized. Both Dien and Aquina knew all to well a great war raged covering almost the entire continent to the south. And when it ceased and peace reigned once more, Dien made her decision. They would slowly at first, begin to mingle with the villagers.

Through the use of scanner information each learned of the changes in customing, customs and idioms. Both memorized what type and the names for the frail crude units used as ground transportation, and the crude type of aerial machine. And while altering some existing garments to conform as depicted, each acquired a smattering of the commerce system. Such as monetary exchange and the fact gold being so highly prized, and the process of trade. And through all this, the obvious sway held by the more affluent, and wealthy natives, ... was Dien thought, highly critical for them. For with this stature eccentricities were excepted, and those natives were not harassed or bothered in any way.

She explained and discussed these facts with Aquina, who agreed with Dien's idea immediately. Dien described what Aquina was to fashion, while she went and procured the raw material. Within several hours Aquina had fashioned ten rectangular molds, each approximately a kilo in capacity. Meanwhile, Dien selected one of the many dozens of stators and carefully cut the core from one. Once in a suitable container heating it to a melted state was easy. She checked with Aquina, then quickly carried it with a small anti-grav pouring some of the bright metal into the molds.

In order to mold all the material, Dien had heated, would require cycling each little mold three times. So the process ended up taking more time than they had originally planned.

Laughing and giggling at their "customs" both exited the compound to waiting animals . . . .

CHAP. 14

Still smarting from their last rebuff by the emperor, the admirals comprising the "circle" decided on another gambit. One senior officer was chosen to plead for their case . . . i.e. "an organized rescue mission."

The officer accompanied by two aides made his way through the large crowds and waited for their appointment. Once the opportunity came to speak the officer was eloquent outlining all the reasons for such a mission. But in the long run . . . it meant nothing . . . . the emperor rebuked him and the admirals.

It was early morning with dew and mist hanging heavily about the ground as they walked, escorted by a variety of small and large animals. Those little or large ones dropping away were replaced by others. Increasing their pace, both eventually came to the scrub line, part of the boundary, and thence to a plowed field.

The path they noticed was more like a road, hard beaten-down earth covered with many different tracks. And continuing on reached a much wider road crossing their smaller one like a "T". Continuing on toward the village they turned at the approaching rhythmic clop, clippity clop coming from behind. The well appointed carriage stopped, and Dien accepted the gentleman's offer. Boarding . . . while the two gray horses fidgeted, and were soon on their way into "town." Driving along, Dien spoke only on occasion as the gentleman did most of the talking. Aquina studied him without seeming too, and was very happy to have a long knife strapped to her leg, easily concealed under the ruffles and petticoats. Dien explained, when pressed, they are on their way to the bank to transact business for herself and niece, indicating Aquina.

The area was quite populated Dien thought, as they passed farm after farm; and even more so the closer they came to their destination. Soon small and medium sized stone and brick buildings, and wood went by on either side. Streets within the bustling "little city" were paved, oil powered street lights and literally thousands of natives. Ships both sail and others lined piers and docks being loaded or unloaded. And finally stopping off at the bank, the gentleman helped them down and inside.

Largely because he eliminated pitfalls and problems with the bank manager, obvious to both ladies . . . . this was one of the privileged class, but even he gulped and momentarily lost his composure when Dien took the three gleaming yellow bars from her stout bag. The manager beside himself to please inspected the "inscribed" mint marks and quickly wrote out a receipt, and a broad letter of credit. Accounts are opened in varying currencies, and he presented Dien with a wad of bills, ... "for the lady's convenience," and had Dien sign for the balance of the amount.

Smiling she divided the bills evenly handing half to Aquina. Filling in the other account information . . . . such as address seemed innocent enough until Dien responded. Dien 'Labr gave her name and spelled the last part of it for the manager. It sounded somewhat different to the two natives, but it was the address that confused and caused their blood pressure to increase. She simply gave it as "the wood." The manager looked up questioningly . . . . "the wood?" "Yes, northeast of this city . . . . within the forest. We, my neice and I, have an estate located at the base of several hills."

The wealthy gentleman recovered more quickly than did the bank manager, and spoke to him. "Come . . . come certainly your not superstitious." "A . . . no . . . no of course not sir." Replied the manager, trying to sound calm, but not quite pulling it off smoothly. So the manager put the address down as . . . . the forest estate . . . "wood." Carefully folding the letter of credit, Dien put it safely in her small bag alongside the roll of currency. "Periodically we shall bring in additional bars for deposit." Beside himself the manager offered whole heartedly his cooperation and support, especially with tradespeople and the like.

When the gentleman asked Dien and Aquina to lunch, she accepted, for both of them. And through his help acquired a hotel suite for their stay in the city, while shopping and making the purchases Dien had hinted were on their agenda.

Of the many shops visited, clothes and accessories accounted for most. Dien had a blaster hidden under her petticoats, so they weren't interested in firearms, but did through the gentleman's guidance purchase a splendid shiny black coach. Course by that time the manager sent messages to all leading tradespeople, shop owners informing them of the identity, and wealth of the two ladies. And around the corner from where the coach sat stood the stables.

Escorted by the eager owner anxious to please the ladies, the small group entered the large stables. Though sizeable only six horses picked up their heads leaving many stalls empty. Aquina turned and went back to the street, where she bought a medium size bag of apples. Walking quickly back to the stables, Aquina went past Dien to the nearest stall. Humming, she talked to the first horse using her unique language, and an apple in the palm of her hand, held it up as the animal gulped it just barely touching her hand. She stroked the long forehead and gently petted the soft muzzle, kissing it lightly, and talking softly.

Aquina did the same with each animal, while Dien stood smiling. To the owner . . . . "I am quite sure my neice will insist on all of your animals." While Aquina busied herself with the horses, Dien paid for them and the coach.

During the dark periods both stayed within their hotel suite whispering, and softly talking until daylight. This routine continued until Dien thought they had everything they needed. Early in the morning, fifth day planetary time, with four horses harnessed to the coach and the other two tethered in the rear, and in the luggage area in back . . . three sacks of oats filled it to the bursting point. While inside every available bit of room was occupied by bundles, boxes, packages and squeezed in . . . . Dien and Aquina.

The driver hired to drive the ladies, and their property to their residence was not at all happy. He like most people in that part of the country was highly superstitious about the "wood;" and here he thought with mounting concern, "am driving straight toward the forest." Indeed, they'd turned onto the small field road and as the coach swayed an jounced along, the long lane began narrowing until only wide enough for the coach. Concern began turning to fear as the coach slowed until the horses were walking leisurely. They passed the scrub line and slowly approached the forest. With less than fifty yards to go the driver stopped, put the brake on and climbed down. He explained and apologized and without another word began running back to the main road. Not until he was well past the scrub and amongst the tilled fields did he show any sign of slowing down. Not able to control themselves both Dien and Aquina erupted into almost uncontrollable laughter. Still laughing they gently eased the packages out of the way and stepped down from the coach. Neither of the ladies worried. Aquina began humming softly as she and Dien walked in front of the horses. They merely followed docile and content.

While Aquina fed the horses and laid food out, and food for the others, Dien went to the quarry for more stone. She discovered many blocks already cut and stacked, but showing wear from long exposure akin to that of the compound's exterior. Before cutting new blocks, Dien began trying to clean-up the surfaces of the old ones. With blaster and anti-grav she cleaned and restacked all the old ones, now satisfied they would fit together properly. Thinking how fortunate it was she had accompanied Roak and Coss'ar to this very quarry, and learned how to cut and shape the hard grayish stone.

Finished with the animals, Aquina attired in riding habit rode one of the two stallions, along "their road" toward the forest boundary. In a light cantor many forest denizens kept pace until reaching the scrub. They stopped and watched as

Aquina, hair billowing out and jumping held onto the horses mane, slowed to a walk. In minutes she turned up the lane leading to the farm house and barn, as many field workers looked on surprised.

It was not her beauty and bearing, but the clothes and riding as a man would . . . . and bareback. Not ordinary behavior and she rode out from the forest. Aquina is lovely and sensuous as she slid easily off the large stallion, landing amid tiny swirls of dust momentarily obscuring her calf length black boots. As she stood gazing over the two medium size fields, the stallion rested his head just over her shoulder brushing the scented hair with his soft muzzle.

Upon her arrival farm hands wandered close and one ran to fetch the owner. He ran most of the way then walked quickly, his wife already watching from the cottage door. Walking slowly he stopped a few feet away bowed with hat in hand, and waited patiently, stealing a furtive glance then returning his eyes once more to the ground.

Aquina turned. "You are the owner of this farm?" "Ye . . . . yes mistress." At that moment a large dog came running out of the barn barking, and stopped snarling at the horse and rider. Extending her left hand, she said a few words and hummed a few soft notes. The dog's demeanor changed instantly, and ran tail wagging furiously, crawled quickly on its stomach the last yard until very close. Still holding out her hand he licked incessantly trying to please. Bending over she made sounds petting and scratching, all the while it tried to lick her hand and face.

Standing . . . . "I wish to arrange for some of this," she pointed to several different kinds of produce. "Oh . . . . every three days." The farmer stammered a little. Aquina smiled and walked over to look at a good size freight wagon. "If this was divided and each of these," pointing again . . . ." Load the wagon leaving it at or just within the scrub line. Do this every three days. Do this! She picked up a handful of carrots and brushed them off. Noticing the tub of water next to the small cart began to briskly rinse the dirt from them. And turned . . . . began to feed the stallion, who gulped and chewed until in seconds her hand was empty.

After petting and stroking the long forehead, she turned to the owner who instantly bowed. Taking some bills from under her waistband counted out the amount. And finding it came to within two bills of the entire sum in her hand, shrugged handing all of it to the surprised farmer. And as he thanked her many times, she in one fluid motion swung her right leg up sitting calmly astride the exquisite white horse. He looked up, with hat in his hands fidgeting, and hesitated then stammered again. Looking down she smiled, waiting expectantly. "You . . . . you are from the forest?" The farmer asked, still fidgeting. Aquina nodded yes. "I have lived there since all the land was . . . ." She moved her arm, "as the forest." The farmer backed up, mouth open and eyes wide and knelt quickly. When he looked up the horse was lazily looping away, the young woman in perfect unison with the horse with some mane in one hand.

In very little time a large garage and stable had been erected. And after Dien extended the energy field, a routine of a slightly different kind set in . . . . Each cycle of which began approximately every twelve to sixteen days, which is equivalent to about the same number of weeks planetary time.

Beginning with a large deposit equal to or greater than the first time, shopping although held to a minimum, still required help to load the now familiar carriage. Recognition was from their many dealings with the myriad of shop owners, tradespeople as well as virtually everyone whom they came into contact. And of course the farmer told others, and they told still more.

It spread by whisper and is kept always "close to the vest." Usually neither Dien or Aquina left the forest except in the coach. Each time the driverless carriage would exit the forest stopping always immediately at the farm. And quickly running to the carriage was the eldest son to act as driver, although he never used the reins to steer or control the animals. He was riding on top reins in hand strictly for the sake of appearance, and to aide Dien and Aquina while "in town." The young man held an envious position, and received a fair amount of attention from his peers. Adding to the youth's enjoyment was the money he was making. And as time went by his wage was increased with the corresponding increase in responsibilities.

Many times the routine cycled while their wealth leaped geometrically, and increasing . . . . their reputation as well. Not in print, but very low key, on the personal side done without fanfare and sometimes without apparent notice. Usually it was the working class and especially the poor, for they always lacked the resources to fight life's calamitys and disasters. Such occasions were often far flung, and ranged from a person with a broken limb, sick, aged or infirmed always received a specific quantity of money. It was handled by the bank and always with honesty and dispatch. The manager dared not to do otherwise. If it was a barn or dwelling leveled by fire or storm . . . . there would always be ample lumber and other material sitting neatly stacked the following morning. Soon after the appropriate workmen would arrive at the location and begin work. And always the same whether building, livestock or whatever . . . . money, material or livestock, it was replaced. The recipients had only to sign that work was completed or livestock was received.

So, it was the sight of the unmarked gleaming black carriage pulled by four white horses instilled a good deal of heart-felt emotion. And wherever they went it was noticed the horses never had bits in their mouths, but a kid of open bridle, which was similar to its normal counterpart, save there not being any bit. This left Aquina able to feed them apples, carrots, or whatever unhindered, and it was of course more enjoyable for the horses.

CHAP. 15

Planetary time slipped by . . . . it is six months into the thirties, and life stayed essentially the same. Aquina is in appearance equivalent to a voluptuous sixteen year old, to the natives she had not changed at all nor had her "aunt." Whether going to the city, along country lanes or on the road . . . . gentlemen and men in general tipped their hats bowed and always a few words of greeting. Women were no different, but kept their hats on, courtsied, waved and always a short chat. The street vendors, who always had some of their children to help and learn the business, were especially watchful. For Dien and Aquina would always buy something from each of them. One of Aquina's favorites . . . warm pernuts, she has a passion for them and pretzels, chestnuts, warm apples and many others.

That particular visit did alter the routine, in that Dien discussed with the barrister-attorney, retained several visits earlier at the urging of the bank manager; and asked him to investigate and to recommend a suitable university for her neice. He was able to discuss several noteworthy schools first hand, having had some knowledge of them from direct representation. Extending to Dien some printed matter on each school, she exited saying a decision would be made soon. And that she would notify him on their next trip into town.

Within several months Aquina found herself enrolled in a suitable university in the south. All arrangements were made by the attorney, and seconded by Dien. Aquina said her goodbyes to Dien, baggage was already on the train, and with suitable money on her person departed on her first adventure.

CHAP. 16

Aquina rode in a private cabin and watched the scenery pass excited and full of zest.

In an attempt to maintain control, especially along critical trading lanes, the military assumed responsibility for all scheduling, and routes for both commerce and passenger ships. The situation did improve, that is . . . . fewer ships were lost. There were other benefits such as the amount of good will the military derived from this action; and to be sure the admirals were smiling. It was part and parcel of a carefully layed plan, each ingredient, each move depended upon the people's acceptance and the more empathy shown the military by the citizenry . . . . the more the military courted them. However, as a formality they did petition the emperor each and every star year . . . . and was rebuked each time.

Amongst the arrangements was what the attorney felt were suitable apartments and accounts at a bank close to the university. In her possession, a copy of the lease, name and address of her attorney's counterpart, bank manager's name and address, and the name of her live-in maid. With one long dagger under her skirt and the other safely within her bags, she felt much safer. What she did not know, and was not told, is the attorney and Dien agreed and with much effort and patience found and hired an armed bodyguard. Intending he was to also serve as her driver, for the expensive motorcar purchased through the bank's representative.

Instantly the attorney and banker in Hamburg knew who was "she" and mostly because of their enormous wealth and social status and reputation. It could have been from any source connected to the bank, but the word leaked out . . . . the young niece of the "Labr family was coming to the university. Many of Hamburg's top elite waited at the station to welcome her. From innuendo and the few facts known about her, other than rumors and stories about her beauty . . . . the family is titled; but she didn't use hers . . . . it was always "miss." The very fact of a hyphen in front of her last name clearly indicated a title, as far as the elite were concerned.

They still wondered outloud as the ponderous machine began braking, no doubt the engineer tried to smooth it out, but didn't succeed to well. Just as the train stopped the short line of cars lurched, drawing angry stares from several of the blue-bloods on the platform.

It is the fall season and a little cool, and Aquina is glad she decided on the black light wool dress with ruffle bodice and black scalloped jacket to match, a medium wide black hat with turquoise piping and accents, and black gloves, and shoes. Not only this outfit, but all her clothes reflected the latest style. In all, she brought two large trunks and three smaller bags.

Helped down from the car by a grateful attendant, she stepped onto the platform, and said . . . "thank you." The small crowd pushed forward and introduced themselves individually and by couples. Single men plainly stared, as did the married men. Most of the women were either jealous or felt their clothes to be out-of-step, or both. But were forced to present themselves graciously. Many young high-born women also presented themselves, but their handshakes and expressions spoke more sincerety.

From the corner of her eye, Aquina noticed a tall man overseeing her luggage being loaded into a large impressive looking motorcar. Minutes later still talking with the young ladies and some of the single young men, the tall person walked up to her standing stiff and precise about half-a-pace behind her. The young women said they would get together once Aquina was settled. She turned and appraised him . . . . black hair, hazel eyes well spaced and intelligent. A square chiseled jaw and a prominent scar running left side high cheekbone to the ear, a trim body perhaps just under a hundred kilos. And she sensed the military in him . . . . it was strong and carried with pride. She let a slight . . . . the barest hint of a smile begin then stopped.

Looking past him and slightly to one side, she saw the motorcar. While she slowly walked toward the large machine, he thought she is the most beautiful woman he'd ever seen. He had tried to appraise her as she had done to him, but once past the awesome figure and childlike face . . . . the eyes . . . . he could not look into those terrible pools of blue fire. Like trying to . . . . to look at lightning but different . . . . a subtle difference he couldn't fathom. Instinctively, and in a second . . . . two he realized take away the money, social status, breeding . . . . she would lead and he a professional soldier . . . . would follow.

He chuckled to himself, couldn't wait to see the chagrined faces on those snobbish bitches and bastards at the university's two sections when they attempted to play their games on this newcomer. But the man also knew she would escape almost all of it because of wealth and her position. Still though, it would be a wonderful thing to see.

As she walked the train's personnel, had lined up moments ago, took off their hats, bowed and all said . . . . "Have a wonderful year . . . . highness." His eyebrow went up considerably as she turned. "And you, have a wonderful year, thank you." He quickly looked around fairly sure no-one of importance heard the word, but still he couldn't be sure. The feel and weight imparted by the luger under the carefully cut jacket was suddenly more comforting than ever before.

"Is this yours?" She looked at the name on the hood crest, "benz?" Bowing slightly at the waist. "No ma'dam . . . it is yours." "Mine? Ohhh, I see. It was Dien, or maybe the bank manager." She continued to look at him. He smiled slightly half bowed with a firm click of his highly polished boots. "Ma'dam . . . I am Kurt." She nodded with a smile. Running her gloved hands over parts of the machine admiring its low sweptback, sleek lines, the way fenders sloped down into the running boards, and the low swept curve to the trunk; the gleaming finish and black cloth top covering the elegant wood and leather interior. "It is impressive Kurt." "Yes ma'dam. This motorcar is one of the most advanced, well made, powerful and expensive machines available today."

In minures they are powering through the city, the busy streets alive with commerce as was normal for a large city like Hamburg. Aquina leaned back in the seat enjoying the opulence as Kurt pointed out some of the area's and buildings, and among those passed several belonged to the university. As Kurt continued on the area became progressively more and more affluent, until slowing to a crawl, he turned left into a semi-circular driveway. Kurt shut the motor off, brake on, and quickly walked around and opened the rear door. Extending his hand, she accepted stepping carefully on the cobblestone drive.

She met the staff in the entrance-way; the butler, personal maid, two maids for the house, chef and assistant, kitchen help and the gardners. While looking over the house the luggage was unloaded, brought upstairs and opened. As Aquina investigated the modest gardens and trees in the rear of the house, many of the staff watched. Kurt stood at the rear entrance keeping her in sight. Smelling and a gentle caress, she examined flowers, trees and listened to the birds.

Meanwhile the city's newspapers society columns were full about her, and facts much as attending the university received several columns. Glowing first hand reports, speculation, Aquina's description and that of her car, and of course the upper crust ladies talked of little else. The single gentlemen discussed her as well, with respect and desire.

Her staff quickly learned many things. First, she wasn't a snob, a little aloof perhaps, but not snobbish. Second, she is highly intelligent, interested in almost everything and for the most part considerate. They learned she is as complex as she is beautiful, and that, she is anything but frail . . . . displaying a good deal of physical strength.

A variety of classes were scheduled, more in a way to discover her range and depth as a student, than to actually impart any meaningful information. The next three years would take care of that burden. Academically she was either first or second, socially it was rather boring. Those functions she attended were basically school oriented. However, there are many that were not connected to the school, such as the opera, ballets, balls and dinner functions.

Always dressed to kill in the latest enchanting creations, she dutifully attended these social functions with Kurt as escort. When asked why, she should accept the private box at the city's premier opera house? Kurt replied . . . . "Your status Ma'dam. It would appear at the very least . . . . ah . . . . unusual." "I see." Was all she said, except for a loud sigh of resignation. Kurt sent a message to the "Labr family attorney.

An answer arrived late the next day. Although it did answer his question as to protocol. He, the attorney, had seen confirmed documents and birth records, and deeds tracing the family to a Nordic king and queen some years before 475 AD . . . Since that time there has been no less than eleven kings and princes binding the family together ever since. Kurt read it over again twice, then immediately sent for one of the city's best jewelers. He'd chosen from the selection an elegant diamond tiara. And sent a message to the opera house, informing them Her Highness "Labr would attend the opening night performance and party afterwards.

While Kurt made preparations for his own formal wear, he briefed the personal maid and the entire household staff. Returning immediately to the lecture hall, where she would be in attendance for a class, and stayed with her as was fitting.

Several hours later, after a light snack, Aquina was ready in a floor length white gown highlighted with gilded thread, strapless, long white gloves, diamond earrings, and of course the tiara. Descending the staircase was an experience for Aquina with almost everyone watching. Kurt held a three-quarter length white satin cape trimmed lavishly in white ermine.

The motorcar gleamed in the moonlight, the powerful engine whispering its muted cadence, she thought much like a stallion ready to run.

Meanwhile the opera house staff prepared the box in accordance to the message received befitting the stature of the expected occupant. Only a short while before the doors opened was everything pronounced ready, even to the single red rose held by a slender crystal vase.

As the orchestra tuned up people began filling the available seats and boxes not previously reserved. Of the later . . . . those occupying the boxes from the back of the house represented lower echelon nobility and while the forward, or front box on each side was always reserved for the highest of the aristocracy. For this opening night performance a purple velvet cordon was hung across the stairs leading to the two front boxes, one on each side, double and triple tiers of boxes running from there to the rear of the large "house" used other stairs. Slung on the outside or front of the two first or lead boxes was draped a purple drape, gilded and usually displayed a coat-of-arms. Kurt sent as part of the message a drawing, a copy of the one sent as part of the attorney's reply.

In front of the opera house, Kurt held Aquina's hand lightly as she exited looking the crème-da-la-crème of the blue bloods. He escorted her slowly through the near vacant lobby up the stairs to the mezzanine, and thence to the cordoned stairway guarded by a uniformed attendant. A salute and he pulled it back, as she slowly climbed the stairs. With the exception of whispers and an occasional cough it is silent.

Softly lit with an oil lamp the large booth had only one chair and a small table upon which rested a silver tea set. She walked into the booth and stood for a second looking over the enormous audience. And opposite her a prince, who had arrived early specifically to glimpse the reported beautiful "Labr."

The prince stood smiling, as the entire audience stood, and bowed in Aquina's direction. She smiled and slightly dipped her head . . . . did an elegant half curtsy. She stood up smiled and sat down as Kurt held her chair. Kurt stood behind her in a military like stance, comfortable to maintain, and still be ready. And within seconds the lights dimmed. Kurt turned their lamp down himself.

The first act became the second act before she could understand the words, and what was being said. While she followed the action, the prince watched and stared at her. Trying to be polite he would momentarily watch the opera, but his eyes gravitated back to her. As the second act became the third, she found herself looking at him as well. However, she only did it twice; the first while he was looking at the stage, but the second instance she looked . . . . he caught her. Aquina continued to stare for a second, smiled and slowly turned to once again follow the lead tenor.

It seemed only moments to Aquina and the performance was over. She watched, and as the prince stood to applaud, so did she. Kurt leaned forward . . . . "Your highness, excuse me . . . a note." "Thank you . . . Kurt." He handed her the note taken from the silver tray, and watched the uniformed attendant walk away . . . . just in case. She finished reading, smiled and nodded toward the prince. Immediately he was up out of his chair exiting the box with his confidants. She began to move as Kurt reached for her chair holding it, she turned and walked slowly out of the box. Taking the steps two-at-a-time, confidants behind him, the prince slowed to a walk drinking in her loveliness as he approached. She offered her hand . . . . he accepted gently letting his lips brush her glove, bowed as she answered by her graceful half curtsy. He was young hardly more than her apparent age, and talked too much.

The party was large and held in the elegant ballroom attached to the opera house. Entering, those present observed necessary protocol. She and the prince began to dance. Much of the evening was spent dancing, several of which she enjoyed with Kurt. Taking time out to rest inbetween, and while sipping champagne met and chatted with many of the city's aristocracy. At a fashionable hour she nodded to Kurt and taking her leave from the prince, departed.

That evening set the tone for not only the first year, but the three to follow. Inbetween returning "home" for holidays and summers, each return was a joyous homecoming not only with the forest dwellers, but in and around the ever expanding city. And of course, she spent a great deal of time talking with Dien. Not only what she had seen, heard and did, but those things she wanted to do . . . . her plans. Dien explained referring to the initial message from Kurt, and why she sent the "information" in that particular form.

Aquina sent word ahead of her planned arrival. Riding the same train, as she had done so many times before, knew virtually every one of the train's personnel. They marveled at how not one hair had changed. And as she had done each year, she again gave substantial envelopes to the senior conductor, steward, and the engineer. Those were shared-divided around the train proportionately.

It is September '34, and with one degree in her hand, she was returning for another. Aside from resuming her studies, living in the same mansion, and Kurt, she learned a good deal of the new political party. The substance of her first hand knowledge, and suspicions were sent home to Dien in a regular flow of letters and pictures. At first the only contact with them was socially, the opera, ballet, parties and other social gatherings.

By the end of '37 the prevailing tension and suspicion grew almost palpable. But, Kurt's devotion to her helped enormously, and the wealth, social status helped to isolate those close to her. Especially advantageous to Kurt, who as she found out was a young brash up-an-coming officer during the first war.

Stress . . . . she didn't like it. As a result she attacked the courses and subject matter at hand. Aquina no longer kept up the pretense of sleeping during the "evening rest periods," but instead rested after six periods. Kurt quietly, surreptitiously looked in on her during each evening, sometimes more than once. Catching a few hours inbetween proved exhausting, but kept up until there was no doubt in his mind. She simply did not require sleep like other people. And faced the realization of other differences, such as her physically showing no advancement from sixteen to twenty-one. Albeit the transition isn't large, but there do normally exist noticeable differences. All Kurt noticed was the slight altering of attitude and behavior, and that was brought on by experience . . . . a thing internal not external. Then there arose the fact of terrible eating habits. When everyone ate normal meals, she simply picked eating really very little and in a normal week's time, he counted possibly four half-way normal meals, no more. After thinking about it for many hours, Kurt finally gave into frustration and passed the whole thing off to her family's "genes" and Nordic upbringing.

During the first five months of '38, several important things occurred. First, she submitted to the appropriate professors one thesis in science, and a long dissertation on military history. Politically the situation was explosive, and becoming rapidly worse. The new party was solidifying its position using frightening methods, with equally frightening results. From what she had read and heard they were rapidly taking total control, re-arming and conquest. Aquina knew of at least five girls who had left school because of the political situation.

Aquina suspected no pressure or demands had been made because of her being so close to finishing this latest degree program. However, word by way of telephone had been sent. Kurt received it from the university saying her advanced degree would be ready for her signature on the morrow; and the other accompanying certificates would also be ready. Kurt explained . . . she would be expected to join the "party" immediately afterward.

Looking back . . . . she smiled thinking about the course of action begun almost six months ago. She had systematically depleted the various bank and trading accounts, with the exception of a thousand marks remaining in her cash account, and hid the entire heady sum within her bedroom. Unbeknownst to her, Dien had pulled and liquidated-closed almost three-quarters of the accounts held by the various banks and trading houses spanning several countrys. In total . . . . tens upon tens of hundreds of millions of krone, dollars and pounds sterling had been pulled from varied banks and trading houses from all over the continent. What remained of the liquid assets, all had been transferred from countries in the south to the local bank, and banks in England. All the hard assets outside the country had been sold by mid '38; and with the exception of one property, all had been eagerly purchased resulting in an overall substantial increase of profits.

When Dien, from a much worried and harassed bank manager, and the now two attorneys, met with her advisors and explained. She not only explained, but predicted a ninety-eight percent probability of war. It occupied the entire morning in which Dien suggested they should pull their personal fortunes as well. They discussed it at some length after her departure, and ended up following her example. Dien's prediction of war between '39 and '40 was as events verified . . . . accurate.

It is Thursday evening after dismissing her personal maid, she began packing everything except her oldest gowns. Within the smaller of the two trunks went part of the money, jewelry et-cetera . . . with clothes on top. Balance of her currency, except a large wad of bills, was hidden amongst the remaining pieces of luggage. While a good number of outdated gowns still hung in the closets all the dresser draws were empty.

Quietly she rang Kurt out of a disturbing dream, and fifteen minutes later admitted him to her suite. With nothing more than a transparent negligee covered by a revealing robe. Aquina preceeded him and sat down in the sitting room located next to the bedroom. Looking past her he saw the smaller of the two trunks, and all the hand luggage. Kurt nodded only slightly as a knowing smile covered his face. She indicated the couch next to her, and he sat with a look as if to say he knew what she was going to do. But . . . it began on a tact he didn't expect. Aquina gently squeezed his left hand, motioned for him to sit as she stood walking to the liquor cabinet. Pouring a healthy amount into two glasses, she turned and walked back making no attempt to close the loose robe.

"You are half jewish . . . . aren't you?" He nodded assent. "Then you wish to avoid them probably more than I." "Yes ma'dam, I must at all costs."

"Good." And standing very close to him while he sat, she whispered. "As you can see, I'm packed ready to leave." Continuing to whisper . . . . "You must escape, as I must; and I want you to be with me. Will you come?" Kurt leaned forward kissing her navel through the filmy material. "Of course, I will." He uttered huskily.

"Quickly then . . . . pack everything except your formal clothes. Leave them, but pack all your regular things. All of our baggage must be in the benz before dawn." Kurt stood looking at her for some seconds, smiled and went quietly to the door.

Twenty-five minutes later he re-entered silently, walked through a succession of rooms and entered cat-like, and stood transfixed by the vision before him. He watched as she, clad only in a satin clinging teddy, bend-over to put on a half-slip, again stoop and stepped into a light colored skirt and fastened it, slip into a light blue blouse and turned facing him . . . . the blouse wide open. He slowly covered the intervening distance, she said softly. "I like your eyes on me. Do you . . . . I mean . . . . like watching me . . . . dress?" For an answer . . . a small groan escaped his throat, and leaned down a bit kissing her gently. He broke the kiss smiling, wondering at her innocence.

Buttoning the blouse, she quickly tucked it under the skirt and donned the matching jacket. Slipping into a soft pair of loafers, she grabbed one end of the trunk as Kurt grabbed the other. Careful so as not to bump anything they slowly made their way down the back stairway to the side door. Once in back of the machine loading the trunk was easy. Three more trips and every piece of luggage was safely in the car's trunk, or back seat and floor. In ten minutes both are once again sitting in her suite.

With a sigh of relief, Aquina filled two glasses with cognac handing one to Kurt. She took a sip and whispering . . . . "We'll have breakfast and leave early, but not directly for the university. I shall bring several books with us and will be reading when you make three stops." Kurt raised an eyelid. "First stop, will be for wine and such." She took out a wad of money, splitting it, handing a healthy handful to him, and put the balance back under her waistband. "Buy six large bottles of a good wine, and at least three or four bottles of cognac. Second stop will be for bread and cheese. I think five or six long loaves, and say ohhh . . . . ahhh a sizeable piece of good cheddar. And the third is for flowers . . . ." She winked at him. "And you know who gets the flowers." She said smiling. "No-one will suspect this is anything but a romantic weekend." He chuckled . . . "Very good, ma-dam. It should work. But how far do we take this, just in case?" "As far as you wish."

Aquina touched his arm, then his chest and moved it up and around . . . . "I wish to learn only from a special kind of man." She uttered low and softly. Her other purpose crystal clear to him, now. "And if I should forget myself while in passion . . ." She had her hand under his shirt and suddenly turned well manicured nails into his skin . . . just enough. "I may forget as well."

"You would make an excellent military officer." Kurt replied with a smile. And to say thank you, Aquina planted a kiss just below the hollow of his throat.

Both stayed up and awake, adrenaline still pumping keeping both alert full of energy. Looking at her watch, she decided it was late enough and picking up her jacket, slipped into matching heels. . . . and strode purposely through the door. Not her walk nor gesture indicated the planned adventure. Arriving downstairs she encountered her personal maid just coming upstairs. Aquina quickly stalled that and instead gave her the day off. Offering the excuse . . . . "I shall be at the university until almost evening saying goodbye to friends." It allayed suspicions and bought them some time. Downstairs in the diningroom Kurt was crisp, although, she noted some redness to his eyes. And as usual she ate one egg, one piece of toast, a small glass of juice and hot tea. She had almost finished. "Kurt." "Yes ma'dam." "Please bring the motorcar around. There are some errands to do before I arrive at the university." "Yes ma'dam."

Fifteen minutes and they are pulling out of the driveway. Twenty minutes later Kurt parked in front of a liquor distributor, and purchased six bottles of their best rhine wine, and six bottles of the best cognac. Packed in two wooden boxes properly cushioned with ice packed around them, they are loaded into the front of the benz. The next stop was only moments away as Kurt bought half-a-dozen varied types of breads, and a small ring of cheddar, and another of swiss. He put it all, with a quantity of olives and pickles in a basket with some odds-n-ends, and loaded them in the front seat as well.

The third and most enjoyable stop was for the flowers. He eventually returned with several dozen long stem roses. Kurt explained as he ceremoniously gave them to her, the shop owner and employees were gawking through the glass. Aquina leaned over the seat and kissed him slowly . . . sensuously, in full view of the stunned onlookers.

Taking their time, Kurt doubled back toward the university, and as always parked in the same place. He escorted Aquina like any other day, but it wasn't like any other day. She stopped to chat with various friends, as he watched with approval at her cool calm manner. She parted and waved to other friends and walked directly toward the director's office.

Kurt looked on smiling as she signed her name many times. Aquina shook hands with the director and the deans of each department, while an aide inserted the degree and certificates into a heavy paper folder, then into a leather binder. Not until she and Kurt exited the main office, did she begin to get nervous.

As they walked to the benz, she was positive every eye is upon them. True, there are some people looking, but not for the purpose of spying. Once in the back seat, Aquina began to slowly relax. Especially after Kurt began moving through traffic, the main northern artery. During the fourty minutes it required to leave the city they discussed their necessary route.

CHAP. 17

Kurt maintained an easy pace of between thirty-five and fourty m.p.h. and "ma-dam, I believe we have about one hundred-eight miles to the border; but, I think it wise to stop several times off this road, not only for you to relax, but also to maintain our charade, and eat." "That will be fine Kurt. I would like to continue now until we have at least an hour's distance inbetween us and the city." Kurt nodded and smiled, as he glimpsed her taking off her jacket.

During that hour, only two vehicles passed them . . . . a farm truck and a dispatch rider using a loud two-wheel vehicle. They continued on for twelve minutes before coming to a side road leading off into the trees and scrub. Slowing drastically, Kurt carefully brought the sedan into the trees making it totally invisible from the road. Without waiting, Aquina opened the door and stepped out, and quickly opened the front door leaning in rummaging in one bag. Kurt brought out a blanket from the trunk, and had it spread out on the ground next to the car. Looking at Aquina bending over half in and half out of the vehicle was enough to quicken his blood, and more. She handed him a loaf of bread, the two cheese and from the wooden box . . . . two cold bottles of wine. And while he opened the wine, she lifted her skirt pulling the long dagger from its shealth, without the slightest hint of shyness, or self consciousness.

Calmly and with firm strokes, she began cutting some cheese into small strips, and just as quickly sliced up the entire loaf of bread. With a cup of wine each, and then another, and having eaten some cheese from each ring, the knot formed earlier in each of them began to dissipate.

Packing everything together in the back seat, Kurt turned the car around and is once again heading north. A few minutes later . . . . "Kurt do we have enough petrol to cross the border?" "Yes ma-dam, though we must stop soon afterwards." "Good, I'm glad we don't have to stop." Kurt smiled knowing she was getting more nervous and fidgety. Aquina busied herself with holding a cup for Kurt, and fed him some cheese while he drove. It was all very domestic.

More traffic and still more, as they drew closer to the large town directly ahead on the same road. Fourty minutes from where they had stopped . . . . they began encountering the buildings. Slowly through pedestrians, farm produce carts, and around some parked military trucks and smaller vehicles, minutes later he began to accelerate smoothly, gradually trying not to draw undo attention.

Just out of the town and up to fourty-five m.p.h., Kurt let up on the accelerator keeping their speed at that level. Seven minutes and the large fork in the road lay directly ahead. "Kurt go left." "Yes ma-dam." "Okay, according to the map we have an uninterrupted road to the border." Fifteen minutes and the bridge across the canal loomed into view. Once clear of the bridge, Kurt accelerated returning to their former speed. And fourty-one minutes later stopped at the border. The gate across the road and three guards barred their way, and with the detestful symbol on their arms were checking identity papers.

Aquina handed Kurt her papers, and while he had his luger in the right hand, ready in case of trouble. Aquina leaned back in the seat casually sipping from the wine filled cup. One guard was standing in front of the benz about twenty feet away against the gate. His weapon slung over his shoulder and laying against his back. The other guard appeared to be sleeping within the small brightly striped little guard hut. Walking toward them is a different sort; the guard's uniform is more modern than he was used to, but the sergeant's insignia was the same.

When the guard saw Kurt's identification . . . . he instantly sprang to attention and saluted. "Heir captain." "Morning sergeant." As the sergeant looked at Aquina's papers he did a double take at the name, title, and face. The guard smiled. "A pleasant duty captain." "Yes, a small reward for many years of service." He saluted Aquina and held it for the captain, who nodded in acknowledgement. "Pass captain." "Thank you sergeant." The gate was raised and in seconds they are across the border and accelerating. Around the corner . . . she clapped and cheered. A few miles and they pulled into Bov, rested, ate, and drank and found enough petrol to continue to a larger town.

About twenty minutes and a road running off close to parallel with the main road advertised a town and petrol. It is much bigger poised on an inlet, part of a fjord, quiet and friendly. Kurt stopped the car and went around and helped Aquina out of the back seat. Her hair . . . . free and moving in the gentle breeze as she walked around the small area stretching. It is then Aquina noticed the coat-of-arms on the car door, she studied it . . . . and decided she approved. She shared the heritage of Roak more than she knew, at that point in her life, wearing-living it.

Kurt brought out several five gallon cans, and using a funnel started to pour petrol into the tank. Some townspeople passed bowed or curtsied acting shy and unsure of themselves. Aquina slowly smiled while some cats, dogs and other small animals congregated around her. She paused played a little, then continued toward the village's main house. A combination of church-meeting hall, and in the entrance . . . . a very old wood carving. Its colors bright and well maintained, shiny from countless layers of wax, and many hours of hand polishing. Gently, Aquina ever so softly brushed it with the finger tips of her left hand.

She whispered. "The three boys were dear and good . . . . they captured my likeness fairly well." And a small sigh of rememberance. "Blissful days, beautiful and an innocent world, when it was so nice and simple." Aquina turned, standing . . . then kneeling three older men, one woman and many children. They stared wide-eyed in wonder, not able to speak.

"Though war will come, I will be home in the wood; and will be through the area helping." She took three thousand krone placing it in the elder's hands. "Use this for your people, and I will bring more." She smiled, turned walking slowly back outside retracing her steps to the benz. In little more than a minute, possibly two, all they heard and saw was the sleek benz purring moving slowly at first then accelerating rapidly toward the main road.

Looking at the map, she measured as best she could. "Kurt . . . it's about thirty miles from that town to our turn-off. We go through a small city and immediately after turn left heading west." He nodded, a thoughtful look on his face.

A few minutes past noon they encountered the cut-off, and Kurt dutifully slowed, turned and accelerated back to their normal pace. Soon with only perhaps fifteen miles covered, Kurt slowed quickly pulled over onto the side, until the benz sat motionless hissing and gurgling. "It is overheating badly, ma-dam. I must allow it to cool before we can go on." Kurt replied, looking in the rear view mirror. "Will it be alright?" She asked, as Kurt was already out of the seat about to lift the left side of the hood. "Yes ma-dam, in about an hour. It must cool down until I can lay my hand on the engine. And we will need water." "Ohh." She said, hopping out of the car, and quickly into the front where she emptied the two boxes of bottles. Much of the ice had melted, but a fair amount remained. Working as fast as she could, she emptied the two large jars, one of olives and the other of pickles onto some paper. Kurt watched as she crammed all the remaining ice into the two jars, and set both on the running board directly in the warm sun. Looking down smiling . . . "there. And soon we'll have water."

It only required a few minutes and they sat on the blanket bread, cheese, wines, olives, pickles and the sound of chewing mingled with some conversation. Two bottles layed emptied on the blanket as Kurt reached for another. He filled her metal cup and refilled his own, and a few minutes later refilled them again. "Hmm . . . . it's so nice and warm." And without any apparent thought, Aquina undid the blouse and shrugged it off. Only the thin filmy satin bodice remained with its dainty edging and lacing running from the bottom of her seemingly frail rib cage to end in an elegant little bow inbetween her large lush breasts. She sat demure bewitching him. His mouth dry . . . . feeling as though filled with cotton, he tried to speak, but only a soft croak came out.

Aquina stared into his eyes only a foot or so away, and slowly undid the dainty bow at the top. It came free and the lacing pulled out of the top two holes on each side until the force and weight of her breasts was free and at rest and equal. Kurt inched even closer until their hips touched, and slowly put his arms around her back. Delicately touching his face . . . "my first name is Aquina." She uttered softly, looking from his eyes to his lips.

Kurt instructed and learned, and Aquina learned and learned. They took from each other wrapped in blissful repture for over two hours. Thirty minutes more found both lovers dressed, and Kurt pouring the water into the radiator, while Aquina packed up what remained of the food and wine. Kurt was taking it easy bringing the sleek benz up to their former speed. Soon they began passing farms where people waved from the roadside. More farms and still more people stood on the roadside. Just before they came to the "woods road," . . . Kurt exclaimed. "Crowds ma-dam . . . . hundreds of people." "What? Ohhh . . . . yes I see them."

Kurt slowed, and slowed still more . . . then only a snail's pace as he turned the crowd parted people smiling, and scores were crying, waving as he rolled to a stop some yards up the freshly graveled road. Aquina stepped out to see the farmer's family, field hands running down the road toward her. She turned toward the large crowd, walked around the car into the open. Kurt stepped out, but stayed standing next to the fender, and watched.

She recognized many of the faces, except they had aged some ten years, others eight years since she had seen them last. "What is wrong?" They all bowed, curtsied . . . . a self-concious shop owner stepped forward. "We heard on the radio they closed the border this noon. And everyone everywhere throughout the countryside worried if you would be able to return to us."

She pointed to Kurt. "Kurt helped me to escape this very morning. But we developed trouble with the motorcar." As if to cooperate the radiator hissed and gurgled. As the crowd more or less encircled her they chatted, she answered some questions, and asked some. She assured them of her well being, and that meetings would be held soon at the city's large municipal hall. And as the crowd began to disperse, Aquina walked over to the benz. In the interim the old farmer and son, who now had half grown children of his own, had begun helping Kurt tend to the radiator.

It didn't take long to fill, and while getting back into the benz, their stares followed. The older farmer kept muttering. "Not a day has she aged. Over twenty years and more . . . ." His son stood next to him. "I know pa . . . . I know." He uttered solemnly, reverently looking wistfully at the car disappear beyond the scrub line.

"Kurt slow down a little please, and don't be alarmed at what you might see." "yes ma-dam." Looking thoughtfully in the rearview mirror, watching occasionally as she quickly looked out one side and then the other. Adjusting the mirror, he saw several large wolves gently lopping behind the car. And as minutes passed the number of animals, and the number of species increased as well. With the compound finally coming into view, Kurt slowed to a bare crawl. Aquina easily noted the tension in his voice. "Ma-dam, a solid wall of animals. What do you wish to do?" "Try and get as close as possible to the large doors on the right." He nodded. "Yes ma-dam."

He was able to do exactly that, as animals parted only to surround the benz. Kurt was about to object, but was already to late, she had opened the door and stepped out. The previous level of noise was subdued compared to the crescendo of noise that reverberated in and around the car. Raising arms and hands the noise seemed to drift away. So enthralled in Aquina's ability, Kurt didn't notice Dien walk around the corner to stand by his door.

Humming, she touched and petted dozens upon dozens of small animals of varied species. And they in turn scurried out of the way when the larger species gradually pushed forward. Wildcats and lynx some just down from the higher hills and crags were purring, mewling loving every second of attention. Some minutes later a big gray mature timber wolf ambled forward putting his nose in her hand. She continued to hum and talk to them as tails wagged, sometimes she would laugh or giggle, and as the wolf licked and was petted dozens of others came up close to feel her hands. Aquina paid attention to all of them only to be replaced with larger carnivores. A few males and more female bears with cubs slowly came up to her sides rubbing, licking her hands and face. Sitting down tired of kneeling, she paid attention to the cubs who are terribly affectionate. And eventually the horses. Only now instead of the original six, there are eleven adults and four colts of varying ages.

And as before, she kissed each on the muzzle, gently petted and stroked the long forehead of each. And while she continued to lavish affection on her animals, and birds of prey, and others, Dien introduced herself to Kurt. They chatted for quite awhile until Aquina finished, and the two hugged for a joyous reunion.

CHAP. 18

During the ensueing hours, Kurt not only was surprised at the informality, but marveled at the avant-garde dwellings and décor, and appliances . . . . in short, he sat looking around discreetly and listened. Having already carried in the food stuffs, wine and cognac from the car . . . . and the baggage. Kurt ate and drank while listening to the flow of conversation. Though most of it was finance, some did deal with armaments. That was his forte. "My neice has mentioned on more than one occasion . . . . of your having been a captain in the infantry." "Yes ma-dam." "Our country has very few trained soldiers, and I fear the scurge from the south will over-run us as they've done to Poland, and other sovereign states. We therefore are forced to adopt the practices of the raiders." "Raiders, aunt Dien?" "Yes Aquina." As she patted the top of Aquina's right hand. "Be happy you don't know of them."

"Kurt . . . you will know best what weapons a band of men will need to hit the enemy fast and hard, while moving from place to place quickly." With a broad smile . . . . "That I do, ma-dam." "Good. Make a shopping list of everything you feel we shall need, plus spares. I believe it will be at least three maybe four years in duration. We have a friend who owns several good ships, and some worthwhile men." "How much do you wish to spend, ma-dam?" Kurt asked eager to begin. "Whatever is required, but everything must be of quality." "Yes ma-dam, it will be." Kurt replied with a twinkle in his eye.

Dien watched Aquina watch Kurt. And with a definite smile began making her own plans. Namely an impregnable warehouse . . . . and became lost in her own thoughts and plans.

Kurt began writing, listing, and mumbling about men, some clothing and helmets maybe, rations, trucks, hand weapons and automatic weapons, and heavy-vehicle weapons et-cetera. He calculated what a squad would need for such an operation, assumed emergencies and then multiplied for a minimum of a hundred men. And the more he thought about it . . . . realized they would face several armored units, and couldn't imagine how that could be handled without something heavy. He thought of mortars, but decided they wouldn't be sufficient.

He picked up the glass of wine that Aquina was keeping full and began pacing around the large room trying to think. Back and forth until finally he stood still, and with a broad grin, and snap of his fingers . . . "Ahhhh yes . . . . yes tricky, but it hopefully will work." Kurt sat down and began to write and didn't stop for some time.

When he was finished, and had set aside the writing, Aquina showed him a "room." Kurt passed off the weird and strange furnishings, and what not, as one of the perogatives of the wealthy.

Early the following morning with Kurt driving, the trio exited the forest heading for the city. With his revised list folded in his inside jacket pocket, Kurt smiled during most of the short pleasant drive. Although they had to wait for the bank manager, and their friend, who owned the shipping company, it was not spent in idle chatter.

Dien spent the time looking to certain clothing wholesalers and merchants for bolts of varying kinds of material. Aquina handed Kurt a letter authorizing him to buy, and contract using her name, and she went around to the many food wholesalers; farmers in town, feed and grain wholesalers, making purchases and deals. Kurt went to all the three gun shops, and purchased their entire stock of certain weapons, ammunition and other supplies. Included were several long range scope equipped rifles. With that completed, Kurt went about buying every large truck he could find that was for sale. Those available that weren't for sale he promptly hired. Hiring the sons of vendors and those out of work, Kurt put them to work loading the trucks and driving them.

At the appointed hour the trio joined the bank manager and ship owner within the banker's private office. Before they began with the purpose of the meeting, both admitted to having taken the lady's advice given earlier, and the meeting was underway. It lasted most of the day with Kurt doing most of the talking.

While explaining the urgency involved, and their projected requirements . . . the ship owner smiled divulging the names and locations of three trusted arms dealers. Kurt divulged the one he knew, and together they split the list in half between the two smaller dealers, and gave the total list to each of the large principle dealers. Both Kurt and the shipper used the phone in the office to contact their people. First the independent agents were notified to . . . "alert their compadres for orders; but in the interim to pick up and secure everything of value, and await his ships. Written orders to arrive by courier."

Regaining their seats interrupted the ladies and banker, Kurt remarked. "Well the word has been sent, and our couriers will leave this afternoon."

The next topic was men. Men for an underground fighting force. "Especially the unemployed, some dock workers, timber men and so-on." Kurt said. Back and forth they discussed it at length. Finally a number was agreed upon. They would try for the figure of two hundred men; and then see from that point. . . . how many would be practical. Later when the meeting had been adjourned, the ship owner went about speaking to leaders of the docks, farmers, and other workers.

Returning to the wood, Aquina and Kurt went about looking for places close to the scrub line all around for observation and listening posts. In the interim, Dien carried and stacked all the leftover blocks not used when she had built the stable-garage, on the side of the compound facing the hills.

With binoculars Kurt investigated sites between the city and the forest first. And gradually he and Aquina with many animals in tow, widened the area of their search. On the other hand Dien, with three freshly charged blasters, set about cutting blocks as if there was no tomorrow. Abutting the new blocks against the existing compound's north wall, short and equaled thirty yards wide, and having gouged the ground approximately layed twenty-five of the enormous two yard long blocks end-to-end on each side. Once Dien had four course of block on top of the base, she began enclosing the end leaving a six yard wide opening. She went back to the quarry and began furiously measuring, cutting and moving them to the side . . . then cutting more, many more.

The light began to fade and with a sigh, she picked up the discharged blasters, and the weakened anti-gravs returning to the compound. Immediately she altered the field to cover and wrap the additional structure. Instead noticed the warning on the strained generator, Dien put a second unit on line . . . . in tandum effectively eliminating all strain entirely. She connected the blasters and anti-gravs for re-charging, and had closed and locked the door when Aquina and Kurt returned. It was then . . . . she heard the unmistakeable sound of many trucks.

"Aunt Dien, I've brought in the trucks from the scrub line." Aquina said to Dien with a wink. "Ma-dam Dien. Where do you wish the trucks?" Kurt asked. "Come, I'll show you." "Yes ma-dam." Kurt replied, bowing and went outside talking to the drivers and helpers. Seconds passed, Dien walked outside and motioned to Kurt, who then called to the drivers motioning them to follow. The trucks creaked over the slightly uneven ground.

Kurt followed Dien thinking only this morning the outside compound wall hadn't been this long. Looking back and then forward craning his neck to see the wall's end through the rapidly darkening sky. He thought to himself. "Dammit! It must be almost half again bigger-longer than when he looked early this morning."

At the end of the wall he motioned to the trucks and they began to pull up and around, while two shined their headlights into the doorway only to rebound again and again off the highly polished walls. The four large flatbeds backed in against the long wall, one after another, so about four sometimes five feet separated them. These held dozens of hundred pound sacks of various grains, feed and corn. He immediately waved in three equally large trucks, six ton capacity each similar to the first four, they backed all the way to within ten yards of the end wall. Quickly men began jumping down as the trucks were shut off, and they commenced unloading. Loaded with different kinds and sizes of lumber, as some men carried tool boxes, and belts that were tied around their waists. All the scrub and what-not was pulled up, and discarded as stakes were cut and lumber set-up on edge after Kurt measured off a specific distance. Stakes were driven and nailed holding the boards steady and secure.

Kurt, after he was satisfied with the progress, motioned for two more large trucks, one with bags of cement, the other with sand, tools, big tubs, wheelbarrows and other miscellaneous tools. They backed down taking the place of one empty truck as it drove forward next to Kurt. Calling the drivers together . . . . "Go back in this truck load up and each of you bring back a truck that's full." With few words they were in the truck and heading for the exit.

Dien and Aquina looked at the flow of activity impressed with Kurt's handling of things. He pointed out to the ladies, after he bowed, which of the trucks they owned. "Those four and the four being unloaded over there, plus the one leaving now, and the one coming in now." A large flatbed with short sides came in and began turning around. Dien and Aquina saw a large tank with the word "water" on it sitting directly behind the open top cab, and the stacks of wooden crates and boxes piled up behind the tank. It stopped almost immediately as several men including the driver began unloading the wooden crates.

The ladies noted the care employed while handling the various crates. They were stacked neatly and carefully against the wall . . . . all by themselves. It is painfully obvious what the crates held, and as Aquina looked at them, she felt a chill . . . . and for a fleeting instant felt afraid.

She watched as two men carrying three small beams layed them down spread and made them parallel. At the same time two more trucks came in, slightly smaller than the first units, stopped next to the beams. Within minutes men are off loading large rolls of heavy canvas. The second truck held smaller rolls of lighter material, dozens upon dozens of rolls and all were stacked on top of the canvas.

CHAP. 19

They watched a steady stream of trucks coming in, many of them held drums and a slightly smaller size drum, but only the smaller size was unloaded. The trucks laden with larger drums backed in and parked against the wall by the entrance, with the drivers climbing down walking over to Kurt. Two walked over and climbed into the large trucks formerly holding lumber, now empty with instructions to return the trucks for loading. Then drive loaded trucks back and so on . . . .

Aquina is pleased to see boards in place almost up to the first parked truck and closed off. Sand was being spread and raked smooth, while the men mixed and dumped cement so they could shovel and rake it smooth ready for the finishers with their floats. She noticed how thick they were making the floor, and correctly guessed it was because of the expected weight, and a margin plus for permanence.

And she watched Kurt supervising for awhile, then another truck or two, would roll in and he would pitch-in helping to carry whatever it was holding.

This went on and on, hour after hour until the dawn was well advanced. All the lumber already unloaded was stacked neatly against the front wall just down a little from the stacks of canvas and cloth. Before they stopped in the morning many of the trucks had been moved out of the building. And as the close to fourty men staggered out into the warm morning sun, they are pleased with their progress. Two ribbons of cement side-to-side, only separated by a greased line of boards, each section thirty feet wide, and one hundred in length, all floated and left to cure.

At that moment Kurt, Aquina and Dien came around the corner carrying two very good size, deep cooking pots with steam leaking profusely from around and under the lids. Once bowls and spoons had been stacked along with dozens upon dozens of loaves of bread, butter, salt . . . Dien held a large ladle in her hand. "This is very thick and hot, and everyone must have two of everything, and Kurt has a large barrel of ale on that vehicle behind you."

The men cheered a little and immediately formed a line. As they came through their demeanor changed. They are shy, humble as young school children, where only moments ago totally different . . . as strong men, boisterous and proud forgetting for the moment where they are. With each holding a large bowl and spoon, Dien filled each with two full ladles, and Aquina passed out the bread cutting it uniformily. It was so laden with vegetables, pork and chicken the broth had become almost as thick as syrup. Kurt was last, and as the others had done, he also said ma-dam twice. He still found it difficult to look at Aquina's eyes with everything they had shared, he still couldn't.

Dien spoke a few words to Aquina . . . who nodded picked up a bowl and poured a small amount, and with bread and spoon sat on the grass eating quietly. Unaware fourty pairs of eyes followed and watched her. In minutes two bear cubs came scampering around the corner, calling and running straight for Aquina. And promptly jumped, rolled wanting her to play, and from the building's corner lumbering slowly came the enormous mother.

The men sat frozen, staring not wanting to even breath hard. It had no sooner came up behind Aquina and put its head over her shapely shoulder, when several others appeared ambling over for affection. The men watched stupefied as she put the bowl down petting the cubs, and then spoke a language none of them had ever heard before, except Kurt. He'd seen this before, but it still held him in a firm grip of wonder and fascination.

The large bears made a variety of noises, while she petted and scratched, and she spoke back and forth. With the exchange continuing the men looked at one-another realizing finally . . . . she was talking to them. Petting each one again . . . the bears began walking off, only to be replaced by many varieties of small animals and birds. Hundreds came representing a kaleidoscope of color and variety. From high overhead hawks and falcons swooped down landing on the ground within easy reach of rodents and other natural prey. But one large very large bird screeched high above them, a bare speck high in the sky. Quickly, Aquina wrapped a towel around her forearm, and held it up calling. She started to sing . . . . and in only a few seconds the bird began spiraling down slowly, an artful dance of grace. Holding up her right arm it came up canted its wings, fluttered its large menacing talons out and effortlessly landed on her arm.

Truly magnificent as the men let out a long "ahhhhhhh," akin to a long sigh. Aquina hummed while the enormous bird of prey turned its head, the large curved beak opening and closing. Slowly she walked over and with the ladle put some meat and vegetables in a bowl. With her left hand, she picked up some meat blew on it trying to cool it, then held the chunk close to the formidable beak. It touched the meat, the beak opened but stopped. Aquina spoke and hummed, blew some more on the meat and tried again. This time the beak opened took the meat from her fingers and gulped it down. More sounds from the bird and she hummed, until seconds later it spread its enormous wings and off it went gaining altitude fast.

The men are held spellbound as a steady parade of animals, almost all natural enemies of one-another, co-existed in peace, came to her. Both the hunters and the hunted have equal rights, and all came; but perhaps it is the huge pack of large timber wolves, and the wildcats and lynx's that worried the men the most.

Visibly afraid to varying degrees the men watched and listened. From several different points there came the baying call of the wolf. Large groups-packs broke from the forest yelping and barking running pell-mell for Aquina. She kept clapping her hands laughing and calling to them. And behind them came the females with pups. Breaking their run only a few yards away, began running around her rubbing and kissing, while she hummed and talked to them.

Finally, she raised her voice. Watching with rapt attention the men witnessed a large gray male bark and growl. And watched as the huge accumulated pack assumed a pecking order sitting on their haunches forming a loose circle around Aquina. She sat down smoothed the loose skirt and held her hands palm up. Instantly the leader layed flat crawling forward a few feet to rest his head in her lap. Bending Aquina hugged and petted him crooning and answered soft sounds with her own.

She patted the ground with her right hand and the wolf responded immediately sitting on that very spot. Females began slowly walking forward between the males with pups in tow. Petting each female in turn and the pups, everything went smoothly until the last female. A little smaller and lighter in coloring came forward with three pups. But one is clearly a runt and undernourished . . . weak . . . . it could hardly walk falling frequently. It was also snow white in color. Aquina followed the pattern hugging and petting the bitch, and petting the pups. The little white pup made its way to her skirt and fell. With her nose the female nudged and pushed the little pup into Aquina's lap. Humming, she rested a hand on the pup, leaned and hugged the female, and answered the soft sounds made by the she-wolf.

Aquina spent several minutes talking and singing to the leader and pack. After which she began referring to the men behind her, and especially Kurt. She stood up cradling the pup and walked over to Kurt with the lead wolf at her side.

"Kurt. I have explained you are the leader of our men, and like him . . . you report to me. In this way he will feel comfortable, at his ease with you, and trust you as an equal. It is necessary he accept you, and after smelling . . . pet him and share your food, and we'll all be allies. Almost all the forest carnivors come here, and I feed them. Now, the bears accept all of you because I do . . . . but the wolves are different. They know something is amiss or else none of you would be here. But above all else, all of you must not under any circumstance kill, or hurt, or injure, any animal within this forest or any other." Aquina explained.

She continued. "I can't stress this rule too strongly. And remember their pecking order is not unlike the chain of command in a military. Their well organized, swift and mercilous. On the other hand they're equally capable of great affection and loyalty. They're very intelligent and learn quickly. I think that covers everything. So, please."

Kurt sat slowly as the wolf came up to him smelling his hair, ears, neck, clothes, back to his neck, hands legs, feet, pants and finally the face. Within seconds a large paw is lowered into his hand. Kurt smiled and slowly with his other hand began petting the paw, and equally careful began to gently stroke the head.

The men let out a collective sigh, seconds and the pack quickly came up doing the same thing to all the men.

With the departure of the wolves and other animals . . . breakfast bowls are filled again, bread and more ale.

"Kurt." "Yes ma-dam." "Please take the benz and stop at the nearest farm and purchase baby bottles, and try for several quarts of goat's milk. Contract to buy the milk every two days." "Yes ma-dam." In minutes the benz disappeared heading for the main road.

CHAP. 20

Meanwhile both couriers arrived at their destinations, spoke with the agents in question and dissemination of the orders as instructed took place. Adhering to their employer's instructions each sent off a coded wire. And afterward immediately began rounding up everything they thought valuable to a small group of armed men.

Upon receiving both coded messages the ship owner was understandably pleased and convened a meeting of his captains. With explicit orders for all five of his ships steamed out on the first tide.

While hundreds of miles in the other direction orders of a different kind had been issued. Orders had filtered down to the appropriate staff command generals. The wermacht was to move and occupy the northern peninsula country immediately north of their border; too hold and continue to move north and occupy the two extreme northern countries.

At the same time to move and occupy the small countries to their northwest. The planning began with the normal zeal and desire for perfection, and ruthlessness . . . . trademarks of the nazi.

Finished, the men moved everything outside temporarily and covered the stacks, and piles, and drums with canvas. All the parked trucks were moved out as well. And with Kurt's timely return, leaving his bundle and a gallon container with Dien, plunged back into the effort.

Hurrying into the "house," Aquina began warming some of the milk as she cut a miniscule amount from a selected "vitamin," mixed it thoroughly into the milk, rinsed the bottle and filled it, put the nipple on it . . . . a squirt . . . . she smiled. Holding the pup in a comfortable position held the nipple close then rubbed the nose ever so gently. "Ahhhh," she said as the little mouth opened. In went the nipple and the milk. Aquina went outside slowly walking and sometimes sitting humming, singing until the pup had finished about half the bottle, a little cough-like burp . . . and then sleep. This was the norm, four times daily ranging from half a bottle in the beginning to a whole bottle week's later.

Soon after his return the first of the trucks began arriving. On some "'Labr" in bold latters appeared, on others the lettering was on a temporary sign type of thing. One truck carried steel sheet and beams, partly because someone hadn't seen columns holding the roof and thought they would be needed. But Kurt told them, he had been told by Dien, the structure didn't need them, which caused some momentary consternation.

Despite their superstitions the entire remaining floor area had been graded with sand and cement mixed, poured and floated. And in the interim trucks rolled in with more steel in plate form; and cement with sand, lumber, petrol and food, dairy products and grains, barley, oats, and corn in one hundred pound sacks; and potatoes, peas, beans, flour and salt in fifty pound bags.

Aquina showed Kurt where most of the grains could be stored in the stable's dry storeroom, and on the other side housing their carriage, and the car . . . . a massive freezer and next to that . . . . an equally massive cooler. All the dairy products, potatoes and such went there.

The last truck came in carrying a great deal of wire and telephone equipment. Immediately, Kurt assigned eight men the task of stringing multiple wire from the main road all the way to the compound. Wire was strung to each observation point, plus a line from the warehouse and so on.

Unseen, Dien measured off and marked the ground for another structure equal to the size of the stable and garage. Calculating the number of blocks needed, she stopped almost in mid stride and decided to erect an additional structure. And with short stakes marked the new building's position and positions for two large sewer tanks.

Everyman not working with the cement, Kurt shifted to digging the two holes, and two deep trenches four feet deep under where the proposed wall was to go, graduated down to the tank level.

Those men digging the two holes and trenches finished three hours after those working on the cement. Large bore black iron pipe had been layed with main connectors coming up to just below ground level with tee's on top. The new construction would establish a large "L" on that side of the compound. With the existing stable and garage at twenty yards wide and thirty long to conform to the existing compound. Dien planned on the larger and longer addition to share the thirty yard long wall. With a common wall arrangement she didn't need to cut out or transport as many blocks, especially when considering the number of doorways.

So, with the men returning to their families that evening, Dien seized the opportunity. Equipping herself with blasters and anti-gravs, she headed straight for the quarry, and began carrying blocks to the site. The moon's brilliant glow made the job not only quicker, but substantially safer. She repeatedly thanked the ancient-ones as she worked, for the foresight to cut a quantity of blocks over and above what she had needed for the warehouse.

CHAP. 21

The animals had long since vacated that particular piece of ground as Dien stacked the surplus totaling eighty block . . . she adjusted a blaster and gouged the ground effectively cutting trenchs along the outside walls of the garage, and the new barricks-training, storage building. Once the trenchs were prepared, Dien practically ran back to the quarry and frantically worked the cutting jig back and forth, up and down.

She rested for a few minutes after cutting almost a hundred additional blocks. Dien then stacked the new ones off-to-the-side affording more working room. Taking a sip of beitra, carried on her belt courtesy of Kurt's gift of a new canteen, she began setting the blocks into the trench fusing them in places as she layed and butted them together. Counting the garage at twenty yards wide the large building at thirty yards wide ate up the blocks quickly. For each long wall soaked up twenty-five block, while the short wall, incorporated the six yard doorway used only seven blocks; and the remaining of the long wall forming the inside of the "L" was ten blocks. And allowing a doorway of two yards meant fourteen blocks were necessary for the end.

The first course used as a footing absorbed eighty one of the two yard long blocks. Setting all of the hundred-eighty, or so, blocks in place, she returned to the quarry walking much slower than she had originally. When the first rays of dawn lightened the sky, Dien put down the hot jig, and began transporting the two hundred thirty blocks to the site, five more than her design required. Realizing, she had perhaps two hours planetary time, Dien rested a few minutes, uncorked the canteen and filled her dry mouth with soft beitra. The slight burning sensation felt good, and discarding the near discharged pair of anti-gravs reached and strapped onto her wrists a fresh pair. Taking a deep breath she started in stacking, butting together and fusing them . . . as she progressed . . . After all were in place, Dien stacked the five extras outside the entrance, and up to one side of the compound's entrance. She cut off the surplus at the entrance, looked at the written measurement of the steel beams seen earlier, and measured off marking off each spot. Using the blaster sparingly cut six inch recess holes for the beams. She calculated they would meet exactly in the middle using a third section.

Finishing all the "drilling-notching," the smaller section as well, she carefully picked up her "tools" trying not to overlook anything. She glanced frequently at the road thinking it was time for the trucks to appear; but didn't see or hear anything except birds and small wildlife. In seconds, Dien is inside and successfully avoided Aquina and Kurt. A brief visit to her bio-compartment and into bed, falling into a deep exhaustive sleep.

Reading Dien's note, Aquina smiled appreciatively, and held the smile as she studied the sketches. She folded the small sheets slipping them into her pocket as she walked outside. With the pup fed and scampering after her the morning could be enjoyed. Warm breezes brought sweet delightful aromas, and saying out loud . . . "Hmmm the fragrances of summer, . . ." its so beautiful here." "Yes ma-dam, it is very . . ." Kurt replied with a huskiness in his voice. She turned smiling into his face, and turned back at the sound of many slow moving trucks.

It was readily apparent to Aquina there had been much talk amongst the men, because she raised her voice to the animals to vacate the immediate close area, for it was not just her trucks and a few from the city alone, ... but a substantial convoy.

Kurt began waving the trucks into a line starting from the corner of the warehouse on down to the new section, facing Aquina, and the compound. The immense addition caused a good stir as the men climbed down from the trucks. Many of which were loaded with brick, cement bags and sand, lumber, iron pipe, and like material. Drivers came up to Kurt saying their good morning to Aquina, first, now holding a feisty pup, and Kurt second. He was handed all the bills and papers regarding all the materials and supplies thus far delivered.

Standing in a rough line the men many of whom brought sons, stood whispering hats in hand . . . . waiting. The fourty-odd men who are of the first group stood more at ease than the others. Kurt spoke to the first group assigning tasks in the warehouse, while those expert with concrete went into the new structure. He then shifted his attention to the newcomers spending time and effort explaining the why's and what fors. When he split up the line into groups each with assigned tasks, three men and two boys walked up to him explaining they are cooks and bakers, and pointed to the two medium size trucks on the end. Once Kurt realized it was stoves and an oven, and paraphernalia, he had it unloaded and positioned just inside the doorway of the new structure.

Aquina looked on as four men and a boy ran to a large empty truck . . . got in and drove slowly toward the main road; returning two hours later totally laden down with sacks of coal. A makeshift kitchen was assembled enabling the men hot meals on a continuous basis.

Six weeks passed before all the construction was completed. Racks and shelving and bins for a variety of goods occupied the warehouse except for a wide center aisle for the trucks. The new garage was functioning for welding and general maintenance work on the trucks and other vehicles. The large new addition, "the barracks" was the last. Two stories high with windows only on the top floor is an imposing structure, equipped with small two and three room suites, allowing for the expected migration of women and children because of the war. Equipped with two large bathrooms one upstairs and one downstairs, the bottom was earmarked for the men, complete with kitchen and dining hall, with basic lighting throughout.

CHAP. 22

It was the last bit of the summer before Kurt began the training. Consisting of tactics used by the now proposed enemy, and then how they could fairly expect to counter and circumvent those tactics. He explained at length over and over what they could do . . . . and must do, not only to survive, but also to hamper their foe, keeping that force off balance.

During this interval, Dien wasn't idle, but working during the "dark rest periods," and when Aquina was sleeping. Disconnecting one of the serviceable robot battle guns, plus the necessary controls proved difficult, tedious and time consuming. Using the jig in the quarry she cut large thin rectangular slabs mounting and fusing them where the outside wall and end-stable wall joined directly behind the rescue ship, forming a large turret about some three yards square, and a yard an-a-half high side walls.

Dien finished mounting the gun, though connecting the controls required more time. A week remained of august when she had the installation totally finished and connected to the C'pter. Immediately, she widened the aperature allowing the gun more latitude of movement. Dien felt substantially more secure, now they were virtually impregnable. The field surrounded them totally, and nothing could approach . . . . no weapon or assault force mounted by the natives could stand against a single battle gun.

First Friday of September, not quite midday and Aquina finished feeding the wolf pup, who is now substantially bigger and heavier. In the act of sipping from a glass of wine the phone rang. Answering it on the second ring, she said very little for most of it, then . . . "thank you. We'll be leaving here in ten minutes. Yes, aha . . . . see you then." Aquina quickly rang next door in the barracks office, interrupting Kurt at the black board illustrating a particular method of infiltration.

When she told him the good news . . . . two of their ships have arrived he is ecstatic. Putting down the phone he ran around and into the main part of the building. "alright, two of our ships are in!" Met with a good cheer. "All drivers to your trucks, twenty-five of you stay here and unload the trucks as they come in. You know where everything must go. Rest of you fill up those trucks, you'll help unload the ships. O'kay lets roll. Wait not you cooks, our people will rotate so everyone has hot food." Kurt said. The cooks didn't like being left out, but admitted they had a job to do as well.

Dien came outside to stand next to Aquina, and together they watched the men running to the trucks filling them and began turning around heading for the main road. Every vehicle except the benz headed for the city. The remaining men opened the warehouse side door and got ready to unload trucks.

The work was slow and arduous, because much of the cargo on one ship is large and cumbersome. Indeed the entire forward half held ten wheel trucks, six wheel and six smaller light trucks. The aft sections held crates and boxes of mortars, heavy machine guns and the like. In seven-and-a-half days the ship is empty. Across the pier the sister ship carried blankets, medicine, a hundred tons of wheat, and automatic arms totaling fifty wooden cases of sten and burp guns. In addition Kurt noticed twenty wooden crates of luger and baretta hand guns. The entire forward half of the ship contained ammunition, one hundred-ninety tons to be exact.

With an additional sixteen trucks on the pier, a corresponding number of men had to be taken from the work parties. Resulting in the off loading taking just that much longer. Thirteen days working ten hour shifts were spent before everything was clear of the ships. Almost immediately the first ship was moved out into the harbor to anchor, with another ship low in the water barely able to make the dock as the tide was against them. The mooring lines barely secure, Kurt and his men swarmed aboard the ship like army ants. Five days became six working around the clock, but the third shipload of clothing, diesel fuel and gasoline found its way to the warehouse and barracks. Partitioned off from the rest of the warehouse for petrol storage was an area already well stocked with both large and small drums. With the recent ship load the area was packed, crammed full before a-third of the drums had been off-loaded. Therefore, loaded trucks with drums were parked on the side out of the way.

It was the twenty-third, and other things besides fuel was sitting on trucks parked on the warehouse's front side. All the space in the stable and around the carriage was crammed to the ceiling with sacks of oats and the like. The benz was moved outside and covered with a tarpaulin. In its place they stacked bales of hay as tight as could be managed. Both storerooms in the new garage was stacked high with replacements, parts and fifteen gallon drums of engine oil. The barracks top floor was used to store all medicine, blankets, clothing and all the rifles and ammunition purchased by Kurt from dealers in the city. While the warehouse itself was crammed to capacity with wheat, guns, ammunition, fuel, cement and sand, lumber, some steel, flour, canvas and cloth, and salt.

All the trucks arrived, but the men were exhausted, some to the point of collapse. Several had to be carried bodily into the barracks. Those who tried to eat wound up sleeping at the tables. For the following day-and-a-half most everyone slept, some were able to reach the dining tables only to stagger back to their bunks.

While the men are virtually incapacitated, and Aquina was busy with the animals, and her wolf pup, Dien began at dusk. She thought to herself, there was only one place available, and still be and have protection of the field. And having taken the time to move the trucks quickly and silently, she measured off the sixteen yard width from each corner. The long front wall of the warehouse eliminated a good deal of work, thinking she'd cut few necessary for the front entrance. Dien did however end up putting an access door of normal width in the rear wall thereby making it easier to gain entrance from the barracks.

Dien used most of the evening cutting blocks changing blasters frequently. Just after midnight, she started transporting all the slabs; and as on previous occasions gouged out for the first course of block layed, then fused each together. Continuing to lay and fuse blocks and trimming the excess at the entrance, and rear door openings, she finished just as the first dim light of dawn could be seen. Picking up after herself went into the "house" and augmented the field, enveloping the new addition.

Later that morning Kurt was up early, and as usual went outside to look around. Staring him in the perverbial face was the brand spanking new warehouse. Muttering to himself . . . "No dammit, I'm not going to get upset. Afterall there is nothing unusual here . . . . buildings made of immense stone blocks appearing out of no-where over night." Kurt shrugged his wide shoulders and groaned, retreating back inside the barracks. "Ahhhggg . . . . what am I doing here?" But he realized it was a rhetorical question. He knew outside of God . . . there wasn't a force powerful enough to make him leave "her" . . . .

And as far as he could tell all the men shared his feelings.

On the thirtieth, word came the last two ships had begun coming into the harbor. With every truck still loaded except for one small four wheel light truck, everyone looked first at the week old concrete floor in the new warehouse. Given the go-ahead the heavy trucks began rolling in laden down with large drums of petrol and oil. One after another they came in and were unloaded, only to leave immediately for the city, and the waiting ships at the dock. And by the time all those trucks holding drums of petrol both large and small had been unloaded, sixty percent of the allotted room was filled.

At a little before noon all the surplus petrol, lumber, ammunition, wheat and flour had been unloaded onto pallets, each in its own particular section.

With lunch out of the way a different twenty-five stayed to unload as the rest climbed aboard trucks heading for the city, and harbor. In the course of unloading not only did they fill the new warehouse to more than capacity, but stacked much of the wheat, corn, barley, ground flour, olive oil upstairs in the barracks. While surplus rifles and ammunition was kept downstairs occupying part of the rear wall.

Middle of October and the first snow didn't help matters at all. But the ships had been unloaded and paid for, and that was the important part.

CHAP. 23

During the winter and into '39 they acclimated themselves to surviving in the cold snow and still be able to fight effectively. This was kept up religiously all winter. Only Dien was excluded. Aquina participated in almost every exercise. Keeping her company around the clock is the wolf pup, who by now was nine months old and fast outgrowing that state where it could be called a pup. Already almost fourty-five kilos in weight, with large paws and entirely in white. Aside from the dark gray or light black nose, he blended into the snow with an eerie effectiveness. Snorting and sniffing in the snow . . . he could always be found next to or frolicking with his mistress.

With the winter on the wan life returned to the previous status-quo. Until the first week in april '39, and what everyone had planned and worked hard to prepare for . . . . happened. Those wearing the swastika poured over the border in strength; and at the same time their ships entered the harbors disembarking some troops. As they took over the city, and the immediate countryside, the capital, Kurt stressed caution and patience.

For a little over a year they watched, planned, and studied the way the invaders deployed their troops and armor. The autumn of '40, they made contact with the resistance from two other countries. All during this period the invaders were becoming more and more vicious. Mass arrests became frequent and their patience was at an end. And at the same time the nazi's became more and more interested in the forest. Especially when they couldn't take photographs, "always hung in shimmering mist," and large . . . very large.

Meanwhile, star month after star month, their carefully laid plan which had been carefully nurtured, began showing signs of picking up momentum. With methodical and relentless work and care their machinations behind the scenes started bearing fruit.

Aquina's "pet" was almost two years old, but is of an imposing size and approximately sixty kilos . . . . perhaps more, with a disposition to match. The one other thing always with her is Dien's miniature recorder. And she used it to keep track of Kurt's plans, lectures, and some general information about tactics. She played and listened over and over again learning, memorizing Kurt's lectures and stratagems.

A late word reached Kurt's office from a nervous elder priest in one of the churchs close to the harbor, just southwest of the forest. He said . . . . He'd overheard, on purpose, a probe or a reconassance of the forest was to be made without delay."

All the lookouts were told to be especially alert for the invaders. And indeed in the early morning two lookouts picked up a small enemy column, only three vehicles. In minutes twenty heavily armed men and one equally heavily armed woman accompanied by a large white animal, hid themselves and prepared to take-out the small column.

The scrub was thick on either side of the road, and as the vehicles continued on, the officer and those that could hear above the vehicles heard nothing, absolute quiet. They kept going unaware of the pairs of angry canine eyes watching them, dozens of pairs. First, the twin 50 cal. machine guns on the half-track brushed against some low slung tree limbs. In seconds the cab of the truck hit the same limbs, but with a lot more force. Instantly a nest of very angry hornets dropped into the truck's open rear amongst twelve startled enemy soldiers. Pandemonium reigned as they screamed, hollered while scrambling out of the truck. The driver was not forgotten either, as he fled with multiple stings. No sooner had the soldiers hit the ground flailing the air, when half the pack attacked. By this time those in the officer car and half-track got down running, guns at the ready; but they never reached the source of the blood chilling screams. Hiding on either side and stirred-up by the sounds of a "kill," they attacked swiftly and brutally.

Almost in the blink of an eye it is over. And in the quiet still air the wolf pack gave voice to their customary howl . . . . Those farmers and others close by heard the screams and growling, and many faces went white with fear. Then the sound of the wolves.

While Aquina calmed the pack, Kurt assigned men to dig some decent size holes on the side for the bodies. All the weapons and ammunition were taken and put into the half-track, as the area was picked up and checked for debris. Not quite an hour and-a-half later, Kurt had a driver back up the truck while he slowly backed the half-track off the road. With Aquina and some of the men holding aside the scrub, he backed it in nice and snug . . . . well camouflaged from even the outside scrub much less the main road.

Kurt sent the small staff car and truck to the compound with orders for reinforcements and supplies, and special orders to the garage. Twenty men loaded up mortars and ammunition, satchel charges and food in containers onto the truck; while the welder and mechanic mounted one of their heavy machine guns.

Returning they set up positions just within the forest line, while the truck and some light machine guns were situated strategically through-out the scrub. In several places men had satchel charges ready, grenades, and extra ammunition for their weapons. With the six mortars zeroed in on the main road and the plowed field off on the right, Kurt began to breath a little easier.

Kurt knew he'd deployed his force as best he could, and hoped the nazi's would be over confident to the point of making a mistake. He expected perhaps two tanks and three or four trucks filled with troops. However, what the lookouts reported early that afternoon illicited a worried frown from Kurt. He counted a few minutes later five tanks, two half-tracks, one leading the column, and six trucks with troops.

He gave the order to fire to the mortar crews, who kept up a deadly barrage for some two minutes; resulting in the rear half-track and first troop truck being hit directly. Numerous explosions around and close to the trucks killed or wounded a good percentage of the troops. The lead tank lost a track from a mortar hit effectively blocking the road putting its big gun on a bad angle . . . . so it was useless. The four remaining tanks turned quickly heading for the scrub at good speed. What infantry remained ran to form up behind the tanks.

Kurt gave the order for the other mortars to fire, while the camouflaged half-track chopped up its enemy counterpart. Being off to the side on an angle the gunner used the twin fiftys and began annihilating the troops moving up behind the first tank. The commander inside must have seen because it veered to the right coming head-on and fired. Kurt jumped partially clear, but the three others were killed instantly.

Immediately the heavy fifty on the converted truck opened up on the troops killing or wounding almost all the troops remaining behind the first tank. The action was taken up by the repositioned mortars hitting the track and engine compartment knocking it out of commission. But three panzers kept coming firing steadily. And as they came, mortar rounds kept raining on and around the troops taking a terrible toll.

Each panzer was within ten or fifteen feet of the scrub when the machine gun crews hidden and camouflaged opened up on the remaining troops. With that as a diversion several men lit off the satchel charges throwing seven of them at the three tanks. One tank skidded into a quick turn with the explosions blowing off the track and ruining some bogie wheels. The two other panzers continued on rolling over the charges to be thoroughly destroyed. When the machine guns ceased there wasn't one soldier still on his feet.

Kurt went hobbling around counting and talking, taking stock of damage. They had eighteen dead and eleven wounded counting himself. After almost twenty minutes of relative quiet the hatch on the disabled tank came open, and the crew coughing and wheezing climbed down and started to run only to be cut down by a machine gun.

Some of the men loaded their dead onto the converted truck and the wounded. Kurt sat in the cab grimacing and insisting that he should stay. Aquina stood by the door and smiling sweetly said, "no." And before Kurt could utter a word the truck started into the forest.

CHAP. 24

She stood there watching the truck disappear with their dead and wounded . . . . and something changed in her. Many of the men watched and saw her hands form fists. She began issueing orders in a very hard and angry voice, telling which men were to stay by their guns, and those others to follow. And they did without a word, with guns at the ready.

Slowly and methodically, with Aquina in front, they began checking on the dead enemy soldiers. Most were dead, but occasiounally she saw movement and quickly let go a burst from her weapon. Several times she chopped a wounded soldier with a burst from her sling held burp gun. And as she was finishing the converted truck returned with men, ammunition, food and equipment to replace what had been lost. One of the men came up to her reporting the truck returned. "Fine . . . . send it out here and pick up all guns, ammunition belts, and grenades." "Yes ma-dam." She turned. "You eight men come with me."

The eight followed her again without a word as the truck came out on the field with the man handling the fifty caliber alert covering the road. In a few minutes they came to the main road, saw nothing coming and crossed. Sneaking around the last truck, she came upon a group of wounded laying on the grass. There is perhaps twenty-eight men, and when she took them by surprise, and the white wolf next to her growling, snarling . . . . a couple of them dove for their weapons. Aquina cut them down and those wounded next to the offenders. Unslinging her other weapon pulled back the slide and cut down every single man. "Check all the others and kill any you find alive." Walking up the line of vehicles looking at each one in turn, making up her mind as she went.

She had just passed the fourth truck, and a blood soaked hand holding a luger . . . . shaking, wobbled and fired. Hitting the fender the bullet richoched cutting-gouging a line across her lower back. "Aaaachgg!" She cried out. Instantly the wolf was on him tearing out the throat . . . . the scream dieing, reduced to a gurgle. Quickly several men gathered around her while others sprayed the dead with hot avenging lead, then stood guard as the others very gently and gingerly picked her up.

Tears ran down her face, but not another sound escaped her lips, as the converted truck rumbled across the field racing for the road. Pushing aside weapons, grenades and belts they layed Aquina gently on the truck's wooden bed propping her head up with a vest. The wolf squatted down by her legs, a little whine and a whimper, its ears back poised to attack anything, and the men knew it all to well.

Trying to smooth out the short ride, the driver pulled the truck over as soon as he arrived inside their defensive line. Gentle hands picked her up carrying her up . . . . carrying her over to a cool spot under a large oak. Immediately one of the men with some medical training came over . . . . "ma-dam, I must uncover this." "I know . . . . go ahead." She said in a throaty voice teeth clenched tightly. Ever so gently he moved her over to rest on the left shoulder. Loosening belt and the snap letting the slacks come down a little, moved the shirt up revealing a long nasty gash. The medic let out a sigh of relief. "Wheeeew. It isn't serious ma-dam." Working while he was talking . . . . "I will sprinkle some sulphur into this . . . . now a bandage, and its done." He lowered the shirt appreciating the glimpse of soft golden tan skin, and rolled the slacks back in place though he didn't snap them shut, but left them loose.

Made as comfortable as possible, the wolf sitting next to her, the medic brought two plates of food . . . . one for her, and one for her white companion. Before eating . . . "Driver." He came over quickly. "Yes ma-dam." "Is there chain or towing cable on that truck?" "Yes indeed ma-dam, and a strong winch." She nodded. "The four trucks out on the main road. Take some men and tow them to the compound." "Yes ma-dam, right away." She called one of the other men. "Yes ma-dam." "Either of those two tanks with smashed treads . . . can we get one serviceable, you know so it will move under its own power?" "I will take some men and check them, ma-dam." "Good. Let me know one way or the other." "Yes ma-dam."

It turned out none of the tanks could be made to run, so she had the men dig several large holes on the plowed field's outer edge, and all the dead littering the field and road were thrown in and covered. Meanwhile one-by-one the four trucks, which had all sustained some type of damage, were towed to the compound.

At the same time, the local farm people gathered agog over the demolished truck, half-tracks and the wrecked panzer sitting on an angle just behind the half-track. But when they saw the one crippled panzer and the three burned out hulks of tanks . . . . many stood with mouths hanging open. Aquina's friends, the farmer, now rather old and frail, and son began recounting the battle to everyone as they stood gaping at the smoke billowing from the three wrecked tanks. And all the while wolves called back and forth from different parts of the forest.

Aquina had finished eating and delegated four heavy machine gun crews and two mortar crews to stay, a total of twelve men on four hour shifts. And when three trucks arrived everyone plus their weapons, less the first twelve, returned to the compound. As soon as the trucks stopped, she hobbled in followed by the acting medic and two Kurt designated as sergeants. Visiting him as well as the others made her feel better . . . . much better. Of course everyone had heard about her wound. "It's not serious Kurt, and wolf avenged me. Didn't you fella." As she bent her head . . . . the animal emitted a soft "whooof" and began licking her ear, smelling and licking, his tail sweeping the floor energetically.

Prior to the first part of the winter, Aquina planned, and led two raids. One in their city to the west, and the second in the junction city, at the junction of their main road and the main north-south artery, destroying fuel and ammunition storage, several small vehicles, many trucks along with four tanks . . . and numerous soldiers. And managed to mine large sections of the scrub.

CHAP. 25

However the winter was especially severe that year with but few sorties carried out. Instead it was a war against the snow and cold. Especially for mechanics who worked long hours protecting the vehicles. Carpenters made dozens of small and medium wood shelters, boxes, pallets that were covered or with liberal amounts of straw strewn inside. The field and compound was alive with varying species of animals. Everything from wildcats to bears down to the little rodents. Untold thousands gathered, lived, ate and kept warm in extremely close proximity with one-another. Though some came and went, as the wolf packs, deer and the elk, the place was alive with activity.

Early '41, it was Dien who actually drew first blood for the year. The C'pter announced approaching aircraft. She ordered "lock-on automatic selection." With direct hit followed by direct hit all six dive bombers exploded, with only bits-an-pieces falling to earth. And this was from a distance of seven miles.

And not merely once, but often it was the same. There was no flack to warn the pilots, nothing . . . . only watching in horror as plane after plane exploded without warning. After many such occasions the Nazis circumvented the forest area circling around at eight miles. Still they were destroyed . . . at fifteen the results were the same, at 35, ... the same.

During the spring, summer, and fall they conducted dozens of small night raids in which the nazi's lost both men and large amounts of material. Up and down the coast, in small and medium towns and cities, they harassed the enemy unmercifully. But it was not without casualties, and many owed their lives to the skill of Dien.

Aquina had been wounded twice during raids that year, and Kurt was wounded once. The weather was fair, and she was maturing a little more, and her wolf is full grown and loved to run.

About the same time the invaders increased their pressure and harshness proportionatly. Women and children began filtering, gravitating toward the forest. The lookouts passed the word, and Aquina or Kurt would meet them at the scrub. Women were just as terrified as the children even though a man's voice would calmly talk to them, reassure them that everything was alright, and they were to stay there until met by the ma-dam. In any case they always stayed rooted to the spot, sometimes glimpsing a wolf or bear. Usually it was Aquina who met them. Many times she would simply stand and smile, while surrounded by a pack, the white one always at her side . . . . usually sensing the fear hanging around the women . . . . would walk forward a little, wag his tail and offer a paw. Aquina's presence had a calming influence. She'd speak to the animals who would sit and watch . . . then speak to the women and children calming and explaining how this worked in the forest. Most were wives and families of the men; who moved upstairs with their families in a room or sometimes two.

Toward the fall of '41, the frequency and severity of the raids increased, and many times Aquina would play back a tape critiqueing her own performance. By the time snow arrived, they were down to seventy-five men; but hard resourceful men who knew how to fight and survive. The children went outside only on occasion, as they helped their mothers keep the barracks clean, wash and the other myriad of things that needed doing. The older boys learned how to clean weapons and maintain them while a few helped in the garage.

Early '42, sometimes during snowstorms, but always at night they made food and fuel deliveries to towns throughout the peninsula country. Of course with the coming of spring and summer life loosened up a little for the people.

It snowed one last time and Aquina seized upon the opportunity. Quickly with two trucks they launched an attack upon the newly replenished garrison in the city, and the rebuilt fuel bunkers. Using silencers their mechanics constructed, they infiltrated the city . . . . inside the nazi perimeter to find the two lookouts lax in their duty. Two spanking new tiger tanks sat in front of the principle entrance to the barrack's entrance, headquarters, parking enclosure, and warehouses.

It is a few minutes to three in the morning when the guards and sentrys on the tank turrets are knocked out. Quickly jumping up on each turret two men using silencers killed the partial crew in each tank. Quietly three of her men jumped into each tank, Kurt was in one of them. Sneaking around each corner five men in black started laying primed satchel charges, and starting from the back working toward the entrance, planted their charges.

The snow came down harder as the wind picked up as seconds ticked off . . . . a deafening barroom hit the resistance hiding on the roadside. Tanks began blowing up . . . . the night sky turned red and white, the wind was turned back as successive blasts ripped open the parking area destroying the walls and helping to destroy the headquarters and barracks. Kurt immediately moved his tiger out onto the road, and swung the huge 88 cal. gun around. "Boom . . . . explosion. Boom . . . . explosion. Boom . . . . explosion." Again and again he fired decimating tanks that didn't initially blow up from the satchel charges. The other tiger tank began firing point blank range at the barracks and headquarters. Those few troops that escaped the buildings were quickly gunned down by the resistance.

In seconds, Kurt turned the tiger around then flipped open the hatch. "Follow us down this road. We'll take-out the bastard's fuel storage." Aquina smiled and was so excited, she jumped down from her tank and climbed up on the other tank, and kissed Kurt full on the mouth, then quickly climbed down. He radioed the other tank explaining what they were going to do. Both machines jerked forward with Kurt in front flying no flag. Aquina in the other tiger . . . . the men falling in behind the two land juggernauts in good spirits, but grim ernest faces alert for the enemy.

Five minutes later they turned the corner on the harbor road to see two ships each flying the nazi naval flag moored to the pier. Obviously, when the explosions started they had stopped unloading. But they saw and for a moment confused about the tanks . . . until Kurt opened-up, blowing the radio room and part of the bridge off the one ship. The other tank followed suit knocking out the entire bridge and radio room. Aquina quickly climbed up on the top of her tank, and took hold of the twin fifties. While on the other tank, a sergeant followed her example. Both of them began raking the decks of both ships, while their men ran down on the pier crushing the last bit of resistance. Kurt immediately brought the turret around and started killing off and exploding the enemy machine gun emplacements around the fuel storage area. The other tank blew up a recent 88 cal. gun emplacement, and some anti-aircraft guns.

Meanwhile, the men had swarmed aboard the two ships killing almost all remaining crew onboard. Code books and captain's papers were taken especially the shipping manifest from each ship. When Kurt read them he "whooped" for joy. "We've hit the jackpot!"

Aquina told one sergeant . . . . "Call the compound. Every man and every truck to help off load, except those on guard duty. Then go through the city ask for help unloading these ships, and tell the people as soon as the area around the fuel storage is secure, we'll be handing out fuel." And in comparatively short time men and women and older children began coming down the slight hill in droves. They were scared and uncertain at sight of the two large tanks, until Aquina was seen plainly on top of one holding onto the machine gun waving them on. Then they rushed to the pier, hundreds cheering.

The snow slowed considerably as citizens began the laborious task of unloading, This left the armed resistance to assault the fuel storage bunker. A short period of intense automatic weapons fire followed, then quiet. All together . . .

it had been their largest raid and the most important, insofar as captured arms, equipment, a costly set-back for the enemy, and the enormous morale boost to the city's population.

Trucks with the "L" on their doors arrived. One after another, many captured vehicles among them, a steady stream some filled with armed men while others were empty. Hour by hour it continued as the night gave way to the dawn, and the snow tapering off to a sprinkle of flakes.

With full dawn, Aquina sent fifteen of her men up to the scene of the carnage the night before, to relieve the men up there holding the perimeter. And small groups of women and children brought hot food and drink to the armed men, and especially those in the two captured tanks. A few stayed by each tank occasionally handing up hot tea, coffee, and biscuits.

Large trucks with empty drums were loading-filling up with fuel at the bunker, as people from the city brought carts, wagons and cans to be filled. Once the few trucks pulled out, the townspeople pushed in. Those trucks made their way to the two tanks to replenish the fuel, and bring their tanks up to full, then made their way to the pier fueling the recently unloaded trucks. There are only four, each with a heavy machine gun mounted on top; and filled with stacks of new tires already mounted on rims. But possibly the best or most important find was the two half-tracks. They came off slowly and carefully. Loaded with spare parts and sundries, they were fueled and started, then moved over to the side to warm up . . . .

Truck after truck was filled, twenty-four in all, with guns and ammunition, departed immediately for the compound with a half-track in front of the convoy. The balance of the half loaded ships consisted of food, meat, wheat, and such; and as the meat came off . . . Aquina called out to the sergeant.

"All the food goes to our people in the city." He waved. "Yes ma-dam." Carts were filled and wagons, a certain amount to each building and group of buildings.

All that day and into the night the unloading continued, and well into the next morning. That afternoon with assurances that everything of value had been unloaded, and food had been evenly distributed . . . Aquina gave the order to pull out. And with one half-track in front the convoy of trucks began pulling out . . . . until only the two tanks remained. The city's inhabitants shrank back well off the pier, as Aquina spoke into her headset. Immediately each tank moved further to the side along the wharf until well aligned with the outboard side of each ship. Each tank fired point blank into the aft section, setting off large explosions which ripped the ships apart. In minutes each sank to the harbor bottom effectively blocking other ships from using the pier. The tanks internal machine guns chopped the few Nazis in the water, to be followed by the other tank. Kurt swung the turret around and sent a shell into the fuel bunker exploding the entire depot.

Immediately, Kurt jerked forward slowly retracing their way back to the east side of the city, as inhabitants waved and applauded. Rumbling and clanking along with many of their men behind turned the corner into groups of cheering armed men, who joined their comrades behind the two tanks. The tigers were so big each one nearly spanned the entire road, huge clanking armored monsters with the enormous large and long cannon. Obviously the word had spread about the assault on the nazi headquarters and the barracks, and the destruction of the panzer group located there, the capture, unloading and destruction of the two ships; but, most of all people came to the road to see the two captured tanks.

It was their biggest raid and the most damaging to the nazi occupation forces. They had lost dearly and immediately began more mass arrests, pillaging-burning and other methods equally vicious. In answer, more and more raids occurred and still more planned. The Nazis paid dearly in both men and material. Even during the winter, blinding snow storms and ice, the groups commanded by Aquina and Kurt continued to cut into and savagely harassed the enemy. This was kept up for many months . . . hitting the Nazis from the northern most point of the peninsula to the border in the south. From the western shore to the eastern island groups facing the Baltic.

CHAP. 26

By spring, early '44, the compound received a message from the resistance to the southwest. "Too expect an allied agent by parachute." Dien immediately informed the C'pter, and changed the settings accordingly. Several days later . . . Aquina waited with the wolf just south of the hills . . . the agreed upon landing site. And at the appointed time heard a solitary plane approach. In minutes a parachute appeared in the moonlight, and in seconds the plane banked sharply to the left leaving the area quickly. As soon as the aircraft was beyond her imposed cordon, Dien reset the automatic settings on the C'pter.

The wolves found him first, sitting growling at him, and he remained still, only blinking his eyes moving nothing else save for shallow breathing. The agent could never remember being so terrified as he was then. He recognized them correctly as timber wolves, and expected to be torn to shreds at any moment. But as he looked up . . . his eyes went wide as a lovely vision was running toward him. The moonlight highlighting her blond hair, then he saw the awesome white wolf running next to her, and wondered if he hadn't lost his mind. He heard some strange language and the wolves gathered round her wagging their tails, kissing as he watched her pet and fondle each and every animal.

Some moments passed and he watched her intently, staring until she came over to him . . . "Are you alright?" She spoke excellent English. "I . . . . I think so." "Good come then, and carry that thing with you." She pointed to the parachute. They began walking and she hummed, as more and more animals came out to greet her, and walk or prance for a short distance.

Although the agent had his doubts they arrived in short order to be ushered inside the barracks office. Once in the lighted office the agent was even more captivated, and was however doing his best to relate the important information so critical to the war. "Because of your successes against the Nazis, we need you to coordinate your efforts with us and the other allies. The first week of june, this year, will occur a massive allied landing on the channel coast of this continent." He said continuing. "We need you to hurt the Nazis here as hard as you can so they will take hopefully a full division, or at least a few regiments sending them north to hit you. This makes our job easier. Don't worry, as soon as we've started pushing inland the division, or whatever, will be pulled back south to counter our push. But by then we will have had time to increase our strength."

Aquina looked at Kurt and smiled innocently. "Oh, I think we can do that." The very look on her face and inflection in voice, assured the agent.

During the ensueing weeks of april, the agent was forced to stay as no boat was available to take him back. So he became a member of the group as an observer, and saw first hand proof of the wild rumors which had spread across to the allies . . . of the destruction of a panzer group, and the capture of two tiger tanks intact. Kurt called the lookouts and tank crews to warm up. "They will be there in short order."

Of the seventy-two men, thirteen were recovering from wounds, ten sat in the scrub at their guns, which left a force of fourty-nine. Aquina made it an even fifty. They piled into three trucks along with the ammunition. The Englishman noticed the large shells in the truck, but decided against asking the question. Now the three trucks came to a stop in the clearing and stepped down the agent saw pallets holding drums of fuel, and excited men. Then he heard the throaty growl of powerful diesels and looking around, in the twilight just before evening, his eyes widened at the two obvious sources of the growl. Men were passing the large shells up and inside with care. His throat went dry as his mind recognized from intelligence reports . . . . tigers. And as he looked around, saw two half-tracks hidden amongst the scrub.

He was impressed. And watched with admiration and a tinge of jealousy as Aquina climbed up on the lead tank. He watched Kurt get up on the second as he and fourty-two men in three trucks got ready to move out. Loaded with mortars and ammunition they moved slowly out of the scrub along what the agent learned is "woods road." He saw some farmers waving silently as the two tanks rumbled past shaking and vibrating the ground on their way to the main road. Once there the speed picked up significantly. And as usual Aquina had Dien's recorder.

It didn't take long to cover the thirty miles to the junction, and turn south to the junction city's reinforced nazi garrison. It is two hours after dark, and as the tanks continued boldly on, Kurt standing up through the hatch spoke into the radio waving telling them his two tigers needed fuel, were getting within point blank range of the tank and half-track on either side. Without warning, Aquina fired converting the panzer into flaming junk, while Kurt took-out the half-track instantly. The three trucks pulled over with the men pouring out running out and around in two groups according to plan.

Meanwhile, the Englishman watched as the lead tank obliterated two 88 cal. guns by running sideways then turning right angles and still firing. A second tank began coming through the entrance-way firing until Kurt hit it under the turret causing it to explode, and block the exit. While obliterating the sand-bag machine gun nests their men were assaulting each flank. Aquina was coming around chewing up the enemy with machine gun fire as a tank began coming over partially crumbling the brick side wall.

"Wait . . . . let them work somemore . . . . now!" The tank's big 88 cal. Sent a shell into the underside blasting it apart. Then she set about blowing open an entrance through the wall. "Don't go through instead turn right." "Yes ma-dam." A sharp right turn and she brought the turret around at ninety degrees facing the wall at a distance of fifty feet . . . . point blank range. "Boom!" Round after round at about twelve foot intervals blasting large sections into small rubble. After the third one, there sat the rear half of a panzer lying in ambush for a tank to go through the previous opening. Quickly Aquina's men reloaded, and indexing the turret a few degrees fired point blank just as it began moving. But it had no time and no luck as the 88 cal. round slammed into the tank's rear half.

"Back up, back up . . . . give us some room." "Yes ma-dam." Backing more than a hundred feet, she looked through the cannon sight her hands each on a squeeze grip, and squeezed her hands together simultaneously sending an 88 cal. calling card into the headquarters building. She indexed to the right and squeezed off another round. The entire left half of the building collapsed.

"Ma-dam, one of our men coming." "Alright," she said throwing open the hatch and stood up. "Ma-dam our lookouts have sighted a column of two half-tracks, three tanks, and three troop trucks about four miles from here." "Alright. Tell Kurt to take up a claw ambush, and kill any troops remaining; all of you get behind the building and throw grenades around. Sucker them into our trap." "Yes ma-dam." Pleased, the man ran off. "Quick get us into the woods here and down a bit." "Yes ma-dam."

Without wasting time the driver turned and drove fast crushing brush pushing his way yards into the woods, but parallel to the road. When they stopped, a good field of fire at about four hundred feet from the wrecked tank at the entrance, and they are still well hidden despite the brilliant moon.

The column gained the crest of the hill and instantly saw large fires, men running and small explosions. From in front, the half-tracks pulled off onto the side letting the tanks on through. And they came on fast, firing near constantly. Behind them, the two half-tracks and three dozen or so men. Continuing their charge the three tanks ran abreast passing Aquina's position at a good clip. And a few yards behind . . . . the half-tracks and men.

On the opposite side from her, that tank exploded just as Aquina is squeezing off a round. The nearest tank to her exploded, and just before she was ready to shoot again . . . the center tank had continued on and started to turn, when Kurt's second round smashed into the rear. Aquina sent her next shot into the half-track nearest her. Seconds before mortar rounds rained in on the troops as machine gun fire from Kurt's tank and her's decimated the three dozen troops in a murderous cross fire. Kurt didn't have a chance to shoot at the second half-track as an incoming mortar round made a direct hit, and another hit the cab.

Ten minutes perhaps eleven, and it was over. "Take us out of here." "Right away ma-dam." "Re-load quick." She threw open the hatch and stood up gasping for air, the over-powering stench of cordite was getting to her. Kurt came out of the woods and joined her on the road. But instead of stopping, she did a hard left running down the road at full speed. And sure enough the three nazi drivers were beginning to turn around, when they spotted the huge tiger barreling down the road with its cannon pointed directly at them. But what really caused them to stop is the effect of seeing the woman holding the twin fifties. Blonde with hair billowing out behind her making-projecting the image of an avenging spector. Aquina returned fifteen minutes later preceeded by the three trucks. The casualties and wounded were loaded onto the two trucks, but before they departed, Aquina had her driver move over . . . . she squeezed off one round into the already decrepit structure causing the balance to collapse.

At eleven-thirty p.m. farmers along the western road were wakened by the rumbling sound, and the vibration. Soon the unmistakeable clank clank . . . clickity-clank . . . clank-clank of tanks pulled people to their windows and doors. As they looked . . . . shining in the moonlight their headlights barely piercing the dark of night, afforded an air of detached reality. Especially in that there was no other sound, save that of the massive tracks and diesels. After that night, Aquina made plans to increase their raids. April became may and total captured vehicles was impressive. In fact, she had accumulated more vehicles than she had men to "man" them. Down to fourty-four, she reduced by half the number sitting at guard posts, which brought the number to fourty-nine. Two days later thirteen former wounded rejoined the group, bringing the total to sixty-two. In all, they have thirty machine gun equipped trucks, four half-tracks each with two mounts each with twin fifties, and the two tiger tanks, plus a dozen small miscellaneous vehicles. And imposing force unto itself.

CHAP. 27

During that time they ranged all over the countryside, north, south, west killing Nazis and blowing up vehicles, taking fuel and ammunition then destroying what was left.

But for several days in may, there was little activity, instead Aquina poured over intelligence data about the only real nazi garrison remaining in the peninsula country. And that one located on the peninsula, controlled the main road, and bridges across the numerous islands leading to the capital. If they could destroy that garrison it would thoroughly cripple the Nazis within the country. They'd tackled larger targets with success. For one thing, they have two tiger tanks and some six older panzers, plus half-tracks and other lesser vehicles.

Located just west of the city, the only one on the large intervening island of Fyn, connected to the big island of the capital by ferry service, the nazi garrison was reported to have high walls, and aside from the armor, some two hundred troops, or more.

Of course during all skull sessions the Englishman was present trying to be helpful wherever possible. And in the wee hours of the nineteenth, all three in the barracks office agreed. The plan was set, and they drank to it, with the toast given by Kurt. It was a little after three a.m. when Kurt woke the mechanics and helpers. And when fully awake, and coffee in hand, he explained what was needed. Handing the senior mechanic the long range thirty cal. hunting rifle with scope, Kurt indicated silencers would be needed for twelve such weapons.

With five trucks warming up, the entire two floors of the barracks started buzzing with activity. Wolves were up and running in and out excited, sniffing and whining at the kitchen door, and outside barking chasing each other. As the two sergeants stood within the office doorway, Kurt rang the "tank pit." "Warm up the tigers." That brought smiles to many faces except the women, who worried for their men. Among them Kurt selected three four man crews explaining they would learn in three days how to drive, aim and shoot from a tiger tank. At which time the training began in ernest.

Early in the morning may twenty-second . . . they are ready. The day is devoted to filling the tigers with fuel and ammunition, topping off seven trucks and loading two trucks with large drums of fuel. Each man carried extra ammunition, grenades and saw to the loading of mortars and ammunition, and many satchel charges.

Kurt and Aquina held two intense briefings during the day stressing certain information. The entire force departed at eight p.m. with seven trucks, both tigers, six older panzers, and all four half-tracks. They crossed the bridge killing silently the sentries on duty, and arrived at twelve-fifty with no moon, and lights on in the headquarters silhouetted the guards beautifully. Nine guards patrolled the small field bristling with tanks. "Holy mother," muttered Kurt into the headset, and of course Aquina heard him. She spoke to him the same way. "They're bringing in reinforcements from the south up through the islands and across Fyn to attack us from the rear. That bridge we passed is the vital link." They gazed upon many dozen tigers and eighteen older panzers. And they are parked in parallel lines facing one-another; and God only knew what was on the far side of the wall. With perhaps fourty-or so feet separating the two lines, it is considerably less than point blank range.

Only one tiger was occupied, as a man sat up on the turret talking to someone inside, laughing heartedly. Signals were given as one of her men, and one of Kurt's scrambled out quickly, and joined up with the three tank crews and split themselves into four three man and one two man crew ready to jump on five tigers. The nazi climbed from the tiger and unexpectedly two more came out. All the marksmen were in place, and suddenly twelve muffled pops. The last person in the lead tiger stood up curious . . . . pop. He would never be curious again. As the crews sprinted the few yards to the tigers . . . they changed their plan just a "little."

Just as the tank crews began running . . . . nine men came across the road throwing satchel charges under the older panzers. Meanwhile three men jumped into the first tiger and loaded, as eleven other engines started, and the line of tigers began to rumble as the older panzers began exploding. The three in the lead tank swung around firing.

The shell impacted the archway above the entrance causing the collapse of the entrance.

Aquina and Kurt began shelling the barracks repeatedly as their four half-tracks pulled over to the side so the rapidly approaching line of juggernauts could pass safely through. Each twin set of fifties opened up on the barracks, headquarters, and pill boxes. A tank maneuvered into the opening, firing directly into the first half-track exploding it into fragments. Kurt sent a round into the opening, but didn't stop it until the three resistance in the former lead tank sent an 88 cal. bill into the enemy tank's forward flank.

Men . . . . nazis began pouring out of the courtyard, and sent mortar rounds ranging . . . catching some of the resistance, but not seriously. Kurt, Aquina and the third tiger tank used inside machine guns on the enemy troops, while firing round after round into the headquarters, barracks and the high wall surrounding the inner courtyard.

A third of a mile away the city's inhabitants were wide awake listening to the mortars, machine guns, explosions and the unmistakeable sound of big 88's firing continuously. They looked out through spy glasses and binoculars and such. The lucky ones passed the word. "Tanks are firing on the Nazis." Aside from the reign of terror imposed by the Nazis their military might was finished.

Meanwhile round after round was sent into the barracks, headquarters until they collapsed then chopped the wall collapsing it on many of the defenders. Hammered and kept down by the half-tracks, tanks and mortars, the resistance gradually outflanked the nazis securing the armory, and fuel depot located well in the rear, and off to one side. Their automatic weapons fire and grenade attack finished the battle.

The entire garrison of some five hundred, only thirty survived, and some of those were wounded. Kurt interrogated the prisoners as Aquina stood with her long dagger held menacingly in the right hand. When the first officer, a lieutenant refused to talk .... she calmly walked up to the man ... looked him in the eye ... and drove the dagger into his groin. At once the room was deathly still, filled with the screams of the dieing soldier. "Take the carrion out!" Two of her men scrambled to obey. She walked up to the second nazi whose eyes are filled with fear, as Kurt asked him. "How long the reinforcements had been there?" The officer groaned then his voice croaked, as Aquina put the knife gently into his groin. Quickly he started talking. "They had arrived only that afternoon, late, it was dark when he pulled into the yard."

Aquina smiled at Kurt, and exited the courtyard. It was two a.m. as the Englishman walked up keeping in step. "I wish to extend my congradulations and my admiration for a bold plan brilliantly executed." With a wave of her hand indicating her men. "Only because of men like these and Kurt were we able to succeed." The agent smiled as Aquina walked over to the fuel truck. "There are a lot of generals who would do well to emulate this woman." He thought to himself.

Too a driver and young helper .... "Start refueling all our tanks, trucks, half-tracks, and the captured tanks. Then restock with ammunition." "Yes ma-dam, right away." She walked over to the side counting four casualties and seven wounded. At that moment a sergeant ran up to her. "Quick ma-dam, Kurt needs you at the fuel and munitions building." She walked past the big steel doors and stopped staring, sitting in the middle are three half-tracks, and behind each was what Kurt .... shouted .... 88 cal. field guns." Each half-track was loaded crammed with 88 cal. ammunition. On her right hand side is a fourth trailer at some 3000 liters, then weapons and spare parts, et-cetera. The entire left side was ammunition.

She went outside giving orders, as Kurt climbed into the first half-track driving it out, around and onto the road, to be followed by the other two in only some minutes. The several dozen tigers were parked in a line sitting on the side with the lead crew of three standing easy, keeping guard, while the eleven others ran over and climbed into the nine panzers sitting in line on the field. One had been scarred, but is fully functional. The three half-tracks moved around and regained the road pulling over in front of the tigers. At the same time the nine panzers pulled up and stopped behind the bigger tigers.

"Sergeant, patch in a phone." "Already done madam." "Thank you." She said with a smile and picked up the phone laying in the truck's cab. When finished, she'd ordered every truck plus some small vehicles with women volunteers, and all the black paint, some light blue, food and all the wounded who could drive a truck. In the interim the fuel truck went dry less some few hundred gallons. Kurt had loaded on the trucks all the individual drums and the refueling commenced until finished. The fuel level on every tank, half-track, and truck had been "topped off."

It is four-fifteen a.m., the third week in may '44, they began filling each tiger and panzer with a full quota of ammunition, in fact each tiger is given twelve extra rounds of 88's. Half-tracks are loaded and the fifties on each truck had many extra cans apiece.

Aquina roamed around with burp gun suspended on its strap as most of her troops slept. Those on perimeter and guard duty had slept first, then relieved. At six-ten a.m., she splashed water on her face and patted it dry, and pleased to see everyone up. The fuel truck had already discharged the empty drums, and all the wounded, and casualties were in the back. The other six trucks were turning in a large arc lining up to load munitions.

CHAP. 28

Sentry's at the bridge called to say their convoy was coming through, and many were loaded with women. But as they rounded the slow curve drivers slowed gaping at sight of the tanks. Even though they were waved on through, they gaped . . . . women were stunned, overwhelmed. All of them thought much the same. "Ma-dam and Kurt departed with two tigers and some six older panzers, four half-tracks . . . . But they counted six half-tracks half with big guns behind them, several dozen gray tigers, nine smaller panzers, and off to the side ma-dam's and Kurt's tigers, and older panzers.

All the women and the trucks holding the paint dropped out of the line parking across from the tanks. Although it was thought the paint won't last . . . . it did. And while they were painting and slopping it on, loaded trucks went by heading for the compound. Seven trucks, big ten wheel things were packed with mines, weapons, ammunition, and drums of fuel.

One truck had only half a load of drums with weapons filling the void, whereas the truck in front had a full load of drums, and pulled the large fuel trailer. Everything else was emptied out of the storage building right to the bare walls, and carried to the compound along with the women.

Aquina is pleased standing in front of her tiger, a stunning black all over with a blue "L" on the turret's two sides. The others are similar.

It is eleven-thirty a.m. as the column began moving west. Coming around the slow bend at twenty-five m.p.h. plus caused tremendous rumbling and vibration. Diesels in the tanks sang their throaty growl loud and clear, and the trucks and half-tracks added their music in between. She turned on the recorder capturing the symphony . . . . her smile is infectous as she experienced the rush of excitement from the sound, and vibration of her tiger.

Coming to the bridge, she bade them cross two-at-a-time, and once over . . . . pulled over, waving them on and . . . "pull off and stop." The last truck was crossing . . . "Sergeant, take the truck with the mines and plant a . . . pattern on either side of the road. Use them sparingly, we will no doubt need some later." "Yes ma-dam." While waiting most of the men ate, slept or talked in low muted tones. The sentrys and their equipment was loaded . . . . "We're finished ma-dam." She nodded. "Good, and sergeant take what you will need of the plastique and destroy the bridge." "Right away ma-dam."

They began pulling out, it is two-fourty in the afternoon. They drove a little faster to make up time. A quick left and right, at the intersection and the entire column headed toward the city located at the junction about two miles south. Aquina speaking into her headset had the column slow down to a crawl as she ordered the last three older panzers to take up positions at the intersection. Resuming their normal speed the column didn't slacken off until a few minutes later entering the city.

Aquina and Kurt sat up on their turrets as citizens applauded, moving slowly toward the city square. When citizens looked and saw different insignia on the tanks, they literally poured into the large open square. Following the example of the elders, and waved as the tanks came closer. It was obvious they had heard of the battle, and of course the demolition of the garrison outside their own city. Many started remembering Aquina from times past, as eager hands handed up food and drink. She passed it down to her crew and accepted a cup of wine from some young adults. Probably the women were the most affected, they swarmed around her tiger shouting to be overheard above the diesels.

Many shouted along the column gradulations as every tank and vehicle is handed food and drink. Some shouted . . . . asked who was in command? And everyone on the half-tracks and tanks pointed forward. When Kurt was asked by a crowd . . . . he smiled pointing to Aquina. The women and girls felt more important because one of their own commanded not only one tank, but the whole column of tanks and fighting men. Elders and city religious leaders swarmed around her tank, as she gave the order to shut off the engines. People stopped shouting when the roar of the diesels ceased.

"Ma-dam, you look familiar . . ." Asked one of the elders as others shook their heads and the crowd nodded assent. "I am Labr, from the forest to the west, by the harbor city." The elder's eyes were wide, and he stammered bending low at the waist in a humble bow. "I have three tanks standing guard at the crossroads, and will alternate with others. Would you see they get hot food and drink." "We will yes . . . a pleasure for our countrymen . . . highness." Although he said the last word softly . . . the crowd heard. Aquina smiled. "Thank you elder." He bowed again.

Looking down, she told people to get back from the vehicles, and looking back stuck her forefinger up moving it around fast in a tight circle. Instantly the tanks and other vehicles re-started including her own. The people stood back as the column moved forward slowly as they swung through parts of the city heading south. The elder quickly told the crowds again about the three tanks guarding the crossroads.

Driving south they occasionally passed small groups of people waving. At five-twenty in the afternoon, she had everyone slow down, while her tiger pulled off to the side. As Kurt deployed the tanks in a crab ambush position and deployed their men for the night, Aquina headed for Abenra. The elders from the junction had called every town and city along the way letting them know who was coming, and with what. The tiger clanked along at seven m.p.h., she thought about the past and how oddly things had turned out. She could now see the buildings and the townspeople . . . . and yes there was the church still as she remembered. Almost abreast of the small building, she had her crew skid a partial turn and stop.

Aquina climbed down amidst throngs of subdued people murmuring, whispering, and pointing. They bowed when her feet touched the ground as many wept openly, and hesitantly touched her hands . . . and arms gently as if to confirm she is real. Smiling, she walked to the church entrance as two children quickly opened and held the door. Aquina nodded to each touching both on the head then walked into the vestibule. The carving was still there, a faint smile . . . . a touch, and she walked inside confronted by a room full of people. The priest explained. "These elders and fellow priests had gathered from small towns and hamlets throughout the near countryside." With Aquina's attention on the priest and elders, she didn't really notice the several women examining her attire.

The slacks are definitely snug around her full hips and crotch, but the leather belt cinched them tight around her comparatively small waist. And located somewhat low is a two inch leather belt holding a large officer's holster with snap closed, packs threaded on the belt for extra clips and a long dagger. Add to this a black wool blouse covered by a black leather vest with an unusual number of pockets, and a large pair of binoculars hanging from her neck laying on her breasts at a crazy angle. The women did not fail to notice the calf-length glossy boots, and felt a little uneasy feeling the aura of leadership, or power, ... or both that emanated from this person.

Separate elders began speaking similar things. "We all have young men strong . . . . good people, who want to fight." "But there is an excellent chance they may die." Aquina said softly-firmly. With hats in hand, they said together. "But you fight . . . ." A stillness filled the air as she looked at them.

"Very well. I am sending for supply trucks, the smaller ones will take you to your villages and return with those who wish to fight. Now to other matters. During the past fifteen days has there been any Nazis through here?"

"Yes, yes ma-dam, one car and truck with wounded officers, but both were badly damaged; and the men were very, very nervous. They stopped and took petrol looking up and down our street as if they expected something terrible to appear at any moment." The priest said.

"Hmmmm . . . . well, they've had plenty of time for . . . . wait a moment . . ." She started giggling and holding both hands up cupping her face . . . "Oh this, this . . . . is fantastic. Don't you see? This is late afternoon, and during the wee hours yesterday morning my force destroyed the nazi garrison on the island of Fyn. Now, they arrived about six maybe seven hours before us." She continued, the room deathly quiet hanging on her every word.

"According to reports, we expected to attack a force only three times our strength, but instead suddenly faced with fifteen times more tanks and hundreds and hundreds more in manpower. Those escaped Nazis did report to their high command, and a retaliation force was sent, ... but not from the south . . . but the northeast. Yes, the ferries slowed them down, and then negotiating through the capital across another ferry, and finally to their garrison on Fyn. And by now they know I've destroyed the garrison."

She looked out the window and was thinking out loud. "They've been beaten off our peninsula, defeated. Their anger and bruised egos will cause them to compound the defeat. But they will come, but from the south, and I'll be waiting for them." Aquina shook herself from her reverie and . . . "perhaps until our supply trucks arrive . . . my men would appreciate coffee if you have some." She asked.

"Certainly, ma-dam, our folk will be there soon." The elder said. "Thank you." Aquina replied.

Without speaking, she exited smiling walking through the open door to a much enlarged crowd. There was little fanfare as she climbed up on the tiger; but the facial expressions said things they could not express verbally. They shrank back from the tiger as both diesels woke up with a roar. She waved as it moved forward slowly turning to retrace its short route back to camp.

Before she finished the call to the compound for a supply convoy, nervous townspeople challenged by a strong perimeter began walking slowly into the camp pushing little carts and carrying boxes. Men, women and some children stood shyly gaping in wonder at all the tanks and armed men. All those who had been in the church and outside the crowd . . . . came; plus many others as some handed out little cakes and pastrys, while others served steaming hot coffee. Aquina was studying a chart under an oil lantern, when a small group of teens stood quietly until noticed. Looking up after a few seconds. "Hello." Aquina said smiling. The young ladies said only . . . . "ma-dam," and curtsied a little. The young men said. "Evening ma-dam," bowing their heads. They had hot coffee and pastries, and as she sipped and ate . . . the young people studied her as best they could with only the lantern for light. But although she looked their age, they realized this woman was, had to be many, many times their age. And the way her own men treated her . . . . they knew this night would remain with them for a long time.

Most of the townspeople and all the elders were still in the camp when word came from look-outs. "Supply convoy was coming in . . . ." As the convoy pulled into camp one could hear many words of exclamation from elders and townspeople alike. Eighteen large heavy trucks, plus seven smaller four wheel vehicles loaded to capacity, came to a stop with the lead driver climbing down handing an envelope to Kurt. Opening it slightly, he walked over to where Aquina was still looking at different charts handing her the inventory. Examining it, the list . . . . she began issueing orders. Her first concern was the two stoves loaded from the city on a trailer constructed by the welders and mechanics. The trucks pulling it were loaded with bags of coal, and the trailer loaded with large pots and pans, plus other miscellaneous peraphenalia. Walking along, she looked at some of the loads then glanced at the list. She gave orders for all small trucks to be unloaded, then had each of the seven visiting elders say how many were in their village. Aquina then had each small truck re-loaded and in some cases, the truck held so much . . . an elder while sitting in the cab had sacks or bags piled around his legs and one or two in his lap.

An hour and twenty minutes later, nine-fourty-five all the small trucks departed for their respective village. Immediately, she began with three heavy trucks, making each approximately equal and allocated the three to the small city on which outskirts they now camped. With instructions to the drivers to parcel it out according to buildings, familys, et-cetera. Repeating the process but utilizing four trucks, Aquina had them return to the city at the junction, thence continue to the compound to reload. With eleven remaining four held land mines, which were parked over on the side out of the way. Of the number brought with them and the additional convoy . . . . eighteen fully loaded trucks remained, with over three-quarters of the contents in the form of ammunition.

Around one-fifteen in the morning the first truck returned with four young men and two slightly older. And by two-ten a.m., all small seven vehicles returned. She had Kurt and the sergeant take their names and work with them, Aquina layed down for a nap, and wasn't awakened until six a.m. "About two weeks to go," she mused.

With only minutes remaining until they pulled out, four trucks honked their horns coming to a stop abreast of the tanks. Handing several sheets of paper to a sergeant they assumed positions at the column's rear. And in due course covered the intervening distance, until she knew the last curve in the road was coming up at which time Aquina signaled to slow down and pull over onto the side. They hugged the inside of the beginning curve. Dispatching a sergeant and several men, Aquina intended to find out what was awaiting them at the border . . . . before they swung around the curve into plain sight. She wanted no rude surprises. Some thirty-three minutes later they returned. "Ma-dam, three panzers, and a half-track, and perhaps thirty men."

"Alright sergeant, take six more men with three machine guns and return where you can command good ground cover, and wait for us to take their tanks." The sergeant smiled . . . . "ma-dam." The other sergeant was told to take twenty men with five machine guns, and go through the woods entering up the road aways and work their way down and cover that flank.

Speaking into her headset. The sergeant puts the range at just under two hundred yards. The four tigers directly behind Kurt raise your elevation for two hundred and a hair. When, I give the signal, you'll lay out a barrage, but only one round each. I repeat, one round each. Kurt and I will go in fast and hit them while they're off balance." Aquina waited another eleven minutes to give the men time enough . . . . she turned, sitting on her turret, to look behind her. Kurt was thumbs up and smiled. The four behind him also gave the thumbs up sign. She disappeared inside closing the hatch behind her, Kurt did the same, and shouted into the mouthpiece. "Now!" At that instant her tank and Kurt's jerked out onto the road while four 88's . . . calling cards screamed ahead seeking the unwary. Two shells landed inbetween two tanks damaging their tracks, the third scattered a handful of troops to the wind, while the fourth fell slightly short. Meanwhile, Aquina said. "Pour on the coal," and sighted on the undamaged panzer and fired. Both Aquina and Kurt are within one hundred-thirty yards and accelerating.

The panzer she targeted exploded into fire and debris. But the other two were able to each fire a round, one missing on the far side, however, the other shell hit within the track and bogie wheels next to Kurt's seat. Not knowing about Kurt, Aquina continued on loading and firing destroying both of the damaged tanks. Certainly those behind the machine guns did their part, she turned destroying the half-track.

It was over all to quick with only two flesh wounds amongst her men, but in Kurt's tiger . . . . her driver stopped in a tight skid turn a few yards away as her people already had the crew out. The driver was only superficially wounded, the loader . . . . a few cracked ribs, and a broken leg . . . . but Kurt was dead. Covered by his blood soaked jacket laying within the shadow of his tank, Aquina slowly sank to her knees . . . . her left hand stretched out not quite touching his chest, Slowly leaning forward . . . . hand gently touching, she began to cry. This her mentor, lover, friend . . . . the pain is terrible, as if a hole had been torn in her chest. "My darling." The men looked away . . . embarrassed having had no knowledge or suspicion of what they had meant to each other.

Aquina knelt no more than eight or nine minutes . . . then almost painfully, she stood. Not bothering to dry still wet tears, she looked up at the sky, eyes open, for about fifteen seconds.

Her gaze returned to the road and the wide rolling fields on either side. From the forest-like wood on their right came the loud howl of a large wolf.

The men sensed something had changed something unusual had been wrought, but what . . . . most only looked at one-another, and maybe were a little afraid. In a hard voice devoid of emotion, she gave orders for Kurt to be taken back and buried alongside their other fallen comrades. And for a tiger to come up and slowly push the damaged tank. Now, it slid sideways less than a yard until the resistance was great enough that the damaged side began rising off the ground. She watched it rise and when level shouted. "Stop!" "Now stones a lot of them . . . jam as many as possible under this thing." When it had been propped up . . . "Sergeant, a slightly curved trench, here. Have it dug half-a-yard deep and wide enough to have two rows of drums fitting snug together. Then, I want those boulders over there dragged and positioned in front, using smaller ones to build up the wall's height. As soon as you have that completed, cover the wall with some dirt and scrub so only the cannon barrel projects over the top." "Yes ma-dam right away." He had seen her face and shuddered, and the uncharacteristic tremor in his voice, began issuing orders.

She had the other sergeant start topping off the tanks using the drums; and when empty, were to be cut partially open on one end, then put in the trench and filled with dirt. "What will not go into our vehicles pour into the tank trailer. Then have some of our helpers pick-up all weapons and ammunition from the enemy." "Yes ma-dam."

Walking along the column now that it had come in close, . . . "You and you pull out and tow those cannon over there, and over there. See that opening in the trees?" "Yes ma-dam . . . gulp." "Rehook the cannon's carriage to the front of the half-track and push it in there. Set it up so it covers that entire area, and camouflage it thoroughly." "Yes ma-dam." She had the other driver do the identical thing on the opposite side. Waving to the cooks. "Come." Nodding they followed. "Alright, we're back a little bit, but still close enough for the men. This cleft in the trees, put your stove trailer here and your truck, park that here facing the border. I want the trees to dissipate your smoke as much as possible." "Yes, yes ma-dam." "Start cooking as soon as you've set up, the men need something hot. Oh . . . and always have some coffee going." "Yes ma-dam."

Because the large inlet on the left or east side of the road came in so far there were perhaps only two hundred-seventy to three hundred feet of wooded area spanning the distance. Too cover she had three older panzers, one a few yards from Kurt's tank located within the wood, and one on the end close to the water, and the third located in the middle. Young helpers swarmed around the tanks camouflaging them with brush and limbs of trees, tied, pulling them down and across effecting excellent blinds. They did similar things to hide the heavy machine gun nests inbetween the tanks.

But the right hand side, or western side, meandered into the distance like an undulating snake for almost two miles before joining with low lying marsh and thickly overgrown acreage. And along the coast was only a narrow old wagon road, now hopelessly overgrown and in near total disrepair.

CHAP. 29

For a good while townspeople from Bov, had watched from the roadside waiting to help, but not sure humble farmers would be appreciated or needed. Sitting on her turret, the tank in reverse backing up to where the others sat, she noticed the groups of men, women and some a little younger. Aquina called down and immediately the tiger's engines went silent. They recognized the insignia and the woman; and quickly the men and young men removed their caps. Aquina saw the picks and shovels. "Do you wish to help?" All of them nodded, smiling. "Have you eaten?" Most humbly said no . . . "Alright, that trailer, see over there by that truck, all of eat and then there will be work for you." Each of the group thanked her as they crossed in front of her tiger.

The engines re-started and signaling the column, she rumbled forward the others following all except three, which she had signaled to stay on the side. Turning right going around the smoldering tank debris, she went slow and about seventy feet down from where the 88, was now "dug-in" motioned for three tigers. They immediately pulled out turned and backed inside the tree line a few yards. Another fifty feet . . . another three tigers and another eighty feet, another three tigers. Aquina then called a halt as a section of forest appeared to move out into the field, judging it to be only several hundred feet wide, as she saw open field through the trees. Standing up on the turret, she confirmed it . . . she motioned for two tigers and two older panzers on one side of the point, one opposite with two tigers in the middle. Fifty feet down she signaled for the last two old panzers and they backed in as the others.

Signalling for the seven other tigers to stop, she turned left running out into the open along a dish-like depression which hid her totally from the large fields, the road et-cetera. It is a shallow grass covered trough paralleling the road for over a mile-and-a-half then curved slowly to the west getting more soggy and then an open marsh area. Aquina didn't go beyond that point, instead backed up until on solid ground, tight maneuvering and returned to the group. She outlined to all the crews of the seven unassigned tigers about the trough, and went into detail about strategy. So the seven sat in a line at the trough's shallow end, a few yards from the extended bit of forest. Two four wheel trucks serviced the "squad" of eight with food, coffee, fuel when needed and ammunition. Other four wheel small trucks serviced the tanks and machine gun crews sprinkled inbetween.

In numerous clearings close to the tanks were located the crews with the larger mortars. Meanwhile the Englishman was looking around and talking to the sergeants as Aquina's tiger came back doing a "good clip" coming to a stop only yards away from the cook truck.

"Sergeant!" "Yes ma-dam, here" "Alright, put that third 88 beast, field piece right there behind these few trees. Set it up and calibrate for . . . ohhh about one thousand yards." "Immediately ma-dam." "Keep the half-tracks close by in case we have to move all three quickly." "Yes ma-dam."

Too the other sergeant, "take this chart and all trucks carrying mines, go out five tenths of a mile from Kurt's old tank, or eight hundred-eighty yards and plant them constantly shifting your patterns. Also put the tall grass tufts back around the top so the enemy won't detect anything out of the ordinary." "Yes ma-dam. But the road?" "As indicated, mine about a thirty-five foot section, because as you can see, the areas immediately next to the road for fifty feet further up are mined. So when they stop the column and we shoot . . . . and they try and go around . . . . well, I'm sure they will see our little prank. Now take every helper, and our new volunteers and plant all areas as I've indicated." "Yes ma-dam. I will start right away." Aquina smiled as he walked away pulling men from other wotk details, and that plus drivers and others. As night fell, she walked the camp and the line of tanks drinking coffee sometimes standing for long periods watching the field.

It is dawn, and the day came and went with all of the work details completed except for the mines. Working parties didn't finish those areas until eleven-fifteen. And lookouts had been up in the trees since the outset on rotating shifts but still nothing. The next day went slow and tedious; and the next day started off the same way until a few minutes before ten a.m., lookouts called down to a sergeant sitting on top of Kurt's tank, wearing the headset, that a very large force is coming along the road. He called to Aquina whose tank was going down the trough ahead of her group. "Keep me informed." "Yes ma-dam."

Some moments later the lookouts called down again . . . "Three columns of tanks totaling about one hundred twenty, one on either side of the road, and the center column occupies the road with half-tracks in front, speed about thirty m.p.h . . . There are roughly six or seven hundred men marching slightly inbetween the columns and behind them. Wait . . . oh-oh, the're setting up five very large field pieces." All of that had been given to Aquina. "We'll take the field pieces, shorten mortar range to a thousand yards, and concentrate on the tanks." Aquina ordered. "Yes ma-dam." The sergeant replied. Aquina opened her hatch and indicated to the others. "She and the second tank will take the east column, the last three would take the column just above them, and the middle three would take the road column. Chop up the field gun crews and the infantry with machine gun fire." She gave the sign and eight black tigers moved up the trough, up the sides quickly.

They could hear explosions as she turned going up the side of the trough leaving the marshy ground behind. As she and the other tigers gained the top and increased speed they fanned out firing their inside mounted machine guns forward, decimating the surprised gun crews. As she watched aiming on the rear tiger in the east side column . . . and fired. Her line of defense fired their opening salvo accounting for several tanks, blocking the road, and a few in either side column. The enemy was firing back slowly finding the range, as some of the front line was hit in places.

Her companion tank knocked out the second one, as her first shot killed the last tank in the column. Firing again she ran back-an-forth aiming and shooting. So were the other two groups, aiming, firing scoring hits rapidly in each column. Many of the enemy tanks were caught by the big mortars and the 88 cal. field pieces. Soon though the mortars stopped as the three groups of black tanks dealt out death and destruction on an ever increasing scale.

Within seconds the enemy panzers were in the mine fields. Tracks blown off immobilized them where they were and quickly destroyed by the defending tanks. One older panzer in the tree line took a crippling hit, a couple of trucks, and some men wounded by shrapnel, but the 88's and the defending tanks continued to score hits on tracks and other areas of enemy tanks, good hits which bogged them down. Most of the enemy troops were dead or dieing, some crushed by the oncoming tigers in the rear. Not until it was much to late did the enemy realize they were being killed from the rear as well as the front.

Seeing many, many tanks disabled obviously by mines and dozens and dozens exploding and burning, and no radio word from the field guns . . . the tank commander made his decision. Quickly opening his hatch, he stood up arms up and out. Speaking into his headset ordered all his surviving tanks to surrender. One by one, then by two's and three's their hatches came open, men standing with arms raised.

The nazi panzer commander's eyes widened as recognition hit him, looking at the eight black tiger tanks. Albeit black with a strange insignia, but definitely his country's tanks. The black tanks rumbled . . . a throaty growl of impatience as the hatches remained closed. An eerie persistent feeling swept over the commander . . . as seconds ticked by . . . snap, click . . . click . . . clank. A hatch opened and a man quickly climbed out standing behind the twin fifties ready in case of trouble. Then in rapid succession hatches banged open, all except one. Slowly it opened and Aquina stood, then sat on the hatch rim. For several seconds, she spoke into her headset as three trucks and four half-tracks started down the road, only to stop minutes later. Men with shovels and bayonets carefully and painstakenly removed the mines from the road.

Meanwhile, all tank crews abandoned their machines and stood in a group. "Sergeant, take two men and unload all the cannons, secure the breechs and secure the hatches." "Yes ma-dam." Finishing his task, the sergeant and the two men returned to their tank as the three trucks pulled up. One truck emptied out along with their sergeant. "Ma-dam." "Check them for weapons, sharp objects, papers and identification and strip them. When your satisfied they can have their pants nothing else." "Yes ma'dam" She turned around some and watched four of her half-tracks, each slowly pulling a very large field gun climb back onto the road heading toward them.

"Sergeant, how many do you count still intact?" He started walking counting as he went . . . "Ah, fourty-six ma-dam. And I think some of these others can be repaired." "Perhaps we will. But for now have some of our men drive these tanks across our line. Try to clean them up, and perhaps some black paint can be found." "I will do my best, ma-dam." Aquina smiled, knowing just how resourceful the sergeant could be when given a job that had to be completed.

Aquina watched men scramble aboard the tanks, and one half-track pass them on its way over to the rear to pick up and tow the remaining field piece. Turning, she looked at the dozens, burning and smoking hulks, when an obvious thought struck her. "Oh! By the universe!" She exclaimed into her headset. "Form up and follow me fast. Load and be ready for action." Her tiger roared off, watched silently by the nazi prisoners, and their colonel . . . pitching forward and then back as it gained the road followed by seven others.

Looking at the fast moving tigers heading south, the now ex-commander nodded slightly realizing they would in all likelihood not only find the supply column, but take them without a shot being fired. He is disgusted, not only with himself, but the asinine idiot who issued the explicit orders for an all out blitz. He, a newly promoted colonel, would have saved his main force and sent a small probe instead, avoiding this very disaster. He had voiced objections, but was quickly overruled, by a general who was basically weak and desperately in need of a victory. For this blunder the Fuhrer would probably order the general shot. He knew to continue thinking about this would only lead to despair, and already he has a bad headache.

Heading south at thirty m.p.h., they'd been on the road for only a couple of miles . . . . rounded a large corner bursting suddenly upon the nazi supply column. Brief spurts of machine gun fire and the survivors surrounded, and covered by their brothers two partial crews searched . . . killing several who hid around the trucks and trailers. All weapons had been collected and the prisoners searched; as others looked through the cabs for papers, inventory records, or anything similar. The tiger closest to the curve in the road sent a message for as many drivers as possible.

Meanwhile townspeople from Bov, and others close by filtered into the camp wanting to help. Many helped with the two dead, fifteen seriously wounded, and the numerous men with superficial wounds. Small groups looked from the prisoners to the open expanse of field strewn with wrecked tanks many of which still burned, and the dead. Hundreds upon hundreds littering the area from a battle that would be long remembered. Captured tanks sat in a long line in plain sight of the town as people began sweeping them off preparing to paint them all black. Two damaged trucks were towed out of the woods, and left on the roadside with two going in taking their place.

A truck crammed with twenty men arrived with their weapons, and were immediately told to drive full trucks back and park outside of camp. While that was happening the sergeant and his men took the prisoners into the woods and disposed of them with quick bursts. At one p.m., in the afternoon a truck with the same men pulled over onto the side behind the first one and as before each climbed into a truck or half-track following the lead truck north.

Once the battle's outcome had become fact, news of it spread, north, south, east, and west by that afternoon, . . . it had spread across most if not all of the countryside. The Englishman sat still trying to accept what he'd seen happen with his own eyes. She had beaten the cream of the reich's panzer divisions. Because all told, according to his tally, their modest, but awesome force defeated and absorbed a full panzer division, and about one infantry regiment. Now they are even more powerful than just this morning . . . . since capturing four dozen more tigers, and five more large field pieces. And now a captured supply column, he sat numb as trucks passed, half-tracks pulling medium size tank trailers, two pulled large earth moving dozers and still more trucks.

He got up slowly slapping his thighs once. "Good show . . . damn glad she's with us and not against us."

CHAP. 30

Receiving the news, from the city a few miles south of where Aquina captured the supply column, the nazi general was stunned at the loss. It represented a terrible blow to their ego's, the morale, and not to mention the accumulated cost in men and material, it was staggering. The wermacht general staff immediately replaced the general, who days later had been mysteriously found shot to death in his country home.

The truck reappeared and the last sixteen trucks plus those used to ferry drivers headed north, with the eight tigers bringing up the rear. By that time dozens and dozens of volunteers had arrived and are helping wherever asked. Lookouts called down from their tree top perchs. "Truck column coming followed by eight black tigers." A small cheer went up as many dozens and dozens of expectant faces craned their necks to glimpse the victorious tiger tanks.

She sat in her usual place . . . on the hatch rim, as did a man in each tank behind her. Slowing steadily the trucks went through the beginning of their line. She pulled out in a skid turn stopping temporarily waving her tigers on into the camp. Coming around smoothly, no jerking motion, the driver pulled in close to Kurt's old barricaded tank and shut off the diesels. Swinging her shapely legs over, Aquina climbed down and accepted a hot cup of coffee. She sipped closed her eyes and swallowed. "Ahhh . . . ." "Good?" Each of the sergeants asked. "Good," said Aquina with a smile. A few more sips . . . "very good."

"How many casualties and wounded?" "Two dead and thirteen seriously wounded ma-dam." One sergeant replied. "It could have been worse, much worse. Put our people in three trucks with orders to pack up the welders and mechanics, with their equipment and return as soon as possible. Send with the trucks our three reserve panzers, and a half-track with an 88 field gun. The three will take over at the junction, while those three have been relieved will secure the woods road with help from the field piece and half-track." "Yes ma-dam."

Speaking to the sergeant, "start refueling and loading ammunition, as we need to be ready at all times." "Right away ma-dam." He said hurrying away shouting orders. Walking around the tank . . . . townspeople smiled, waved and nodded as men and boys pulled their hats off, bowing their heads as she passed.

Continuing on to the few tables set up on two sides of the cooking trailer, she poured another cup of coffee. With the exception of so many people watching her, it wasn't unlike normal camp routine. The prisoners were becoming a problem.

She is short handed as it is, so around-the-clock guards to properly watch one hundred-four enemy soldiers was out of the question. Then there is of course the food problem, she didn't want to have the task of feeding the enemy. "Sergeant, split the prisoners into two groups. Take the first down to the water over there, strip them completely . . . . point out the distant shore . . . . and let them go." "Yes ma-dam. But it has to be a three mile swim, or more, and the water is still very cold." "Tsk, tsk . . . . how true. However, we'll do it anyway." "Yes ma-dam." The sergeant said . . . The colonel jumped up demanding to know where his men were being taken. "I'm sending them home." Aquina said with a smile. He opened his mouth as if to speak, but changed his mind.

Finishing her coffee . . . . Aquina waited until her men returned for the second group. Then and only then did she walk away. The colonel at first experienced a few seconds of panic, the resignation. He didn't blame her . . . to be honest, he realized the circumstances could easily have been reversed.

Too the resourceful sergeant. "I have a big job for you." "Yes ma-dam," said the sergeant. Pulling out a chart, she showed him the small road about three or four tenths of a mile north of Bov. Showing him how it runs west until intersecting with the north to south shore road. Pointing to the junction and the border being only four or five tenths of a mile south. "This is all heavily wooded, and with five tigers, a field piece with half-track, you should have no problem in holding it secure. Take a few dozen men and three trucks. Load all your ammunition in the half-track, and some mortars, and machine guns, plus food into the trucks. We will keep two small trucks running the road constantly." "Thank you ma-dam." Aquina nodded. "Take five of the newly captured tigers." "Yes ma-dam."

Having eaten the small column departed at four-thirty in the afternoon. Experiencing no delays save a narrow road the small column arrived at the border on the shore road at five-fourty, and immediately began barricading portions of the road . . . . then dug-in for the night. During the following morning they finished setting up the field piece and three tanks, keeping two mobile, and the half-track.

The balance of the day for the main camp went normally, with one notable exception. South of them the small city experienced a brief bombing run. Though it lasted only minutes the damage must have been extensive because of fires lighting up the sky for most of the night.

Bright and early the next morning, Aquina spoke with her one remaining sergeant, and in do course promoted him to "second in command." And from his recommendations, . . . she promoted two from the original group to sergeant.

It is noon and both refueling and loading of ammunition had been finished, along with the painting and insignia work. Aquina was thinking to herself . . . "The camp is much larger crowded in fact," looking around catching many townspeople watching her as they went about their tasks. Most, she had never seen before as the newly appointed officer, as yet unspecified rank, walked up to her with two cups and a pad of paper in hand. Handing a cup to her, he discussed the list of names in his hand. "I have names of one hundred fourty-seven of our people who've asked to join our force." "Excellent, we can use them. Assign driving duties to those who can drive, and ammunition loaders . . . try to free up as many of our fighting people as possible. Until more people come in try to maintain three to a tank. Reorganize our present crews so that each tank has an experienced driver and gunner. Assign the previous truck drivers and helpers as machine gunners and loaders. Then shift these new people to the trucks and other duties, such as picking up all the weapons, and ammunition from those dead soldiers on the field. "That has already been done. Ma-dam." Replied the officer smiling. "Good, then have a few men who planted the mines stand out there while the helpers pile bodies on trucks. Use one of those dozers to dig a large mass grave, and bury all the dead." Aquina instructed. "Yes ma-dam."

As dusk fell almost all necessary work had been completed. Where here-to-fore there had been clearings of varying sizes now were filled with green tents. Women gathered, and from the large rolls of gray canvas cut and sewed a large tent-like structure . . . and when in place braced properly . . . covered the cooking trailer and serving tables. More latrines were dug and walled in with thick brush and scrub, as more and more people appeared. Small trucks ferried supplies to the tank group guarding the western road. And with the trucks running back-and-forth, word came of a large influx of people wanting to help. Inasmuch as there was a good deal of birch and other such trees, tents were made using the gray canvas splotched with black in irregular patterns. The twenty-second through to june witnessed a continued procession of volunteers entering both camps; and a substantial increase in the frequency of air raids. Sometimes three, four a day with the small city to the immediate south being pulverized, plus loud booming in the distance, mostly to the south and east. The Englishman had departed for home on the eve of the twenty-second.

CHAP. 31

Friday morning, june second, Aquina lead a force south to the small city. Two black half-tracks each with two separate twin fifty mounts, courtesy of the welders and mechanics, eight tigers plus four trucks of men. A half hour in front of the column her men, twelve strong, did reconnaissance and called back via field phone, saying "only token resistance had been found." Entering the city from two different converging directions, they quickly dispatched the Nazis. While the men searched buildings for Nazis, supplies, radios et-cetera, four small planes dove coming in very low. Many of the men saw them as Aquina aimed and fired into a building collapsing it completely. To the lead plane the black tigers stood out like beacon lights against the ruin in the city; and radioed his find back to the group leader. To the incoming bombers the squadron leader radioed that the city such-n-such was now occupied by a column of black tiger tanks from the north. They swarmed around giving reports to the bomber wing of damage sighted, and "fleeing refugees heading south."

In seconds the line was broken, and one by one the four spitfires dove wobbling wing tip up and down. Almost all of Aquina's people who could cheered and waved. When that group returned home, they weren't at all bashful about their sighting the black tigers, and going into detail about the ruined city. The allied air ministry discussed these developments at some length.

Meanwhile, Aquina had looted and literally destroyed the city burning most of it, and established a hard perimeter three hundred yards south. Calling for reinforcements, she immediately marched and struck the medium sized town just east of the city . . . . repeating the devastation and ruin.

On the fourth of june, at six a.m., she began assaulting Husum with three 88 field pieces, a dozen tigers and six trucks of heavily armed men. At the same time the sergeant, leaving a small force with two half-tracks, pushed south with his tanks destroying both towns on the shore road, and met Aquina's force at Husum. From the lengthy bombardment by both field pieces and tanks, it resulted in little more than a cake walk. Her men looted the city for supplies of any kind, destroying a few ships in the harbor and systematically burned everything remaining. Tired they slept in shifts, while waiting for the supply column. With its arrival they refueled, loaded up on ammunition and started out immediately heading due east. The sergeant with some reinforcements established his perimeter at the junction outside Husum. And with the road and approaches mined it was quite secure from attack.

At four-ten a.m. in the wee hours of june fifth with fires still raging in the city from a recent bombing run, she sat with two field pieces and eight heavy mortars, and twenty tigers. On the north road one field piece and twelve tigers, plus several mortar crews. Four-twenty a.m., brought word from two fifteen man reconnaissance teams, which had been through most of the city. One of the men stood next to Aquina's tank as she climbed down to hear him.

"Ma-dam, on the other side of that building . . . . there . . . . yes that one, is a large grove of trees. Spanning across those trees is camouflaging net and underneath are eleven tigers, large field pieces and half-tracks. Most of the Nazis are trying to put out fires, saving papers and such. We overheard them talking about reinforcements. It seems that the last bombing run destroyed the barracks and headquarters. They have no tank crews, all were killed in or around the barracks." The man's broad grin was catching. She put her hand on his shoulder. "Now where do you suppose there would be crews willing to unburden those poor people. Tsk, tsk." Her grin answered his.

"Take enough so you've three to a tank, and one driver for each half-track, and beat it back here as quickly as you can." "Yes ma-dam." An additional twenty men were added to the two groups of fifteen, and they melted into the night. It is four-fourty-three a.m. She had the word passed. "Stay alert, we don't want to fire on our own people." They waited . . . twenty minutes, thirty, fourty minutes . . . and just as she looked at her watch for the umpteenth time . . . explosions and the unmistakeable sound of tanks. From the sound they were closing fast, and finally in the dim moonlight, she picked out a column of panzers heading their way firing on the city behind them. Aquina gave the order to commence shelling the city.

In a few minutes two half-tracks passed quickly followed by four tigers, then five half-tracks pulling enormous 150 mm. field guns, bringing up the rear . . . . seven tigers. Aquina gradulated them. "Save the 88's . . . set up these big guns quick." Drivers moved the large guns into position and in quick order had them set up ready for action. Their range of 22 miles, so great the barrels were pointed level at the city. With ear plugs in position, she gave them the order to fire.

The concussion was enormous followed by instant impact. While entire buildings disappeared in clouds of fragments. Again and again the guns fired, two in rapid succession then a short pause while two men loaded the heavy shells onto the automatic feeding trays. The five massive guns were leveling approximately three or four acres at a time. Fires broke out everywhere as the guns from the north road began firing steadily. It was five-thirty a.m., with dawn well on its way . . . when she called to cease fire. From the north road the force split, four tigers slowly headed into the city, while the others ran east at speed reaching the long serpentine inlet and followed that into the city.

Aquina began coming in on the west with twenty tigers chopping up resistance easily. The black half-tracks sat amongst the captured equipment, while alert men standing at the multiple fifty's guarded against possible flankers. From their vantage point a considerable part of the inlet was only about thirty yards behind them and the large bridge, and main artery south was open for many miles. They, as Aquina, thought constantly about expected reinforcements, and trying to be prudent, left two tigers at the large bridge to guard it against any surprises, not knowing her men had repositioned the 88's to cover the main road south to the bridge.

From the inlet approach the four tigers, and twenty men eliminated machine gun emplacements, and captured the dock area, and warehouses killing several Nazis as they tried to plant explosives in the same warehouses. The four tanks from the northern end did their part sweeping . . . . effectively eliminating resistance. With the tanks spearheading the drive, men checked those buildings still standing for nazis and sympathisers. Those that survived were gradually swept, herded into the city's approximate center and shot.

Reports began coming in of blank searchs and with the passage of an hour with no Nazis found, Aquina called "cease fire." Only the east section of the city was still intact reported by some men loaded down with wine and champagne. Aquina called down accepting two bottles. "Make sure each tank has a bottle." "Yes ma-dam." Handing an open bottle down to her crew, she began with a liberal swallow of the bubbly. She paused . . . when the field phone now sitting on top cradled in the hatch cover . . . bleeped. "Yes?" "Ma-dam we are down at the docks in front of several warehouses. We have a surprise." "Leaving now will be there soon." Moving her headset back into place, . . . "lets go, reverse back to the docks, and the bridge." In seconds, she and her guard tank meandered around piles of rubble getting progressively closer to the docks. Rumbling through the quiet deserted streets, she thought of Kurt. Only the screaming sound of aircraft impinged on her mind snapping her back to reality. Squinting, she saw large planes at comparatively low altitudes, and six fighters buzzing the city. Using binoculars, Aquina picked out the English insignia, and alerted her people, that they are allies, and not to fire. It was radio silence for the bombers, so the fighter squadron leader didn't expect an answer. "This is wasp squadron leader . . . . Tiger Lady has Schleswig."

The bomber crews . . . many smiled while most just nodded. That was how the allies had identified her, the Nazis however referred to her in considerably less flattering terms. Too her people, she is more than a folk hero, even to the resistance and underground in other countries, she is a folk hero. Aquina's most ardent supporter and spokesman is the English agent, at least out of her own country. He detailed his personal observations, and accounts from his written diary not only to the air ministry, but the admiralty, and the war office. High echelon gatherings, parties, and such he often answered inquiries about the celebrated lady. On many occasions the agent would relate an eye witness account of a battle, most especially the one on may twentieth. In which her tanks, all captured from the Nazis earlier, were outnumbered eight to one.

Running low on fuel the fighters returned to their base. Whereupon they immediately notified their superiors. "The Tiger Lady, sir, has taken Schleswig, and the city west of that, establishing a hard line across that area approximately twenty-four miles south into enemy territory." That word when received at staff meetings caused quite a stir. That was late afternoon, . . . june fifth.

CHAP. 32

Meanwhile, Aquina arrived at the dock and warehouse area. "Well sergeant, what do you have to show me?" The large double doors swung open to reveal eight bofors guns, and an even dozen twenty millimeter guns all in partial crates. She looked around the building, and saw ammunition for the crated guns, a considerable amount. She walked out and around into another warehouse and saw large drums of fuel, and some oil. "I counted them ma-dam, there is one hundred fuel, and twenty drums engine oil." "But for what sergeant?" "For these ma-dam, over here." She walked out of the warehouse following the sergeant out onto the dock. Aquina saw them immediately. "Ohhh, but why would these be here?" Indicating the five large gunboats tied up and nested to the dock. "I don't know for sure ma-dam. But as you can see these small ships are gray. In this small warehouse are a large number of drums containing black paint." "Ambush?" "Yes ma-dam." The sergeant said. "I believe part of the reason for the reinforcements, they were going to land troops behind us where the bay comes in just north of the border, at night." "Makes sense. And certainly those guns while light . . . would supply a good deal of firepower." She chuckled to herself. "I think we shall go along with these preparations, but it shall be we who do the ambushing." Aquina said firmly.

Aquina quickly regained the turret, and began speaking into the field phone. Calling for reinforcements, and as many helpers as the base camp could afford, plus transport trucks, and speaking into the headset ordered all gray tigers and half-tracks to the dock area. "Sergeant, when they get here have the men start painting our armor. We can leave the gunboats for the helpers." "Yes ma-dam." Too her newly promoted sergeant. "The town east of here on this inlet, assemble five tigers that are refueled and loaded with ammunition and take the town. Secure what supplies are available and destroy it unless something is found noteworthy." "Yes ma-dam."

Sipping champagne, she looked up at the sound of approaching aircraft. Dozens of bombers were heading back, and some were flying lower trailing smoke and fire. "Allies," she said to no-one in particular. Looking through binoculars, "different from the Englishman, but he said they are compatriots." Aquina began counting parachutes as the people abandoned their aircraft. When it became apparent they would land several hundred yards to the south . . . "start em up, lets go! You men into that half-track."

Aquina with two tigers following, and a half-track loaded with armed men rumbled across the large bridge accelerating racing south. Two other black tigers raced after their leader in case of trouble. Two nazi half-tracks accompanied by three large trucks headed north to take prisoner the allied flyers when they landed. Still hundreds of feet in the air the airmen looked down in dismay at the half-tracks and trucks coming toward them.

They landed amidst low scrub, some on the field as several hundred feet away the gray half-tracks were closing fast surrounded by a good number of nazi troops. Although some were wounded, the flyers had their side arms ready. One officer yelled . . . "duck!" The high pitch whine of incoming shells began exploding tearing up the half-tracks. All of a sudden loud crunching with the sound of scrub being crushed . . . . as only about twenty feet away a huge black tank burst through roaring out in front of them machine gun blazing. In seconds other black tanks literally burst on the scene easily destroying the half-tracks, and killing all the nazi soldiers.

On the lead tank they heard a hatch clang open, and a woman stand up with binoculars shouting orders, as other black tanks and a black half-track arrived. The airmen watched stunned from the suddenness of the attack, men were running some toward them, while others started picking up weapons, grenades, and ammunition belts from the dead enemy soldiers. As they are helped into the half-tracks, they saw the vision still sitting on top of her tank, as it and two others roared off down to the road, and the three enemy trucks. A spurt of machine gun fire and then all is quiet once again. Gaining the road slowly, most looked back and saw three enemy trucks coming up behind them with the enormous tigers bringing up the rear.

Crossing the bridge the airmen gawked at all the black tiger tanks, field pieces and the column of gray tigers being even now painted black. A few pointed to the large gunboats tied up to the pier. They saw the trucks and tanks stop, but their driver kept going. All of them grew very quiet . . . . the devastation and ruin registered on them . . . . heavily. After a short while the half-track stopped in front of a building, fairly intact . . . a hotel with restaurant and bar. They'd been inside only a few minutes, when both another yank crew and an english crew were ushered inside. Gradulating each other, the topic quickly changed to the woman on the tiger tank. One would think each was a suitor in competition for her affection. Service people in the hotel began feeding them, biscuits, soup and some meat.

It was obvious to the airmen the resistance fighters were expecting someone. An hour passed, as evening announced its arrival with twilight, at six-thirty p.m., and the building began to vibrate. With dust floating down from the ceiling and lamps shaking . . . two tanks stopped outside. Cats and dogs came out from their little sanctuaries running pell-mell for the entrance. Aquina entered confronted by the animals. Smiling and getting down on her knees, . . . she petted and played with them for several minutes as the large room full of men looked on. She spoke to the people in aprons, who quickly began feeding the animals. Flanked by many of her men, Aquina walked into the dining room, and looked at the airmen for some seconds. They in turn gawked and stared. Some of the airmen quipped, whispered . . . "I'm in heaven." "Ohhh, I'm in love." "Blimey, a gueen." "She's a knockout, gorgeous." Much of it had to do with her age, or rather the lack of it. However, they all were of the opinion she couldn't be more than eighteen or nineteen.

One of the sergeants addressed her, and spoke the first word in English. "Ma-dam, I've ordered refueling, reload with ammunition, and the painting is continuing." "Good sergeant."

The airmen understood the informality amongst the men, but paid close attention to the display of defference and honor the men showed the young woman. Then like a common thought the whisper went around the room. "It's the Tiger Lady." "Pardon?" Aquina said. All the officers saluted and introduced themselves. "We, or rather ma-dam, it is the name by which you are known to the allies." "Ohhh, I see," with a small smile. "My name is 'Labr.'" One of the English officers sucked-in his breath, stood at attention, bowed and softly said, "Highness." The others looked at him somewhat quizzically. "Ma-dam is a member of the oldest royal family in existence . . . save possibly the English monarchy." The flyers suddenly became a bit self conscious.

Meanwhile the appropriate allied commands had been notified their missing men had parachuted to safety just in front of. . . . and to the rear of positions held by the "Tiger Lady."

June sixth . . . . passed with the status-quo still normal. Working parties hurried with their tasks especially the painting, and mounting the new guns in the proper places on the gunboats. That in itself was not finished until evening. The supply column arrived late morning, and seven trucks immediately departed heading west with escort. All the flyers fit and able pitched-in with truck loads of volunteers painting the boats, unloading trucks laden with foodstuffs, and reloading them with all the left-over ammunition from the gunboats.

On the ninth, all airmen were trucked west to Husum, where they went aboard a fishing packet. With the tide they were on their way west.

CHAP. 33

The next several months continued much as before, only the air-raids fluctuated. During which Aquina, and her men were responsible for saving the lives of many allied flight crews, as well as dozens of individual flyers. And the Nazis were far to busy with the allied armies on two separate fronts to worry about Aquina. Summer changed to fall, and fall to winter; and those months were put to excellent use. She solidified the line making it hard with large areas mined. Field pieces are solidly entrenched and virtually all the armor was in position, supplied with truck convoys.

By November, she and her men carried out raids destroying the railroad, and towns along all the main and secondary roads. On the east road all the bridges had been destroyed for those across the canal. They had shot-up or bombarded, sacked or burned from the west Eider across to the Sorge, Wittensee, and straight across cutting the road and railroad . . . as well as the towns on the east shore.

In December, Aquina regrouped her forces, and advanced pushing the hard line south on the west, until firmly entrenched on the Eider river across to within three miles of Rendsburg, and the entire canal east to Kieler Forde. Reinforced by recent captured equipment, Aquina assigned to her deputy the execution of the crab, her favorite method of assault.

During the wee hours of the twenty-first, they sat poised to push-off. That Thursday morning, like so many that month, it was snowing steadily adding inches to an already thick blanket. In position on the east and west approaches to the city were a total of thirty tigers, eight half-tracks and seventy men split evenly. On the north road . . . the same except a hundred men, with her in the lead tank. Several miles to the east a similar force was ready to take the large principle bridge over the canal. Their signal was the first 88 mm. round. At two-twenty a.m., east and west pincers began their almost silent approach. Wind muffled the diesels to a large degree, while the new and old snow cushioned the normal harsh tread noise.

Both pincers closed with fierce fighting form both man and machine. Warehouses, fuel depot and demoralized units . . . . while the last vestiges of a panzer division fell into their hands during the first half hour. Nazi defenses were initially strong until 150 mm. rounds began to systematically reducing buildings to rubble. With whole facades, and buildings falling on them, and bursting asunder, it didn't take long for them to flee. Unfortunately headlong into the black tigers already at the rear controlling all avenues of possible escape. The end was both swift and final. What few pockets and remnants of the enemy survived were in due course routed and killed.

Aquina quickly strengthened her position. Supplies were distributed and individual pieces of captured armor were moved into the warehouse, and converted. Up and down the "line", she joined her people in celebrating the holidays. Just as well because the weather was totally vicious during the last of December, and well into January '45.

Hampered by bad weather in the form of snow, the rain, briefly back to snow, and on again-off again, freezing weather made their push to the west slow and arduous. Not until march thirtieth did they finally come upon the mouth of the Elbe river. Immediately the sergeant requested reinforcements. Aquina complied with forty black tigers, half-tracks with 88 mm. field pieces, a twenty truck convoy with fuel and an additional hundred men.

In the interim, she pounded Kiel into oblivion using two 150 mm. field pieces, and three 88's.

April fifteenth . . . . a nazi grand admiral escaping the red onslaught from the approaching army to the east returned to Flensburg with a modest force at night, recapturing the city's center. Immediately, some of Aquina's people, helpers and volunteers were captured, but no armor, and only some hand weapons to speak of. Within hours the whole entire group along with the admiral was surrounded by reserve armor units of Aquina's force. The Nazis could do nothing, or go anywhere. And they realized, they were alive only because they held some captives. In loose communication with the stranded and cut off nazi group of officials in the northern island capital of Aquina's country; he was trying to find a graceful exit from the predicament which could only get worse. And sight of the black tigers sent not only a chill down his spine, but his men as well.

Midday on the nineteenth lookouts sighted enemy divisions, and armored, and infantry strengthened by panzer brigade bombarding positions south of the Elbe. The sergeant heavily reinforced the only bridge crossing, over the canal, located within plain sight of the Elbe. When Aquina received the report, she hurried to the sergeant's location with fourty tigers, three half-tracks each pulling a 150 mm. field piece, a fuel trailer, and drums, and twenty-five trucks loaded with ammunition and other supplies. Sitting on her tank, the light blue flag flapping high in the breeze from the radio antenna, quickly issued orders for the big guns to zero-in on the enemy guns and tank concentrations. She had the 88's set up in two groups and spanned out her tanks.

Across the river in command cars and tank units . . . . english officers noticed the furious activity. The english field marshall was notified by subordinates, and told his officers and commanders to look for a black tank flying a blue flag or bunting. When notified of its presence, the field marshall ordered all commands to take notice of their unexpected ally, and not fire on them by mistake.

Observing the nazi's strategy, Aquina ordered her tigers to approach from the river bank, and the second section to attack the rear. She ordered the big guns to fire, dropped down slammed the hatch shut and charged ahead. By the time she reached the bridge's apron on the far side, she'd already scored twice. Up to thirty-five m.p.h., her tanks virtually streaked across.

Meanwhile, the gunners and allied officers watched the slaughter. At first elated and cheering, but after some minutes . . . they watched fascinated by the spectacle. It was a total rout with english infantry, and tanks on the same side pushing north and the black tigers attacking ruthlessly from the side and rear. Their machine guns cut through the infantry like a giant scythe. Across the canal, field pieces chewed up the panzers near the English lines, and the nazi 88's were mere toys against the 150 mm. rounds. Outgunned and demoralized the battle was short lived. Nazi tank crews abandoned their equipment sometimes only a split second before an 88 mm. round crashed into it converting the once proud machine to flaming junk. And there was a great deal of such junk, the black tigers killing tanks and crews like a school of maneating sharks in a feeding frenzy.

Those Nazis still alive ran toward the English lines throwing down their weapons screaming-running for their lives. And many didn't make it, instead were cut down by the black tigers. For some time the enormous guns were silent, now moved ready to be re-coupled to the half-tracks.

Aquina, and her deputy, both tigers parked on the side, opened their hatches standing up savoring the cool air, and watched the mop-up operations. Speaking into the headset issueing orders, she hardly noticed the English infantry moving up to help in mopping-up the area. But when a group of small vehicles came toward them it was different, especially since several tanks accompanied them. Because the English tanks immediately swung their cannons to the rear, or passive position, it was clear this meeting is important to them . . . . so she tried to be pleasant.

She signaled the driver and both diesels were turned off seconds before a group of smiling officers began applauding. Aquina swung her legs over and stood on the coaming covering the treads, just as the junior officers stood at attention as several majors and colonels came forward with an obviously high echelon officer. All the officers were struck by two things, youth and her physical beauty. The field marshall was no exception, although he didn't suffer quite as much. A senior colonel stepped forward and introduced Aquina to the field marshall, and visa-versa.

She exchanged pleasentries with the field marshall, who then departed after a few minutes. About fifteen minutes later while talking to the group, her deputy interrupted with news. A quick consultation, and Aquina took her leave. The men were disappointed, but at least they had the opportunity to meet the celebrated "Tiger Lady." Looking down on her belt as the driver reached thirty m.p.h., she flicked off Dien's recorder. Aquina squinted a little heading back until across the bridge. Three-quarters up along the canal shielded by groves of trees and scrub, is the camp. In her absence a spatious tent had been erected amidst some large firs. Her deputy held the flap as she walked in to find two rooms. The first or outer room held an oblong table and three chairs, and a small desk; and beyond through the second flap . . . . a sturdy bed, but comfortable looking with clean sheets, pillow and blanket. A small dresser stood in the right hand corner with a straight back chair next to it. Opposite the dresser stood a sturdy night table with an oil lamp resting on top. Aquina looked down and suddenly realized, she was standing on a wood floor. She turned slightly smiling. "Thank you Klaud, and thank the men for me." He smiled and bowed his head . . . . and said quietly, "yes ma-dam." That evening the entire camp is in good spirits. Aquina sat and ate a small plate, chatted a little then walked to her tent sleeping the entire night.

The twentieth and twenty-first were spent clearing up odds-n-ends of maintenance, as it rained steadily the entire area was socked-in.

With dawn of the twenty-third, the allies had secured all of the city of Hamburg, and its environs, and formed a line from the northern city limits to four miles north of Itzehoe, to the canal.

At one-thirty in the afternoon an English staff car was stopped at the bridge approach for an i.d. check then passed across. Enroute to the camp, the major couldn't help but gawk at the dispersement pattern of tigers. And before arriving at the entrenched camp, counted well over a hundred tiger and panzer tanks, twelve heavily armed half-tracks, with 88 mm. field guns in tow, and in another grouping to the rear, ... a group of half-tracks with truly enormous field pieces, a truck convoy of some thirty trucks, fuel trucks with trailers, and other interesting sights.

Aquina was in the first room of her tent, reading over fuel stores and anticipated fuel requirements. She heard the staff car stop outside, and stood waiting by the open entrance as the major walked around the car heading in her direction. He stopped a few feet away at attention, saluted . . . . "Ma-dam 'Labr, a message . . ." Bowing slightly, he handed the note to her. "May, I wait for a reply ma-dam." She quickly scanned the neat script. "Yes there will be an answer." Rereading the note, Aquina smiled at the flattering prose and immediately sat to pen a reply. Handing the note to the major with a smile. "Thank you major, and I shall expect the vehicle at six-thirty." "Yes ma-dam, and thank you." He said with some emphasis.

After his departure, she had a sergeant dispatch a driver to Rensburg for her travel bags and things left there when she decided to head the reinforcement column south. Calling her deputy, Aquina explained the invitation, and that he will be in command until her return. On an area map, she pointed to the estate, where the dinner was to be held. "About fifteen miles from here, and almost one mile south of this small city." "Yes ma-dam."

She realized in her haste virtually everything, but a skimpy travel case was in Rensburg. And with a sigh, Aquina bent over picked it up off the floor, opened the loop-like latch and slowly began emptying the contents on the bed. "Hmmm . . . . brush and comb, hair pins, ahhh style comb, face cloth and my cream." She opened a small jar and shook out a vitamin promptly swallowing it, recapped the jar returning it carefully to the recess within the bag. With a sad distant look, Aquina reached down picking up an ornate rosewood jewelry box. Touching-caressing it and wiping away several tears, she opened it slowly. The black velvet bundle was opened one side at a time. Sniffing-wiping away tears, she touched the tiara, and earrings, although, she had paid for them, Kurt had chosen them . . . . for her.

Aquina was suffering from fatigue, but it represented only a portion of the problem. Hence the underlying reason for her acceptance. Perhaps for this one evening . . . . to forget the war, and the killing, too feel . . . too act like a woman again. Aquina needed it badly, far more than she realized.

One sergeant called-out asking to be admitted, and when she said, "Yes." They brought into the inner room a white bathtub setting it down next to the dresser and chair. She thanked them as man after man carried in two buckets of hot water. And when full the sergeant departed closing the flaps behind him. Unpacking from the bag scented soap, perfumed bath salts, and a face cloth, she began stripping.

Fourty-five minutes later, she toweled herself dry, and wrapped her hair. Sitting with a large towel around her it required only moments to set the long flowing tresses, and apply make-up sparingly. While it seemed forever waiting for the driver, Aquina busied herself with paper work.

A few minutes after five the driver returned with everything she had left behind. And by five-fourty, Aquina had some of it put away. Between brushing her hair, getting dressed, in a floor-length black silk gown with semi-close fitting skirt, ruffles extending from the shoulder down around the sumptuous bosom. As she admired her reflection, and put on a long diamond earrings . . . . the field marshall's own staff car approached the bridge.

Fingers with freshly done nails deftly positioned the tiara, and pinned it securely in place. Touching up lipstick, and additional sprits of perfume, three-quarter length matching cape trimmed in black fur, and she is ready.

Aquina heard the car stop in front, and with a last glimpse in the mirror . . . . grinned, picking up her purse, flipping up the hood, and slowly exited the bedroom. Her high heels told the deputy of her approach, and he quickly pulled back the front tent flap. Heads snapped up, some mouths dropped open as men stared in open admiration. Extending her gloved hand the major helped her down the six inch step from the tent's wood floor to the ground, and the several yards to the waiting car.

In one fluid motion, she is sitting in the spacious rear seat as the major joined the driver up front. As the car turned and headed for the bridge, eight freshly washed black tigers pulled in behind . . . her tiger with the telltale flag was first in line behind the car.

The drive was a treat for the two men, while, she is lost in her own reverie.

CHAP. 34

Within the spacious mansion dozens of senior allied officers listened to the orchestra, drank and joined in conversation many checking and re-checking the time. The field marshall no less affected, added to the air of expectancy. All the service people, orchestra were regular enlisted ranks. And the only females present were the countess, who owned the lavish estate, her sister, and one daughter.

At seven minutes to the hour, the sound of tanks was unmistakeable, and grew progressively louder. They were passed on by guards, who seeing the "Tiger Lady" sprang to attention saluting smartly. Six of the eight tanks did not wait, but followed the car up the massive circular drive. The last two tigers assumed a defensive position on either side of the entrance. Pairing off, as the car came to a stop at the front portico, split up three on either side of the drive, and shut off the diesels. Officers at the windows remarked out loud about "her escort."

It is impressive, but no way as much when compared to the person. Several majors came outside as a seductive nylon-clad leg appeared. Aquina exited on the arm of the major, and slowly, looking regal walked to the door. Inside a butler bowed then helped her with the cape. Flipping the hood back had more of an effect than she had anticipated. The countess, who was walking toward her for a greeting is almost stunned to see the tiara, and only then did she recall the princess from years earlier in Hamburg. Recovering her composure almost immediately, the countess curtsied and bowed. "So good to see you again highness." "Thank you countess. It has been some years." The countess standing . . . . talking, as if an old friend to royalty, where in actuality they were only acquaintances, since the parties and theater in Hamburg." Aquina said. All the officers were numb with surprise and pleasantly shocked. The countess noticeably trying to get into Aquina's graces went on an on about the prince, who was so captivated with Aquina . . . . was left stammering at a party. Although she looked almost dowdy next to the princess, the countess is an accomplished hostess, and as they walked into the large dining room, she had officers introduced in turn. They all bowed, and tried valiantly in some way to outshine their fellows. Walking slowly the officers became more-and-more senior until only the field marshall remained. Aquina nodded slightly and smiled, "Field marshall." He bowed and holding her hand brushed his lips lightly.

"A pleasure highness." "Please call me Aquina."

In minutes, she found herself seated in a comfortable chair with the countess and others nearby. Senior officers were seated with the others hovering around seeing to Aquina's every need and whim. Champagne flowed like water, and with it . . . . questions. Almost all of them were directed at her. Explaining how while going to the university in Hamburg, she had met the prince. When she mentioned her bodyguard, while at school . . . she explained about Kurt, and the sadness registered itself on her exquisite features. The men were sorry they asked, but she kept on. "Kurt was german and a captain of infantry at the end of the last war. Not only a capable bodyguard, but complimented certain courses, especially when my aunt and I began our buildup. We had imported small arms before the war swung into high gear." One of the colonels asked. "Princess, if I may. What kind of arms?" "Oh . . . some trucks, mortars, automatic weapons, some heavy machine guns, explosives, food and fuel, steel and some lumber and grenades. With that you can count seventy-five hard men. At one time because of a few casualties and wounded . . . we were reduced to about fourty some odd men. After many battles and skirmishes, and had re-patrioted tigers, and some older panzers, we engaged the nazi garrison on Fyn. Expecting a force three times our number, but instead they'd reinforced earlier that day . . . . and encountered almost brigade strength." Her look became distant. "The nazis experienced a hard lesson that night." Many of the men swallowed with difficulty. Aquina continued. "Kurt and I regrouped adding captured units to our force, and their entire storage, weapons, and fuel depots. We formed up and ran south to our border. With minor preparations, Kurt's tank and mine charged the tigers and half-track at the border. During this relatively minor operation, Kurt's tiger was hit in the forward flank assembly. One man was lightly wounded, a second with serious wounds, but Kurt was killed. Your probably aware of the following battle from the agent." "We are indeed." Replied the field marshall. "How many Nazis do you calculate north of the canal, Aquina?" The field marshall asked. "None. Unless one counts the miniscule group at Flensburg, and some of my tigers have them surrounded, and penned-in. There is . . . oh . . . a few still in the island capital . . . . but that's all."

Almost every man is speechless, the field marshall was incredulous. "My Goddd!" Exclaimed the officer.

"According to reports there was one infantry division, one armored panzer division, and at least one possibly two brigades one of them comprised of tanks."

Aquina sipped daintily from her glass, and smiled sweetly at the multitude of faces. And slowly shook her head, no.

"Then, Aquina, where do you keep the undoubtedly hundreds of prisoners?" The colonel asked. "We have no prisoners." "But the agent clearly recorded some prisoners taken after the rout of the enemy above Flensburg." "Quite so, we did. But gentlemen with less than a hundred men, most of them in my tigers, at three to a tank, I could not keep them. Nor could I allow them to go free. You on the other hand have tens of thousands of troops, great numbers of mechanized and armored units, plus huge massive stores and supplies to draw from. I do not, but am forced to take it from my enemy. So . . . . I consigned them to the ultimate authority. Half of the group at a time were shown their native land. They had but to swim the fjord."

The field marshall spoke. "It is . . . . it is, but such is this war. In your circumstances, I'd have no doubt done the same. However, your continued run of success speaks louder than any mere oratory. I wish to seize this opportunity, and thank you for your sudden and thorough aid . . . your attack of several days ago saved many allied lives." The field marshall stood and held his glass in the position of a toast, bowed slightly to Aquina as did all the officers, and drank.

Dinner was announced, Aquina immediately turned speaking to a major. "Would you have the staff take hot food to my men . . . on the tigers?" He bowed slightly smiling. "I will see to it personally dear princess." Aquina smiled and nodded. "Thank you major."

The field marshall extended his arm, Aquina stood putting her left arm through his and walked slowly into the lavish formal dining room. He immediately sat her on his right, while the countess, as hostess sat opposite, at the table's far end. Seating was by the alternate method, when possible, thereby affecting a slight mix. Conversation was light and brisk between the preliminary first and second courses. Aquina ate sparingly as was her habit. Most if not all the officers would look trying not to stare, but found it difficult not to look. Without exception every person found her to be an enigma. Her obvious tender age simply did not allow for, nor explain her academic credentials. And yet a colonel had checked the supposed facts on record. And the records were clear, and quite specific. And verified not one, but two degrees of achievement, which only added to the confusion. As the facts suggested, and eyewitness accounts i.e., the English agent, appeared to verify, . . . the princess is far more unusual than any of them had supposed.

Aquina's senses were alert, as she picked up on the subtle change in the field marshall's curiosity. All doubts evaporated when his next question inquired about pets, . . . if she had any, what kind et-cetera? She in turn shifted her answers to the evasive and giving no answers, save that yes there are puppies and kittens, but were now close to full grown. Shifting his stance the field marshall attempted a soft more gentle probing. When that didn't yield the hoped for results, he decided to dispense with the questions rather than antagonize the princess.

An hour later, Aquina exhaled slowly trying to rid herself of renewed anxiety. The sound of her tigers was comforting allowing tension to ebb off. Thinking . . . relaxing the questions, and change in mood, she realized and resolved to always to be on guard against intrusion. Preoccupied, she noticed the bridge crossing, and snapped out of her reverie just before entry into the camp.

A gracious parting by the major helped to restore her mood, and decided to get a cup of coffee. Making sure the hood was up all the way, she raised up the gown a bit, and walked over to the kitchen tent, being careful not to allow the heels to sink into the ground. Sipping the hot coffee, and carefully putting the jewelry away, undressing, and et-cetera, was under the covers and asleep all within twenty minutes.

On the twenty-fifth the allies continued their push east and north meeting only token resistance. And by may first, they had covered the entire lower area of the Holstein, and arrived and took Lubeck on the second of may. Also on may first, in the afternoon, had retaken the surrounded center area of Flensburg without a shot. May third the replacement for the grand admiral petitioned for a surrender. May fourth, all principle parties were present in varied localities, and the overall surrender was signed, to be in effect on may fifth, at 8 a.m. However, one nazi admiral did not arrive to sign the surrender until the evening of may fifth.

When written word came, verified by allied commanders, Aquina was in her tent doing paperwork, the bane of every field commander. She had to read it twice, as tears persisted in blurring her vision. Looking at her second in command. "Contact all our units and men along the canal, to pack up everything, and form up on the north road. Proceed to this location at best possible speed. Stress normal defense posture. And remind them this is still a military outfit." "Yes ma-dam." With his departure, she opened the bottle of champagne which appeared from behind her deputy's back.

Walking after changing into clean clothes, Aquina interrupted their celebrating. "I share your enthusiasm, but remember there may very well be some Nazis still around who haven't received the news. Now break camp, and load up. We will wait here for our people from the canal area. Sergeants, start refueling all vehicles, and load up." She motioned to one sergeant. "Yes ma-dam." "Start calling the cities and major towns at home, in case they haven't heard." "Yes ma-dam."

Her tiger tank is first in line behind a half-track with the others lined up to the rear. She looked around as the camp was rapidly broken down and loaded onto trucks. At nine-fifteen a.m., the camp had been loaded, and while waiting for their compatriots, talked and gestured about the war.

"Sergeant?" "Yes ma-dam." "Have you notified the compound?" "Yes ma-dam, we were able to get through." "That's good. Is everything loaded?" "Yes ma-dam. All except the warehouses." "Hmmm . . . yes, I think so. Sergeant reload everything from them as well onto the trucks." "Yes ma-dam, right away."

Dozens of men formed lines, while in some cases trucks backed directly into other warehouses. And while her deputy saw to the smooth loading of sacks, bags, crates, and drums, she looked over the inventory. At twelve-thirty sentrys informed one of the sergeants, who in turn brought the news to Aquina of the rear or canal units approaching. The moment they pulled up to a stop behind the first column, men jumped down to help. Within the hour, vehicles and tanks began assuming the proper positions. "Sergeant, you've counted every person and vehicle?" "Oh yes ma-dam, everyone and every vehicle is accounted for, and present." "Well done sergeant." He nodded, and to her deputy . . . "Arrange them so there are three half-tracks in front, followed by all the tigers, fifteen half-tracks with the field pieces, all trucks and fuel trailers, then the remaining fifteen half-tracks in the rear." "Yes ma-dam."

CHAP. 35

At one fourty-five they were formed up in one continuous colossal armed column. Sitting atop her own tiger, she gave the long awaited signal. And one by one each vehicle started moving north at a sedate ten m.p.h. Around piles and hills of debris the column snaked its way out of Flensburg. Once clear of the city, she ordered them up to twenty, passing the stretch of road where the large enemy column had been captured. As the half-tracks rounded the bend lookouts in their accustomed positions picked them out as well as the lead tiger.

Soon those on the ground were able to pick out vehicles with their own field glasses. Moving briskly in the breeze the blue flag rippled as the vehicles exited the wood line to the open field. Water glistened on the right reflecting the early spring sun. And ahead, she could make out movement at the border and smiled.

In many parts of the world, people were dancing in the streets, drunk, hugging and kissing, ... incredibly happy and thankful to God. Although areas still raged with war most of the world was again at peace.

Closer and closer to the border they rumbled on clanking along, the multitude of tanks adding to the roar. Aquina spoke into her headset giving the order to slow to eight m.p.h., because of the crowds. An enormous number of people were at the border waving and cheering; from older people to mere youngsters as the column began to cross. She held up her arm to stop, and each tank on back the person sitting or standing at the hatch did the same all the way to the trucks, and further yet. While people gathered around shaking hands, kissing the drivers through their own personal hatchs, ... Aquina called to the sergeant. Not able to hear his lovely commander . . . jumped up on the tiger, and shouted. "Are you loaded up and ready to pull out?" "Yes ma-dam." "Good, pull into formation at the rear, with trucks behind the half-tracks, and your panzers bringing up the rear." "Yes ma-dam," shouting above the crowd.

People stood back a little as diesels reved and vehicles began moving. Slowly at first barely able to make any headway until the crowd shrank back. Aquina had them accelerate slowly. Their progress was slow with groups of cheering, waving people every few hundred yards, throwing flowers onto tanks and other vehicles. And it continued that way until the lead half-tracks were abreast of Abenra. There . . . . entirely across the road . . . . people, hundreds and hundreds more blocking the road. From surrounding towns plus large Abenra itself, they came crying, cheering, and waving. Young men and women climbed up on the tanks, and half-tracks, and trucks et-cetera, on down the line giving the resistance members flowers and drink.

Finally at about three-fourty the column started moving north again, and glancing at her watch, Aquina realized they wouldn't make the compound. She moved the column up to fifteen m.p.h., and tried not to slacken the pace. But it seemed the further north they went, the greater size and frequency of the crowds. Until five-fifteen p.m., still two miles south of the junction city, lines of people on both sides of the road became constant, increasing in size, until reaching the city. At which point the crowds reached mob proportion.

Aquina called to the rear of the column instructing them to come around onto the field, and make two lines. And although it took some shouting the crowd moved away from the right side allowing the long line of tigers to pivot, and move from the road onto the field forming two lines of black. The trucks, both large and intermediate sizes, closed inbetween and behind the tanks as the immense crowd surged in-and-amongst the now parked vehicles. Speaking into her headset, standing on top while her crew climbed out and down, she directed the food truck with its cooking trailer forward to occupy the center. Dozens of people began helping; while some were erecting tents, starting the stoves, moving coal and some wood, sacks and bags from supply trucks, personnel tents, and her own was set-up in front of the lead tiger. In a fraction of the time it normally required, the camp is up; and putting her headset down on its hook inside the turret, she closed the hatch and climbed down to eager waiting hands, which lowered her gently to the ground. Many of them cried with joy as flowers are thrust into her arms, and men bowed and shook a hand, a clasp on the shoulder. Women curtsied sometimes hugging her while older children able to get close hugged her around the waist.

Not only her machine, but all the vehicles were heaped with flowers as wine flowed and laughter, smiles, cheering and singing ruled the camp. Vast numbers of people numbering in the tens of thousands swarmed the fighters as each is fetted and cared for in style. All that evening, she is fetted by a sizeable number. It was questions many in fact, wine or cognac, and food was brought for her. Sometimes the crowds sat quietly watching, or followed as she walked the camp checking on her people. The young are in awe of her . . . . the parents entranced knowing a little better, and more of this woman than the young, she so uncannily resembled.

Through the entire night and into the wee hours the party continued, but began loosing steam around dawn. Not-with-standing the entire camp was struck, and loaded and formed up ready to move at a few minutes past nine. In minutes the ground began vibrating as the column rumbled across the open ground to the road. Rumbling into and through the city, the cheering started anew. Flowers slightly wilted from the past day's festivities and celebration were from people in high windows and roof-tops. Thousands of people lined the road north of the city to the junction, and west, so that their speed, instead of being increased had to remain the same. In certain places their fifteen m.p.h., rate had to be reduced as in the junction turning left, were forced to lower to eight m.p.h.

The units at the junction went in behind the column as it passed laden with flowers and sentiment. Crowds slowly dissipated the further west until passing the road sign announcing the harbor city. From there it increased little-by-little until suddenly new crowds came into view.

Thousands from the harbor city and surrounding towns swarmed around the intersection of the "wood's road" to the extent of almost choking off both the roads entirely. Parting reluctantly, the column started turning right slowly penetrating the enormous tide of people. Almost one at a time half-tracks and tanks turned the corner heading toward the scrub line.

With a few yards left to maneuver, Aquina ordered the half-tracks to turn, split evenly on either side in rows parallel to the scrub. Almost five rows of tigers, and older panzers of thirty each, then the half-tracks pulling field pieces. Old panzers and half-tracks some with field pieces lined up as men emptied out of trucks, tanks, et-cetera. She ordered the cook truck in the middle, and tents erected. And like the preceeding day, there was no shortage of eager willing hands.

She dispatched two empty trucks for the families, and her aunt Dien. Not only the families, but the cooks came as well. And Dien, when she arrived the crowd gave way . . . . for several seconds they looked and studied each other . . . as Aquina broke into tears throwing her arms around Dien. Dien at once recognized some of the danger signs, and tried to comfort Aquina, but always mindful of the crowd around them. Most of the people wept with her, part in relief, and part because of empathy toward them. And gratitude for all the men who came back whole, and the surge of pride for a leader who vanquished an invader.

Dien recognized the symptoms . . . that Aquina had become a statistic, as surely as if she had been mortally wounded. Aquina held onto Dien with one hand, while sniffing and wiping away tears with the other. The crowd had quieted substantially, and experienced a moment of discovery . . . . for that brief moment in time they saw a very frightened young woman, scarred from the war . . . . cry with relief. Dien had an arm around Aquina's waist while she wiped at a few remaining tears and forced a smile.

A young woman came forward with flowers, while another handed Aquina a glass of wine. The smile deepened as people shyly came forward congradulating her mumbling heartfelt thanks. And as Aquina finished the wine, there was no hiding the trembling in her hand. Immediately, an older man came forward gently held her free hand kissing it lightly, and mumbled his thanks. Straightening he looked at her, eyes filled with moisture, and smiled as another quickly stepped forward repeating the action. Another and another came forward . . . . a continuous line, while a young person filled the empty glass with cognac, not once but several times. Each instance when the glass was empty, within seconds it would be refilled usually with cognac.

It didn't take long for the strong brandy to react, as Aquina slowly began to relax. And the more at ease she became, the more high-spirited the celebration became. The entire afternoon and the greater part of the evening flew by unnoticed because of the party mood.

Starting the following day several tanks and half-tracks each with field pieces were parked within the scrub. While some including Aquina's tiger were parked alongside the compound, and warehouse, as various trucks were driven into the warehouse and parked. Others were parked in rows outside waiting the results of the meeting and the phone call inside the barracks office. For the meeting, Aquina had been joined by her second-in-command, and all the sergeants while the men sat on the barracks side of the large windows with their families. They had received some of the logistic problems, and were closing in on the one remaining glitch. At that moment the phone rang.

The sergeant sitting closest answered. "Yes?" His eyes widened handing the phone to Aquina. "ma-dam, a parliament minister." "Thank you sergeant." Aquina took the phone and quickly pulled off an earring and listening . . . "Hello? Yes this is she. Thank you, we had our share of luck. Ah-ha . . . yes, I have surmised as much." Some minutes later she continued. "I cannot of course make any promises; however, I believe most of my people will accept. What of my officers?" Seconds later . . . "I will speak to them on your behalf. Yes, ah-ha, I will do that . . . yes at approximately ten a.m. Yes thank you again, goodbye." Aquina returned the receiver to its little cradle and sat for some seconds looking at her officers the smile widening.

She explained the phone call, and its ramifications for them, and the others if they agreed. And while the barracks full of men, and their families looked on, Aquina began pointing out facts in favor of the minister's proposal. After some moments they agreed, after which, she and the officers went into the barracks and explained in detail not only what they had discussed, but also the minister's proposal.

An hour passed at which time the families discussed it privately with their men, the single men discussed it amongst themselves. Those waiting outside were given the identical information. She stood chatting with individuals answering questions and trying to clarify some of it for them. As it turned out Aquina didn't have long to wait. Of the four hundred-fourty men present, both inside and out, fully three hundred-twenty-five decided to accept the minister's offer; that is "to serve in the newly reformed army along with their tanks and half-tracks, with pay and rank alongside the same officers that they're accustomed to, plus gratuities. Most of the balance of one hundred-fifteen opt'd to return as quickly as possible to their farms, fishing, lumber, and other livelihoods. But there is a fair size group, including some family's, who had lost their husbands, or sons, and were not sure what it was they were going to do. Aquina went to this group first.

"Please sit with me." As the adults sat in a semi-circle the children fidgeting . . . . and suddenly in a rush it was out in the open. "Without their men-folk they couldn't survive in their present positions."

Aquina found some were farming, and the rest fishing families. And asked questions concerning the sizes of the farms and the fishing boats. She found all of the farmers owned their land, and only one fishing boat amongst those who fished was not owned by the family in question, but by the bank. From that family, she obtained the bank's name and all the necessary information. The fact it is one of the banks she did business with only made her decision easier.

She spoke to the mother . . . she said, "come with me for a moment." "Yes ma-dam." The older woman, and mother followed Aquina to the office followed seconds later by her several children. Aquina dialed the bank and once the manager's familiar voice came through, she gave firm instructions concerning the vessel, its name, the family who worked the boat, and other particulars. "Now Sven, I wish to pay whatever is outstanding on that boat . . . yes that is correct A fuel bill . . . I see, yes that as well, and put it in the mother's name. Yes, ah-ha here speak to her yourself." Aquina handed the phone to the shocked woman, who spoke hesitantly to the bank manager.

In a comparatively short time it was accomplished. And in similar manner she saw to the needs of farmers, the other fishing family's, et-cetera, with funds for seed, equipment, extra help, supplies, and in every case a medium or heavy truck. The fishing families faired much the same except, it was money for maintenance, bait, fuel, equipment, supplies, extra hands and a suitable truck.

The larger group comprised of families with all members intact, were next to be compensated. For the farmers, she provided seed, fertilizer, and supplies comprised of food, along with some other essentials. Fishermen received similar assistance as did those who's livelihood involved lumber; and in every instance Aquina assigned to each family a suitable truck. And of those tank crews and others joining the military, each received financial compensation.

She still has thirty-two heavy trucks plus fuel trailers, and an ample supply of fuel stored in drums. The small warehouse still held an overflowing inventory, with but one yard wide aisles crisscrossing enormous stacks of material. And those trucks given away were the first to be unloaded, then reloaded with the supplies earmarked for each family. As for the three dozen remaining trucks . . . those city men, former drivers, remaining drove them into the large warehouse, and began to systematically unload them and stacked the cargo.

It was very late when the drivers finished their task. In the interim the medium and small groups departed after saying their emotional goodbye's. Only the large group remained, and that night while the barracks was alive and echoing to laughter, and conversation . . . Aquina visited the small hill-side cemetery. Joined by multitudes of wildlife, she "talked" to each one, but spent the greater portion of the evening next to Kurt's stone.

Sitting outside . . . . the benz shined in the morning sun as did all the tigers and half-tracks. With her own tiger and one half-track in the warehouse, and having refreshed herself . . . . and now in appropriate clothing was in the act of stepping into the benz when her deputy interrupted.

"Ma-dam, please." "Yes Olaf." "Ma-dam, we . . . . I mean all of us wish you would ride on top of the lead tiger . . . . in your rightful place."

Her lower lip trembled ever so slightly, then moved as a faint smile lightened Aquina's features. She nodded, and turned in time to see a bright blue flag being tied to the tall antenna on the tank. Only this was different. Picking up the black a-line skirt, she began to climb up, but stopped before continuing up to the turret. Undulating in the breeze, and on both sides, Aquina saw the coat of arms adopted so long ago by Dien. An ancestral long ship . . . . bow view under full sail, with long oars out on either side. She felt the rising tide of emotion, and holding the skirt climbed up on the turret swinging nylon clad legs and black high heels down into the turret. Adjusting her position, she smiled down into three equally happy faces.

The blue silk blouse off set by the black suit jacket really set off the outfit. Olaf climbed up on the second tank and awaited the signal. Aquina waved to Dien, nodded to the driver half in and half out of the benz, and turned to look at her men on the turrets. One hundred eighty-five of them. Her eyes went from one line to the next, and in each case their nod . . . . from each tank leader.

She gave the order . . . . first the benz headed for the beaten-down forest road with the tiger carrying her only several yards behind, In a well ordered procession each line of tanks fell behind the preceeding one, until they stretched out for seven tenth's, or so, of a mile. The last tiger in line had just begun to crawl as the benz exited the scrub, with the rumbling monsters close behind.

The mercedes well out on the woods road, and the armored convoy followed the thirty-two half-tracks pulling field pieces to join the line behind the last tank. Radio broadcasts from the capital almost the entire previous day caused the woods road intersection, and the main road east to be mobbed with people waving. On the main road throngs of onlookers kept back off the road, so the column could pass unhindered. Of course it didn't stop them from voicing their admiration. Accelerating to fifteen they made good time.

Although large crowds gathered around the intersection, and the dog-leg leading to the main artery heading east, the column had no problem winding through the junction and dog-leg. She found the once destroyed bridge had been temporarily replaced with a floating pontoon bridge; and men are removing the last of the mines. Aquina raised her hand to them in passing. After a mile and one tenth, she slowed to a bare crawl allowing those coming over the bridge singularly time to catch up.

Formed up again into a proper column, she accelerated up to their normal pace. In many areas townspeople gathered waving, and cheering as many merely waved mouths open and eyes wide at the spectacle. On both sides of Odense crowds were as thick as the tigers. Slowing to fifteen, they roared through the city only to speed up again once beyond the city's population areas. At twelve-fourty-five the column slowed as Aquina arrived at the ferry landing, and smiled as two large ferrys waited. The captains and crew shouted, waved and are cheering wildly. The car was quickly waved on first, Aquina's tiger second, then followed by two more. They began across at a sedate speed low in the water, as the other large ferry followed only fourty, or so, yards behind them. On the opposite side the entire town had turned-out to watch and welcome the resistance fighters. Many eager hands caught thrown lines, as the ferry nosed into the landing. Safely off, she pulled over to the side directing the tigers onto the roadside with instructions to move up slowly as others came off the ferrys.

In all they made more than thirty trips with tigers, the last one had several half-tracks on board. Five additional trips and the entire column had been brought over before Aquina resumed her normal place in line.

Sjaelland reflected its greater number of towns, and small cities by the continuous lines, with people crowding and trying to get a glimpse of the tanks, and the famous "Tiger Lady." Along the route especially around the two cities before the capital, it seemed the crowds swelled into horde-like proportions. In some areas maintaining a set pace was difficult. It seemed for every mile covered beyond Roskilde crowds grew geometrically. She slowed to ten m.ph.

The amount of open dryland south or around their route was virtually non-existent. However, northwest of the city's lake area, a wide road led off to two small fields. Aquina had the idea of parking the column there thinking it easier for the new army to take delivery outside the congested part of the city. Aquina was amazed at the behavior of her normally conservative countrymen. The crowds became noisier the closer they ventured toward the capital. As she waved the clamor seemed to increase, and so did the volume of flowers.

She found herself ordering a further reduction in speed, a result of people swarming in closer than was safe. There were no accidents, but she was still concerned even at eight miles per hour. Soon the eight became five as they moved into the outskirts of the capital, and the streets and roof-tops of short buildings were alive with people. Flowers rained down adding to the substantial amount already covering much of the tank's surface. She turned to look back and every vehicle, she could see was being inundated with flowers. Her benz was no better off, as the driver turned on the windshield wipers to open a swath in the blossoms. She had flowers covering her abundant tresses, shoulders, some caught between blouse and jacket, and the turret on which she sat.

The crowds increased and so did the number and size of the buildings. Between the cheering and shouting from the crowd, and the growl of her tanks, she could barely think. Deeper and deeper into the city she progressed, though slower than before, down to less than five m.p.h., Aquina began noticing some military personnel sprinkled throughout the crowds. And in minutes, she could see a portion of government square. The parliament buildings, palace, opera theaters, and banks surrounded the square, and lined a portion of the larger avenues coming into and circling the large fountain and monuments.

She took a deep breath at sight of the large open space beyond the human roadblock. Putting on the turret headset, she ordered a gradual halt as the benz had already stopped. The entire almost mile long column sat as units in the rear also stopped, she began looking around for an explaination. Almost instantly a ranking army officer approached shouting to be heard over the crowds. Aquina motioned for him to come up, and he did with surprising alacrity. In seconds he respectfully relayed his instructions. She nodded self-consciously . . . he saluted, then quickly climbed down.

Aquina explained the movement to the column, i.e., they are to circle the square, and turn in making two rings if necessary, while she and the benz occupied the open area amongst the monuments. With a hand signal from the officer those blocking the entrance to the square parted moving back applauding, many with tears streaming down their faces. The benz began moving forward her tank immediately followed as did the other tigers, each in turn, but instead of coming straight out as she did, they turned to follow the street winding around the square.

Something happened . . . . the extensive crowds quieted as she moved to the center. The benz stopped on one side of the center monument, and she on the other as the armor followed the curb line similar to a parade of awesome pacaderms. Coming full circle the lead tiger turned left a few yards, and kept going as more and more tanks then half-tracks entered the square, In mere minutes all of the vehicles had entered, and Aquina called a halt, took off the headset and swung ler legs out of the turret taking a few steps to the front resting her arm on the cannon's barrel. The three crew climbed out, and all one hundred eighty-four tigers turned their cannon barrels toward her and lowered them in salute.

She could no longer control the wave of emotion and tears began to flow freely. More or less at that moment the huge crowds began anew their collective cheering and shouting. Crews from each tank climbed out to stand on their machines waving to the crowds, One of her crew began taking the blue flag off the antenna. Seconds and he had it folded, and coming slowly around the turret bowed his head putting the flag in her hands. As the three crewmen began applauding, the now familiar officer caught her attention. Helped by the crew, she climbed down and was promptly introduced to the two dignitaries, and other officers present. While meeting these people, the noise of the crowd continued though not as heavy . . . . and she began to calm down.

Walking with the group, and clutching her flag . . . . the benz quietly followed, turned at sound of the tigers revving in time to see them exit the square. Aquina waved realizing a large chapter of her life had ended. And for a second she felt regret for although it was a grizzly heart rending time for her . . . she felt strangely at peace sitting on top of her tiger. Instantly memory re-asserted itself, her tiger was still at home, at the compound. Aquina smiled as she kept her hand aloft, a salute to the departing column. On their way out each man on each turret held his arm up, and each driver on the half-tracks.

The afternoon and evening went quickly. She recieved a standing ovation from parliament, was fussed over during dinner, and even more so at the theater. She had been fitted for a gown that afternoon, one of light blue, and her waist encircled by a black sash. With a new tiara, she attended dinner sitting on the crown prince's right, parliament figures on her left, and so on . . . And after the first dozen, or so, toast's she lost track of things. Dancing and the theater only added to her flow of adrenalin. Almost to a person, they marveled at her youth and vigor.

CHAP. 36

Nine a.m. the next morning, and with purchases in the car, she said her goodbyes, and stepped into the benz. Smiling into the rearview mirror the driver started off smoothly winding effortlessly out of the city. With head against the cushion and eyes closed, she tried to relax. She didn't see people waving at the car, or those a distance away looking at it as they removed their caps. The car's motion lulled her to sleep, and to dream of the forest animals, solitude, gathering herbs and berries, and once again tending to the welfare of her animal friends.

She wanted life to resume its peaceful unhurried pace, for the world to forget and leave her in peace. But, it wasn't too be. Aquina failed to realize how famous a person she'd become. Aside from the tens upon tens of thousands, who held pictures taken of her in various locals, she is not the sort that could travel without being noticed. She possessed that rare indefineable quality of adding a certain brilliance to any room, or area that she might be in at the time. But although those represented substantial reasons . . . . there is one infinitely more substantial and powerful. Some refer to the force as "fate," to her, it is the universe. She regarded these omnipotent forces as representative of the diety.

Too Aquina, the all pervading force of the universe is God to her; the only thing of religious significance taught her by Dien. Dien used names for agents of the universal force terms long honored among the tucanans. That same force decreed a vastly different life for Aquina, one such as not even thought of in her fantasys. For if she did they had no substance, no connection with reality, as it then existed around her.

Aquina was still sleeping as the driver pulled off the road slowly bringing the car to a gentle stop. Those waiting on the ferry landing and inside the small ticket hut noticed the car, and walked over not quite sure if they recognized it or not. Not so much the car, but instantly recognized the young woman sleeping in the rear seat. The ferry was docking, and with ticket in hand the driver entered the car, softly closed his door, and moved the benz over to the ramp. She stirred a little as the car rolled onto the ferry, and just as quickly drifted back to dreamland.

The balance of the trip was uneventful, in that she did not waken until their arrival at the compound. And that wasn't by the driver, but her "white watchdog." No sooner had the driver managed to round the car and open the door, and the wolf jumped inside licking Aquina's face with enthusiasm.

In the days that followed, it seemed normalcy returned, but it is a false fascade. Dien used the C'pter to answer the phones and list all calls as she endeavored to handle all their business affairs. With that in mind, she handed the solicitor a margin of authority to handle certain types of inquires, while she made substantial deposits, and authorized the banker to work with the solicitor-attorneys regarding the establishing of two new business's. One is in trucking, and the other in coastal shipping and fishing. To that end the five former nazi gunboats were ferried around the large peninsula to the harbor city. Once docked, literally . . . . workmen swarmed aboard attacking their assigned jobs with gusto.

But as days became weeks, Dien clearly recognized the signs of inner turmoil and stress. It seemed sun and the animals had little lasting results, as Aquina is still ill. Dien was mulling the problem over trying to find an answer, to suggest some course of action, but nothing came to mind. A few more evening periods came and went with no change, and no clear ideas. However, at their very next meal, Aquina suggested something Dien thought might possibly work, i.e., a trip . . . an extended holiday cruise. Dien liked the idea immediately, and chastised herself for not thinking of just such a remedy.

They established an itinerary to include rail, cruise ship, and lastly air travel for short distances. And while Aquina decided on what clothes to pack, Dien went into the city to meet with the attorney and banker. She gave them each a copy of Aquina's itinerary and asked about what currencies would she need. Almost thirty minutes lapsed while Dien chatted with the attorney, the banker walked in with several fat envelopes each containing a different currency, each in equal amounts. Although a few were not as fat because of the exchange rate, each held the equivalent of ten thousand dollars. Aquina would have English pound notes, French francs, krone, and dollars.

Packed and ready, she had everything including both lugers with plenty of ammunition clips, one knife, and "wolf."

She decided to bring him for companionship and protection. With the packing completed, Aquina changed her clothes, and wearing only enough for modesty sake gave "wolf" a bath.

Four p.m., the next planetary afternoon, she is ready to leave. Bags are on the train along with two trunks, the wolf sat next to her on the platform, while Dien said her goodbyes. It seemed so long ago, she was on this very platform saying goodbye on her way to school, Aquina thought to herself. Waving to the driver, she gave Dien another hug, and turned quickly boarding the train. A conductor helped her to the reserved compartment quite conscious of her identity, and the wolf's presence. She was barely seated as the conductor hurried along to spread the news among the train's old and new personnel.

A steward returned fidgeted with his tie and jacket for a moment, then knocked lightly on the door. The wolf growled slightly as Aquina walked to the door opening it to confront an old steward. "Yes?" "Pardon . . . your highness, tea and cakes." "Thank you steward." She waved him in and laying the silver tray on the small table couldn't help but stare at the wolf on his way out.

Six p.m., Aquina changed trains at Hamburg, and while all her baggage was transferred conductors from one train talked to those on the other. A normal enough practice, except this time, Aquina is the subject of conversation. Only once during the trip to paris did she leave the compartment. She told the animal to guard the room, and she would bring back food. Hiding one of the lugers in her handbag, Aquina exited locking the door.

The corridor was narrow . . . well lit by the abundant windows, and blessedly empty. She didn't appreciate curiosity from people especially since the war, and walking through the salon car didn't improve her mood. The five men present whether holding a brandy sniffer or newspaper looked up the instant she entered. Almost en-masse they stood, while she walked past them, the air became scented with her tantalizing perfume. Just before reaching the door the steward behind the bar hurried over to the door saying . . . "allow me . . . please your highness." Aquina smiled, . . . "thank you steward." As he opened and held the door for her the "gentlemen" felt like clods with their feet in clay. She stepped through and the steward pushed the tiny buzzer located near his left hand. The door to the dining car is held for her by one steward, while two smartly dressed waiters who stood next to an elegant table. Set apart from the others by a freshly prepared center piece, and rather prominent place card, the waiter held one of the richly covered chairs.

As ten couples watched intermittently trying to maintain an air of discretion, and still satisfy their curiosity. She enjoyed a light dinner with a good wine, and just before finishing asked the waiter for a soup bowl filled with one-an-a-half pounds of lean roast beef, not to hot, with a small amount of gravy, but no salt, and a small bowl of ice cream. Both waiters appeared confused until each realized it is for "ma-dam's pet." It seemed only seconds since walking through her compartment door, when she heard the familiar discreet knock usually announcing a steward. Opening the door, Aquina smiled inwardly from winning the wager she set for herself, when the steward rapped lightly on the door. She accepted the tray from the smiling steward, who closed the door for her, and she quickly lowered the bowl for her "companion," who began gulping the contents before it reached the floor.

With the exception of a bottle of vintage champagne there were no further interruptions, and the solitude was a welcome gift. She finished the newspaper, and opened a section of it in the corner for the wolf.

Aquina awoke early . . . the sun streaming through the curtains enveloped her face in warm brilliance. She was ready to depart a full hour before they arrived in paris. The express amid a great deal of screeching brakes and swirling clouds of steam, stopped quite smoothly. Immediately people began walking off as two porters split Aquina's trunks and hand luggage, while she walked slightly in front with the wolf on her right side. Just before reaching the identification area she stopped at a booth and purchased a newspaper, speaking fluent French.

Walking through the bustling station, she marveled at the large number of allied soldiers. Some were positioned around as guards, while others filed through from trains as she was doing. Near the identification-customs area allied officers of varying rank were positioned at strategic points.

Aquina's passage through the rail station caused something of a stir, not only because of the wolf, but herself as well. She was definitely causing a bit of a sensation. So much so the booth and counter she headed for seemed crowded by a rather large group of officers all looking in her direction, some with sexual desire, others because of that indefineable aura; and all looked from her to the wolf, and back again several times.

She handed the agent her papers and without looking he asked. "Your purpose for visiting france?" Aquina smiled. Behind her the porters tried to signal the agent illiciting a threatening growl from the wolf. Opening the i.d., folder he glanced at the photo within noticing the delicate tiara, then her full legal name. With a deep internal groan, the agent looked up with profound apology written across his face. "Please excuse me you Highness." Aquina smiled. "I am here on holiday, and call me ma-dam. No titles please." The agent bowed smiling self-conciously. "Thank you ma-dam 'Labr." He returned the i.d. folder, and held open the gate for her, and the wolf. On her way out many officers in close proximity saluted as she passed.

Once outside all the luggage and such was loaded onto and into a taxi then a tip for each porter, and she and the wolf are off into traffic. In a comparatively short time she arrived in front of a sumptuous hotel. She was registered and in an elevator in record time. Accompanied by the concierge and several bellboys, Aquina is shown to the suite of rooms reserved for her ahead of time. In fact, she hadn't even passed through Hamburg on the train, when the attorney placed the call to the hotel. She tipped the bellboys, and also the concierge, even though that part was not usually done, who were about to leave when the hotel's manager stood in the half open doorway. Announced by the concierge, the manager entered followed by more bellboys carrying flowers and champagne.

The manager welcomed her in flowering praise, speaking of her exploits . . . the manager noticed Aquina grew uncomfortable and instantly altered the subject. Though the concierge and bellboys listened with fascination at what the manager was saying, as they'd all heard of the "Tiger Lady." Their thoughts were expansive one second, and small introspective the next, not realizing, but trying to guess the reason for her "holiday." And while she put down her bag and removed a light summer jacket, the manager asked if she wished the chilled champagne opened. "Yes, thank you." Quickly with practiced movements he removed the cork. She nodded, when asked if he should pour . . . a pause . . . and handed her a glass, bowed standing . . . beaming as she savored the contents of the chilled glass.

When she looked up the concierge was just leaving. As a matter of course the manager asked if there was any additional service he or the hotel could perform. She mulled it over for a second or two then mentioned a need for a person to act as secretary and guide. The manager happily replied, he knew of several proper young ladies and would fetch them immediately, with Aquina's permission. She nodded with a smile, and bowing the manager hurried from the reception room.

As soon as the door closed behind him, Aquina almost ran to the bedroom and rapidly delved into certain pieces of luggage withdrawing the other luger, and all the ammunition clips, knives, and what-not, and quickly hid them underneath the first mattress beyond the fold in the sheets. Standing, she walked into the large reception room leaving the opened luggage in the bedroom. Aquina had begun to refill the glass with more bubbly, and petted her white companion, when she heard a gentle rap on the door. "Entre." The door opened and an older woman entered in a light colored dress, curtsied. "Your highness, I am Margot, senior of the maids. May we unpack your luggage?" "Yes." Aquina replied.

She noticed in the manner and speech there was a definite note of respect, and as three young maids came in and quickly curtsied, and stood quietly . . . . their eyes and manner suggested the news was already known throughout the hotel.

"This way." Aquina said, walking through the sitting room and into the bedroom, leaving them to their work and gossip. Within the hour the manager had returned with two young ladies in their teens. After perhaps twenty-five minutes in which Aquina had spoken to both, and realizing their lean financial plight, she simply couldn't accept one and not the other. She called the manager and informed him of her decision, at the same time establishing a working relationship with the two students. They understood about shifting their responsibilities on a rotating basis, and Aquina explained what they could do and couldn't do around the wolf.

For the next six weeks, native time, the girls rotated jobs taking turns guiding the ma-dam around paris. With the wolf always with her and the newspaper hounds sniffing out the story, Aquina was still a celebrity, and becoming more so rather than less of one.

They sometimes made it a threesome, and the wolf, sightseeing or eating at sidewalk café's, and all the while quiet fuss was exhibited. On occasion it broke out into boisterous displays, but they were few, and usually in good taste. Quite often both young ladies accompanied Aquina to the theater for a play, or ballet, and always received a standing ovation from the assembled crowd when she entered the box. It soon became troublesome and annoying, no matter where she ventured the curious, the autograph seekers always seemed to find her.

Her luggage was made ready, and she concealed the weapons carefully, handed each of the young ladies-students an envelope, paid the hotel bill and with luggage in the taxi, quickly found herself once again at the train station. However, this time she boarded a short ferry train, that was one of only a few cars, which is able to roll on-board a large ferry for the passage across the channel. A change of trains and once more she was on her way.

And of course the English read newspapers containing news from the "continent," as do most native civilized people. She had been recognized when changing trains immediately after the ferry ride and on the train itself. During the war the newspapers often carried news of the "Tiger Lady," and here she was, finally, where they could see her in the flesh . . . a real person.

Aquina had resigned herself to the fact of being watched, and sometimes stared at by the curious and others. Once ensconced in a fashionable suite of rooms, she sent a cable to the bank at home for funds to be transferred to a suitable bank. The manager complied almost immediately giving the bank full disclosure, and Aquina's whereabouts. And the hotel true to form wished to cater to her every whim, except she didn't present them with any. She often called for food service from the kitchen, basically for the wolf, and formidable amounts of champagne and cognac.

Several times she placed calls through the hotel switchboard to the better steamship companies, but all said much the same thing. "None of their better cruise ships would be finished with the conversion from wartime to peacetime use for another four months." Of course the hotel management was aware of these developments and others seemingly unrelated. Other than for newspapers, which went up with the twice daily dining cart ladened with food for the "dog" champagne and cognac refills, and on occasion a small salad. The hotel's only contact with Aquina was through the daily maid service. And when each morning the maids knocked and were bidden to enter, they always found the young princess on the bedroom terrace wearing only a peignoir reclining on the chaise lounge sipping champagne. The wolf always sat at her side watching the maids carefully. This routine lasted for almost three weeks native time.

CHAP. 37

Morning of the twentieth day, Aquina exited from one of the elevators and approached the concierge inquiring about maps of the city. He and those at the admissions counter across the lobby breathed a tremendous sigh of relief. A good many of the hotel patrons were also looking and whispering. An indepth story had been publicized the day of her arrival including pictures depicting her and the wolf. So it wasn't likely she would be able to go anywhere unnoticed. Taking a deep breath, she walked toward the entrance. Doors are held open and Aquina strode out standing under a portico planning on taking a taxi to the bank. However, instead of a taxi, a gleaming black Bentley stopped in front of her. With nary a sound the hotel doorman opened the rear door, and with a smile, she stepped inside . . . the wolf already occupying the floor leaning against shapely nylon clad legs.

Aquina gave the bank's name and address to the driver and relaxed occasionally looking at buildings and pedestrians. She petted, and talked to the wolf, and was rewarded with a wet tongue. The ride was all to short, and obviously expected because there were a number of people at the bank's entrance waiting. They made the morning very nice with an armful of flowers, champagne and a great deal of attention. Introductions of the bank officers and when finished . . . . a familiar person stepped forward. He bowed and "Your Highness." "Andrew." She sighed with obvious pleasure. "I am so glad to see you well." She said with a broad grin, and a warm voice. "And I you, your highness. When I learned of your wounds and still carrying on the fight . . . I tried to get permission to give you aide; but it was not possible." "I am recuperating well enough." She said with a grim smile. "And I see the wolf survived." Andrew remarked looking down as he bent over a little. "Yes he did, as did all the others in the forest." Aquina spoke in her strange language, and slowly the wolf moved forward a little lifting his right paw. The agent took the paw gently, shook it a bit as if shaking hands, and let go.

"If your free . . . I wish to ask a favor of you." "I am one of your most ardent supporters, your highness. Whatever you might ask of me, I will do with pleasure." Andrew replied and bowed. Her face flushed a little. "I have some business to transact. We can then discuss this over tea." "My pleasure," said Andrew with a bow and an infectious smile.

It didn't require much time, Aquina signed with flowing script for the accounts, and the cash she wished to use immediately. Shook hands with the manager and walked out to join Andrew. A few minutes and all three sat comfortably in the Bentley quiet and serene as it covered the distance to their destination. It is one of those proper establishments catering to the genteel, and aristocracy of English upper crust society, where tea and small pastries are the only fare. The results of that chat was evident almost immediately. Andrew began the following day acting as guide pointing out the most noteworthy parts of London, and as days became weeks he broadened the area to include those places outside of London. And by the time weeks changed to months they were going further and further afield.

They began staying in inns and such, and it afforded Aquina a period of unexpected pleasure and happiness. Ordinary English countryside folk came to know her, and their initial consternation or confusion changed to affection and occasionally wonder. Especially during those instances when Aquina had an opportunity to be around animals.

Among the more desired attractions for Aquina was stonehendge, a short distance east of Shreton. They stayed two days and from the outset, her warm personality and candor overcame their shyness and reserve. Forced to accept most of the bad manners of tourists, were pleased a person of her station took such an interest in their village and main attraction. The folk paid special attention however, when several notoriously ill-tempered dogs chained around in back of the barn met her by way of the wolf. During and after her encounter with them the behavioural changes was nothing short of remarkable, such that the owner of the inn was able to bring the three dogs inside. At varied times the wolf joined the dogs in chasing games, running across the meadows to the extent of laying down on their sides exhausted, panting too tired for any further action.

In the interim, Andrew accompanied Aquina to the time worn circle of monolithic stones known as stonehenge. Andrew looked on in fascination as she went from stone to stone touching, caressing each as though a living thing. She felt almost the same degree of warmth from all the stones except two, and these Aquina deduced must be the entrance. Standing outside in front of the "portal" with eyes closed, she raised her arm palm up and forward, and still Aquina was half-a-pace from the stones. The huge grayish white slabs towered over her, some with obscure etchings partially erased by time.

She had spent several hours studying the symbols in puzzlement as if having seen them in a dream, but could not pull the memory forward to her mind's eye.

Carefully a third of-a-pace each step . . . she drew even with the stones then slowly inbetween them. A fragrant breeze stirred the long tresses as Andrew stared. Barely breathing his excitement fueling more adrenalin. He knew this was not allowed, no-one to his knowledge had ever attempted such an act in quite the same way. Andrew inhaled a few deep breaths to calm down, an effort to control the pounding in his temples. Another step and she stood within the circle listening, clear of the portal, and the breeze felt stronger.

Aquina opened the left hand realizing it was clenched into a fist, and let out a deep sigh, and gazed upon the stone pedestal, and the small slab it supported. She walked toward the old stone senses alert to every possible nuance. The small steps she had covered to stand solemnly inchs from the slab. Slowly, hesitating, she layed the right hand palm down on the slab. There were no fireworks or other manifestations such as Andrew half expected, but the sound of a low sigh . . . . one of pleasure was to Andrew almost equally significant. She felt warmth, and a vibrant tingling sensations through her palm and fingers normally there should be only cold lifeless stone. And after some moments, Aquina retraced her steps carefully. Their return to the inn and dinner was to Aquina the cap to a beautiful day. In her upbeat mood, she didn't notice the quiet faces around her, the shyness and reserve had returned.

Mid-morning the next day, Aquina re-entered the circle. As on the previous afternoon they'd been alone it being still an "off year." People were still trying to shake off the war, and for that Aquina was most grateful. She behaved and conducted herself the same way as the day before, touched the center slab resting on the pedestal feeling warmth, and the pleasant tingling sensation. But unlike yesterday instead of just her hand, it began to rapidly expand-flowing until she felt aglow captivated by the all encompassing vibrant warmth. It filled every part, every hair and cell of her youthful body.

Andrew stood much as he had the previous day rooted to the spot, staring, unable to avert his eyes. He felt no breeze, nothing . . . . it was quiet yet the long tresses of her hair moved seemed to undulate like the motion of a wave; she continued to stand in front of the stone ten minutes, fifteen and gradually lifted her hand from the near ancient slab.

Upon exiting the circle, Aquina paused next to Andrew who still hadn't spoken or smiled, as if to say, "I understand." But he didn't understand, and equally positive he could do nothing about it if he had understood. By the time his reverie evaporated, Aquina was already sitting in the back seat. And rather self-conciously he opened the front door and slid in behind the wheel, pushed the starter button and managed the bentley onto the road. Without asking, Andrew pointed the bonnet back to the inn.

Just as the inn filled the windshield, she mentioned, "because of the early hour, they could probably get back to London before evening." Andrew mumbled his approval, and quickly entered the inn, saw to the luggage and payment of the bill, and returned to "her" to await the few seconds for the luggage. Less than a quarter-of-an-hour and the black bentley was pulling away from the inn.

Laying on the floor the wolf would gaze at her sometimes for several minutes, lick a paw then return its gaze to her face or hand. This kept up for most of the ride, and not only the wolf, but Andrew looked repeatedly into the rear-view mirror.

Andrew recalled the previous day and added the facts from that morning's visit to the stone ruins. His conclusions were obvious and irrefuteable. Either she had sampled some unknown thing or communicated with something, or possibly both. But of what was causing her pulling back, the lack of her outgoing jovial manner, had been stopped, and was convinced Aquina had been given a new start. He realized the knowledge and understanding of what happened was far, far beyond him; but thanked the lord, she had been spared, if indeed it had been dangerous.

CHAP. 38

On her arrival at the hotel those acquainted with her behavior remarked at the subtle change, how the eyes sparkled, the spring in her step, and the infectious smile. Aquina, accompanied by Andrew, the wolf, and baggage re-entered her suite, and in only minutes is visited by the concierge. He bowed handing the note to Andrew, who in turn handed it to Aquina, and waited for a possible reply.

She read it quickly then returned it to Andrew, and with a smile instructed the concierge to contact the cunard line accepting the suite as described in their note. With the departure of the concierge, she asked Andrew to arrange for the transfer of all baggage to the ship. She quickly went into the bedroom and packed the small jewelry case into the false bottom of her cosmetic-overnight bag, including those weapons she hid under the box spring. The small bag she kept out with her purse, and rejoined Andrew who was in the act of pouring champagne. While sipping from her glass, Aquina gazed at Andrew through thick lashes, thinking about him in a way exceeding the bonds or morals of their respective social stations.

With early evening all of the baggage, except the overnight case had been ferried to the cruise ship. And Andrew departed after accepting Aquina's invitation to spend a quiet day aboard ship after the completion of necessary errands. She finished the champagne and retired early.

True to his word, Andrew presented himself at the agreed hour, and saw to the few remaining bags, while Aquina satisfied the hotel bill. The bentley waited purring quietly in front. And without any fuss they were off to the first of her errands. Andrew guessed correctly as they rounded the corner for the bank. Once she was out of the car, and into the bank it was twenty-five minutes before she reappeared outside. And with the cable office only a few minutes away, she decided to stop and send a cable to Dien.

Minutes before eleven a.m., the chauffer angled the bentley off the service road, into the main terminal parking area thence into the two lane shipping and baggage area. The chauffer opened the door initially then surrendered it to Andrew, and opened the trunk for the porter. Aquina stepped out of the car with the wolf next to her only to be confronted by dozens of photographers. Andrew carried the small case, while she prevented the wolf from tearing into the shouting crowd of reporters, as the porter followed with the one remaining piece of luggage.

A formidable group of ship's crew and a few officers opened an aisle through the crowd, as the captain and senior officers gathered to welcome her aboard. She responded cordially, and in due course was shown to her sumptuous suite after accepting the captain's invitation to share his table. While the porter surrendered the baggage to a crew member, Andrew followed close behind "number one, the exec," led the way up several deck levels to the uppermost passenger area. Only eight suites occupied the deck, shared with a v.i.p. type lounge, and an expansive sun deck.

The suite is large and airy scented by many variations of flowers in large bouquet displays throughout the sitting room, dressing room and bedroom. And while Andrew opened the chilled bottle of french champagne compliments of the captain, the wolf roamed through the suite smelling and challenging anything that might be there. Aquina discovered all the trunks and baggage had been unpacked, and neatly put away, into dresser drawers.

She and Andrew chatted sipping champagne oblivious to the stories even then being prepared for the afternoon papers, and other tabloids. That afternoon, not only was there a sizeable story on the front page, but virtually the entire society section was devoted to her holiday, plus pictures. The front page story explained, Aquina had booked passage with cunard for the first post war pleasure cruise. It largely referred to the society section, which recapped how she had met Andrew. Delving into his reports, not only the fighting, but about the woman behind the public fascade. Reporting her age at nineteen to twenty, the story went into depth about why she was known to the allied armies, and her countrymen as the "Tiger Lady," Several pictures depicted Aquina sitting on the turret of "her tiger." The others were even more graphic showing her tank in the canal-Elbe river battle; and pictures by english battle photographers and eye witness reports, and those words from the famous field marshall, made for sensational copy.

It continued to discuss her methods capturing the first models of the dreaded tiger tank, and in the process crippling and annihilating nazi garrisons throughout her own country. Word for word they printed the glorious account of the rout experienced by the waffen SS panzer brigades of which she either captured and/or destroyed their entire force. Those unit s captured were repainted black with blue insignia and put immediately back into action against the Nazis. On and on it went, saying how she held no rank, but her men, sometimes precariously few in each tank, and support troops, followed her and took orders without question. All this was followed by a section devoted to the accounts of downed allied pilots and flyers who gave their own eye witness reports. Especially the crew who were about to be captured by a nazi half-track and a few squads of troops.

Andrew finished reading the paper, and reached for his glass and while doing so saw the look-expression of resignation on her face. They chatted for another several hours, and in part, Andrew succeeded in calming her ruffled emotions. He departed quietly soon after saying his goodbyes. Moments after Andrew's departure the exec. called respectfully asking if she wished a steward and menu. "No thank you. I believe, I shall dine with the captain." "Yes, your highness." He hung up the phone and quickly told the head chef, and the head steward, all the while on his way to inform the captain.

Recalling the captain's words . . . "the formal dinner hour normally begins at seven." She decided on a medium blue satin strapless with short white fur cape, sapphire and gold earrings, and a single star sapphire necklace. A steward had delivered cut meat in a bowl moments earlier. She petted the wolf, a kiss and Aquina exited her suite locking the door behind her. She dropped the keys in her small purse next to the derringer, make-up, lipstick and a tiny vial of perfume, and walked the twenty yards to the first stairwell. And one more, a semi-circular descending staircase forming an elegant entrance to the enormous sprawling first class dining room. Every seat at each and every table was filled as an air of festive expectation filled the room.

It is seven-twelve as Aquina's blue high heels caught the attention of the purser. A second, two, and she came into full view and with a few steps remaining, a ship's bell rang out its music in the form of two single notes. All the ship's officers present quickly stood as did every person in the dining room, and began to vigorously applaud, as Aquina stepped off the staircase. The captain had walked into position in time to bow, and escort her to his table, and the applause didn't taper off until she was seated. At which point everyone did the same.

She is positioned on the captain's right, and at her request lifted the fur off and onto the chair. A small hint of a sigh could be heard from the males, as well as many of the women, who were less endowed. Some of them kept glancing repeatedly at her gown. Dinner was punctuated with a generous amount of conversation, and a good deal of dancing afterwards interspersed with drink and dessert.

That evening set the tone for much of the cruise. Not only in so far as dinning room etiquette, but the respect and treatment afforded by the other passengers. She is immensely popular with the crew as well, partly from taking few things for granted, and displaying an interest in daily life aboard the huge ship. However, some merely wanted to oogle her figure, and often had their chance when she would wear risqué bathing suits, while lounging on the sun deck.

CHAP. 39

It is late in the year when the cruise began, but warmed considerably as the ship steamed its way further and further south. Soon they rounded gibralter for the beautiful dazzling mediterranean. The holidays were spent around the greek islands, and by January twentieth had Alexandria, Egypt in sight. She caused no small commotion, but was prudent and stayed in the more english parts of the city.

Aquina decided to change her itinerary, and had all baggage transferred to the principal hotel in the city's best area. She bid those on the ship a "bon voyage," and without delay booked passage on a large packet. It seemed a fair number of the english couples, swiss and several dutch were also booking passage on the very same ship. They met and talked socially as most stayed in the very hotel Aquina was staying in, and was a natural basis for becoming acquainted.

At first none of the couples recognized her, not until they began boarding the ship two weeks later. The packet had similar accommodations, but not as elegant or spacious. Everything was scaled down in size compared to the cunard, but it is comfortable and clean. She had no sooner come aboard and checked-in with the purser, given her stateroom keys and if she wished to dine at which of five tables. That area of the ship is incredibly jammed with people, and just as Aquina was deciding on which table, the captain came out from the office, and loud and clear . . . "Her Highness will dine at my table." Well it was as if everyone was struck by laryngitis. People turned gawking, some whispered. Aquina, with a mental sigh, "thank you captain." He bowed slightly and escorted her through the throng of people out onto the deck, sun and breeze highlighting and moving the waves of her hair.

The ship got underway only to put into Port Said later the same day to pick up more passengers, but departed again this time for the suez canal. Although the ship was a good deal slower the view and the warm sun more than made up for the ship's lack of speed. They waited their turn and soon entered the main portion of the canal. Traffic was heavy, and the passage slower than normal, as the heat increased so to did the liquor intake of the passengers. Toward evening the following day they had just passed the swing bridge; and by mid-day were entering Lake Timsah. From there the passage went more quickly, with the ship entering the bitter lakes area by evening. And the following day, an hour earlier the ship's bow began biting into the Gulf of Suez.

During the three days for the ship to steam south to the straits, the heat seemed to remain, and during lunch the captain announced they had passed into the red sea. From there it was seven days to Port Sudan, which was reached in the afternoon. It proved to be uneventful as only cargo was off-loaded, and the captain immediately put back to sea in a fruitless attempt to make up time lost at the canal.

Another week the ship passed into the Gulf of Aden. This passage enabled Aquina to make friends amongst many of the families. Enough so, when several asked her to disembark at Mombasa with them, to visit and see some of the most beautiful vistas in Africa, she agreed. A few families lived together in Thika, in a ranch style compound, which they explained was a few miles northeast of Nairobi. Some others lived in Fort Hall under similar arrangements, and Kijabe, where they owned and operated a general store. And still others operated ranchs outside of Naivasha, Embu and Nakuru. Three families owned and operated a business trapping animals for zoos, and two others were hunters, who organized and led safaris into the bush.

Their stories of the bush, and animals excited her and through the narrations, Aquina asked numerous questions. Those of the families with young men who were onboard, had long since fallen under her spell. Something Aquina did quite unconsciously through body language, she exuded a natural heady sensuousness that proved devastating to young males, and tantalizing to the more mature man. But she made no outward overt sign to any married man, a thing the wives came to respect, and with no small amount of relief. They could control their husbands for Aquina helped by the way she spoke and her behavior, but the young men were beyond the control of their respective families, and it fell to Aquina to exercise judgement.

Each and every family extended an ernest wish, an open invitation for her to visit, and stay as long as she wished. Every family had their respective motives for most it was friendship, others hoped for investment money, still others hoped for a possible laison with a son or nephew. A few merely wished to show off their ranchs and land hoping for an ardent spokeswoman in Europe.

But for her part seeing the scenic country . . . . it was the animals. She heard so much from these people about the awesome animals. Aquina felt a need to try. She accepted as due course her affinity with animals, and some reptiles at home, but Africa . . . . ah well here this place would furnish proof. Dien was the only person that treated her as a normal person; but others rarely did, almost always the feeling of not belonging . . . the feeling of being outside. Aquina thought . . . "only Kurt let me in, made me feel wanted. He accepted me . . . . for me."

She, in that moment sitting on the bed, realized and admitted to herself . . . she is different. It was little things added together, childhood memories inconsistent with apparent age, the compound and the ability with animals. Tears began to well up and cascade down youthful cheeks, and chin as she sobbed softly. The wolf jumped up on the coverlet laying down against her body.

The period of self-pity didn't last to long. Reason impinged on her conscious mind, and with a sniffer of brandy calmed her nerves a-bit, even to the point of philosophizing. The places and animals the couples talked about would furnish undeniable proof. And if she was indeed different . . . . well, that would simply . . . . be that. Aquina decided she would do and live with her strangeness as best as possible.

With the weather improving calming the sea to a smooth glossy surface and having off-loaded many tons of cargo, the packet increased its speed by a small margin. They passed into the indian ocean with the bow biting hard into the water. It was a few hours past dawn on the sixth day, when the ship stopped at Mogadisho. Some people she hadn't met disembarked along with a fair amont of cargo. That evening they departed with the tide for Mombasa.

The morning of the third day, at nine-thirty the ship made a wide turn to starboard going around the point making for the channel. It is shaped very similar to a three-toed foot . . . . the harbor, and a small harbor tug puffing away sounding and looking like a cartoon caricature of what one expected a tug too be, came alongside. It touched the packet's bow and began huffing and puffing, from the little horn, a beep-beep—sounding all the world like a child's toy. Standing at the railing with the wolf, she felt the packet's bow turn to starboard close to the dock, and clapped her hands, applauding. A white man stripped to the waist covered in grime, his dirty slacks spotted with liberal amounts of grease looked up, and snatched off an equally stained navy hat, and bowed. Aquina giggled and waved then turned walking the main deck toward the salon gazing out at the harbor. The man's eyes didn't leave her form, but followed . . . joining her growing legion of admirers.

Returning to her cabin, Aquina packed the few remaining things, closed everything and locked the bags and trunks. Checking the luger in her purse, and petting the wolf, she exited going directly to the main salon.

The crew was busy unloading the ship and the salon was a beehive of activity, with her friends making arrangements with dock people for the movement of personal baggage. As she walked in the wives gathered around with some of the men, and they decided, with Aquina's o'kay, where she should visit first. They agreed on Naivasha, enabling her to be inbetween most of the compounds, thereby making it more easy for visiting. Aquina smiled, ... it was settled. She carried the one small bag containing the false bottom, and shoulder bag purchased on-board, containing purse and sundries. Everyone's bags and luggage had been taken to the freight platform at the train station, the wives including Aquina went shopping. The lay-over time went by quickly. She bought wine and food, and reframed from purchasing some other things on advice from the experienced wives. Aquina was advised to wait until Nairobi, where most things are cheaper and more readily available, and of course it meant less to carry.

Apparently the representatives from government house were late, but easily learned her whereabouts from pedestrians and other natives. The natives had never seen a white wolf, not to mention untethered. Then visualize the effect Aquina instilled in the natives. Fact of the deference shown by white people, her appearance especially the eyes, but the shocker came when she spoke to the large animal in a totally strange language, and the wolf answered . . . . Only to be addressed again. Anyway, the representatives introduced themselves, and asked about her plans and pledged their support, and that of the counselor general.

They occupied every seat in the two cars with humidity adding to the discomfort and among other things . . . . she noticed dozens of European newspapers in the various shopping baskets. A wicker type with two strong handles each held a variety of merchandise. She discounted the coincidence watching the countryside as the train gradually moved up to what she later learned was only thirty miles per hour. As cool air rushed in she took off the short jacket and loose scarf flipping up her hair to allow the breeze access to her neck.

While natives both stared or merely watched, she poured some cognac, and listened to her new friends occasionally asking questions. As she did, a dainty forefinger in the liquor, and held it up speaking to the wolf. Who made some noises . . . . shrugged her shapely shoulders and sipped the cognac while wiping off the wet finger. Finishing the cup, Aquina poured water into it from a bottle, and soaking a linen hankerchief began to gently comb the forehead area gradually dampening the fur. The change over the animal was enough to start tongues whispering, although a few especially men thought the princess pampered the animal. However, the natives took a totally different tact altogether.

Moving along in one motion and then another, the train continued on, until nine-and-a-half hours later they arrived in Nairobi. Disembarking most went to the hotels accompanied by their luggage, and some others stayed at the exclusive clubs. Aquina stayed at the hotel with the others carrying the one piece of hand luggage, and the shoulder bag. A few of the wives came in just as she finished bathing, and was in the act of dressing. Staying in the outer room they chatted while she finished. And when Aquina walked out to meet them, their reaction pleased her immensely. She wore a white suit, an a-line skirt 2" below the knee with medium side slit, silk beaded blouse and matching jacket, heels, pearl earrings, and selected make-up. Holding her white purse the group walked downstairs, the wolf content on the bed, kept watch in the cool set of rooms.

Each husband waited with bar glass in one hand then escorted their wives to one of the several large round tables.

There was certainly no shortage of young men viaing for the honor of escorting Aquina to the chair set aside for her. As it turned out she accepted one on each arm, and enough left over for two to hold her chair. The owner-manager was on hand to make sure everything went off without any glitchs.

The dance floor was full after dinner as one after another, the young men asked Aquina if she would dance. And sounds of conversation mingled with the music, with her usually as one of the topics. After begging off from any further dancing, she asked the wives their advice about what to shop for in the morning. And together she made a list including clothes, supplies, and artist materials, and some bush supplies. She asked about transportation, something discussed back-and-forth until the men spoke up giving advice born of considerable experience.

Wearing only skirt and blouse, and flats, Aquina joined the ladies for morning tea, they had breakfast, and departed to "raid" the stores. With a fair size group of ladies accompanying her they made one of the major banks their first stop. It was this bank in which most of her new friends transacted business, so Aquina felt this would be her choice as well. Sitting in front of the manager's desk, while the group either stood, or sat, she gave him the names and addresses of the banks her family owned, and those others they did business with, and the names of the managers. She also divulged the attorney's name, et-cetera, to the manager who quickly and somewhat nervously looked up the information he sought in a handsomely bound ledger. The group quietly exchanged surprised looks especially when the manager spoke. "Opening an unlimited line of credit, and cash . . . . ?" He looked up politely. Aquina thought for a few seconds. "I think fifty thousand english pounds, and I have been advised the english land rover is one of the best vehicles for this country." "Yes, yes . . . . it is Your Highness." The nervous manager said. She gave the dealer's name and asked the manager to arrange purchase of a new vehicle, and that she will select it herself as soon as she finished at the bank. The manager asked about cash . . . . Aquina said, "ten thousand." She signed her name several times and that was that. The majority of the group were speechless, the others found their throats suddenly dry. Their next stop was the dealer, who minutes before her arrival received a call from the manager; who wasted nary a second explaining who was coming, and why.

When the group arrived in older vehicles owned by members of the group, the dealer realized she had been given advice, and for that reason didn't try to sell the light model, but instead let the princess choose. He and the group plus a crowd of native blacks looked on while she kicked, looked and had the bonnets raised looking at the various engines. She quickly narrowed it to one vehicle somewhat larger, and definitly heavier than the others. This one she looked at carefully noting the multi-fuel engine, larger radiator, larger heavier tires, the two bench seats and the eight, or so, feet of cargo space, all enclosed by a heavy steel body. The top is covered by a heavy canvas, which could be rolled open at any time. A large winch graced the front and rear plate steel bumpers, and a formidable pintle hook on the rear helped to convince her. She noted the cradles front and both sides for water and fuel cans, plus spare tires. The dealer was surprised at her apparent selection, but was pleased to answer her knowledgeable questions. In response, he pointed out the large twin fuel tanks, and selection valves, a built in water tank, and the extra heavy duty transmission with two extra low gears. Aquina asked for the keys, and in a few moments started the large rover easily, then engaged the clutch listening for unwanted noise.

Many of the native population understood english, thereby understanding what was said, passing and translating for those who didn't.

"How is it you have experience with heavy trucks, your highness?" Members of the group tried to get his attention to shoosh his idiot mouth. "War forces people to do unexpected things." "War? Surely your highness was far removed from that horror." She looked at him for some several seconds . . . . her face showing a steel hard malevolence. "You will no doubt recall the seven nazi waffen SS panzer divisions." "Why, yes of course. Those were the most powerful tanks ever made. And then they improved on that with the dreaded tiger panzer tanks." He looked unhappy at the rememberance. Aquina looked at him with a cynical smile. "Well Mr. Binder, my accustomed place during the last year-and-a-half of the war was atop the turret of a black tiger panzer, and have destroyed, or absorbed one entire division of the waffen panzers, and at least one or more brigades. That and the capture of dozens upon dozens of benz six and ten wheel heavy trucks, dozens of half-tracks, and that is my qualifications, Mr. Binder.

Her face mirrored the pain and sorrow of the war. Her hurt came through loud and clear as the wives quickly came forward to console her. "I'm alright. It will pass." The dealer apologized feeling like a clod. "Forgive me, please . . . I did not know . . . . you were she." His regret appeared to be genuine. Aquina nodded toward him and climbed out of the large rover. "I've decided Mr. Binder. I will take this machine." And in a voice with menace. "Have it oiled, greased, filled with gas and water." The dealer was definitely listening. "I will pay for the following spare parts and supplies." In the same hard voice, she quickly rattled off a list ranging from dozens of extra jerry cans filled with fuel and water, extra tires mounted, tarps, cases of oil, batteries, and wheel bearings and grease to name only part of the list. With the understanding, she will pick up the rover serviced and all spare parts ordered in approximately two hours.

The entire group moved on to equipment suppliers, and the more specialized clothing stores, for the families needed to replace certain items those things broken or exhausted. It was her first exposure to something akin to dungarees, and although they proved to be tight, she pulled out a dozen all the same sand color. Aquina repeated with shirts, although she strained the buttons, light pullovers made of mesh material, bush jackets and vests, bush hats, twill shorts, thick and light cotton socks, and three pairs of calf-length boots. Plus, she purchased several bottles of a sun lotion, sunglasses, a package of salt tablets, and other sundry necessities. Afterward everything was wrapped and packed in two large cartons, paid for the items accepted an itemized receipt, and was assured everything will be ferried to the hotel.

All the ladies then strolled next door to join the men, and afford their illustrious friend the opportunity to purchase the bigger more cumbersome articles of equipment. They had a display set up for new customers, which helped to aid her in making a selection, from the average tent to cooking utensils. Instead, she purchased the large two room tent with awning, and everything else on display, and holding her chin by crossing the arms, looked around.

Just a hair over two hours the group stopped in front of the dealer. Aquina went inside the office, and was met by a gracious Mr. Binder carrying a clipboard. "This way your highness. The rover is ready, washed, fresh oil, and all the spare parts, and supplies are packed in wood boxes in the back." "Very nice, thank you." She said. He showed her the garage, and all the black natives, and those few white people stopped whatever they were doing to stare. They of course knew who she is, and how their boss made a twit of himself earlier. She asked about the trailer. "Oh, well mum, that was George's idea you see. He is right of course, your purchases plus luggage wouldn't all fit into the rover; especially if the tires, and extra gas and water cans were packed in the back area. We'd like it mum, if you'd use it as long as necessary." "I will . . ." And turning nodded. "Thank you." In ten minutes, Aquina signed all the documents including registration, and the itemized receipt. Binder backed the rover and trailer out of the garage all gassed up and ready to go.

Taking a deep breath, she followed the group back to the equipment store, where the entire small mountain of purchases was split between the trailer, and the cargo area. Their next stop was the hotel. She made "sweet talk" to the wolf, who gave her an affectionate welcome, while native porters carried the trunks and baggage down to the rover. It seemed everybody knew which was hers, and she shrugged not thinking to much about it at the time.

While paying the bill the desk-clerk showed her the two large cartons from the clothing store. Carefully the porters packed everything leaving only the front seat vacant. Aquina and the wolf, her shoulder bag, and the case with the false bottom, and a basket of fruit and wine compliments from the hotel occupied all the available front seat and floor.

In surprisingly little time they headed northwest out of the city. The wolf was excited and so was she. The drive was simply exhilarating as they passed open land as far and further than the unaided eye could appreciate, and occasionally natives waved as they passed. She started to sing and kept on switching from one language to another settling on the "special" language eliciting a bark, low moan, a low or soft whowl, and some other noises from her white companion.

The road was pretty good and they maintained a decent speed, which Aquina clocked. An hour and ten minutes later the convoy turned off to the left at the sign, "Stockton Compound." From that point, she clocked another almost six miles before she saw the large lake through the gorgeous woods.

CHAP. 40

At twelve-twenty-five they arrived approx. one and-a-half hours from Nairobi. A sizeable crowd is on hand, and she noticed a number of vehicles parked out of the way, and estimated around fourty white people and almost an equal number of black natives began gathering around. She noticed, while getting out the "natives" were running about doing menial tasks, handing out cocktails and tending a huge barbecue-type of open pit cooking. The wolf hopped out, and Aquina accepted a glass of red wine from a waiter, and found herself surrounded by smiling people. The wife of Stockton . . . . Lois, quickly began the introductions.

Aquina learned they were friends and neighbors of those at the compound, as Lois showed her around the huge "U" shape. There are five low rambling ranch houses of wood sitting securely on stone foundations, covered with a strong looking thatch. Each had a wide porch extending across the entire front of the house, white posts and railing, and shrubs forming a border in front of each porch; and surrounding the houses extending out to the vehicles, and the whole compound was grass, rich and vibrant in color.

"Lois this is just lovely, and the flowers are beautiful." It was then she saw the name sign affixed to the right front post of the middle house forming the base of the large "U", in bold letters. It has her name without the double "H" in front. Lois instantly picked up on the error, and was about to reprimand the head man-native when Aquina put her arms around and hugged her, as women often do . . . "Thank you Lois, so very much, titles can be so cumbersome. Please call me Aquina." Lois had tears welling up in her eyes as she returned the hug. That type of reserve, and tension brought on by protocol with titled people largely melted away, and the others warmed immediately although there were boundaries of familiarity which they still would not cross. She met many of the natives especially the four servants who were very pleased to meet the young white princess of which they'd heard so much about from other natives, and overhearing the conversations of the white people. She met daughters and sons and gradually relaxed and became more at ease. Lois's husband, a Major Stockton, respectfully interrupted, and asked for the keys to the rover. Explaining the boys will unload, and begin the unpacking. "Thank you major. I'm forever taking the keys from the ignition." She opened her shoulder bag, and searched for the keys, and the luger slid into view. "Pardon me Aquina, but a gun?" Asked the major, a bit surprised. "Yes. A habit from the war." Lois tsk'ed, tsk'ed her husband.

"May I," asked the major? "Certainly." Aquina said, holding the polished weapon by the barrel, and handed it to the major. His respect for her grew, as it would in that kind of way when a woman especially a young one, displays respect for a firearm. As his eyebrow arc'ed up, a good sign to Lois, noting the pristine condition, and the safety was on. "An officer's weapon, nine millimeter." "The nazi colonel was pleased, and relieved, when I accepted it from him. An SS panzer brigade commander, and I think as sick of the war, as I."

Her look of regret passed, and she smiled as the major handed the weapon back, saying . . . . "an elegant weapon for an elegant lady." Aquina smiled.

The rover was brought up close to the door, and gradually unloaded by some men, and a few of the native women, while the party continued. And Lois continued to show Aquina the compound, explaining where things were located, such as the machinery shed. Things, such as their schedule for going into town, for food supplies, or the general store at Kijabe, owned by a few of her new friends, or bringing the wool into sell after the shearing. Such duties as branding, and herding were explained, and inbetween, Aquina asked many questions.

Many of the natives had set up tables, and during dinner the flow of conversation continued unabated. The wine warmed her, a comfortable mellow feeling began settling-in and, she decided to go slow on the drink. Quite a few questions came Aquina's way, and she answered them truthfully, although at times, she omitted certain facts still being cautious. They asked about her home, and "the wood," she so often referred to, and the wolf, who at times would bark and chase a small rodent around playing only to stop and pant. Aquina answered describing the forest, and its inhabitants going into detail about the packs of wolves, as if all of the wildlife were personal friends, and she their protecter. She unknowingly or perhaps because of the wine, reinforced this by explaining how they put out great quantities of food during the winter for all the animals. She described the compound, how old some of the sections were, and how new are the others, and included the warehouses and garage, . . . the barracks and other smaller areas. She also described the deep cold fjords with their majestic cliffs, and the hills to the north. Aquina turned to look into the distance. "Each landscape has its own intrinsic beauty and appeal. I like this . . . . it is so vast one cannot help but feel the challenge." The major piped up. "All of us have experienced and know that feeling. It stays with a person."

While the dishes were cleared away questions continued on both sides as the guests began to describe their homes-compounds. A few minutes before five p.m., the guests began with their goodbyes and departed. The four families including the Stocktons continued to sit with their illustrious guest trying to get better acquainted. They were thankful for the time shared on the ship, but they felt there was a great deal they still didn't know, and it made them curious.

The men soon gathered talking about a trip around the two camps that are always set up, and going, and for the shifts of men checking the herd keeping watch against predators and poachers. She overheard part of it then, Lois pointed out the native quarters, and the barracks where it was explained the working "hands" stayed. Walking a little further Lois pointed out the corrals, and the shearing shed, a medium sized barn housing horses, and used for storage, and pens with chickens with roosters.

Sitting around the table finishing their drinks the men, and young men, watched the ladies walk back with mixed emotions. It was getting late and the six children were already sleeping, tired and worn out from the trip. The seven teens, the boys sat with the men absorbed in their own erotic fantasies, and four girls walked with their mothers listening and trying to learn.

With everyone again sitting together conversation was limited to the herd, and camp inspection, to begin the very next morning . . . early. Naturally, Aquina perked-up asking if it would be possible to go along. The men seemed carefully neutral looking to the major to decide. He in fact didn't say no, but instead outlined the difficulties, and lack of conveniences for a woman. She smiled, but in a way that all the men found disquieting . . . . the type a parent would use with a child. It was settled, Aquina was going with them. She excused herself and with Lois walked toward the "guest house." The gathering began breaking up, Stockton stood watching Aquina's back thinking . . . it will be interesting.

With the wolf alongside they entered the rambling guest house encountering four tastefully dressed natives, two men and two women. Lois started with the older man introducing him, his position as houseman, the almost equally old man in whites as the cook, and the two ladies as her maids, also pointing out they are a family.

The house appealed to Aquina immediately. With the parlor or living room area dominant with the front door, and all other rooms opening to or from it depending on one's point of view. A sizeable kitchen shared the front half, with an almost equal size dining room separated by a half wall. The rear half held the large principle bedroom with a smaller one opposite sharing the "loo" or bathroom inbetween. Aquina liked it immediately with the size, and it is airy and bright with plenty of throw rugs and a liberal amount of well padded furniture. She sat on the bed appreciating its firmness, and loved the large deep closets flanked by large dressers. Lois showed the mesquito netting and how to let it drape around the bed, and hang it up on the overhead rod when not in use. And much to Lois's pleasure, and the four servants, Aquina commented on how happy she was to see everything unpacked. Disregarding the two large cartons sitting on the floor still bulging with recent purchases; she nodded at things hung in the closets, dresser drawers full with everything systematically arranged and folded. She noted the boots, and other shoes were arranged on the floor with hats, purses, and other such things on the top shelves, and her personal bush gear in the large closet in the parlor. In fact, Aquina commented enthusiastically about the entire house, and its cleanliness, which caused Lois to beam with pride, and the four natives as well.

Her small case aside from the two boxes, was the only bag not unpacked, and learned it was because "they are personal Ma-dam Sa-b." She smiled at the two black women, and began to put all the cosmetics on the small table located against the back wall. Aquina was tempted to leave the case on the chair, but decided to tuck it away in the closet. And she did, but took out all the weapons she expected to use. The other luger held in the glossy black holster, and belt, and her sixteen inch sword knife, and its shorter eleven inch brother. Leaving the other luger in her shoulder bag, she took extra clips out of the case, locked and put it on the closet floor.

She spent the night reading occasionally pouring a little cognac into a glass, but closed the cover soon after the first rays of dawn. She cleaned the glass and went into the bedroom to change. Pulling out two of the "V" neck shirts made of one-eighth inch mesh, she set them aside to pack, and put on a bush shirt of light cotton pushing in forcing the second and third buttons to close. As an after-thought . . .

Aquina reached for the small portable sewing kit, and with an impish grin, she tossed it on the mesh shirts. Next, she picked up one of the cotton duck canvas slacks with thigh pockets. Stepping into them and sliding 'em up was easy, but, she had to pull and twist-a-bit for them to fit over her full hips and tush. Her problem stemmed from hips slightly more than ten and-a-half inches more than her diminutive waist. The waist buttoned well enough, and threaded the attractive leather belt through the belt loops, cinched it tight. Not having a full length morror, she didn't realize the slacks, although feeling snug around the crotch, and her "bottom" looked as though she had been poured into them. She slipped on the calf-length heavy grain snake-proof boots, and began on the large knife filled scabboard. The gun belt was last, the holster part resting on the flare of her right hip. She cast a blood stirring shadow to any male with her mouth watering figure, most especially clad in the tight shirt and slacks. A shorter woman could not carry such measurements and still maintain the grace in each gesture, and movement that is one of Aquina's natural attributes.

The two black natives stared from just inside the doorway as Aquina packed, not able to help themselves. The two women following them, whispered scolding, but they stood for some seconds looking then quickly went about their duties. One of which called for them if not to assume the duty of packing, then at least to help and tidy up the room. It didn't require very long to fill the canvas duffle bag and load it, the shoulder bag and artist materials into the rover. She put the large knap-sack, and a few cosmetics and other sundries into the rover, and considered herself ready.

When asked about breakfast, she mentioned toast and tea or coffee. And noticed the head man pouring gas into the rover with a large funnel, then watched the wolf eat voraciously. She had just finished the cup when the headman walked-in bowed slightly saying he checked the rover for fuel and water, included two cans extra water, and two extra bags in the back. The extra cans he put in the cool fuel shed with the other cans and tanks.

She had started a second cup when the major stood in the open doorway and rapped on the door panel. With an open smile, he said good morning to Aquina, the four natives who happily chimed in with their greeting, returned his gaze to the body thence to her face. Aquina was just finishing her second cup, dashed into the bedroom for the bush hat, and joined the major, who was standing on the porch. He was looking at the wolf that was already sitting on the front seat waiting patiently for his mistress.

A few minutes later, she followed the major with one other vehicle behind her, as they exited the compound around the corner clump of trees following a well-worn "road" across the course grass. It is only about six-thirty, she smelled the sweet odor of flowers, grass and a multitude of airborn aromas from animal and scrub. She loosened the string loop under her chin, and let the hat fall back a bit, and began to hum. At intervals, she broke out into song usually ballads, or folk songs from home. Her's wasn't a soprano type voice, but one would mistake it for that of a professional, as it is clear with considerable range, and did not waver, and she is able to exercise a good measure of control. And there was no doubt she has the lungs for it, but perhaps more important, . . . Aquina truly enjoyed singing.

Her voice went up the scale as she belted out a cabaret song in French. The next one is an Austrian national song about the mountain edelweiss. A beautiful piece of music, and she switched to german . . . singing with gusto and feeling. Several more in English and finally in that unique tongue, she sung and weaved melodys that could not only be heard . . . . but felt akin to a caress, a sensation bordering on the sensual. It was plainly obvious to the men in front and in back . . . it is a woman's voice, and not one failed to enjoy the music.

They had been driving about fourty minutes, the slightly rolling country dotted with scrub, and patches of trees, and thicket. A good deal of it is covered with a tall sand colored grass about two feet high. The camp was barely in sight when the loud sound of multiple shots, rifle shots could be heard. Moments later they careened to a stop by the tents, a bullet ricocheted off her fender just as the rover stopped. She shouted to the wolf, and jumped clear, and scrambled for cover. Aquina already had the luger in her hand, and seeing the major motion to her . . . . she got up in a crouch, and ran toward him zig-zagging leaping the last few feet. Landing next to him. "You alright you highness?" "Fine major, just angry." The men who had been in the camp looked at one-another surprised and asked one of the reliefs . . . who she is.

The wolf came on the run hunching-down next to her, and petting him began using "that tongue" talking to him. He uttered half growls and a snarl, as Aquina pointed to the clump of trees up on the slight rise about two hundred-fifty or sixty feet in front of them. The wolf darted off into the tall grass, and disappeared.

While she waited, the major commented about the herd scattering from the shots, and it taking days to gather them together. Any further comments were stilled as several bullets spattered the earth around them. They were effectively pinned down. With that realization, Aquina thought of something else, and asked the major if this could be a diversion, a stratagem, while other poachers grabbed off what remained of the herd. Startled, surprised, and angry, he didn't think of it, Stockton uttered an oath under his breath, assigned a few men and all the native blacks to stay, while he and the other men made it to the land rovers amid ricocheting bullets.

Without mishap they took-off with tires throwing sand and dirt rapidly putting themselves out of range.

Aquina asked if there were any rifles around. She learned two white men had been wounded, and one had a rifle, a thirty cal. carbine obviously from the war. One of the natives squirmed on his stomach and retrieved the carbine, and brought it to her. "All of you stay here and occasionally fire a few rounds at the poachers." Before they thought to protest, Aquina had crawled into the tall grass with the carbine cradled across her arms.

The sun was warm, and she is soaking wet from perspiration. And for what seemed an eternity came upon small bushes not quite half-way to the clump of trees. Stopping for a minute, she smiled when the men started shooting only to stop seconds later. She was equally pleased to note the poachers were content to stay in the same place.

Again, she began crawling elbows painfully sore, and her blouse-shirt almost entirely open as buttons gave way because of scraping on the ground against sand and stone. It took over another half hour to work her way around their flank, and behind them, where, she found the wolf crouching waiting for an opportunity to attack, or his mistress.

Aquina is behind them on their left, and up into a crouch slowly made the thick scrub, and a tree directly behind them about fourty feet. She cautioned the wolf, and knelt in the proper firing position. With the safety off, she sighted on the white man sitting on the extreme left . . . for the lower left shoulder blade. Her right forefinger caressed the trigger, and the carbine coughed a single round. Quickly to the next person, without taking time to aim caught the second of the white men in the back; but the others, native blacks were turning. She fired in quick succession hitting only one of the three, then dove to the ground rolling. Filling her hand with the luger, and aimed for the two natives, who were shooting in her direction missing with the first two rounds. A white streak entered her peripherial vision springing taking down the one native stifling a blood curdling scream.

Aquina kept firing hitting the last native twice, once in the chest and once in the stomach. The wolf stood next to his kill, and raised his head letting go with the age-old howl. She went about the task of picking up the rifles, and their other weapons, and noticed her badly damaged clothing. Quickly stripping the shirt and mesh "T" off, Aquina peeled off the almost severed bra discarding it with a shrug, and with alacrity, donned the mesh "T" and the now buttonless shirt rolled it up a bit knotting the shirt-tail tightly around her bare midriff. While it didn't cover much of her large breasts it is blessedly cooler from the five inches of exposed midriff.

Picking up the rifles slinging one over each shoulder, she began to carry them and the holsters. A rather attractive ivory handled machete was also on the pile cradled across her arms. As she stepped out into the open the younger men came on the run cheering, with the older members coming more slowly, waving.

Seconds later the men gathered around her taking the weapons off of her arms, all except the machete. One of the natives offered to help with the weapons over each shoulder. "Here take this one . . . I'll keep this sten." He nodded several times eyes wide grinning politely looking at the blood spattered wolf, and her dirty sand filled clothes. Plus the fact they'd never seen so much uncovered tan skin before on a white woman, especially one so well "proportioned."

Aquina handed the carbine to a young man, while most of the others already had picked up a rifle. Those that didn't at least had a pistol and holster. She was too busy examining and then cleaning the sten sub-machine gun, which the slide is positioned forward has single round capability, to notice the looks and smiles as the men were wavering. They are all to painfully aware she is royalty, and were a little shy, and definitely unsure of themselves. Somehow the young men felt inept and clumsy around her, and had a difficult time relaxing.

She realized to late they are intimidated, and shrugged dropping the problem from her mind . . . . at least for now. Many in the camp watched as she with quick sure movements reassembled the freshly cleaned weapon, put in a fresh clip then made sure the safety was on, and turned her attention to the luger. She didn't clean it but simply snapped out the magazine, walked over to the rover, and dug into the shoulder bag. A second or so and she pulled out two . . . . put one in the luger, and the other in her right thigh pocket.

Aquina did leave the ivory handled machete in the rover though and turned returning to the small stool on which she had been sitting. The camp's headman bowed presenting her with a hot cup of tea. "Thank you." He nodded grinning from ear to ear.

While she drank the tea more and more vultures gathered to feed on the carrion. The wolf came over sitting next to her stool making little sounds. She got up and retrieved a shallow bowl from the rover and her canteen, returned to the stool pouring a liberal amount of water into it so he could satisfy his thirst. In one swallow the cup is empty, and saying politely . . . . no to another, walked over to the table by the cooking tent and washed the cup, and put it down inverted on the table.

Virtually nothing she did or said went unnoticed by the native black people, and their quiet acceptance of her caused the young white men to be even more withdrawn.

Aquina went quietly into the tent where both of the wounded layed on cots with a native for each trying to keep them calm with cold or rather wet cloths on the forehead, and seeing to the dressings. She knelt by each looking at a leg wound on one, and a shoulder wound on the other. A few seconds with each, and she knew if they didn't get medical help soon it will be bad, maybe even too late.

Walking out of the tent, she spoke to the headman and immediately walked over to the young men sitting with the few older married men. "I want to apologize for appearing withdrawn and ill-tempered," They all looked up in mild surprise, as Aquina continued. "I came here in desperate need of a holiday, while this sort of thing was certainly not in my plans." Several of the men tried to speak up, but she motioned for them to wait for a moment until she had finished. "However, I was trained and am familiar fighting in that way, you on the other hand . . . are not and would most certainly have been wounded, or killed. And we have enough wounded already.

Besides, none of you have ever had to kill before . . . have you?" They all nodded "no." "Now, if those men do not receive proper medical attention soon it will be to late. I need four of you to carry them gently to my rover. A few others can shift all my things to the cargo area . . . now quick, lets go." Aquina clapped her hands, and everyone began moving at once, and soon both wounded men were loaded into the rover. She had suggested to the others, how to set up sentrys, and of course tell the major everything, especially, that she was taking the wounded to a doctor.

Climbing into the rover with the sten gun, she pulled away from the camp bringing the speed up to almost fifty. Aquina leaned on the horn as she drew close to the compound, and quite naturally women and children, everyone came out on the run. Coming to a stop she quickly filled in Lois, and asked about a doctor. Lois said for wounds that serious they would have to be taken into the hospital in Nairobi. Wives were screaming and crying as Lois said she would radio ahead.

Aquina gained the main road as quickly as she could trying to smooth out the worst bumps and ruts on the way. Once on the main road, she quickly accelerated up to fifty, then fifty-five. Lois, in the meantime contacted the hospital, and then the district police. Although she had to honk the horn frequently, she didn't slack off on the speed, but kept going. And fifty minutes later was squealing rubber careening down a couple of streets braking in front of the side entrance of the hospital marked, emergency.

While the men were in the operating rooms, two young men took shifts pacing, while Aquina, the wolf, and the other two young men sat on a long wooden bench waiting to hear what the doctors had to say. She got up and walked down the other connecting hallway to get some coffee, and stood by a window looking out thinking to herself. In the interim a district police lieutenant walked in and began talking to the young men jotting down facts and related information concerning the events up to and after the shooting. Only one of the young men however . . . was present at the camp during the night, and early morning when the incident first started.

Aquina went to refill her empty cup when two off-duty nurses walked up and a little shyly . . . . if she would care to freshen up in their lounge and bathroom. It broke her out of the reverie to the present. "Yes, I'd like that." She took stock of her clothes and, "ohh, I must look a sight." The nurses smiled showing her into the bathroom where she was able to wash the dust and dirt from her face, arms et-cetera. Feeling refreshed, she went back to the coffee urn, and brought the nurses coffee chatting until the doctor came out looking for her, and the others.

It was apparent the two wounded men would recover, but due to substantial blood loss, and the surgery, would remain at the hospital for at least two possibly three weeks At which time the two doctors will re-evaluate their cases. The two men had been sedated so waiting to visit was pointless. With a sigh, Aquina turned to go and almost bumped into the lieutenant.

"Oh, excuse me your highness. If I may have a few moments of your time." "I have no time. These young men have mentioned something about your questions, and I am not interested." She replied coldly. A cold anger began seething becoming hotter until, she turned and stared into his eyes. The lieutenant's eyes opened wider and blanched as if struck by an unseen force deep in his conscious mind. At the same instant he stepped back shaken averting his eyes.

Aquina began walking toward the side exit, called behind her for the young men to follow. More than a little anxious they quickly fell in behind her not wanting to look at the police lieutenant. Without a word they piled into the rover, only a half bark from the wolf broke the silence inside, as she backed out of the small parking lot. Aquina half turned and spoke to them in back as she negotiated traffic. "We are stopping at the gun shops." They looked at one-another, and two began to voice their position of not having brought money. In a much softer voice, she explained it would be a gift from her.

Most of the shops were located within a city block of each other, and it was in front of the first shop, she parked leaving the wolf to guard the rover and its contents. Not until visiting the third shop did she see anything note-worthy. Hanging on one display stand were several weapons left-overs from the war, plus larger game rifles on display behind the counter.

Her attention centered on a sten, virtually identical to the one she left in the rover, a nazi burp gun, and a sniper's rifle with a top quality scope. She inquired of the man behind the counter if the owner or manager was in the store or closeby. "At your service your highness." He said with a broad grin and bowed. "Primarily, I am interested in those weapons on that stand." He smiled, . . . "yes M'Lady." While Aquina and the owner/manager looked at the weapons and answered her questions, the four young men were engrossed looking at glossy 8x10 pictures hanging up behind the counter. Of the many, they stared at only three. The first depicted a tank battle, and printed on the bottom was the date, and the word "Elbe." The second showed a woman sitting atop an enormous tank, with the inscription . . . . "Tiger Lady." And the third was a shot similar to the second, but showing Aquina shaking hands with the English field marshall. Aquina made up her mind, and purchased all three weapons on the stand, plus a considerable quantity of ammunition for each. At her insistence each of the young men selected a rifle, and ammunition, and she paid for the entire lot. Just before departing, she consented to autographing the pictures, while the "men" loaded their purchases into the rover.

CHAP. 41

They had been out of the city only minutes, when she began giving instructions. "Open the boxes marked clips, those marked for the sten, the burp gun, and the mauser. You will find the many boxes of ammunition are labeled for each weapon. Wait for a minute, and I shall do one of each." While she said the last few words, her foot came off the accelerater and onto the brake, slowed, and braked to a stop on the roadside. Getting up and turning in the seat, she showed them what to look for, and how to fill each clip until they could do it competently. "Open one box of ammunition at a time careful how you rip open the foil." They nodded assent, and started filling clips. "A little attention to her white four legged friend, and they were off, but this time Aquina stepped on it wanting to make up time.

Three-thirty . . . . quarter to four, she honked the horn as the vehicle stopped in front of the compound. Getting out she told the teenagers to stay put, and continue to fill clips. Aquina walked over to the converging group of women and children, and told them what the chief doctor had said. It is blessedly good news for everyone, especially for the two wives, and the children. Aquina hugged the two women and quickly got back into the rover, rounded the clump of trees and raced off into the distance.

Those at the camp, major and the others had returned only an hour before, saw the rapidly approaching dust cloud, and within minutes they sighted a vehicle. Closer and closer until it was recognized as belonging to the princess, and many felt easier-not so jumpy. But the rush of adrenalin is strong . . . . not from apprehension, it was anticipation. For, she represented not only a challenge, but an enigma, her youth and physical beauty, and the body all combined to make her extremely desireable. And lastly, she is a young woman, who had been given wide acclaim, and lauded for her courage and convictions. Each of the men wanted her, or failing that . . . . just to be with her.

She came to a stop and parked next to the other vehicles only too be enveloped by the camp, including the native blacks. Getting out of the rover, Aquina leaned over holding out her sten to the major, who smiled, and thanked her with a warm hug. While she left the sniper's rifle on the seat, she gripped the other sten and burp gun handing them out to the mature men of the camp. "There are boxes of clips and ammunition for each weapon in back there." The others began unloading some of the stock ammunition distributing it according to the major's orders.

Aquina started to tell them about the two wounded men, their status relaying what the doctor had said, and the fact she had stopped at the compound relieving the anxiety of the wives and children. The headman brought tea to her, bowed and . . . "Ma-m Sa'ab." She thanked him, and with the "first swallow" closed her eyes, . . . savoring the taste. And while enjoying her tea orders were given with several natives setting up her tent with its canvas floor, with surprising alacrity, and good humor. They set up the cot, chair, knap-sack and duffel bag, the shoulder bag, and the wooden attaché-like box of artist supplies, and paper.

Looking inside the tent, she noticed they had hung up the fine netting over and around the cot complete with pillow and sheets, with her things stacked in the corner neatly side-by-side. The outer room had already been claimed by the wolf, who immediately had walked in and layed down. Without the awning up it is really large, easily three-quarters again bigger than any of the others; except the cooking tent, but with the awning adding eight feet equaled a little more than twice any of the others.

Aquina was admiring the tent, the first time she had seen it up, and liked the size. It is situated to one side of the camp, that part of the camp dominated by the native whites, and only a few paces from the native blacks. A system she often thought was unnecessary and unfair.

At dinner, she is seated opposite the major with the others inbetween on both sides. The cooking tent was by far the largest, actually a small half trailer open on the long side, which was located the stove, and all the heavy supplies, with the body of the tent attached to the single wall on the trailer, and the balance set-up and braced in the normal fashion. The meal consisted of beef with a type of sweet potato, and a local vegetable served with wine, and afterwards, tea. Conversation remained light during dinner, but turned serious with the serving of tea. Plans were made to gather as many strays as possible.

And time was of the essence, not only because of poachers, but the many predators that would take an even greater toll.

Agreeing with the major, Aquina stayed within or close to the camp along with the native blacks and three of the younger white men, While the larger group rounded-up the scattered herd. Watching for poachers and predators became a full time job for three of the older men.

Thereafter the days were largely uneventful except for chasing or scaring off occasional predators, and visiting the other camp, where the herd was perhaps a bit larger. The major drove inbetween sometimes taking Aquina along, always armed of course, "showing her about," and affording her the opportunity to meet the other people. She hadn't realized it at first, but the major and associates possessed a much larger operation than originally assumed. And most afternoons, she walked a number of yards from the camp to sketch, always with one of the men to stand guard even though Aquina carried the mauser.

She wanted to start early, the sun was high and warm, and the men were busy shifting supplies, cleaning weapons as one shift relieved another. With the rifle over one shoulder, kit of materials held in the left hand and the stool in her right, she is ready to go. Some yards from camp Aquina put the stool down and the box laying the rifle next to it, and with the board and paper resting on her lap, began sketching some grazing wildebeast in the near distance. So engrossed in faithfully capturing her subject, she didn't notice the old male lion enjoying the shade provided by the scrub not twenty yards on her right side. As the sketch took shape and substance, she began humming, and in minutes started singing softly. In that strange tongue, she sang a ballad, and then a love song. The lion is old and because it was slower hunting hadn't been successful, and it cast hungry eyes at the careless human. But raised its head quietly, confusion mixing with the hunger . . . It turned its head to an fro trying to locate the sound, which stirred familiar sounds from its near past. It looked but didn't see a pride or another of its kind, only the human. Wearily he rose to his feet remaining quiet, and shook himself off and slowly, noiselessly approached the human taking advantage of every bit of cover.

The closer he went the more familiar, the clearer the sounds as some are universal with all species, and with that familiarity came a kind of understanding. He is very close to the human and smelled the scent finding it different than his own kind, but not unpleasant, and craning forward uttered a soft mewl. A little startled, Aquina turned almost eye-to-eye to the mature cat.

Immediately, she began to speak affecting a sing-song tone and extended her right hand. She was concentrating staring into its eyes, and tested several words to find those with the most influence or those sounds and tones illiciting the most favorable responses. In less time than it takes to discuss it she discovered the proper tones, the proper inflection to use. This didn't mean she would stop trying, it represented after all only the first step. Feeling the tone, the strength of the sounds and their inflection . . . . and the energy radiating from her sub-concious, as it did, everything surrounding her whether awake or sleeping, the large male reacted better than she hoped.

Aquina could not help but notice how thin the big male looked, and turned picked up the meat sandwich, she had made earlier. And holding it in her open palm held it under the formidable mouth. In a wink the tongue came out . . . . jaw opened, and zip it disappeared.

She quickly packed everything together holding the kit and stool in one hand, and under the arm with rifle slung over the same shoulder . . . . and slowly walking toward the camp. She knelt talking to the big male, and was answered by guttural sounds, a soft mewl, half growl or sort of "humph" only louder or sometimes softer with each a different meaning. And with her empty hand gently stroking the head giving the cat encouragement because of its unsteady gait. At just that moment, her customary guard came jogging into view provoking a roar of challenge from the cat. As if struck dumb, the black native stopped dead in his tracks, mouth wide open, eyes wide with wonder mixed with fear. Ever so slowly the native began backing up calling into the camp. Aquina told him to calm down, and tell the cook to put out a hind-quarter off to one side. She successfully made the large male understand . . . the growling stopped, and its murmuring became much softer.

Everyone came into view trying to look, but stayed discreetly out of the way as the cook's helper laid a fat quarter down on the grass. Those present watched with fascination huddled together and peering around tents held almost spellbound by the "event" unfolding before them. Sniffing and growling the old male tried to go faster, but its legs and hind quarters are weak from hunger, and gave way. Aquina knelt and with conjoling and trying to lift him, and slowly he got to his feet . . . . and staying next to him, holding him, she led the starving cat over to the meat. Laying down on its stomach it began digging into the tender meat, and the large fangs began tearing out large pieces, which disappeared instantly. Continuing her monologue, Aquina got up from the sitting position next to the lion and slowly went for a bowl.

The men white and black stared at her open mouthed incredulous as she nonchalantly picked up a deep bowl filled it with water, and walked carefully balancing the bowl made her way back to the cat. Still talking, she regained the position next to him putting the bowl of water on the ground.

Aquina quickly spoke, and the wolf answered drinking from its own bowl. Coming up for air the lion moved a little lapping up water as if dying of thirst. Soon it stopped only to begin cleaning its mouth and jowls, the tongue working with an almost industrial efficiency. In a few minutes the lion turned to her its head well within arms length. Aquina held out her hand palm up . . . . and calm, and docile it licked her palm then leaned, looking down, rubbed its forehead against her hand. At that instant, as if a signal was issued, the wolf walked over to her other side and one specie came to accept the other.

The men realized they have witnessed a thing unbelieveable, strange . . . . a happening none of them would ever forget.

From that moment on . . . . Aquina's life had substantially altered. Now there could be no mistake, she thought to herself. Henceforth, she will pursue this ability and train herself, learn the subtleties of "it". For there was no error, there existed something within, a power . . . an ability . . . . she shrugged, and smiled. Whatever it is, she must nurture the ability and strengthen it. Still smiling and petting the lion on one side and the wolf on the other, she felt pleased with herself.

Her existence had changed in another way, seeing it in the faces of all those that happened to be around her. A rover was dispatched to the compound for a meat supply, and the news was told to black and white alike by white men and black. The other camp was told and from thence it moved outward, to the Bantu, and other tribes especially the great Masai.

The great test of old, was for any masai male youth, was to face a lion with but spear and shield . . . . face the awesome strength and courage of the lion, and kill him. They believe by facing the lion and killing him the youth assends to manhood, assuming the cunning, strength, and courage of the great cat. This was reserved only for men, they disbelieved the rumors, and the talk from the "others." But that was not the end of it, as more and more eyewitness accounts were told and retold around the tribal villages.

Many days passed and instead of returning to the compound, Aquina stayed traveling wider and wider circles. Until two men began following at a reasonable distance in her rover acting as protection and support. She carried no rifle, but did have her big knife and the luger in its customary holster, plus a full canteen. Although only about eighty degrees, she kept the bush hat in place, but took off the shirt knotting the arms around the waist leaving on only the mesh "T" shirt. Her subtle light tan became more golden, the hair . . . . a lustrous tone made the streaks showcasing her long tresses more stark and pronounced.

Aquina felt free and unhindered by the constraints of a society she didn't entirely understand. And to display her feelings, she often sang in songs, in every language she knew, and then remembering her purpose slipped into the one tongue which brought the most pleasure. And the lion recovered its strength, and bristled with vitality unusual in one so old. Its eyes cleared, and the mantle of dark and light fur became more healthy looking and it added weight restoring the animal's symmetrical balance.

Very often substantial amounts of short trees and scrub were encountered, thorny bushs . . . scrub, lush green areas teeming with monkeys, and whole varieties of birds. Many times she was observed by startled natives as well as wildlife. Her song attracted so many different-divergent species, she found herself overwhelmed.

As more days past the two men in the rover became three, then five, watching and some from the camps took turns taking pictures. One specific morning the rover was joined by the district police, a lieutenant and a captain. They chatted with Stockton, and the others and spent long intervals looking through binoculars at a lone woman walking with a small pride of lions. Flanked by a large male and a white wolf, the pride walked close as they watched her pick-up one cub, then another going through all . . . . one by one. Her voice, clear and vibrant, could be heard for a fair distance.

Those in the rovers picked out of the green lush foliage a group of five masai warriors, standing stoically shoulder to shoulder holding their long spears straight up and down in the one hand, shields in the other, all resting the blunt ends on the ground. The Europeans exclaimed softly and remarked as only the police had seen masai warriors of such high rank. Their plumage and multi-colored clothing bespoke their status, and Aquina did see them; but before she could utter the only words she knew in Swahili, a greeting, two young male lions burst from the undergrowth some twenty yards to her left-front. The pride quickly moved around on her sides as a terrible roaring challenge was issued from the newcomers. Instantly the big male at her side was up answering the challenge.

Aquina stood and raised her right arm pointing as she yelled at the two young males.

What transpired next amazed even the masai. The two challengers blanched as if physically struck, and all the lions around her layed close to the ground, including the big male and the wolf. She scolded the two newcomers, who slunk forward on their stomachs, heads down each uttering small cries. The pride was silent, even the cubs were uncharacteristically quiet. All the white men looking on . . . . each trying to understand what they were seeing. The masai too had similar problems, only living much closer to nature, and the wild . . . . they better than the Europeans knew just how special . . . . this happening really is, and its significance to them.

She softened the tone, dropped the hard inflection, and held out her right hand. Both groups masai and Europeans stared with mixed emotions as the two males now on their feet came within arm's distance and stopped. Extending both arms palms forward perpendicular to the ground, she resumed talking to them. Slowly each rubbed their snout and then the forehead. The pride gathered around as before with the cubs returning to their normal vociferous habits.

Inbetween the sing-song words, Aquina paused and turned to her right. She stood and held out her right hand greeting the five masai. They knelt, laid their weapons on the grass, stood and walked slowly toward her. She took a few steps toward them, but stopped, still standing amidst the pride.

"Blimey." The police captain said. He called for everyone to continue taking as many pictures as possible. She spoke and the lionesses parted, and ever so carefully . . . . each step the masai walked brought them deeper inside the pride. They slowly knelt and then stood up not wishing to make any sudden moves. The native in the middle spoke identifying themselves, and asked her a question. She was confident about its meaning, and simply nodded yes. He immediately removed one very ornate necklace and with much care slipped it over her head. Aquina raised her right hand as if to shake hands, the native gently grasped it in both hands and kissed the thumb. Each of the four others repeated the solemn ceremony, said a kind of salutation, and started to back up, slowly. They knelt on both knees twice, while backing up until reaching their weapons. Raising their spears in a salute . . . . they disappeared into the bush.

Days that followed proved the men wrong. They were sure nothng could surprise them anymore, but she managed. Aquina cavorted with all kinds of animals including giraffe, leopard, water buffalo, zebra, antelope, rhinoceros and the great elephants, plus the tree monkeys, chimps, occasional babboons, a wide variety of birds and the multitude of rodents. But some instances were especially strange . . . . the animals would gather, hunter and hunted together.

CHAP. 42

The days turned into weeks and the "magic," her influence spread amongst the animals geometrically and the native blacks. And proportionatly the whites as the curious and meddlesome tried to see her. Those who couldn't or were thwarted by a growing allegiance of followers attempted many types of chicanery in an effort for pictures or story. For instance, few of the Europeans said anything and no-one from the two camps, or the compound said or divulged any information. The natives were considerably more obstinate since the return of the five masai. Each is an underchief to the head or big chief, who took considerable pride in the telling of their experience. It spread like locusts through the masai nation, and the other tribes.

Her first trip back to the compound since the poaching incident was not only a little unusual, but very moving, not only for those at the compound . . . . but Aquina felt it as well. She made the trip to replenish the stock of paper, tins of salve, sulphur, salt pills and brought dirty worn clothes back to exchange for new. With the wolf in front and the large male lion in back occupying all of the seat . . . presented quite a sight as she rounded the clump of trees. Children ran inside calling their parents, everyone around or in the compound gathered as she climbed out of the rover, and lifted out the clothes bundle, while the two animals jumped out. The lion instantly raised a paw menacingly with claws extended roaring until she called to him. His change in behavior was immediate, padding over to Aquina and rubbing that long snout against her exposed midriff with the touch of her hand petting, scratching behind his ears as a reward.

Lois saw as the others did, Aquina had changed perhaps lonelier, and no-one missed the multiple necklaces around her neck. She greeted them warmly cutting through the stares and both confused and happy expressions. In her quarters the four natives knelt on the floor as she entered, the two animals following on her heels. She began talking to them calling each by name as if nothing had transpired. They on the other hand treated her much differently. More than anything it was their way of looking at her, and the responses. She wrapped-up the sixty odd charcoal sketchs, and picked up the remaining two pads storing the package on the top shelf in the closet. In addition, Aquina pulled out of the boxes, shirts, slacks and shorts, and more of the mesh "T" shirts replacing what was worn and dirty.

The houseman put everything in the rover including filling the fuel tanks, while she ate the delicious salad prepared by the cook.

Including cosmetics, she took what remained of the salve, but found the supply of sulphur, and other things dangerously low. So, telling Lois about the shortage, she made up a small list and remarked "she would try the general store at Kijabe."

Piling the animals into the rover, Aquina was off heading toward the main road leading to Nairobi. Not long after Kijabe filled the windscreen, and moments after cutting the speed, she noticed the general store set back about fifteen feet from the road. Aquina sighed with relief to see only one vehicle in front. She wanted to pick up the supplies and be on her way. Getting out she naturally touched the door, and felt a living kind of warmth. Aquina paused, then shrugged walking around letting the animals out for air, even though the top had been rolled back.

Entering, Aquina noticed the only other patron busy with a list of her own, and with nary a sound began picking up the items she wanted. It was cool and her friend, Flo hadn't heard or seen her what with humming and stocking a shelf behind the counter. The aromas of seed, cheese, nuts, and herbs all mingled to enhance the homely feeling. She walked up to the counter depositing the tins of sulphur, and a few other items she had chosen. Flo turned and surprise instantly turned to an affusive greeting broken by the shriek of horror from the other person.

The poor woman ran out screaming, ... "Lion, . . . Lion!!!" Padding around the corner of the aisle, the big male sat down next to his mistress, and murmured, and Aquina answered him. Flo stared. "Amazing, simply amazing." She mumbled. Aquina smiled and talked a little with Flo and asked about George, Flo's husband of many years.

While they chatted, and Aquina chose several additional items, the woman's hysterics brought several constables from their office, plus many curious and excited onlookers.

Flo saw the small crowd around the doorway and helped her illustrious friend put everything in two bags. With promises to visit, Aquina walked to the door wolf on one side . . . the lion on the other. The crowd nor the constables offered any resistance when she opened the doors putting the bags inside, and the animals. Aquina walked around to the other side getting in, the constables grinning and bowing, and starting the engine calmly eased the rover onto the main road, and accelerated. It was one of many such episodes, and feeling the need for a change, she graciously departed with warm emotional farewells.

CHAP. 43

Some fourty-five, odd minutes later, she saw through the windscreen a jeep and rover off on the side. Aquina waved and mindful of the loaded trailer slowed before turning. Everything, all her personal belongings, and field equipment was packed in the rover and trailer. She left many tires and other supplies at the Stockton compound including the fuel, water and the lion, who had walked in the direction of a small pride. It was difficult for her, but necessary to leave the lion in its natural setting. The wolf could cope, but Aquina knew the big cat would eventually have problems.

Though a somewhat smaller compound the warmth and enthusiasm was no less intense than that received at the Stocktons. The accomodations consisted largely of a clean airy bungalow, and only one servant, but she appreciated it more for those very reasons.

The compound itself was situated amongst high rolling hills covered with light and dark green foliage broken by sections of lush trees. More to the southwest it appeared more similar to what she had already seen and enjoyed. The "ranch" carried both beef and sheep at opposite ends, with many acres tilled, and bearing a variety of crops. As the major differences amounted to size, and purpose, Aquina blended-in as best as she could. Many of the bags and trunks were lined up against the wall in one room, and preferring to unpack only the essentials, at least for now.

Accepting an invitation to be shown Nakuru, a large town or small burgeoning city depending on one's point of view, with a trio of young people all around her apparent age. She freshened up and changed into clean blouse, and knee-length skirt. Wearing only the necklaces for actual jewelry, Aquina picked up her shoulder bag and walked outside. The trailer had been unhitched and left sitting on the side of the lot, while everything else was carried inside.

Inasmuch as her's was by far the larger vehicle everyone piled in pairing off. Her escort is twenty-one and good looking, but not as self-assured as she would like, or wish for in a suitor. For his part it was much to late. The young man's heart had been captured from the first minute of their meeting. He smiled a lot, nodded and stared at her, and she climbed in behind the wheel, and made no effort to suggest he drive. The insistent feeling of inadequateness did not help his self-confidence, nor the frequent times she caught him staring.

They arrived early enough to have lunch doing so at one of two establishments frequented by the younger set. From their first stop at a traffic sign, they had been noticed by native blacks. Inside the small restaurant, once seated, every native black person passed her table greeting her with a bow, and a masai or bantu tribal greeting. Each time Aquina smiled, and answered with a greeting of her own, and when their lunch was served, she smiled at the garland of small brightly colored flowers resting on the plate surrounding a delicate salad on damp crispy lettuce. She is always the first to be served, and when she was undecided about any desert . . . the waiter quickly excused himself, and reappeared moments later with a plate. The center had small bite sized pieces of different melons topped with ice-cream bordered by two flowers. Thanking the waiter in Swahili, she deftly removed the rather large blue-white clematis and began slowly savoring the melon. Afterwards, she gently wiped off the underside of the two blooms and stems, dipped them in her water glass and secured both together in her hair with a bobby pin. The are striking, nestled over her left ear . . . very appealing.

From the restaurant they first stopped for fuel, shopping followed to be replaced with sightseeing, easily consuming what remained of the afternoon.

The weeks unfolded offering Aquina opportunities with some of the same species she worked with before, and many new ones, notably the panther. There were more leopards as well, along with the elephant and buffalo. But the leopard family, of which the panther is a member, interested her the most. Smaller than the lion, but sleek and very fast, and with habits different than its larger cousin. Of all the cats Aquina cherished the panther . . . . black, with its own behavior pattern, stirred her instincts more than any other animal.

Going out to a line camp, as they called it, she spent many days back and forth into the bush on the pretext, "she was sketching." And during that time, she sang and hummed those sounds associated with the big cats, with no results. That is not to say, she didn't attract wildlife, she most certainly did, but not the panther.

Those in the camp witnessing her "playmates and friends," talked. And the talk spread much further than just to those on the ranch. Ever since she had been inducted into the masai nation as an honorary queen, the natives treated her with a mixture of fear and respect; So it wasn't unusual that they watched her most of anyone. Whenever, she ventured forth into the bush always present, were a number of natives. And they of course talked to other natives . . . . and so on.

Beginning her third week, on a wednesday, she departed early for the bush, with stool and the wooden box filled with drawing supplies. With canteen and gun holster, knife, she walked off through the grass and scrub followed by the wolf. Almost immediately the camp heard the first melody, and as the time slipped by her voice became progressively more faint. She crossed a couple of tiny streams, and one fair sized one before breaking out of the trees into the open. She saw three elephants, two cows, and a small calf, and walking to within about 140 feet, she sat down on the stool. Sometimes, she sang then hummed, changing the tone and inflection frequently as she began sketching. Working rapidly, she had the three animals outlined, and the foliage, and moved to the secondary lines.

Aquina was thoroughly engrossed, working feverishly trying to finish most of the detail before the elephants moved too much. The wolf was watching the two cows and calf . . . . suddenly the wolf whirled crouching down . . . ears back snarling. Just as she saw the wolf's reaction the sun was blotted out for some yards around her establishing an area of shade. At that instant, Aquina felt something gently rub up and down her back.

The few onlooking natives almost swallowed their tongues when the enormous bull came up behind the "lion queen." They watched as she turned around on the stool. No longer humming, Aquina used the same sounds and words that proved so successful with other elephants. But this bull is truly enormous, putting her hands on the prehensile trunk and standing on tip-toes, she still couldn't reach where the trunk joined the head. Each of the tusks came out and down, and up again forming a graceful arc. The massive head lowered, and the trunk wound around her as it continued to probe gathering her scent, and little sounds came from it interspersed with other more urgent sounds.

Moving forward its left front leg, so it was just resting on the ground, she squatted down and looked at the pad carefully. A few inches up from the bottom on the outside, was a blunt end protruding. She took it to be a large thorn from one of the thorn scrub trees, and guessed the bull broke it off while pulling on it with his trunk, or broke it against something. Either way it is infected, and obviously very sore. Standing, Aquina patted the leg with her hand and went back and held onto the trunk talking and making the necessary sounds. It answered with some small sounds of its own, and started rubbing her back with the end of the trunk.

A few seconds and she had everything back in the wooden box, picked up the small stool in the same hand, and spoke to the bull. The trunk came up in a high arc and trumpeted twice. Then another sound lower and less shrill than the first two. In no time the two cows and the calf were joined by the others.

A few young bulls and the rest were cows with sundry calfs gathered on one side of the big bull.

Gazing intently at each, Aquina went from one adult to the next and then the calves . . . a broad grin covered her face, and many a giggle escaped her lips. Thirteen adults and calves extended their trunks pulling in her scent.

Meanwhile the natives had run back to the camp telling everything they had seen and heard; seconds . . . . and the camp, and surrounding area heard the trumpeting. There was no way not to hear it when the distance involved was less than a mile.

Walking a few yards in front of the bull, the wolf at her side, the herd moved unhurriedly, and paused at the larger stream to drink, and wet themselves down. Putting her things down on the bank, taking off the gunbelt and knives, and divesting herself of shirt and boots, she entered the water. At the deepest it is only waist deep, and cavorted around with the adults and calves alike. And while the animals relaxed in the water, she stood on the bank drying off in the sun.

Not quite an hour, and she is ready, and called the bull. The next two small streams were crossed easily, even the calves made it easily, and in minutes they are within sight of the camp. Those remaining in and around the camp . . . shrank back, some just wide-eyed, the native blacks in fear as she came closer. The herd stopped about sixty yards away with the two young cows keeping watch, while Aquina stopped by the corner of her tent. The bull stood quietly sniffing, and watching the small white animal lay down within the flimsy shelter.

Walking quickly to her rover, she pulled out a jerry can of water, and issueing orders to the natives in Swahili, soon had the camp really buzzing. She returned to the bull talking constantly, while opening the "can." With a big show, she tasted it, patted her face and spilling more petted the animal's trunk. A very skittish native bowed, handing her a large round pan four inches deep and eighteen inches in diameter, which she filled; And lifting the trunk put the end by the pan. Still talking with soothing sounds, Aquina walked around estimating where the bull's rear knees would touch the ground. In each spot, she felt for stones and such with both hands until satisfied then thoroughly wetted each area, doing the same for the elbows of the front legs.

Setting the empty can down out of the way, she uttered new sounds, new words, and with a sigh the bull slowly bent its rear legs kneeling in the cool water on each side. Then the front legs, with the enormous elbows sitting in the two little pools, and with a slight grunt the bull is down; but Aquina knew it was a position he couldn't maintain to long.

Changing the tone, inflection to a distinct husky monotone, she kept up the chant until the bull drifted off, "to think of his cows." A native who had put candle wax in his ears as had all the other people from her urging, handed a pair of pliers to her. Aquina quickly cleaned the area with alcohol, and gripping the broken end of the thorn . . . pulled suddenly. She gazed at the thorn, amazed at its size . . . about as big as her forefinger and two inches long tapering to a long thin point, represented by another two plus inches. Working fast she tore off a bit of rag soaked it in alcohol, wrapped it once on her smaller finger and began cleaning the wound.

The native kept looking fearfully at the bull, as indeed everyone kept looking at one-another expecting the bull to roar with pain; but nothing happened, his breathing was normal and very much still in dreamland.

After repeating the cleaning process many times, she is rewarded to see pink flesh and bright red blood ooze into the gradually closing wound. Dabbing at the blood, she sprinkled some sulphur into it, and opened the tube of Dien's special salve. Aquina rubbed it into the wound and around it, and with seven foot strips of torn sheet, she put a bit of cotton on top of the salve wrapping the bandage over it twice tying it secure.

She slowly got to her feet, stretched, and wrapped up her "medical kit" putting it safely away. The native, casting furtive glances at the bull, cleaned up everything else. Wiping the perspiration from her forehead, she filled a cup with cognac, and drank most of it in two gulps. She went back outside and stood for several seconds admiring the bull. A few more yards and standing next to the massive head and trunk, she began humming lightly. As she did, the eyes opened and the tip of the trunk moved once again resuming, rubbing her back.

The difference in the animal's noises wasn't lost on the natives black or white. And the wolf, shaking off unwanted sleep, came over and sat on his haunches leaning against his mistress. With a sizeable grunt the bull raised himself on the two massive forelegs, followed by one hindleg at a time. Still talking, Aquina went around with a freshly filled pan and rag washing off the elbows and knees inspecting the skin for any serious abrasion in the wrinkles. Several times the bull raised its left foreleg each time putting it down with greater force. Only for a minute or so then stopped, letting out a long sigh and other smaller sounds.

Some more sounds, different though, as the camp looked on she went into her tent re-appearing in seconds wearing the sandals given to her by the masai. The men in the camp did a double-take as the trunk went around her waist, picking her up effortlessly. She put one foot on the left tusk and immediately it unwound, curled up a bit . . . . and she stepped on it then crawled quickly up behind the massive head.

Aquina grunted a little doing a total "split" straddling the top of the neck area with her legs. With a giggle and a wee laugh, she waved to the camp, and told the wolf "to stay," and she would be right back. Well she didn't come right back, but spent the afternoon riding the bull. For the men, who had their hearts in their throats most of the time, they smiled nervously shaking their heads in wonder. A few of the men drove back to the compound picking up the families and cameras. Most of the time she was within sight of her friends who snapped away taking pictures as if there was no tomorrow.

She loved it, the view is just spectacular and for all his mighty power, the pachyderm was gentle with her . . . not moving to fast, gently going under trees to feed. And for her part, she cut down small leafy branches for the calves. Meanwhile, as the afternoon dragged on and the shadows lengthened, she turned the animal toward the camp. And the balance of the late afternoon and evening was equally enjoyable. Though each time she had an "experience," it seemed life became just that much more hectic. It reached such a level as too be a definite hinderance. Aquina felt to pressured to go into town, where like it or not, she would be harassed by the curious and meddlesome.

The very next night, while Aquina slept, for what was her normal period, the wolf ventured only a few yards away to relieve himself. Rounding a bush he surprised a medium-sized, very deadly snake. In an instant the snake struck. A few seconds the bewildered wolf staggered into the tent whimpering plaintively. Aquina awoke immediately, got-up and sat down on the floor next to the wolf, and held him. She saw the blood oozing from the two closely spaced punctures and guessed the cause. Trying to check the upsurge of emotion. Aquina began humming then sang in a low throaty voice . . . . eyes filled and spilled over as she lulled her faithful companion to sleep for the last time.

Taking the long handled shovel from the rover, she dug a four foot deep hole. And cradling her friend now wrapped in a sheet, set him down gently, and covered him humming the sounds he enjoyed. Though cold and stiff, she would never forget him, but would remain in her heart as a warm robust member of "her" forest.

She had piled stone to form a small cairn and sat through the night humming. At dawn with swollen red eyes, she went-off by herself, walking, sometimes sitting humming for hours. Although there were plenty around, no animal came close. She walked unhindered though watched by scores of ground and aerial species alike.

Aquina spent the last week of august '46 with them and moved-on to Kijabe for several weeks. And moved-on again the last week of september to Embu. Thence into Fort Hall on october, and Thika in november. The third week in december saw her ensconced once again at the same hotel in Nairobi. She spent the entire week buying gifts for each of her friends, returning the trailer to the dealer, making arrangements for passage on the first decent ship. For Christmas, a wednesday, the hotel launched a sizeable party attended by not only her friends, but many others as well. She gave out all the gifts, and to the family among her circle of friends who had the most need, she gave the rover, and all its remaining supplies.

However, she did keep the black sniper's rifle as well as a quantity of full clips.

She departed Nairobi on the 30 th., closed her accounts at the bank that very morning and boarded the train for Mombasa, and her reserved hotel room. And as soon as she checked-in, Aquina sent a cable to Dien outlining scheduled destinations, but little else. She spent the evening with champagne and her thoughts, and the hustle-n-bustle of the city's activity, that continued well into the late evening.

A bright and early tuesday morning, the 31 st., she was ready. The hotel had all of her trunks and luggage brought to the ship including the black engraved gun case; she carried the small cosmetic case and shoulder bag by herself. Aquina went aboard soon after, accepted what turned out to be a fair size suite and began the laborious task of unpacking necessary lingerie, and outer wear.

She put in an appearance that evening in the dining room and enjoyed the meal with blessed little attention paid to her except for admiring glances from the men, and some envious . . . . from the women. The following morning she stayed in the cabin, reading and filling a number of pages within her diary. A precious collection of both pleasant, and tearful memories, and accurate accounts of her experiences with many varieties of wild animals.

CHAP. 44

That afternoon, jan. 1st., '47, the large packet departed on the tide. This particular packet was both larger and a little faster than the last ship she had been on, and more luxurious. And less than an hour they're underway from the harbor, she stood casually at the starboard rail gazing out at the blue-green indian ocean. The captain politely interrupted her reverie, chatted for a moment, then asked if she would dine at his table on a continuing basis. Aquina smiled, and said . . . "yes, thank you captain." He smiled, bowed his head then walked to the gangway climbing back up to the bridge deck.

Weather is glorious, and the sea calm, and serene, She thought, "how like the big bull . . . gentle and mellow, but a raging deadly force when angered." She smiled and resumed her walk along the deck sometimes lost in thought, reliving recent events.

One week and five hours later the ship arrived at its first port-of-call, Karachi. Very few passengers went ashore as the stop was mainly for the purpose of off loading cargo. Early the next morning, thursday, the 9th., she was awakened by the noises and motion in the ship as it moved away from the pier. At noon, two days later, the ship rounded Colaba Point turning to port, coming steadily around entering the harbor at Bombay. It continued, giving "middle ground" a wide berth, for a bit over a mile. Slowing to a bare crawl, expecting to go inside of Alexander Dock, and therefore into the center of the "terminus," but because of delays in off loading other ships the small tug moved them to the harbor side of the "terminus."

The total lay-over because of delays et-cetera, amounted to ten days, of which, she spent on board ship with but two excursions into the city. And on those two occasions, the captain accompanied her for both . . . . safety sake and his own personal reasons. It was a pleasant experience to be guided around by a more willful man for a change. And when after their second trip ended, and they both stood at the door to her suite . . . the captain attempted a gentle kiss, she made no attempt to stop him. He bowed smiling, and said "goodnight," and began to walk away as she stepped inside closing the door behind her.

Afternoon of the 21st., the ship departed Bombay for Mangalore. A short trip and somewhat monotonous starting and stopping, like a country railroad. Inanyevent the packet arrived at 10a.m., on the 23rd . . . They immediately not only off loaded cargo, but also spent many hours re-loading. She stayed on board displaying no interest in going ashore, but content to watch the activity.

One o-clock in the afternoon on the 28th., the ship again departed with the tide, this time for Madras. Steaming around the indian ocean peninsula in excellent weather, the wind not rising above 14 knots, began pulling into Madras at 4p.m., on the 31st . . . There, it was both to take on passengers and cargo; however, Aquina still stayed on board content, listening to music in the first class passenger lounge.

February 3rd., departed for Calcutta, arriving at 8 a.m., on the 6th . . . She learned from the exec. The packet would remain in Calcutta for two weeks, and asked him, "if he was free . . ." The officer smiled and stammered as surprise gave way to confidence. He readily accepted, and a few hours later was showing her some of the notable attractions. When the exec. had the "watch" the captain officiated, and visa-versa. That is not to say . . . she went ashore every day, on the contrary, many a day was spent reading or she could be found sitting in a chair sketching animals, or a portion of the city.

Inanyevent, the packet departed on the early morning tide . . . . it was the 20th., bound for Rangoon. Although the wind shifted and picked up speed, the weather did not seriously change. Though it did briefly shower as the ship was pulling into the dock, but ended moments later just after the ship's lines were made secure.

It was about . . . eight-fourty a.m. on the 24th., and already she could feel the humidity. As in Calcutta, the captain and exec. rotated showing her only the best parts of the city. Like the other cities, she was struck by the poor, and the wide rift separating them from even the middle class. What she saw, though only a small fragment of the people, left a lasting imprint on her mind.

The evenings, or at least part of them, was devoted to her diary. On the 6th., a thursday, for Singapore.

CHAP. 45

It rained during most of the trip, and on the 11th., pulling in around four-thirty p.m., it had tapered off to almost nothing. Not withstanding, telltale signs of the past war were still plenty evident.

She stood on deck gazing at new construction and further to her right . . . repair work, but couldn't tell exactly what type. The contrasts between the types of architecture drew repeated glances, and occasionally, she shook her head at what appeared to be flimsy structures.

Aquina, soon bored of looking out at the city and shifted her gaze to what was happening on the dock, and the recently secured boarding ramp. At that moment four oriental men came up the ramp carrying baggage, and instantly disliked them feeling comfort in the idea of the luger held securely in her bag. Other passengers boarded, but none of them illicited any special feelings good or bad. With a sigh, Aquina turned to her left continuing her walk. Her thoughts went out to the wolf . . . . she missed him very much. She decided to return to her cabin and relax, perhaps take a nap. Laying down she cleared her mind, and concentrated on the rooms, then outside to the corridor. There was no sign of anything remotely suspicious until in her "mind's eye," she saw the four distasteful orientals in their room several decks below. The person giving orders held a sub-machine gun similar to a sten, while the others held menacing hand guns. She withdrew . . . . and a few heartbeats later opened her blue iridescent eyes. Shaken, not only by her ever growing capabilities, but also at what she had seen. She tried to think of who they might be after, and of course thought of herself.

Her hand trembled a trifle as she poured three fingers of cognac into a glass, capped the decanter immediately swallowing half. Sitting down next to the small bar, she marveled at how much her abilities had grown, as the cognac began to warm the stomach. Aquina realized the task of keeping tabs on the four "brutes" will not be anywhere as difficult for her, as versus that for a normal person. She caught herself, and smiled. "No, she thought. I am not like other's, but strange, and I think getting more strange." And from experiences and what she had already seen . . . . she became progressively more, and more, pleased about her "strangeness."

With that big step behind her, and the acceptance in her own mind . . . . growing . . . . so to did the power. The headaches all but disappeared in the days that followed; and while the captain or exec. Took her sightseeing, she found some things happened without conscious thought. Whereas in other respects, she had to concentrate on a particular thing or action. And each time, no matter how insignificant the gain or success it merely fueled her psyche. The more Aquina learned . . . . the more insatiable . . . . the more willful her mental drive became.

The morning of the 23rd., the packet departed for Bangkok. And all while, she kept the four thugs under almost constant scrutiny.

It proved to be almost two days, to the hour, when the ship nosed into the Chao Phraya, with two small powerful tugs to help the packet navigate the river. A winding, twisting course taking an hour and fourty-five minutes before they squeaked under the only bridge before their assigned dock came into view. Was the 25th., and noon by the time lines were made secure to the main dock.

Before Aquina finished lunch, she heard the sounds of men and machinery signaling either off loading, or loading was in progress. At two in the afternoon, she sipped hot tea, while watching passengers file up the gangway. One after another, and virtually all are orientals, but one in particular caught her eye. It wasn't his height, nor the black simple robe cinched about the waist with black leather, nor was it his apparent lofty age, or his wooden staff used for balance, nor his baldness and long white beard, but it was the feeling or sense of great inner strength and wisdom. A boy of approximately nine or ten, walked in front with the old man holding his hand.

The slight tingling sensation in his mind perplexed the old man causing him to look up. An instant later his eyes came to Aquina, and she smiled into his upturned face. He was fascinated, but only the eyebrows moved. Another several feet and he looked up again as if to make sure she was really there.

Soon both are standing on the main deck, received a cabin number and immediately walked in her direction. With an elegant bow and smile, he addressed her in French. Aquina responded in kind. However, she became curious during subsequent dialogue when the old man kept shifting his gaze from her hair to her eyes, and back again. Seconds passed before the old man and boy went below to their cabin.

Aquina didn't see them in the first class dining room, and assumed they were eating below deck. She finished a light dinner and sipped a delicious white wine while listening to the exec. add additional commentary to a wartime episode shared with the captain. In her mind's eye, she saw the four brutes sneaking down a familiar corridor, then . . . . from a connecting corridor the old man and boy slowly approach. Very convincingly, she feigned a migraine, and excusing herself, and the need for a sympathetic escort . . . . Aquina walked out occasionally rubbing her forehead.

Once out of the dining room and around the corner, she ran for the nearest stairwell. First, second, third deck . . . alighting from the last step . . . she quickly pulled off her shoes and ran down the corridor, athwartship's, down the connecting corridor, and silently leaned against the wall inches from the corner. About thirty feet down the four gunmen were talking loudly at the old man. She had the luger in her right hand safety off . . . . and concentrated very hard getting angrier by the second. Two of the thugs began moaning each holding their head with first their empty hand, then both hands dropping the guns in the process. The one with the sub-machine gun is wincing in pain from a very bad headache, migraine, while the fourth also began moaning. At the precise second the automatic weapon lowered, she swung around the corner firing two rounds. Both smashed into the leader's head killing him instantly. The first two had already collapsed as Aquina walked closer to the fourth man, the old man trying to comfort the boy was not looking, for who looked into the ghastly visage displayed on her face, screamed . . . . and collapsed, dead . . . .

She took a deep breath exhaling slowly, then thumbed the safety to the on position restoring the luger to her bag. The old gentleman bowed twice, and in French, said . . . he would include her in his prayers each day. It was the boy's turn, and he voiced a similar sentiment referring to the old man as "Master Chu."

Aquina wondered . . . . "master of what?" Barely completing the thought . . . . "Several ship's officers, captain included coming this way. Allow me to do the talking." The old man nodded looking at her with keen interest. A few seconds more and the captain, and three other officers jogged around the corner slowing to a fast walk. The officers began checking those laying on the deck, the captain looked on, then directed his attention to Aquina, not so much as a glance at the old man and boy. "Your Highness. What happened here?" He said after bowing. The old man had just been comforting the boy, but snapped his head up looking up with intense interest. His reaction brought on by the captain's form of address.

"After taking two aspirin, I sought this gentleman hoping to ask questions about Bangkok. Before reaching that corner, there, I heard the bolt from that sub-machine gun being pulled back. It's a sound I am not likely to forget. So, I leaned against the wall, drew my luger . . . . stepped around the corner and fired twice, and you arrived only a minute, or so, later." She smiled looking innocent and vulnerable. "And what of these others, Your Highness?"

Several of the officers stood waiting to interject, while the corridor filled with orientals. "Captain there isn't a mark on any of these, but I'd say they died of fright." The captain looked skeptical and unsure, possibly for the first time in his career. He looked at Aquina who smiled and gave only a hint of a shrug from beautiful bare shoulders.

Gazing at the one she had shot. "Your two rounds hit this one in the forehead and face, superb shooting under difficult circumstances. Your wartime reputation, I believe is well founded, Your Highness. Yes . . . . I can easily visualize Your Highness sitting atop a former nazi tiger tank." He paused. "Inanyevent, I shall log this episode and your involvement as justifiable homicide. And I shall notify the city police. There is no reason to bother Your Highness further." Then he bowed, again and began issueing orders for the removal of the bodies.

The crowd of orientals had been chattering back-n-forth excitedly especially when the old master bowed low . . . . the show-indication of honor and respect, to the tall european woman. He opened the door to his cabin, and in french asked her to enter. Aquina nodded and replied she would . . . . and did. It was aglow with soft light supplied by many candles with the scent aroma of incense filled her nose, she thought it a strangely comfortable and secure cabin.

Watching closely for each reaction in the face or hand, each nuance, the old master's eyes followed as Aquina continued her casual inspection of the room. She smiled at the diminutive statue of Buddha, and continued her eyes, her gaze fixed upon a small scroll hanging on the wall. Canting her head first one way . . . then the other, Aquina studied the symbols carefully.

She turned toward the old oriental. "Excuse me, but this scroll looks oddly familiar, and yet it doesn't." Again, she fixed her eyes on it concentrating. The old master smiled faintly eyes twinkled, as hope soared in his heart. He described the scroll and indicated it as an ancient Confucian prophecy. Old hands trembled slightly from high excitement as a delicate rice wine was poured into two tiny cups. She accepted one with a nod and waited, after sitting down, for the master to drink first. Although he said nothing, that simple act of courtesy meant much. After some seconds of not being able to look deeply into her eyes, he averted them taking a small sip from the cup. Still she did not drink.

Aquina sat not staring at him, but studying the smooth face when he spoke. "You do not drink?" "I sense many questions . . . you wish to ask me . . . questions of importance." He nodded. "True, but there is time." She nodded, and with the fingers of both hands on the cup . . . daintily sipped making no sound. When she finished the contents, and had put the cup down, it signaled the start of the old man's questions.

However, he asked only three . . . and to some extent they are enigmatic, and each had more than one part. She thought for some seconds before beginning to answer the first question. And, it seemed to her as though each answer delighted the old master, but nary a sign on his face to indicate the range or amount of pleasure. She did not consciously "feel" his mind, but nonetheless detected the emotion in a small way. When all of her answers were given, the old man sat motionless for many seconds then smiled reassuringly.

The hour was late and bidding the old master goodnight, and smiling at the boy, who was already sleeping, she walked back taking the stairwells up to the main deck. During the brief trek, she tried to analyze why the interest in her, and what was the reason or motive behind the questions. She couldn't find a rational reason, but her furrowed brow smoothed out pleased that at least she had arrived in time to save two lives. That one thought made her smile, and, she started humming a light melody continuing well after arriving at her cabin door.

Four days later march 1st., the ship departed for its next port-of-call, Hong Kong.

CHAP. 46

The five days that followed were pleasant ones, with frequent visits by the old master and the boy. Their conversations were sometimes lengthy and animated, but educational, especially the first meeting after leaving Bangkok. With care the old master explained many things about his native country, Korea. One of those first presented was the unmun, the 24 letter phonetic alphabet. The expert tutelage was rewarded in a mere few hours, as most foreigners picked it up adequately enough after some twenty-four hours practice. Aquina is able to speak competently with only four hours of unbroken concentration, and practice. The sounds are soft with a lilt she found refreshing. Very quickly and skillfully, she spoke the language and it tended to catch many unaware. Of course speaking the language was only the first phase, writing is a whole different thing.

The 6th., of march at 6:30 a.m., the ship entered the West Lamma channel, and began the long turn to starboard docking on the Kowloon side.

Aquina had changed into an appropriate outfit in white with soft blue accenting and stood with the old master as the gangway was lowered and secured in place. Days earlier, she agreed when asked if he might serve as a humble guide, thereby increasing the enjoyment of a beautiful and unique city. The greater part of six days, she spent touring the city, while the early and mid-morning and late afternoons, she could be found sketching any one of the warships riding at their anchorages. Usually during these periods one or more ship's officers hovered around only to glad to answer her questions.

There are two cruisers, and a carrier . . . . and Aquina sketched each one., plus lesser ships. It is however, the carrier and cruisers that captured the lion's share of her interest. Of those ships, she did five or six sketch's each from different angles. Her sketchs became progressively more refined . . . . until they became virtual scale reproductions. And to please the captain, she did two of the packet, which elevated his pride to new heights.

As it turned out many officers from the ships at anchor saw her in different parts of Hong Kong, with the old gentleman, and inquired about her. It happened to be the exec. or number one, from the english cruiser, who provided the information, and her war-time nom de' plume. As it is the english officer had been waiting for the opportunity to broach the subject with his captain. The senior officers agreed, and organized the entire program. It only required the nod from each respective captain. A mere formality, but a necessary one, a thing that could not be circumvented. And as things turned out the captains involved returned to their ships that very evening and found themselves set-upon by their officers all requesting the same thing.

The same evening each of the three captains conferred with each other coming to an agreement . . . they would stand-by for reasons of protocol, but then leave the proceedings in the hands of each executive officer. As befitting the senior captain aboard the carrier, the flagship of the task force, he personally issued the invitation. Aquina was asked to the packet's bridge, where listening on the ship's phone, she happily accepted the captain's invitation. A boat would pick her up at the passenger landing, at 9 a.m., in the morning, a few yards from the packet, and convey her to the carrier, and from there to the other ships.

With Aquina's acceptance each ship mimeographed, from a master prepared by the english exec. officer, enough so that each officer of every ship had three copies. Each ship was informed, that is . . . . each "division" aboard has an officer and a few junior officers as assistants. Each officer held a copy plus the third was affixed to the bulletin board. Through the "squawk box" each crew member went to his division work place. There the officers briefed their men about royal visitors, and this one in particular, and the heavy particulars about this princess, some pertinent facts and a large photograph underneath explaining some noteworthy things about her, and the proper forms of address.

For hours each crew went to work with a vengeance cleaning their ship, after which attention was given to uniforms.

Minutes before the appointed time, Aquina stood on the landing in white silk blouse, dark blue knee length just an inch over the knee, full skirt, and a matching jacket with white scroll-work around each pocket, and with hat and low shoes, and shoulder bag to match. Aquina watched as the captain's gig rapidly approached. Still high on a plane until about one hundred-fifty feet away then it slowed down dramatically. With an expert's touch the boat barely nudged the bumpers, as seamen hopped onto the landing and held the boat as a handsome officer stepped out and saluted. They exchanged a normal enough greeting, but she noticed the nervousness in the officer, and smiled. She stepped aboard, sat, and in seconds was heading out into the harbor. As the gig passed inbetween first a few destroyers, then cruisers as shrill boatswain whistles echoed across the harbor . . . . "Attention to port, . . . attention to starboard . . . salute . . . two!" She looked up at each ship, and saw men lining the sides, on every ship, and the cruisers especially, she thought . . . . "it must be hundreds of men" lined the sides on multiple levels.

The carrier loomed larger until it seemed to Aquina a sheer cliff, only a small part of the mountain, with men shoulder-to-shoulder spanning its length. Again the gig slowed coming closer to the metal landing and stairway. She was helped out by an officer who saluted first, then helped her up the short stairway, the small landing thence through a 10x10 foot opening. Instantly, she is "pipped" aboard as marine guards, a double line, were brought to attention as she walked a few yards more, directed and escorted by officers and marine guards, to an airplane elevator. Whereupon it began to rise slowly. Soon she came into view of the crew assembled on both ends of the superstructure, as a line of officers starting from the elevator extended across the wide flightdeck to a doorway flanked by marine guards. Off to the left a band is playing one of the much loved songs from her country, and rising swiftly up to the flag yard . . . . her country's flag, and a blue bunting just below it, undulating in the breeze.

She began with the captain, who saluted once for himself and crew, the exec. Standing next to her was introduced by the captain, who walked to one side and just behind her. Each officer introduced himself with a broad grin and shook her hand, and to their pleasant surprise, as the captain did, a light firm hand from the princess.

From the moment she stepped through the door into the superstructure not only did the tour begin there, but also a unique education that was to become a passion. Each and every aspect that was explained found its way like photographs, to the mental file in her sub-concious and the same with each space and area shown. During, which she asked many questions and the information gleaned went into the same mental file as the visual data. In a comparatively short time, she learned why certain things had to be done in a certain way, the proper location of supplies, and materials, and matters of ordinance and structural integrity.

It is a few minutes after 11a.m., when the touring party arrived in the vicinity of "officer's country." A short while later she put her bag down and removed her hat and jacket before sitting at the long table. She commented on the large spacious officer's dining room, the table, but especially praised the ship and its crew. A quick lunch and an apertiff, and she departed for the english cruiser.

The same gig did the honors. Though protocol was observed according to the same basic rules, the english take great pains, and provide much in the way of flourishes and pomp to the ceremony. And as in their own royal family, there exists a special place . . . . special care and sentiment for young princess's. But this person happened to be a heroine to them and everything was extra crisp precision about the ship.

Aquina is piped aboard as "ratings" lined the starboard side, and when the order was given for attention . . . . all . . . . many hundreds of pairs of boots and hands slapped heel and trousers simultaneously. She gained the main deck to the boatswain's pipe, and as the ship's band played the same song, as they played on the carrier, she nodded her head, and a slight bow of the head, toward their country's flag displayed from the fantail. Turning a little she stepped off the gangway landing, met the captain and the double line of officers. In minutes she stood within the lounge, took off her hat, put the shoulder bag next to it, and drank the freshly prepared cup of tea.

From the one cruiser to the other, finding them basically similar, but noting the differences and the similarities. The tour and the day wound down, and fourty-five minutes later sat on her bed, kicked off uncomfortable shoes and partially undressed.

The next morning sipping hot tea and stepping outside, she noticed the harbor empty of the warships. And so to did the packet, on the late morning tide after taking on last minute passengers. From the 17th., to their arrival in Inch'on, Korea, the packet's last stop, Master Chu instructed her in her "writing" and the philosophy of the temple.

The day before, Aquina had accepted an invitation to visit and continue her studies at the temple. That evening, she repacked the stalwart trunks tight, and locked each one secured leaving three pullman type and three smaller bags. In the three pullmans went blouses, some skirts, shoes, and assorted underwear, plus almost all the "hard service" clothes purchased in Nairobi. The handsome hand guns and ammunition she loaded into the small case already loaded, with same, and her jewels and currency. With arrangements seen too, monies paid and the trunks stamped, and ticket stubs affixed, were finally moved an hour later to the passenger storage hold, to be shipped home.

Within an hour the three boarded a much smaller ship plying the coastal trade, and departed heading north for Namp'o. They were expected, for as soon as the small ship docked, a small group of monks came aboard. Attired in black and white robes, and bald, they bowed with deep respect to Master Chu. It was at that instant he introduced Aquina to them; however, they being initiates betrayed their emotion as slight though it might be. Their eyes grew a little more open and they bowed voicing an appropriate greeting. She bowed answering their greeting with one of her own. That brought more surprise, as they picked up all baggage and walked slowly down the gangway.

CHAP. 47

Tied to the dock is a sampan type of boat decorated in red, blue, and gold colors, with several more monks on board tending lines et-cetera. It appeared, she had more effect on them when the master introduced her. Varied types of gulls and birds hovered or were flying in random patterns as the boat left the dock, the little engine chugging faithfully. Looking out over the water, and the low flying birds, she wondered why the master also referred to her as "little star." She had no explaination . . . suddenly, a gust dislodged her hat, and carried it wide some yards out into the river. The sizeable pin laid on the deck and was picked up by the little boy, when Aquina ran to the rail. She looked up and with several high-pitch whistles, . . . pointed to the hat riding the little wave crests rapidly floating away. The one large gull arcing directly in her gaze called out with two crys of its own, and with a long sweeping glide canted its wings . . . . fluttered its wings grabbing the hat and gained altitude quickly. A few seconds and the bird arced around one way then another coming in low canted its wings back greatly reducing its speed until almost hovering, dropped the hat into Aquina's hands. Quickly wrapping her right hand and wrist with a heavy rag . . . . and extended the hand in one fluid motion. Instead of the shrill whistle, she made another much softer one rewarded with the gull landing gently on the raised hand.

Every monk looked on including the master and crew, trying to watch and still not hit anything in the river, as Aquina offered a bare well manicured nail up and gently stroked its beak. Changing the sound the bird turned its head to one side then the other, eyeing the small table to her left. Some small chunks of bread . . . . and one-by-one, she held the pieces very close to the sharp beak, and it took each piece from her fingers gently. A few moments and Aquina stroked its head with the same forefinger, changed the sounds and raised her hand. The bird immediately took to wing up, up and flew back toward the main dock.

Aquina picked up the hat and tried to reshape it despite its condition, and the attitude or aura of carefree nonchalance indicated to the master, who's heart is soaring like that of the gulls, that Aquina looked upon the act as a common everyday practice. And as the hours passed, she felt intuitively there was a greater purpose . . . . that she study at this temple, where ever it might be. It seemed as though she is subtlely being manipulated, a sequence of events that began long ago when she was but a child, but the feeling soon passed.

Master Chu watched, observing his initiates and the effect "little star" had on them. With a veiled smile, he visualized their consternation when her full capabilities became known. Chu also realized there was a great deal he did not know about this woman; but, the fact she is "little star" . . . . there was no doubt. Upon their return, he will give thanks to the great Buddha for honoring his humble servant. Their temple, he thought to himself, had been chosen by the great Buddha, and Sien Wou Chu vowed to teach their royal charge everything he and the temple possessed in the way of knowledge.

They passed Songnim, still heading north following the wide river inland. Hours later the wide part of the river ended narrowing substantially, but the boat continued on navigating easily past other boats and miscellaneous craft lining the river. People in other boats bowed as they passed, and Aquina felt their stares. At 2:30 pm., the boat plied the river heading northeast through P'yong-yang; but by 4pm., rounded a bend in the river again heading north. She moved sitting a little lower as the breeze made it more than just chilly.

Around a tight bend at 5pm., and a short time later a dog-leg north again, but soon the boat encountered the river branching off like a "T", and the helmsman went to the right. The countryside is hilly and cultivated dotted with small poor buildings here-n-there. A few more miles as the narrowed river undulated around, and one such bend Aquina saw a dock only some hundred feet from them. With the sun beginning to wan, it is like a rich painting with the colors of robes and dock showcasing each other. A few minutes and the boat was being made secure against the apparently solid dock despite her qualms at its construction.

It was not difficult to pick out the instructors from the students even senior students, and with the bowing concluded, Master Chu introduced Aquina, first the european, or western name and title, and then as "little star." And again she picked out reactions, subtle as they were . . . . but detectable. The instructors and the senior initiates felt the energy that permeated from her, as did the master. And leaving the dock area the crowd made its way up the many steps inset into the sloping hill then began to cross a small meadow . . . and there about eighty yards in the distance rose the stone walls of the temple grounds.

Just beyond, she saw the many tiers of roofs as the temple itself rose majestically above the walls. The tops of other buildings could just barely be seen, and the width and length of the wall before ending gave her the sense of a substantial size or area lay within the walls. The master explained there had never been a female within the temple walls, and therefore a room had been prepared amongst those reserved for instructors and other masters. And to take that evening to think and unpack only the essentials, Aquina allowed her mind unbridled . . . . to roam, to walk the compound, to discreetly touch the minds of others and learn. She slept soundly with a hint of a smile on her lips.

Early the next morning, she was summoned before the council of masters, each an instructor, while Master Chu sat in the center. It is silent, the incense filled her nose as dozens of candles illuminated the stone chamber with a soothing glow. First one master then the others asked questions always in a soft voice, but probing her for some underlying reason. And slowly, haltingly Aquina explained her feelings beginning when she was a child discovering the forest and its animals, and the world beyond the forest. Of animal skins worn by the tribes living on the western shore who were always fighting with spear and sword.

Aquina went on about the animals, going into detail regarding the care, love and protection she afforded them, the realization of the basic law governing the "food chain." And how she made an area, about the size of the meadow outside, where the hunter co-existed in peace and harmony with the hunted. Where in the open courtyard of her home . . . . she cared for the sick, injured, and helped deliver the young, of the great bears and wolf packs, and the birds of prey . . . . And explained how she scared the tribes, and forbade them to enter the forest beyond a certain point, and the forest a sanctuary, where anything other than man would find freedom and safety.

She skipped over the intervening years, accept to explain how she and her aunt gradually made their way into society as the state of civilization significantly improved.

Aquina continued with her school years, and episodes at the Univ. at Hamburg, both the first time and second; but when she referred to Kurt . . . . her voice cracked, and tears dampened her cheeks. Witholding nothing, Aquina told what she felt when he was killed, and the callousness afterwards, the battles and the seemingly incessant killing. The biggest, the most dangerous was the guilt, and how the world would not leave her in peace. They, the curious and meddlesome, always found her, harrrassed and meddled because she is different. Aquina went on about all the noteworthy experiences of her cruise and vacation, from the "circle of stone" in England, to africa's animals and her necklaces from the masai. And concluded with the encounter of the four thugs trying to hurt Master Chu, and the young boy.

After many moments of silence one of the masters, in a voice laced with a high degree of excitement, asked if she wished to join the temple, and if so . . . . why? "Yes." And she paused looking at each of them, "for knowledge and wisdom, the true wealth." "You then agree to place yourself in our tutorage," stated one of the masters. "I will," she said in flawless Korean. A moment of reflection passed, as the masters embraced the sweetness of being chosen to fulfill the "Confucian Prophecy."

At the end of that moment, Master Chu spoke the formal acceptance. "We accept you little star, instruction begins today." Aquina was shown to her room where six loose fitting tops and bottoms, slacks also loose, awaited plus a robe of sky blue for the temple. Immediately after changing clothes, her long tresses were braided into four fat long lines. Afterwards in high-laced sandals, she was shown around all areas of the temple grounds, work-out areas, tumbling, meditation and prayer, animal compound and the weapons areas.

She started in the tumbling area under the watchful eyes of a master. Initially it is by example, Aquina copied whatever was demonstrated and did it well; but, the exercises became more difficult and strenuous. And they to . . . . became easier as her self-confidence increased.

Initially during the evenings, she continued studying and perfecting necessary writing skills. When she had mastered the artful script sufficiently, and had only nuances of the art yet to study, she began every evening, but one for sleep, the seventh or eighth depending on how she felt . . . . with tumbling exercises and practice, and finished with a visit to the animals. Separated from the others in a stout enclosure, a young tigress not yet full grown and not exactly friendly, but it didn't deter Aquina.

On any given night, she hummed, talked and played with the other animals for a time, then gravitated next door. Very quickly the animal not only accepted her as others had, but expected the nightly visits, the humming and "talk," and most of all . . . . the gentle scratching behind the ears, chest, and along the spine on top from head to tail. At the outset, Aquina's nightly practice was done away from the few sentry's and play period, therefore unknown to the masters. Until one evening, the fifth, one master happened to be up. Walking outside, but still in the shadows looked-on as Aquina practiced her tumbling. Hour after hour he watched, much pleased with her progress and continued to watch when she splashed a little water on her face from the small fountain, and with that feeling of soaring excitement inside . . . . he saw her sit against the animal enclosure and speak-n-play with the animals. And next door the large cat was mewling softly. Soon she moved over to the cat, and in the moonlight, sitting in the lotus position, the paw on her knee, Aquina reached inside talking to the tigress in a language unknown to him, but one the cat obviously understood. It murmured softly and licked her hand as she moved from petting the side . . . to its chin.

With the coming of dawn the master stepped inside to quickly confer with his fellows. They tested Aquina repeatedly forcing the development of her mental capabilities, and while doing so knowledge of her nightly workouts and other things filtered down to the dozens upon dozens of other initiates. Her exercise schedule was increased and the periods of reflection, and meditation kept pace. As time passed her popularity increased with the young men learning form her as she learned from them. From the seniors to the new initiates their respect, and feelings grew and continued to grow as Aquina/little star progressed. This dramatically increased when the initiates learned, she rested but once in eight days, and then for only a few hours, and ate three perhaps four times lightly, during each lengthy period. When the masters first discovered her abnormality they instantly recognized the awesome potential in this, and set to work using this period for instruction. She was still however allowed time with the animals.

The months passed, to april, to may and so on. And the passage of time saw her become an "artful butterfly" in gymnastics, Master Wo nodded and smiled. She bowed smiling in return; for to earn the nod and open smile meant she had fulfilled her potential in that art form.

While studies and discussions into philosophy continued, she was introduced to the bow. Though at first, she could barely pull the string back using only physical strength. Aquina persisted with an almost fanatical zeal. She was given certain exercises to build physical strength in the shoulders and arms.

A consistent work-out that yielded more than the just upper body shoulder and arm strength . . . it firmed and strengthened youthful breast muscle, and tissue to a high degree. As far as breast size, Aquina had always been "amply endowed," but many months had increased the blood flow measureably. Consequently the formidable amounts of fatty tissue had firmed, expanded due to underlying muscle development under the breasts resulting in a full "D" going to a bountiful "DD," going from 39" to 41" . . . .

All her activities contributed to the firming, slimming experienced throughout the whole body. Her hips still wide are now firm, legs in general had firmed-up even her tush had tightened to a more natural curve. The face mirrored the strength and vitality pulsating within the body.

As '47 drew to a close, she had mastered the bow, even blindfolded, she could hit any target or combination there-of, moving or stationery. And with the first day of '48, Master

Wo introduced "little star" to the long staff of hardwood and the steel pike. But the new year celebration, jan. 21st., to feb. 19th., briefly intervened. Those days were spent either in the temple, in prayer, meditation or around the several ice-covered garden pools. Where the masters gathered with their students and expounded on philosophy answering questions and explaining answers.

Time slipped by, march, april, and may. June arrived, and during the first week, Master Wo stood nodded and smiled. "You have done well little star. Walk with me." She bowed, smiling, said nothing but, she fell into step next to her teacher. They talked for almost an hour heading steadily toward the work-out area where the "dance" was being learned and practiced. Aquina began . . . . and worked hard displaying the same zeal for practice, and still more practice.

More months passed, with the first dance, lotus blossom, she was introduced into the second, that of "the butterfly." With marked degree of excellence in that dance she was introduced to a total of six more artful dances of grace and power. The schedule is brutal, building stamina, skill, mental discipline, toughening the hands and feet, and above all . . . . tests of will. Her mental prowess and steel hard force of will enabled her to rapidly outdistance the other initiates. Day and night she practiced all the basics, the advanced moves and sets, plus all the nuances of each.

The winter had come, she took no notice . . . . still practicing in light top and pants . . . bare foot. After each four hour period she stopped, stretched and wiped her face with snow . . . then began again. The moonlight became a soothing neighbor and friend during her lonely work-outs. Keeping her mind and consciousness on the exercise, she was only on occasion aware of a master's presence, and in such instances stopped immediately, bowing in his direction.

She had already won the coveted black belt, but as the year turned from '48 to '49 . . . . she is well beyond that point . . . . beyond any and all students.

She is introduced to the weapons, the last area and in some ways the easiest, for her. In days she threw the five or eight-pointed round skurgen with repeated and consistently deadly accuracy, so to the dirka. The two handle and chain followed, and the piock, a miniature sythe with 18" handle, 9" razor like curved blades with six feet of fine chain attached to the handles, the hand claw and corresponding claws for the feet, steel claws enabling one to climb sheer stone walls, and finally the straight sword. A blade 30" long and one inch wide and a razor with thick black handle for both hands, and a square guard, "the katana."

All activities stopped for the new year, '49 . . . she spent large amounts of time in meditation, and many hours within the temple. She exited feeling free for the first time since the war.

Morning of February 20th., Aquina began in ernest. It was clear to Master Wo, little star had already some instruction in the use of the sword. Soon it is march, then april, and bit-by-bit over a long period of months information leaked that little star was indeed in the temple. Small hamlets and villages in the area gave prayer to the great Buddha. And too information found its way in, but not welcome news. The northern communist factions were banding together and amassing troops and war material.

Although the situation continued all the masters upheld the belief no-one would dare hamper or damage the temple sanctuary. Aquina wasn't convinced, and concentrated harder with her practice . . . endeavoring to accomplish more in less time . . . and so she did. When the end of july arrived, Master Chu and the others came to a unanimous decision . . . . "Little Star" was ready.

Master Wo went to her, early on the 29th., smiled and bowed, gazing at her for a few seconds without speaking. Finally. "My heart sings with praise "Little Star". The prophecy has been realized with your excellence." He said softly. They talked for a time not as instructor and pupil, but now as colleagues.

Aquina had been given time to pack, meditate and prepare for the special ceremony. She gathered all belongings and clothes, and in a comparatively short time had the luggage ready to depart. Only the sky-blue robe was left on the spartan bed, planning to wear it when she departed. A short time later Master Wo entered bearing a black silk top and bottoms. And on top was a black belt interwoven with red and blue in bold stitching. This garment, with the tiger-dragon emblazed in scarlet and gold covering the entire back, she is to wear it to the ceremony. Master Wo, with unaccustomed emotion, rearranged her long braids into a cap on top while the ends dangled to her shoulders.

Properly attired, Aquina made her way slowly to the inner chamber of the temple. All the masters gathered forming two lines, one on either side of her. With the end of the prayer a brazier was uncovered, but she made no outward sign, nor was there any inner turmoil . . . . nothing but serenity. She blanked it from her mind, therefore no pain existed. A brand 8" long, a total height of 3" depicting the temple mark . . . . the fighting tiger-dragon . . . . facing each other, was seared into the back of her right shoulder, high and prominent. And so the silk top would not stick to the burned skin . . . a salve, specially prepared for such purposes was applied with a deft touch.

She bent over humming and a little singing said good-by to the animals. Retiring to her room for the last time, she changed into the light blue robe . . . . and sitting on the bed, a 32" long, by 6" by 6" . . . highly polished box, black and handsomely tooled, with an elegant leather sling. Opening it slowly, ... a faint smile at sight of the new glistening weapons, then quickly layed her silk uniform and belt inside. Only the shoulder bag and ornate box remained in the room. She knew the luggage would already be on the boat, and slung the box over her back along with the shoulder bag and walked outside.

The courtyard was conspicuous by its vacant silence. She is alone, everything was in its proper place . . . . but for one item. This was tradition, for no monk-priest was ever gone or separate from their temple; therefore no need existed for farewells. An ornately carved staff of hardwood, black from age . . . . a handsome gift lay against the large doors. Aquina grasped it in her hand, turned and with her right hand said a thing . . . a . . . sign to the animals. Each small one made its small cry, and then the tigress bellowed, the roar echoeing in and around the temple buildings.

A wink and she was silently through the door walking down the path to the boat. Not a sound from footfall or sandal disturbed the air as fleeting memories came forward, only to receed seconds later. She pulled up the hood on her robe, which concealed nothing from her, but did partially obscure face and hair from onlookers. In minutes she arrived on the landing and stepped onboard the boat, her bags in the middle, the crew bowed . . . . then quickly shoved-off heading downstream. And with the prevailing current in the river, the boat's speed was easily twice what it had been on her first journey.

During the trip, she reflected on the steady corroding political picture. And knowing war was inevitable decided to head south and do what she could for the refugee's and orphans.

Arriving at Namp'o, she boarded the afternoon's return run of the coastal freighter. With her baggage in a pile close to the small ship's superstructure, she bid the initiates adieu. Most took notice of the hooded figure in as discreet a way as possible. They knew it was a monk, but the fact of the obvious female form plus the robe's color and the ornate staff indicated a learned-one of high lofty rank, and it confused them. Many women and children sat around the hatches and against the sides, and Aquina scrutinized them and the crew. She noticed one boy of about nine years with a bandaged forearm. Trying to be brave he whimpered from pain. Silently, like the tiger, she stood before the knot of people assembled next to one of the hatches.

Kneeling, she gently touched the boy's hand with her own, and very softly . . . almost a whisper, she spoke to him. The tired pregnant mother woke and tried to move so she could bow, but was stopped gently by Aquina's left hand; and equally . . . gently touched the bulging abdomen. "A healthy daughter who will grow lithe and strong." All were looking-on listening, for the voice is distinctly feminine, as the boy looked at her questioningly. The mother reached out and touched Aquina's sleeve with eyes begging for reassurance, and said her name. "You . . . . carry the staff of a high monk, or high priest and are a woman?"

"Yes." Aquina said softly. "I am called Little Star, from Kodo'Kun temple." Those on either side overheard, and much whispering ensued as they bowed, nodded moving closer to watch and listen. All the while, she was unwrapping the soiled dirty bandage from the boy's arm, she held his eyes . . . cleaned the cut and bruise with alcohol from her bag, and with some of her salve on the wound, began bandaging it with a clean cloth. And not a sound from the boy's lips when she averted her gaze and looked at the mother. "It will heal quickly now." The mother nodded and tried to express her thanks, answered by a nod.

There were many such episodes during the following months, as she travelled south to Kunsan, Taejo`n, Cho`n ju, Kwang ju and Iri plus towns and hamlets inbetween. With her bags in a cart, drawn by two oxen, holding several women and children . . . . refugees. She met soldiers while travelling from city to city, town to town, but these were different than those in the north. The reports of cruelty, torture and indiscriminant robbery and murder caused her more than just concern. Aquina worried for the temple and the masters.

CHAP. 48

In the ensuing months "little star" did much to see to the need of ever increasing numbers fleeing to safety. The winter was harsh, especially for the refugees. She couldn't be everywhere at once, but that didn't stop her from trying. Of course the fact no-one ever saw her sleep, and aside from a cup of soup three times in seven or eight days, or eat as a normal human must . . . . all the talk and whispers helped. Usually no-one saw her come or go, especially at night . . . . and on the few occasions when she sat or meditated and refugees or others watched, animals came, it was treated and savored in quiet dignity.

It became a new year, '49 to '50, and the tension and reports from the north grew steadily worse. The months slipped by, and more and more displaced refugees came swelling facilities to the bursting point. Aquina continued to visit the places she had been the year before, and new localities around them helping wherever she was needed. Other then sending a few cables to Dien, Aquina had almost no contact with europeans. What she did have mystified them even more, than she did the Koreans.

June 25th., 1950, northern troops swarmed over the land heading south. Although partially checked by the courage and resourcefulness of the southern troops, their call for help was answered, in time. And with that answer came much needed supplies from many allies. Much of it in the beginning went to the war effort, but commodities such as medicine, surgical supplies, food and clothing, blankets . . . she not only arranged the purchase, and shipment from close geographically located neighbors, but was not above putting the bite on sympathetic allied commanders.

And as luck would have it . . . some of the allied commanders recognized her, or at least thought they did, but nonetheless word spread amongst the allies. Found usually with refugees, she was also known to frequent the hospitals visiting those in pain. Many sought her as the war went on, including those who were paid to gather news and pry into private lives. But try as they might, she was not found, instead to appear in another locality or appear immediately after the meddlers departed. Of course the koreans said virtually nothing, and it continued . . . . she came and went . . . where she pleased . . . when she pleased.

The hooded figure in light blue confounded the allies, and terrorized the enemy soldiers. She was a spector of doom for the enemy, and for the allies . . . . an enigma. Too a lonely frightened guard or a few men in a trench, she gave comfort in whatever language they understood. Helping them to understand, or pray was the greatest gift, and many allied soldiers reported seeing the robed female figure.

It was during the first year of the war for the allies, that certain prisoners had been taken to a base in the rear for interrogation. And as a coincidence, Aquina was not far away helping to deliver a boy, and tend the sick. At the allied base the interrogators . . . . korean and allied officers were harraging the prisoners with no success. The sizeable room was full, as guards stood with their weapons at the ready in case of trouble. Interrupting the shouting, cursing and confusion a loud bang on the door, loud enough to grab irate attention, and much displeasure from the officers present. With an angry retort the ranking officer ordered the guard to see who it was and get rid of them.

The door opened seemingly of its own volition. Looking up the irate officer stopped in mid-sentence, at sight of the robed figure casually and silently entering the room. The men stepped back opening an aisle, as the korean officers bowed deeply as she passed. Stopping, she put a seemingly delicate hand on the shoulder of a korean captain. "Your wife is well and nurses a boy." He mumbled from emotion his gratitude and prayers. "Give your prayers to Buddha, not me. I am but a humble servant." And with that she continued to walk toward the group of prisoners, who were not boastful or superior, but scared to death. Their fear was readily apparent, however one officer spoke up taunting her. "You have no special power, but made a priestess by those fool monks. We sacked and burned your temple and slaughtered all the monks, and their students." He stood defiant with an expression of contempt daring her to strike him.

A few heartbeats, suddenly the contemptuous officer's body jerked up on tiptoes as if picked-up under the arms. His expression quickly turned to fear then horror, when the clothes around his chest went tight. He struggled, swore and cursed . . . . all to no avail. A second passed he gasped for air as her energy filled the room and the man began to scream . . . . blood curdling screams. The chest was being crushed, as every person could plainly see, but nothing they could see touched him. His screaming continued as those outside the building cringed making the sign of the cross, or prayed silently, inside blood began coming out of the nose and mouth, the hands and arms flexing tearing at the unseen force, the legs and feet flaying the air no longer barely brushing the floor. A few heartbeats and blood ran freely soaking the grayish uniform, then slowly the head began turning to the right . . . . past the point it would normally stop. A loud crack and the grotesque shape was still. It continued to hang there for several seconds then dropped to the floor.

The balance of the prisoners dashed for the chairs, babbling a steady torrent of information and did not stop until divulging everything they knew or overheard. Most of them finished about the same time and stood together sheepishly occasionally looking at the terrible thing laying on the floor. A few heartbeats, and they held their heads with both hands moaning. Quickly it turned to agonizing screams . . . then nothing . . . collapsing to the floor . . . dead. The others begged, whimpered and begged some more . . . . but were soon screaming holding their heads, collapsing in death a few feet from the first group.

When she had turned to leave, their shocked and stupefied expressions greeted her and very few faces did anything but stare. The door opened . . . she walked through, it closed immediately after her, quietly. A second, or possibly two and the guards yanked it open expecting to see her, but nothing . . . and no-one saw anything out of the ordinary. Already with a considerable following by the end of the first year, it grew proportionately as the war continued. The years were not without pain, and great despair, and working with her people helped Aquina deal with her own terrible pain . . . the lose of Kodo'Kun Temple, and its people. But unlike the world war, she now possessed the wisdom, and the serentity to understand, to see a tiny part of the meaning . . . the reasons why it happened.

On july 31st., '53, a ninety day cease fire went into affect culminating in a truce. But the refugee problem was far from over, and she sent a cable to Dien, explaining in part the reason she had to stay. Aquina returned four days later, and received Dien's answer, and a faint smile at the words. "Glad everything goes well, stay a few more months." Actually it was may '58, and the refugee problem had been largely settled, and a sense of normalcy returned. It was time, and with the purchase of some fashionable new clothes, she packed her robes and changed into the chic new garments, and booked passage from Pusan to Tokyo.

CHAP. 49

State of the empire at this point in time was one of massive unrest. Being threatened from without by the raiders, and pirates and other enemies, plus unrest, and in some systems . . . open revolt. It was already known the outer systems had experienced open insurrection. Moreover, the old guard military leaders were showing open contempt for the emperor. The emperor's own court and assembly was rife with paid favors, totally corrupt legal authorities, and widespread gross abuses of power. The emperor was himself old, decadent, pleasure happy, whimsically abusive, contemptuous of the military, and gave power and favor to a select few. Moreover, he refused advice from appropriate counsel, held the people in open contempt, and overly taxed everyone including the nobility . . . . all except a select group.

It was not difficult to see the ruin, but if change did not happen soon all would be lost.

No one person, even the ministers knew how many plots were hatched against the emperor. Each day the intrigue grew worse, every day people were caught, and their plots exposed, with the suspects and other participants executed without trial. And each day . . . . the emperor . . . became more afraid, more paranoid. Until one succeeded and the hated ruler no longer had anything to concern himself, save what judgement had been decreed by the all powerful universal God . . . or Ancient One, as it and the lesser ones are affectionately called.

The official release for the emperor's death, read:

> "Aged emperor Solc'-eo-Hatr, had been repeatedly warned of
> Ill and precarious health for some time. Enormous pressures
> And problems at court, plus too heavy a work schedule was
> Cited as cause."

Of course behind the scenes anyone of a number of people could have done it; or any of the numerous factions by various maneuvering could have made it happen. Inanyevent, it is a blessed occasion for a great many of the empire. But corruption, paid assassins, intrigue and conspiracies of every conceivable kind, espionage et-cetera were now at serious risk.

Immediately a furious stampede for power began amongst the more powerful noble families. Several exerted considerable influence over the other trying to acquire all the support possible. The race quickly, in a matter of weeks, thinned to three families, and then to two . . . . and the struggle continued becoming highly intense.

Wheeling and dealing, the acquiring of power is a deadly ruthless game; and the Tywr family hierarchy well understood and played . . . . classed amongst the most astute. The Tywr's as well as their competition knew the prevailing conditions of the empire, the seething unrest in the people, and quietly bought and used those problems to advantage. An observer witnessing this see-saw struggle between the Tywr and the Colyn'ca, would compare it to a championship game of chess. Each changing their positions acquiring support or discarding one faction, when in conflict with a larger more important one, such as the favor of support from a guild.

Most coveted of these guilds are the traders, the technics, bio-people, and the citizenry (upper echlon labor) guild. The military usually always lent support to whom they thought would at least respect their position, if not openly show support.

As the struggle unfolded most believed the Tywr family was loosing support. However, in a number of small brilliant back room moves, and with the aid of many loyal supporters behind the scene, the Tywr's won the support of the traders and technics together. Some hours more added the support of the military to that of the two guilds.

A few days more and the Colyn'ca conceeded the struggle leaving the Tywr family to become the new ruling influence. Thus, . . . it fell to the elder Tywr to actually assume the throne, Roak-eo-Tywr was crowned emperor without the lengthy ceremonies normally associated with a coronation, because of prevailing conditions throughout the empire. Roak established a young vibrant dynasty. Though the family was much decimated by past border and frontier wars struggling to maintain control of their vast holdings . . . . he partially solidified his power establishing a vibrant new order.

> Note: The transition or interregnum is formally the interval between the cessation of one government and the establishment of another. In this particular instance the interval is usually brief from one emperor to another, passing to the family member in line of succession. But in this case, power had to be won by the family most able to martial required support. Once accomplished, all citizens were expected to swear allegiance to the new ruler and family.

Immediately after the brief, but colorful ceremony there followed two formal festive parties which ran over into the following day. The second day consisted of partially moving into and taking possession of the palace, and its attendant buildings. As if reviewing troops, all the staff of the varied levels and departments were standing in dress uniforms positioned in parallel lines. The new emperor wearing simple blue as he had earlier, walked slowly down each line smiling. Occasionally a handshake, and a touch on the shoulder, as aides read each department, and each name and family. Finally, he was finished and turned to speak. "You are many, but as new things unfold your numbers will multiply. The effective running of this palace is your responsibility . . . . take pride in this. For hard work and initiative there will be rewards. We look upon this palace as not only our home, but also the hub of the government and empire, and must always reflect this attitude." Roak stated.

Day three the emperor, his confidential people already moved in the night before . . . . started with the subtle changes; but it marked the dawn of a new face for the empire. With lists made previously by closely trusted advisers and confidants, the emperor began with the palace itself. All those whose identities and crimes were listed found themselves quickly dismissed and jailed to await trial. Quickly and quietly the purge went on, and on, and was accomplished with surprisingly little fuss or outcry.

The next morning saw the palace pretty much secure, and the emperor turned immediately to the legal and administrative courts. As before . . . . he jailed all those charged to await trail. Virtually eighty-five percent had to be replaced, and were . . . quickly. Within several days all vacancies were filled with known people of quality.

Rumors moved around fast and furious as citizens began learning this emperor meant business, and was surrounding himself with quality people. All over the home planet and system, the emperor's trusted marshalls were acting with swift sure moves. As days passed more and more of the corrupt people were jailed. Of course the marshalls had been weeded through well in advance, actually taking place the day before Roak accepted the customary oath of allegiance.

Within the first six days, thousands upon tens of thousands on every level of society throughout the home system had been jailed. And slowly the purge was extending out to the closest system of the empire. In many cases the quality people ousted by the corrupt were either asked to return, or were seeking those positions again of their own volition.

The first meeting-session of the emperor's court convened on the eighth day, and sitting at the large table's center resplendid in white was Roak. First order of business was the pardoning of hundreds of thousands of wrongly accused people. Spatial media was instantly making the tucanan people aware of happenings as they occurred. In a special ruling, all the persons released were to be given their former property, vocations and or rank restored, plus an amount from the empire in part apology. It was not an isolated case. Many hundreds of like cases were heard and in each the emperor, who always has the last word, handed down sympathetic but fair judgements. All of the people and guilds, without exceptions, were told to clean their own organizations, or the emperor would see to it for them. There was no mistaking the implications.

Reviews for all empire administraters were being enacted, and speeded up as was practical. This presented problems because of the sheer enormity of the empire. Being nine planetary systems without counting the outlying territories, weeding out the bad from the good, administering to all the planets involved proved extremely difficult, and time consuming. Equal in every respect . . . . the enormity of abolishing out-dated laws and regulations trying to standardize as many new laws as possible required more ministers on each level. So that the overall enacted laws of the empire would be uniform regardless of the system one happens to be in at the time, required co-operation from a great number of people.

Of course each system would have additional laws pertaining to them alone; that is expected, as each planet incorporated laws valid only to that planet.

Roak planned to slowly build-up the military, but kept the decision confidential, while earlier plans were being mentally appraised and revised. Moving swiftly through the home system, and almost as fast throughout the empire . . . Roak, his power established began the modernization of the complex machinery that actually ran the empire. Necessary also, was the need to win over the military completely, and there was only one possible way to accomplish that. His plans hastily formed must wait until his position was unquestionable. Roak realized, as his predecessor had not, for a successful rein . . . . the military's support is crucial.

CHAP. 50

She stayed in her cabin during the relatively short cruise, trying to arrange her overly long tresses that pilled high and swept back a little allowing it to hang in waves about her shoulders and middle of the back.

From Tokyo, she booked passage on what proved to be a very luxurious and fast ship to Hawaii. Dien had graciously forwarded to her in Pusan the official new passport complete with picture, and crest inside, plus funds, so now she has two. She still had most of the original money in envelopes, and decided to convert all of it to dollars, and english pounds. Once on the ship it was as if the world had raced ahead in modern conveniences some fifty years since she'd been in Korea, of course it hadn't been anywhere near that, but she was out of touch, and realized if she was to be of any use she must "catch-up."

Her natural tan and addition to other bountiful charms, caused her to be the object of many a man's attention and advances. From almost the first step on board, she found herself saying yes to the captain's invitation to dine at his table. And that evening noticed these men were polished professionals not only of the sea, but women in general.

Though no longer conscious of the tattoo, Aquina always wore a small shawl or matching jacket whenever her shoulders were exposed because of fashion and such. However, it still was seen through transclucent blouses and it showed through cottons, everything except a jacket, shawl or coat. The oriental waiters and those in the galleys and laundry rooms were stunned when those several waiters recognized the mark, and had spread the word. She often went silently and unbidden to the crew's lounge and rec. room and there helped them in prayer, solutions to nagging difficult problems and general discussions.

And all the while, men pursued her lavishing attention and praises, to the point where by the time the ship reached the big island of Hawaii, Aquina had received proposals of marriage, and many propositions. And it didn't stop there, when she left the ship, but continued with an increase rather than a decrease.

She checked into the Hilton, and immediately went out into the city, buying and replacing what was out, and adding to her wardrobe. Plus the fact she really had only leisure clothes, and bush clothes, and resolved to modernize herself . . . . at least in so far as clothes were concerned. She even purchased new risqué two-piece and bikini bathing suits. In all she invested five days, and a small fortune buying slinky, some tight, flowing lingerie, and clothes, then more clothes and of course three large trunks to hold everything.

She stayed until the end of june soaking up sun and swimming. But time was also invested in tours, trips to the other islands and finding gifts for Dien. Through the travel agent in the lobby, she arranged for a ship to Los Angeles, and a flight from there to New York.

Although the ship was different the amorous advances of the men were the same. Finding her suite more than ample, she unpacked a few things filling dresser drawers, and the one large closet, leaving the smaller one empty. Hours later, she dressed for dinner, wearing a jacket matching the new gown and went to the luxurious dining room, and waited for the maitre'd to show her to the table corresponding to her suite. While waiting for the few seconds for the maitre'd, she smiled inwardly as one after another turned to stare. In minutes, she is sitting opposite the captain, who was of old-world charm, and Aquina liked him from the first second her eyes rested on his slightly lined face.

The weather was balmy and the pacific cooperated allowing the ship to make good time. Arriving in Los Angeles, she kissed the captain after a final embrace, and followed her trunks and luggage off the ship.

The baggage claim officer saw to the delivery of the trunks and baggage to the airport. Aquina had with her the jewelry case, the other small overnight case, her wooden weapon's case and of course the shoulder bag. At the airport everything was checked-in on the proper flight leaving only the cosmetic case and her bag to carry onto the large four engine jet.

With the ticket tucked safely away in her bag, Aquina watched through the large window in the v.i.p. lounge, the jets taxi while others streaked across the paved ground lifting gracefully into the air. The lounge is cool and the atmosphere soothing, the music soft . . . glad she followed the impulse to come in and have a drink. The well padded contour chair was comfortable and of course the small round table is at just the proper height. She had ordered an expensive dry rhine wine and sipped watching, fascinated as one plane after the other left the ground.

It was almost time, and leaving a tip under the glass, she departed the lounge walking with feline grace to the boarding gate. A minute or two more and the gate was opened, and following the handful of first class passengers onto the plane, put the case and her bag down filling the window seat. The other's chose from the many empty seats and did much the same thing, or pushed articles in the overhead storage areas.

In what seemed only seconds the plane was airborne, and in customary fashion the captain said a few words then clicked off. The service was excellent, and just as Aquina was looking out at graceful milky white clouds one of the stewardesses brought a chilled bottle of champagne. "Compliments of the crew, Your Highness." "Thank you." Aquina said looking up at the stew. And she noticed a good looking man with four gold bands on his sleeves walk up behind the attractive stewardess. He introduced himself and a brief conversation took place in which, she categorized him as a skirt chaser. With the captain's departure, she sipped the bubbly and day-dreamed interrupted on occasion for dinner and more "refreshments."

As the plane landed in New York, they were only minutes off the schedule. The most pleasant part, she noted, was the escape from the airport with all her trunks, bags, wooden case and the two small bags in the same large taxi, thanks to three smiling red caps, who made sizeable tips for their efforts. In less than an hour, she was checking into one of the best hotels in the city, and spent the evening settling-in, but unpacked very little.

First thing in the morning, fri. aug. 1st., after toast and coffee, Aquina called the cunard line and arranged passage on the very next liner for England. The layover amounted to five days, and to fill the time, she went sightseeing during the day, and the evenings went to the ballet or a play. Inanyevent the short time went very quickly, and in short order and little fuss found herself aboard a splendid ship ensconced in an elaborate suite. And from the first moment on board found herself being pampered and virtually surrounded by people anxious to please.

A maid was assigned to her, but an escort wasn't required as she never lacked for male attention and devotion. She still appeared nineteen, albeit a mature and very worldly nineteen year old, but many mannerisms suggested a woman of much greater age. Aquina realized, a time ago as had Dien, in this time of greater record keeping and preciseness in gathering information, she must be ever more careful. Divulging anything but what people would expect of a nineteen year old was verboten!

Putting aside the need to be careful, or rather in spite of it, she did find the cruise delightful. However, before departing New York, she had cabled Dien giving the ship's name and date and time of arrival asking for one of the large former gunboats to pick her up upon arrival.

At eight am., on the eleventh, faint mist hid most of the english coast as the liner edged-in closer. Several hours and at 11:30 to be precise, the ship was being nudged gently up to the quay, and soon thereafter was made secure. Aquina had everything packed and ready, but is unsure if she should have the trunks and bags moved to the dock, or wait.

Meanwhile five men stood on the congested dock. Though dressed as fishermen, they are clean, showered, shaven and the clothes clean with no hint of fish odor. The older man who was in his late fourty's had the only symbol of leadership . . . an old naval officer's cap, whereas the others wore only woolen watch caps. They waited until the large gangway was lowered into place in the large open cargo hatch door in the side, and waited to go aboard.

In the interim, Aquina sensed the need to go out on deck. And locking the cabin walked a short distance down the plush corridor to the double doors leading onto the deck. Standing at the rail and looking in the direction indicated by her mind's eye, saw the small group of fishermen. Her eyes, the lids narrowed slightly and ever so gently touched his mind; the one with the officer's cap looked up. When his eyes beheld her form high above them, the chest expanded from the sudden intake of air. He raised his hand high holding it for a moment, until Aquina held up her hand . . . . a salute, a sign given and received years and a world ago.

The men of course talked a good deal as they boarded the ship through the cargo area, and the older man recounted again some first hand knowledge about the princess, who they had never met; but learned about through witnesses, and about things that had become lore. Too the older men who served with her, and those families and country-folk who knew the princess . . . . she is the "cat's meow."

But for the young people, too young to really remember . . . she is a living legend. So it is with a myriad of mixed emotions the five men exited the elevator.

At that instant Aquina came around the corner and stopped. The men hurried up to within a few feet, and to Lars . . . it is deja'vu. Recovering quickly, he bowed and "Your Highness." "Lars . . . . you look well, and fit." "Thank you ma'dam. These young men are part of my crew . . . sons of those from the corp." He introduced them, and Aquina shook hands with each. In minutes the men are carrying trunks and other luggage to the baggage elevator muttering to themselves. It required multiple trips each leg of the way, but in about an hour the men had everything on a small truck hired for the purpose, while Aquina sat in a taxi.

Because of traffic, pedestrians and overall congestion, it took about twenty-five minutes just to travel the distance of several piers. They turned driving out on one of them. Coming next to a blue mast and part of a blue and black superstructure, the vehicles stopped on that side. She got out and began admiring the small ship as Lars, and the men started unloading. While she was looking fourty men of varying ages stood almost motionless staring at her, the younger ones with their mouths open, and all after a second or two, bowed at different intervals.

In short order Lars saw to the two drivers and every piece of luggage brought aboard. The wooden staff and ornate box, tied together, and all the other Pullman and smaller bags went below into one of the cabins . . . Left on the deck as a precaution . . . several of the men positioned the three large trunks amidships, covered them with a heavy tarpaulin tieing everything down in case of bad sea conditions. When Lars was satisfied everything was ready for sea, he assembled all the men into one line. Explaining he normally has eight crew, the others . . . two from each vessel owned by the "company." Lars had each man introduce himself and the boat each was from, and, Aquina shook hands with them. Minutes passed and the black ex-gunboat with blue superstructure was pulling away from the pier.

The multiple diesels sounded young and eager as the familiar sound brought back wartime memories, no longer painful but solemn, cherished memories of a great struggle. Aquina stood next to Lars, and asked him a question. "All the men, their families do well?" "Yes ma-dam. The company provides work for many, many thousands of people. From fishing and canning, and boatyards, and now fertilizers, the trucking, many thousands benefit indirectly. Like the leftovers from the cannery goes to farmers and into fertilizer."

Leaving a large part of the harbor behind the throttle was pushed forward, and the former gunboat came up on its step . . . beginning to plane, as if tired of wallowing like lesser craft. The knotmeter kept inching up until it read thirty knots, and once there, Lars backed off a smidgeon on the throttles, keeping the speed at thirty knots. Gentle swells of four feet, and a little more, were nothing and while Lars caught a few hours sleep, his first mate stood at the helm. With the exception of coffee, she had nothing, and except for visiting the head on occasion, stayed on deck or in the wheelhouse.

CHAP. 51

A period of several weeks followed the brief coronation during which time the new emperor spoke to the citizenry empire-wide, via spatial view screens. Of course immediately they saw the obvious differences between the old hated emperor, and the new one. Where the former was fat and whimsical with slurred speech and reddish face . . . . the new emperor is considerably younger, vibrant and spoke with a clear distinct voice . . . a resounding baritone. Though reasonably tall at 6'10", he wasn't thin, but muscular with a barrel of a chest. And watching him the average citizen could see, or sense the conviction, the purpose . . . . it was displayed on the face and in the clear intelligent eyes. He came across to the people with strength and vigor, all of which made for a very successful image.

He discussed several important matters, all of them meant changes will be taking place, in some instances large ones. And afterwards aides began correlating the reports coming in from the home system planets, and on nearby systems. For the most part citizens were willing to wait and see. Roak was relieved, it meant his people would allow him time. And that was the most he had hoped for . . . .

When the military agreed to support his family, they did so knowing he possessed many character traits not found in the previous emperor. Then too, . . . Roak's reputation as a fair man and patriarch of a weathy and powerful noble family made him an excellent choice. But, there was one more reason why the circle of admirals agreed . . . Roak openly pledged to support the military, coming from a man who at one time was a soldier. A very large and powerful inducement. So powerful, the admirals put an indefinite hold on their plans for a military coup . . . They too would wait and see what transpires.

Just one of the many formidable problems facing Roak was the ever present danger of open insurrection, especially in those systems where the raiders were on one side, and on the other . . . little or no empire military presence. Other systems were close to revolt because of heavy handidness and poorly conceived programs run by corrupt ministers, and heavy taxation.

A definite powder keg situation, and . . . Roak knew without a strong military to patrol, and establish a "presence" . . . . the whole damn empire might blowup in his face. He thought it better to set aside this problem until later . . . when there would be time for reflection, and time to plan more carefully.

Still in his inner office, he began looking at lists of qualified and trusted people, that had already been screened, and then checked again more carefully before it was handed to him. From which he selected secretaries, and amongst the "top" list . . . . selected several to fill slots as assistant ministers, and aides. Roak continued this until the administrational load could be split down far enough to initially guarantee more thorough representation and at the same time establish a definite sense of order within those areas of the government. It of course didn't immediately alleviate the staggering schedule of requests and appointments for audiences, petitions, planetary and system officials, in an almost constant parade of diversified peoples and species. All basically humanoid, but incorporating many variations on the basic theme.

But, what it did accomplish even from the outset was to make available more people to help the throngs, making smaller groups according to the specific crises, problems or emergency.

With the indoctrination and briefing well underway for the most recent appointees, Roak returned to his inner office to re-think about the lack of military prowess and the prevailing tension throughout the empire. The raiders were only part of the problem, he had to think of some way . . . . a quick bold move that would defuse the tension and fire the people's sense of loyalty to the throne. While Roak thought about the problem, he absentmindedly filled a goblet with soft beitra, and was about to take a sip when a partial solution occurred to him. Sitting down, Roak quickly signaled for a senior minister. While waiting he quickly wrote out a few lines in neat script, smiling at the anticipated results.

Roak acknowledged the minister and handed him the sheet of pasid to read. The look of shock and disbelief only a nod and a firm order from Roak. And within minutes after the minister departed his office, the note was "flashed to the net," by spatial news. Its meaning, at first, was met with blank stares, and abject disbelief, until the order was repeated several times.

As a result more than half of the taxes levied on the people were rolled back, "until such time as the emperor had an opportunity to review the entire tax structure of the empire." Roak, as he drained the goblet, was hoping it would indeed be a very long time. He had struck a chord. A senior minister hurriedly begged entrance, and after Roak admitted him . . . . "a masterful stroke sire, absolutely brilliant. For the first time in my memory the people of Tucana are celebrating. The crowds in the palace are whooping for joy . . . . it is certainly infectous sire." "Fine, fine, it went over better than I expected. Good, this is exactly what is needed." Roak said leaning back in the form sensitive recliner.

After the minister departed, Roak was again lost in thought. "Only, that appears to be doing well . . . . at least as far as it goes, but there is the whole other side of the problem. And, I need help with that part." He entertained several quick ideas and then signaled for a secretary. Roak quickly wrote the name and habitat location of his old teacher, and handed it to the secretary with orders for the said named individual to be brought to him forthwith. He remembered his old friend in a rare moment of mid-day reflection . . . . an old warrior of proven skill and valor. In all the empire, few are as good with sword and dagger, hence the reason why Barith had been retained as his teacher. And during the course of his instruction, had become an honored friend to the entire Tywr family. In the interim, while Roak remembered pleasant memories, the secretary asked one of the emperor's advisers about who to send. Recognizing the name and habitat address, said he will fetch the old soldier.

Departing quickly the adviser found Barith at home sipping-gulping beitra, and a little "tight" watching past battles on the vid screen. But shook the cobwebs quick enough when the adviser told him who issued the summons. In a little over an hour, while consuming a light lunch in the private dining hall . . . . Barith was announced and admitted into Roak's presence. Roak stood, and while Barith bowed . . . . grasped him by the shoulders and . . . "ah my friend. I understand you have complained bitterly about retirement. I wish you for my senior military aide, with rank and privileges restored." "Of course sire . . . gladly." Barith replied with a broad smile. And within a few hours Barith moved into the palace, across and down the hall from the emperor's main suites and immediately assumed a broad spectrum of duties.

Armed with special identification, Barith very quickly immersed himself in the grueling master schedule that constantly needed updating. Along with considerable influence, Barith also had his share of worries. Only one of which was the lack of almost required time for the emperor to have absolute rest . . . . time for reflection and private thought. Hitherto the emperor had waited until the customary evening interval for reflection et-cetera, before allowing sleep to rescue him from the stressful day.

All of the items on the emperor's daily schedule, was as Barith noted one more, which he did not understand, partly because the emperor . . . it made him depressed. He could easily see whatever the problem . . . it was bothering his emperor. But, Barith kept silent. And thought, "with that many serious empire-wide problems . . . . could be anything." What Barith did not know . . . . the pre-occupation, worry concerned the plight of his nephew lost on a wild primitive planet dozens upon dozens of parsecs away . . . lost, marooned.

CHAP. 52

An hour before dawn Lars came up with three steaming cups of coffee. Aquina accepted one and the first mate accepted the third. The diesels kept purring along beautifully, and three hours from "their harbor" began sighting fishing boats of various sizes. Some were fairly close while others were not, but horns were sounded at their approach, and crews waved, some frantically. The closer they came to land the more boats encountered, and the greeting was much the same.

They are within sight of the long peninsula, and the beacon light on the point. Soon they were abreast of the light, and in minutes Lars began coming around to port. At 9:45 he maneuvered up-against the quay, and the people normally working on or around the docks, and quay, gathered waiting patiently, while the small ship was made fast, and the small gangway put in place. Aquina walked across the gangway and onto the quay greeting the small crowd; while Lars and his men loaded the small truck waiting behind the mercedes.

At 10:20 am., with everything in the truck, she sat in the back seat of the benz, and waved to the people, as the car made its way down the pier and onto the road leading into the city. It didn't take long, perhaps thirty-five minutes, to thread their way through traffic. She noticed while many things had not changed, many others did. Some of the farms had obvious new construction, and looked prosperous, new homes, and children playing here an there.

The woods were still there, healthy and as the car passed, Aquina noticed road signs warning of crossing animals, and other signs warned of dire consequences if an animal should be injured. Slowly they came upon the "woods road," and as the car turned, she noticed some things did change. It is paved with two lanes up to the scrub line, which is kept neat; but the big change was the large wrought-iron gates set into large stone pillars. And to one side a large four foot square bronze plate attached to the left side pillar.

The driver stopped and honked the horn waiting for the caretaker and gateman to come out from the small cottage, sitting behind and within the scrub, and open the gate. While waiting, Aquina got out and stepped over to the bronze plate, and read the dedication. It commemorated the battles fought by the resistance, gave the names of the participants, and a brief account of what happened.

As the gatekeeper began opening the ponderous gates, Aquina turned at the sound of children playing by the large barn, all familiar sights and sounds from the past. The driver held the door as she got in, bowed and quickly got back behind the wheel. Driving slowly through, the older gray haired man suddenly bowed, pulled his hat off, and started clapping as the glistening benz went past him. Ambling into the cottage laughing and weeping, his wife concerned at her husband's antics tried to quiet him. But he continued and first called the compound to let them know the princess was home. After that he began calling the neighbors and the neighborhood farms, and the surviving members of the original group of resistance fighters.

At 11:30 am., Dien was alerted by the business staff, in what used to be the barracks, and was already prepared when seven minutes later the benz came into view. The group of mechanics and assistants quickly lined up in front of the garage area, and all office personnel, some four dozen lined up outside of the building facing the open compound. And likewise those two dozen working in the warehouses lined up behind the building facing the compound and those from the office building.

Every person knew to prepare, having been told by Dien days earlier. The entire area and buildings were gleaming from the intense preparation, and the younger people took their cue from the older members of the staff. For they only had Aquina's portrait hanging in the large open office area, to go by and of course had many questions. Everyone, from all parts of the compound . . . . even the stable hands, grooms and boys were lined up in their "sunday best" waiting . . . . expectantly.

The benz came out from under the trees and slowed gradually coming to a stop in front of the compound. The sound of pounding hooves from a small herd of horses came closer and closer. Dien stood a few yards to the side as the driver opened and held the door, while Aquina stepped out. Instantly, Dien knew the "vacation" had been successful . . . .

Aquina was healed. Dien had been afraid that such might not be the case, but breathed a definite sigh of relief, after a good hug and seeing the serenity and wisdom in the eyes. But before she could say very much, the herd split around the car, and converged on them . . . . her.

The "whinny-ing" and other sounds were all for her benefit, and as two and three at a time pushed and nuzzled up against her. She giggled with delight and hugged each gently, a kiss on the muzzle, and petted their long foreheads. A few words and they're off running and prancing. Aquina looked-up filled her lungs letting it out slow. They walked over to the office personnel first as Dien began the introductions.

Most were barely able to speak at all . . . bowing smiling while heads turned to follow as she went further and further down the line. Thence to the garage personnel, then next to the stable trainer and grooms et-cetera. Then the warehouse personnel . . . . but everyone reacted much in the same way. Those Aquina knew from the war, she called by first name or nickname, as if the passing of time was only brief. She walked back to the benz with Dien chatting when the air was filled with the sound of a howling wolf.

For the moment, Aquina looked at the wide beaten-down gravel covered road curving up to a similar apron spanning the front of the compound, the inside of the shallow "U" shape, and curving around to the warehouses. On the far side ran the long narrow meadow, about two acres in width by about four-an-a-half long. From the tree line broke a large pack of timber wolves, barking, yapping and growling and more barking. She quickly pulled a Pullman size suitcase from the benz, and walked off several yards and sat on the handle of the bag. They ran pell-mell stopping in front of her, barking and jumping tails wagging, prancing round greatly excited. Beginning in a soft lilting tone, she started talking, and immediately the big carnivores quieted, and sat in a semi-circle. Starting with the leader, each animal came forward rubbed its forehead on her hand, a few slurps of the tongue, and she in turn petted and spoke to them. That last realization rocked all those watching except those of the "corp.", who had witnessed this same thing years earlier, for there was no doubt the animals understood, and, she likewise understood them. There followed the bitch's and pups doing the same ritual although the pups sometimes "wobbled" on the attempt.

During the next few hours more wolves arrived, and bears, wildcats, deer, some wild pig, and finally small animals like the rabbit, and those of the rodent family . . . . it had to some extent developed into a very rowdy homecoming.

Little in the way of work was accomplished, it was already after 3pm., when she got up off the suitcase. As for the trunks and other luggage, they had long since been unloaded and stacked neatly to one-side of the front door leading to the occupied portion of the "house." They waited until everyone had departed for the day before carrying the trunks, and such in to be unpacked and sorted. And while unpacking Aquina began relating events to Dien, some of which she already knew. And inbetween Dien related how and what changed during Aquina's absence. Not until well into the next morning did they pause from the task of organizing all the new clothes. Dien asked about the wooden case and staff, and after a pregnant pause, Aquina related all that transpired in Korea.

Dien began to weep quietly as pride, happiness and thanks to the universe welled up and spilled over. Looking at Aquina . . . . Dien nodded and thought to herself, as Aquina kept talking. "The fat is gone, and ohhh such a beautiful body, She is a woman now, healed and mature . . . and the power radiates from her like discarded body heat." Dien closed her eyes and gave thanks, not really knowing to what . . . . but gave thanks nonetheless.

That very morning, Aquina began familiarizing herself with the many family businesses. And in the course of that year, and the next "planet time," she assumed more and more of the work load. In addition, she devoted two hours each morning going through each movement of all eight "dance disciplines," and exercising, plus sword movement. Each evening period, she devoted time for meditation and reflection. And more often than not, Dien sat watching closely as Aquina went through the ka'tahs of all the dance disciplines; but the dance coupled with the sword held her entranced, while Aquina made the sword a blur of deadly poetic motion.

The years '59, . . . '60, and '61, passed as had all the others . . . . quickly, and except for certain happenings within the world of science, Aquina would not have taken notice. Tremendous strides were made by the two chief nations in space exploration. Such things as satellite launchings had already taken place and highly motivated and ambitious people were getting involved. The cry for engineers and specialists were in all the major newspapers and on radio air time. Dien recognized the wistful look on her face . . . . she had to get into this.

In '62, the country, Aquina favored of the two formidable military powers launched an orbital flight that february. She simply had to be a part of this "great adventure." At dinner, she and Dien discussed the possible pitfalls, and the reminder for secrecy. And above all no mention must be made of her war-time experiences. Aquina heartily agreed, and brought up several other points for discussion. With a classic inscrutiable face, she sat quietly amused watching Dien gleefully hatch a plan. "Aquina if we time this properly . . . you could be on your way to school without anyone causing fuss or bother." She explained the plan and the harmless subterfuge, and with the exception of a few points altered, Aquina agreed.

With the passage of mere months the plan was put into motion with a phone call to their senior soliciter. He in turn discusses it with the charge' d' affaires of the appropriate embassy in Copenhagen. An appointment was tactfully arranged with the charge' only after the soliciter divulged tidbits of required information.

A week later at the appointed hour, Aquina and Dien walked into the embassy and was in due course admitted into the charge's office, three minutes early. Armed with her most recent passport, Aquina answered the diplomat's questions totally charming him in the process. In less than fourty minutes they departed graciously with an open-end education visa. And on their way back made plans on what she would need.

The very next "morning," Dien touched base with the same soliciter putting the next phase of their plan into motion. He contacted a suitable counterpart, an attorney known for some years, and knew him to be highly ethical, and more importantly . . . kept his promises. After a somewhat lengthy conversation describing the lady in question, and the reason for her visit, the name of the school, and other equally important information, the attorney readily agreed to represent her. On his end the soliciter had received an estimate of the yearly expenses involved, and the name of a decent reputable bank located within the Cambridge area.

As a result of that phone call a meeting was held between the banker, who instead of a manager . . . was now president of the bank, and the soliciter is a senior partner in his own prosperous influential law firm. The banker, after a disconnection and a few minutes waiting, spoke to his counterpart outlining the wishes of the family, and the projected needs of the princess. Monies were transferred, accounts set-up for personal and school needs, and the assurance of a suitable apartment would be leased guaranteeing all the amenities. And the letter on embassy stationary reached the dean of admissions-office and desk, notifying the school of Aquina's visa status and political status signed by the charge' in Copenhagen.

She packed only her most recent fashions including leisure and swim wear, vitamins, and such, put the wooden weapon's box on the luggage pile, but omitted the wooden staff. And saying her goodbys boarded a flight from Copenhagen to London. From there, despite a two hour lay-over, boarded a transatlantic flight directly to logan international.

Knowing the flight number, and armed with her description, the attorney waited with a woman from his law firm ladened with an armload of long stem red roses. The v.i.p. and first class section of customs wasn't crowded, and he hoped they could leave soon and escape the rush hour traffic. They had rushed to the customs gate immediately after the flight was announced and waiting patiently. As he and the assistant watched . . . a few passengers began approaching the customs counters. A few moments more and a small crowd approached consisting of the captain, and co-pilot plus stewardesses talking and laughing a little with a young woman in the middle.

Aquina walked to the nearest counter and presented her passport, visa and a letter from the charge'. The attorney followed her with his eyes devouring the body before him. As he tried with effort to bring his saliva and breathing under control . . . overheard the customs official. "Welcome to my country Your Highness, and there is no need to check your luggage." She folded the letter, put the license etc. back into the passport, having already stamped it. "Here is your passport and have a wonderful time."

"Thank you," she said smiling. The sky caps followed her through the gate as Aquina looked for the person she was to meet.

Immediately the attorney stepped forward, introduced himself and companion with a bow of the head, and a small curtsy from the assistant all the while trying to control his pounding heart and erotic impulses.

The chit-chat was almost solely about her school, and the Cambridge area as they walked through the terminal, then outside only to stand on slick sidewalks, while the attorney went to retrieve the car. While he was gone the assistant talked about the men there, and college students in particular. It is a large luxury sedan that rolled slowly to the curb, the attorney careful of possible ice, and the sky caps were successful in putting the storage trunk plus three pieces of luggage in the car's trunk, and the balance in the back seat. And with the sky caps paid, they were off . . . out into traffic, and the drive around the heart of Boston, heading for Cambridge.

At 4:30, the large sedan pulled up in front of a three story elegant brownstone, with driveway and garage. Ivy covered much of the front and sides despite the snow, and smoke curling skyward from two of the four large chimneys.

She met the staff, comprising a cook, and two maids, and looked through the first floor and so-on. A bit later they managed with the pieces of luggage and everything including the trunk found its way to the second floor master bedroom. And by six p.m., the attorney and assistant departed, the later to return in the morning, early. Aquina was to meet the dean of admissions at 9a.m., and take the battery of "entrance exams" at 1p.m., that afternoon. After the staff retired for the night, she continued to unpack. And as the last item to put away . . . carefully hid the ornate wooden box on one of the upper shelves.

At precisely 8:20 a.m., Laura arrived, and in slightly under thirty minutes parked next to the administration building. There were students everywhere, and with Aquina in a close custom fitted silk suit, framing a lean lush figure, and Laura is an attractive woman in her own right . . . , but couldn't hold a candle to the princess. Many young men paused to stare, some said hello" and "good morning," and more risqué lines. The ladies couldn't help notice that there were few women on the campus . . . a thought Aquina kept to herself.

The meeting with the dean was pleasant and of course very informative. When asked . . . why she wished to study there, she replied . . . "to be the best . . . one must study from the best." Her attitude and intensity impressed him, but above all it is the maturity and wisdom he sensed in her. But he also felt something else . . . . an aura of something . . . . but he couldn't put a word on it or an identity. In conclusion, she was to fill out the enrollment forms, and they would talk again later.

Aquina went outside received the forms and sat down in the outer office to complete them. The first page was basic and routine such as address, vital statistics, marital status, then sports. Deciding how to list certain activities . . . . she shrugged and forged ahead. Listing principle activities first, she put down martial arts, and next to that Kodo'Kun Master and followed that with fencing and a few others. The second sheet began with languages, she listed six. For headings such as hobbies, she listed animals, board games and riding, ... for special interest, ... she indicated animals and medicine, Buddist studies and philosophy. The balance of the page was the tricky part, education. She delved into her bag for the sheet of paper containing the prepared information from Dien. This was actually done by the C'pter, to be used for this purpose.

The balance of the forms, she was able to fill-in quickly, then handed the completed set to the dean's secretary and opted to wait in the hall. By doing so she hoped to get a better idea of school activities by the trophy cases and activity boards occupying a good portion of the wall space on both sides. It wasn't long before the secretary came out looking for her and found herself before the dean for the second promised interview. He went over the questionnaire with her and with a smile stamped it approved pending the outcome of the exams. They shook hands and reminded her of the entrance exams scheduled for that afternoon.

With a number of hours to fill, Laura suggested shopping as they each opened a car door and slid into the front seats. Their conversation turned to food and money, and wishing to show the princess the better restaurants in the area stopped in front of an elegant french "house" offering supposedly excellent salads, among other things. During their light meal, which Aquina ordered in fluent french as if a native much to the maitre' d's delight, discussion turned to money and that the bank should be their next stop. And it was, Laura showed Aquina the way from the brownstone to the bank, where she signed for the three accounts already opened. One for savings and two checking, one for tuition, and school expenses, and the second for herself, and the house. When she inquired about the purchase of a car, the bank's vice president asked what kind. When she told him a jaguar roadster . . . he thought a moment and smiled saying . . . . he knew of a dealer in the city, and picked up his phone and dialed.

A brief conversation ensued back-n-forth, at times Aquina answered questions as to what color, power, optional equipment in which . . . she opted for all of them, convertible with detachable hardtop et-cetera. When Aquina agreed to the price, plus prep charges, tax and registration the banker told the dealer to consider it sold, get it ready and the princess will have a bank check to hand to him . . . this afternoon . . . at 4:30 . . . ? Very good Her Highness will be there."

When they walked out Aquina had her bank book, two of the small folding checkbooks with temporary checks until custom ones arrived, the bank check for the new car, and a sizeable quantity of cash. Laura aware of the time headed back to the institute's administration building and arrived with only ten minutes to spare. And in minutes Aquina found herself sitting down with the four hour exam, and scratch paper ready to begin.

Her first impression was a small release of tension as the exam was not as difficult as she presupposed and was almost totally relaxed by the time she started writing answers. There are four parts, general was first, english and literature, science, and lastly mathematics. With a smile on her face, she worked swiftly as the procter looked-on amused thinking the young woman falsely over confident. Aquina finished the exam and went back over it looking for errors. And although unsure of three questions, all located in the english section having to do with tense and phraseology, Aquina handed the exam to the procter in an elapsed time of two hours-fourteen minutes. He directed her to wait at the admission's counter or the dean's office for the results.

The procter took out the answer grid and began to carefully correct each segment of the exam. It wasn't long before the "I told you so" smile began to disappear, and a look of surprise take its place. And gradually that was replaced with a grudging respect. Once finished the procter hurried to the dean's office, stared momentarily at Aquina then knocked on the door and went in . . . A few seconds later Aquina was asked to go in . . . both men stood as she entered.

CHAP. 53

The dean began by clearing his throat. "there is no question of your being admitted only your choice of career." Aquina nodded . . . "I see," and for several seconds debated between the three she really desired. Bringing out a large fold-out brochure . . . she looked up. "Ahh-hha, yes these three please." The professor who had proctered the exam looked at where she was pointing, and felt a constricting in his throat. Smiling, the dean tried to explain that each is a four year degree program. He pointed out the courses necessary for each and how they are designed through two semeters per year, with a major course of study and a minor. "And a student would normally earn a degree only in the major not both, especially not three."

Both men sensed the intensity and part of the strength in the young woman. "May I use the summers as a third semester?" "Well . . . yes arrangements can be made, it will require however additional financial agreements between yourself and the professors in question." The dean said with a smile.

"Wonderful! When may I begin?" "The next semester begins in January, and your choices for major and minor?" "Hmmm . . . . aeronautical engineering and astrophysics for my majors, but I want both to be degree programs." "Your Highness, it would mean taking two major courses of study, where a 3.5 average must be maintained at all costs. And even using the summers . . . I doubt its possible. You are, . . . I take it determined." Aquina nodded. With a loud sigh. "Very well, you and the school will try it on a trial basis." Replied the dean. Aquina smiled with half-lidded eyes. "Thank you."

The dean rang for his secretary . . . handed her a form, which indicated the two major courses of study. "Have admissons process this student for those two degree programs, and the office prepare a comprehensive schedule to begin with the spring semester. Oh, and have admissions pull out all the stops on this, with the entire list of lab books, texts and everything else Her Highness will need." The secretary did a double take on the dean's form of address, and left the room quickly. She quickly visited the admissions dept. desk and the offices responsible for course scheduling.

In minutes, she walked across the way and paid her first semester's tuition. And while waiting for the breakdown of the courses and schedule for the semester, she visited the large school store, and browsed. Aquina looked at her watch, and decided there would not be time to shop, when she was due to pick up the car in fourty minutes. She picked up a business card with the store hours printed in two neat rows and returned to admissions. It was 3:55 when a woman came out and handed Aquina the semester schedule and literature containing all the combined courses and course descriptions. With a quick look at the wall clock, she said "thank you" and hurried to the front door.

Laura was waiting, trying to be patient, when Aquina climbed in and Laura wheeled her car out onto the side road. Almost on the dot of 4:30 . . . they arrived, and ran into the showroom. "Whew," said Laura, "in the nick of time." Both ladies hurried, Laura is on Aquina's right taking incoherent steps ontrasting to Aquina's feline-like measured strides.

The owner, manager and six senior salespeople sat in a group staring at the women, especially the taller one. Whispering to the owner . . . "I must be in heaven . . . its an angel," said a staring manager. Aquina spoke a few seconds later. "I believe you gentlemen have a roadster for me?" "We have one prepped, may I see identification?" Asked the owner. "Certainly," replied Aquina and pulled out her passport, and handed it to the middle-aged man. He looked at her, smiled and bowed. "Thank you, Your Highness. This way please." Returning the passport, he showed her down a short corridor and out into the garage.

Over to one side a roadster was being pampered, buffed, while a gray haired man in white coveralls leaned over the engine. The dealer indicated the roadster. "Ohhh yes," and a gentle touch on the fender sent a warm tingling feeling through her fingers. She smiled looking at the wire wheels, knock-off hubs, the tunneau cover and "boot" resting behind the seats, the hardtop and in the trunk, a new tool kit and spare with its own tools. The b.r.g. color was soothing and cool, a nice color for a car, as she stood with one leg out to the side on an angle admiring the sleek lines of the roadster. And while she did, the men were admiring her sleek racing lines. The chief mechanic came up for air, and immediately bowed.

"Your Highness, now it is ready." He said with satisfaction wiping his hands on a rag. Aquina bent over to look immediately joined by the mechanic, who began pointing out things on the six cylinder engine. He pointed to the twin SU carburetors, and other tidbits, the pride showing in his voice. A few minutes and she was in behind the wheel starting the engine, and without hesitation it erupted into life, and settled to a throaty growl. She let it growl for a few seconds listening to the engine then blipped it once, and shut the key off. Returning to the office, Aquina signed the papers, the registration, title and pink slip then handed the check to the manager who officiated. Meanwhile, the roadster was pushed around in front by the glass doors.

When she and Laura departed most of the other people were leaving as well. Laura followed her back to the brownstone to make sure Aquina knew the way. The exhaust rebounded amongst the buildings a little as she gently nosed it into the recently cleaned garage.

Early in the morning, Laura accompanied Aquina in the new jag to the school's large book and supply store, armed with her class schedule. She was ready to do battle with the book shelves, but learned the girls working in the store had already pulled all the books listed for her courses, and stacked them in three cartons. She looked at the 40 odd texts, and over a dozen lab books, and with a sigh decided to purchase the other items and supplies at the store, instead of elsewhere. And the additional supplies including a slipstick, paper supplies, and writing instruments filled another carton.

Both ladies managed, with help, putting the boxes in the car, and from there into the brownstone.

They were becoming very close, for Laura was frequently surprised at the wisdom and tact used by Aquina, and thankful for advice that on many occasions was given so subtlely, she didn't realize it until usually hours later. She helped Aquina turn one of the third floor rooms into an exercise and workout area, and with her friend's urging, Laura began with stretching exercises and then sat on the side toweling herself dry. While Aquina went through the one "dance." Usually Laura sat for an hour, possibly two, enthralled finding it difficult to avert her eyes . . . especially during the body isometrics routine. And those instances when both stepped-out of their briefs and T-shirts or leotards, which Aquina loaned Laura to use. And using the third floor shower . . . were trying times for Laura. She was by no stretch of the imagination . . . a lesbian, but for this young woman, she found herself thinking about it more-and-more. But Laura kept her desire and fantasies under control.

During the entire month of december, aside from Laura's visits and her own workout routines and those they did together, she spent reading and studying with a voracious appetite. She left the lab books for later, and paid attention to the texts themselves. So, when she began the semester virtually every text had been studied, giving her a substantial leg-up on each class and subject matter.

Her first day happened to be a monday, and with just enough time inbetween to make the next class, she was literally off an running. In many of the classes, she was the only female, while in others there was two, three and five young ladies to share the over-abundant male attention. Through most of it, she seemed not to notice the men, but kept her mind exclusively on the subject at hand; which in itself pleased the professors. The dean of admissions had discussed Aquina at some length with each dean of each department, and of course all the professors were appraised of the situation as well. Therefore they kept a closer eye on her work than any other freshman.

From the very first day, she is instantly popular with the girls, and the men . . . . that went without saying. Males were almost always around her talking, asking for dates, invitations for a wide variety of activities. But, she participated in few activities, and those she did attend were usually dances. It was no secret to the campus at large . . . that her curriculum was "heavy." Allbeit some were envious, jealous, but they are in a distinct minority. The overwhelming majority were behind her with help if needed, and a great deal of encouragement.

This continued for the entire semester, and finally late may rolled around and exam time. It was grueling. Aquina finished one exam . . . . checked it over, and then handed it to the procter, only to hurry from the room sometimes running to the next building and another exam. Where others would be finished, she could be seen hurrying from one building to another, or one floor to another . . . . sitting down closing her eyes and visibly calming respiration and nerves. And thereby focusing the mind on the particular task at hand. And this ability by no means escaped the astute professors.

At the close of the second day, she was able to relax. All the exams had been taken and that evening, she slept soundly for seven hours. She was dimly aware the phone ringing, it was a thursday . . . and early. The upstairs maid discreetly knocked and after coming into the room smiled and opened the drapes. After a few words of greeting she mentioned the phone call from the dean of admissions. "If Aquina could come to his office at around 9 a.m."

It is a warm morning and wearing a light summer transcluscent white blouse and skirt, she drove to the admission building after a light breakfast. Aquina parked, smiled and waved back to friends and acquaintances, and was soon inside, Smiling in response to the secretary's broad grin, walked through the open door into the dean's office. His greeting was warm and his mood was decidedly up-beat. "Normally grades are posted in the lobby of each building, as is yours . . . Aquina," after her insistence he address her by the first name, though he still felt a need to say the title occasionally. He cleared his throat before speaking again. "Fabulous, simply fabulous," as he looked at the sheet listing all of the individual exams, instructor, course and grade. "All perfect grades but one, and I believe it was a misspelled chemical name. Inanyevent only two-tenths of a point was deducted. That specific exam grade is 3.98, while all the others are four-o." The dean was visibly bubbling with enthusiasm. "Then, I may continue?" Aquina asked, smiling. "Of course . . . . certainly. There is no doubt remaining in anyone's mind that you can handle the curriculum. I merely wanted to be the first to wish you well." "Thank you dean."

"Oh, here is your courses and schedule for the summer and the name of each professor and his address plus phone numbers." She thanked him and went directly to the admission's desk, where in moments tuition is paid et-cetera. Her education crept forward another notch. Of course to Aquina virtually no time at all had passed.

She visited the store and finding all the required texts, lab books, paper and other sundries packed in cartons . . . . thanked them, paid for everything and left leaving the cardboard cartons behind. Some curious looks and shrugs followed as everyone went about their normal work. About twenty-odd minutes later the loud growl of the jaguar came through the open windows, . . . a car door, and the click-click of high heels, and a light lilting voice singing then humming and back to singing. In seconds the front door opened and Aquina walked in carrying a good size carton. She came in and put the box on an adjacent counter, and reaching in began handing out containers of coffee, and pulled out two boxes of donuts and pastries. "There is . . . ah . . . three cups for each, and plenty of calories over here." The ice was broken, as a ring of laughter filled the store with Aquina handing out more coffee.

Aquina is standing with her back to the front counter and didn't see but heard and felt two heavy-set men enter, their footfalls sluggish and "heavy." She was talking to the girls across from her and . . . "ush, ohhh what a honey. Haven't seen you around here before." Aquina's eyes became slits and the several girls, and the few young men, stared as her face became a mask of stony inscrutiable concentration, and loathing. The two twits came around the counter one put his hand on her shoulder suggestively. "Come to lunch with my friend, and I . . . . we can get better acquainted." She deceptively grasped his wrist with thumb and forefinger, applied pressure and broke it. The crack was audible and so was his scream. His friend came fast with a powerful right, but instead of landing ended in mid-air, her right hand a blow to the underside of the arm breaking it followed by a scream and oaths. The same hand in a sweeping move called "wiping the window" made contact with the man's chin slamming it shut with crushing force, fracturing the jaw and breaking many teeth.

It all happened so quickly no-one had a chance to react or speak, but simply stare with mouths hanging open, looking from Aquina to the two upper classmen laying on the floor then back to her. Those that worked in the store looked at one-another, their mounths closed, but still staring. The young men soon whooped for joy, and hugged the girls looking on while Aquina called campus security.

Three strapping men in tan campus police uniforms entered, assessed the situation and began taking statements, while a phone call was made for an ambulance. Aquina decided not to press charges, but merely wanted the hub-bub to settle down. And it did to a certain extent . . . . that is to say such an incident did not occur again on campus. However, word of the "fight" went through the school seemingly in hours, except for the large percentage away on summer break, and they found out almost immediately upon their return.

In spite of the additional attention Aquina was accorded, she did even better on the exams in late august than the previous semester's achieving a consistent "four-o."

Two other noteworthy things happened during the summer. First, Aquina asked and received permission to use the gym equipment. Initially it was to be with supervision, but after only a few moments watching her tumbling exercises, the instructor nixed that requirement signing a letter to that affect forwarded to the head of the athletic department. Included in the arrangement was the pool. And almost on any given day late in the afternoon, she could be found in a skimpy two-piece swimming lap after lap.

Second, the school began a fencing club, in which Aquina and some two dozen others enrolled. The instructor, a middle-aged french army officer, accepted the administration's offer because it sounded cushy, would keep him out of trouble, and most important . . . it meant a salary. Plus of course it also meant respect, and it helped that he spoke excellent english.

With the first meeting he established the ground rules and explained what the health benefits were, about grace and quickness of the eye. He said after some minutes . . . "Those who have never had a lesson or held a foil, pair off with these practice foils and we shall run through some elementary moves." Being the twenty-fifth and possessing experience . . . Aquina put down the shoulder bag, removed her jacket, momentarily not thinking about the tattoo, and made sure the knot in her halter top was tight and flipped her abundant hair. Some stared for she didn't wear a bra, which was plainly evident. Not because of any sag, there wasn't any . . . but on each side a telltale well formed nipple was trying to push through the white material.

After getting the others started, he asked Aquina . . . . "are you standing alone because of being odd one out, or because you have experience?" "Both," replied Aquina wearing a beguiling smile. He found it and her manner annoying, and said something he regretted later. "We have foil and sabor. Your choice." Replied the frenchman wishing to put the beautiful woman in her proper place. "Sabors." And Aquina went to the bench and picked up one, and began a warm-up. In seconds she assumed a professional stance. Left hand casually on left hip, she went to the "on-guard" position. The instructor returned the compliment . . . touched swords and heartbeats later filled the room with loud clashing sound of steel. The others were totally captivated. These are dueling swords without the protective tips and soon not only the room, but the entire building rang from the sound. The sound is the repeated staccato note of steel against steel. Very soon other students began arriving, as the two kept it up . . . Aquina cool with that enigmatic smile, while the instructor began to falter, perspiring and tiring. It was over within a half hour, and she whipped the sword from his grasp twice . . . and twice allowed him to pick it up and continue. With the constant moving and changing of position all the spectators observed the elegant tattoo on her right shoulder through the blouse's thin fabric.

Another few minutes and she disarmed him again, and with the point at his throat . . . "I yield," said the gasping man. And with that, she raised the sword point about mid way on the right cheek, just below the eye, and with a flick of the point . . . put a small cut on his face. He bowed, and then Aquina offered her hand . . . . the instructor clasped it warmly. The students looked at one-another with a wide array of expressions. "Please, madamoeselle, I must know where did you learn such technique . . . . who could teach you this?" Asked the instructor. "My mother. We share the same first name . . . my aunt's wish at my birth. It is said . . . . I am enough like her to be a twin."

His face lit up. "Mon ami . . . . of course . . . . The tiger Lady." Turning to the crowd of students . . . "The woman, I speak of is the greatest female warrior of the 20th. Century. It is no wonder the norsemen conquered most of the known world, and some of this one, also I think. I remember your mother well . . ." His right hand went up as a sign to heaven. Speaking to everyone in general. "I saw your mother at the Elbe River, the germans could do nothing to stop her, In captured tiger tanks in brigade strength and in the lead tank, she raced across the bridge, her tank firing as it crossed scoring direct hits on enemy tigers and older panzers. While her big guns ripped into the enemy, she and her men cut savagely into the enemy's armored division. That's right . . . a short brigade against a division. The princess destroyed them and the infantry. The nazi threat and strength was broken like a dry twig at the Elbe. The allies had been bogged down, but that ended it there in smoking, burning enemy hulks."

He continued. "I vividly remember the banquet and ball at the chateau the English field marshall used. Your mother was escorted by several of her tanks, and when she walked in ahhh a vision like a queen, she carried herself. I know every man was smitten and the field marshall could not take his eyes from her." "And you mounsier?" Asked Aquina with a smile. He nodded. "I confess . . . . I love your mother still. Everyone who knew or fought with her, loved her . . . . some passionately. Tell me . . . . please. Your mother rules now, certainly?" Asked the instructor. Aquina thought fast. "No, my uncle is king, and my mother over-sees the family business holdings."

"Alas, a pity. I have always felt, to be a good or great monarch, one must first be a great warrior. It is europe's loss . . . . to be sure. Please Your Highness, teach with me, be an instructor?" Aquina looked at the crowd hesitantly thinking it not a good idea, then back to the frenchman. The substantial crowd began applauding. "Very well then, but only if you call me Aquina." He smiled, bowed. She lifted the right hand to shake on the arrangement, but he gently held the fingers touching them with a slight touch of his nose, and stood once again. A slight flush deepened the natural tan on her face.

In the fall followed another semester and in spite of the extra-curricular activities, she scored consistent grades. And at Christmas, Aquina helped to organize a lavish party, utilizing the entire gymnasium.

It is '64, and real trouble reigned again in asia, and slowly some of the joy went out of her. Although each semester continued to reinforce a consistent four-o, she was sometimes preoccupied with the war. She and Laura discussed it frequently during dinner and their ritual workouts. Laura was concerned and frightened for a brother, who enlisted in the army. The fears became worse, and Aquina frequently held her friend hugging, holding her close often with Laura's head cradled on a breast. Laura slowly moved her head brushing full lips across the partially erect nipple. Aquina sucked in a quick gulp of air as the nipple stood at attention. Laura flicked her tongue at it, the kissed it as saliva soaked through the blouse. Aquina said nothing, Laura put the weight of her head back where it was and slowly reached up with her lips and kissed her friend lovingly on the throat. She did nothing else, but Aquina began stroking Laura's head as a mother to a child. In a few minutes Laura sat up with a self-concious look. Aquina smiled, and stroked the back of Laura's head with the right hand. She leaned over and kissed Aquina's cheek then sat up again. Aquina gently touched her friend's mind and saw fear, uncertainty and the overwhelming need to feel protected and loved. Her mind was open and fragile, vulnerable.

CHAP. 54

The attention from Laura continued at about the same level, at least for awhile. At the close of the spring semester, after Aquina finished all the exams scoring a net average of four-o, Laura invited Aquina over to her apartment for dinner. While Laura wore a halter dress, Aquina wore a silk halter short enough to allow three inches of bare midriff above a snug slimming skirt, and neither woman wore a bra. Laura filled the wine glasses from one of three bottles of a dry rhine wine smiling at the thought of three bottles of one hundred proof vodka sitting in the cabinet.

During the course of dinner all the wine was consumed along with a good deal of conversation. Afterwards, while she put on a nice record, Laura started making stiff martinis. This is where Aquina began feeling it mixing martinis with rhine wine was definitely not wise. They both had long since discarded shoes and after several more refills of martinis cuddled together on the sofa, letting waves of soft music flow around them. Aquina still held a good deal of control over herself, and although debating how far to let Laura go . . . could not deny she enjoyed her friend's velvet touch.

Laura with her face again resting on a large breast, sat up a little and put one arm around Aquina's back and the left hand on her friend's satin-like midriff. The head gently like a child, caressed the open skin feeling the strength and well formed muscle underneath, the bottom of the large breast barely brushing the hand. Aquina partially restrained Laura by hugging her attempting to reason softly, gently without resorting to other methods.

Laura's hand already held one breast seeking out gently kneeding and stroking the pleasure areas around the breast. Places known usually only to women, usually ignored or unknown to men. Laura sunk down, raised the hem-edge of the halter, and was just starting to suck on a nipple . . . when she passed out. Aquina carried her into the bedroom, undressed Laura and put her in bed . . . shut everything off, checked the alarm clock and left for the brownstone.

The summer and fall semesters went by successfully, grades were consistent, and the extra-curricular activities progressed well. The fencing club grew in size, and notoriety during this period. During the year Laura became even closer to Aquina, but changes were becoming noticeable. Laura was becoming stronger and more like her old self. And in keeping with the previous year's festivities, Aquina planned, with Laura's help, another party for the gymnasium.

Meanwhile, newspapers continued to run more and still more stories and editorials on the space race. This hype kept gaining in size and momentum over shadowing other news.

But the war in southern asia was fast gaining notoriety. Quite frequently, she sent cables to Dien, and called on holidays.

The year '65, wasn't too much different than the previous one, save the fact of Aquina's increasing school popularity. And because of the vicious winter, she hired a houseman and purchased a formidable vehicle equipped with "muscle", and a plow. She wanted the added assurance of being able to attend classes irrespective of the weather, hence the prime reason for her hiring a houseman. His principle task during that winter was the clearing of the driveway, walks and both front and rear stoops. Through his advice and help, she found and purchased the right vehicle. It was just one of many duties . . . the maintenance of the vehicle and driving her to class if necessary. And the need was frequent that winter as snow and ice continued to accumulate.

Also during that winter of '65, Aquina went out with the frenchman to a variety of places, and uaually as not Laura and an upperclassman she met at the christmas party accompanied them making it a foursome. And because Laura's mental stability increased, she didn't need to "cuddle" with Aquina quite so much; in fact, it was steadily decreasing in frequency and intensity. In her own behavior, Aquina began to relax more, especially after aceing all her exams. And during the summer semester they would use part of a weekend for a picnic, to the beach, or on a friend's boat. Marcel's associate from years past owned a boat which he and Aquina occasionally borrowed. Fairly often they invited Laura and her friend.

The going out began casually enough as two fencing instructors, for she had been officially listed as such soon after the exhibition match when the club first formed. He delighted in not only relating stories from his own experiences about her "mother." He told other anecdotes heard from others, but the fact she would even consent to be out with him . . . was a surprise. For the first half dozen or so interludes, or discussions, he drove her back to the campus, where even kissing didn't take place. She would then take her own car home. However, there came one evening in early june in which they ended up in a drive-in movie. Marcel's car was equipped with bench type seats, and that evening, Aquina had worn a short 2" above-the-knee length pleated skirt, and a black skimpy halter. A good three inches of bare midriff was exposed, but mostly covered by a light sweater. The halter is a brief little thing just barely covering her 41" treasures.

Marcel had difficulty keeping his eyes off her midriff and undulating hips and her well rounded tush. After they had parked in a good spot, with easy access to the concession stand, she moved over next to him, the thighs touching. Quick as a squirrel, he was up an out the car door mumbling something about soda and popcorn. Aquina smiled inwardly, and took off the light sweater throwing it in the back seat. She then lightly rubbed her bare arms, and the seat felt good on her bare back. In fact the black silk hid only the bare essentials revealing a great deal of tan skin. The already short skirt was easily half way up her tan thighs and as a finishing touch, she dabbed some of her best perfume inbetween the large melon-like breasts, behind the ears and underneath her black lace panties.

A few minutes later Marcel returned carrying a light cardboard tray of soda and assorted goodies. After re-adjusting the speaker, he took everything out of the tray putting most of it up on the dashboard. The movie started and when he looked at her for the first time since returning to the car, and saw the mouth—watering thighs, and the proud nipples pushing through the black silk . . . he sighed heavily swallowing hard. Aquina smiled a little, and snuggled up-against him so Marcel involuntarily put his right arm around her shoulder. She quickly slid over the remaining distance. His hand easily layed on her right breast, but instead laid innocently on her arm. Instinctively he hugged her tight against him, not roughly but gentle, painfully aware of the growing erection in his pants.

She put her head back on his arm and let out a little sigh. Marcel could stand it no longer, and turning his head . . . she turned toward him . . . brushed her soft yielding lips, lightly, then more urgently. From lips to her ears licking inside, then the soft inviting throat, all the while his right hand massaged the hard nipple. He felt and instead of finding her thighs soft, they are firm and solid with a velvet surface, and his left hand explored both, moving on up to the lace panties.

Marcel marveled over how she let him take control, too pushing her legs open. With varying amounts of pressure . . . massaged the inviting mound, and the wet recess just below it. When he took his hand out from under her skirt, Aquina softly protested. He quickly opened his pants, and pulled himself out with a sigh of relief. The crudeness of it only made her blood race even more as she tentatively reached out and grasped it, amazed at the heat and the way it pulsated. Marcel was still fondling the right breast with his other hand, as he leaned over and sucked the other aroused nipple. Aquina let out a little squeal of delight, and began pulling urgently on Marcel's large manhood. With her free hand, she grasped his, pulling it back down inbetween her legs. She had never been so on fire before, she loved and craved the hot electric feelings coursing through breasts and lower abdomen. Marcel stopped and sat up, his head back. "I think we should leave." She nodded.

The first feature was over anyway and they departed, driving to Marcel's apartment. He showed Aquina around the typical bachelor apartment. She kicked off the heels, while he mixed two stiff vodka's. Marcel watched her look at the cheap reproductions . . . . marveling at how the enormous breasts sat proudly out firm and jiggling, swaying as she moved. His mouth watered and another erection tented his slacks. This time however . . . Marcel made no attempt to hide it, and walked back into the livingroom. Noticing his "condition," Aquina smiled. "Did I do that?"

"Mon cheri, you are the most beautiful and sensuous woman I have ever seen. Merely to look at your magnificent body and face makes my blood boil." Aquina flashed him a bewitching smile and started looking through the extensive record collection. She found bolero . . . and other similar mood music, and stacked them above the stereo turntable in order . . . flipped the on switch and pushed the selecter. Marcel had come up behind her, the erection pushing into her lush skirt covered bottom. He released the button and slid the zipper down; then with both hands slid the skirt over the gorgeous hips letting it drop to the floor. She obliged by stepping out of it as he threw it on the chair. Hours later the lovers parted.

CHAP. 55

Later that evening, feeling troubled . . . Roak went to the private room that supposedly is a duplicate of the chancel located in the temple. Reserved for the royal family, none . . . . no citizen of Tucana could enter the temple, as its door had been closed . . . and remained thus for untold eons of time. Therefore, Roak felt extremely self-concious . . . . He had not opened his mind or heart to the universal presence since he was a youth; and wasn't really sure he could recall the proper words learned so long ago.

Going into the adytum, Roak stood inches from the low rail resting his hands on it . . . trying to open his mind. Moments went by as he concentrated offering communion, and hoped-wished for his nephew to survive. Roak had very often treated young Roak like a son rather than a nephew. His brother was the overly ambitious one, taking unnecessary risk to further the family's power and influence. The older Roak was the administrator, the organizer of the Tywr family, and thought it strange that now . . . he is emperor. His brother although living was bed ridden, able to get around only with the aid of a robot attendant chair. Because of that he would never be emperor . . . . as there existed legal requirements, as old and firm as the monarchy itself . . . .

> ". . . . any noble person must be of sound body and mind, willing and able to cast off all encumberances, allegiances and loyalties, and to assume the throne . . . . to have loyalty and allegiance only for the Tucanan people and empire."

Very often it was to the elder Roak, the younger looked to for sage advice and counsel, especially when his own father was not available. Such an instance, when after attaining his scarlet cloak, that of a captain in the empire's ground forces. And most especially when as an accomplished young man and the lure/lust for adventure proved too potent to ignore.

A quarter of an hour later Roak re-entered the sleep chamber and dutifully laid down, but remained half awake thinking. Soon his mind began putting together a plan; during which various scenarios began flitting across his mind's eye. However, not all the scenarios were discarded, some were kept . . . . thus began forming into a definitive plan. Roak's mind continued to build on it as the hours passed. And finally in the wee hours, while most of the palace operated a skeleton shift working, ... he awoke. The furrowed brow of hours ago, now smooth, a look of firm resolve on the emperor's face.

Waving on the multiple light sources, Roak sat at a small writing desk and worked feverishly swiftly covering several sheets of pasid (a plastoid material processed into "paper" and several thousand other products) with memorandums, notes et-cetera. Almost an hour later he leaned back and reviewed his work. And satisfied with the results thus far, massaged a twitching muscle in his neck as he waved off the light sources. He tucked away the sheets of pasid, and returned to his sleep chamber.

In the days that followed palace personnel multiplied, appointed from lists handed to Roak by Barith, and some assistant ministers. Those chosen by the palace seneschal and domo were split between the heavily automated kitchen's and the domestic departments. The entire responsibility for maintenance on all levels fell to a separate seneschal. As there was no "lady of the house," Roak is unjoined, these three reported directly to the emperor.

On the other hand those Roak chose were instructed and briefed in order to help administer to the needs of the people. And Roak discussed with Barith, only after the old soldier brought up the point (in a delicate way of course), the recruiting of more personal aides. They helped Roak deal with the mundane, the tedious . . . or helped him to do it for himself.

Of course Barith headed the military branch of the rapidly growing department within the palace. He was assigned junior officers due to the ever increasing work load; but in part because of the confidence and esteem Roak felt for the man. In all their years previous, Roak had never known Barith to give anything but honest intelligent counsel, and is the soul of discretion.

That very afternoon, having only moments ago finished briefing the new junior officers, and left the assigning of duties to his second in authority, Barith walked into the first and outer room of the emperor's sumptuous suites. One of the attendants came out and said it would only be a few minutes. And indeed, Barith had only sat down when the same attendant admitted him to the emperor's private office, part of the first suite of rooms. Observing protocol, Barith continued to stand because Roak is standing. On the desk rested a scarlet bundle, and on top of that . . . . a tiny box.

There were few instances in Barith's long distinguished career in which he felt both nervous and excited . . . but this was definitely one of those times. Roak walked around his desk. "This should have been done years ago, my friend." Roak took off Barith's collar insignia and opening the tiny box, dumped its contents into his hand. In a second or so, the new captain's insignia shined brightly from Barith's collar. Roak turned and held the scarlet cloak while his friend doffed the old one, and accepting the new one and fastened it secure to his tunic. Barith's throat was dry and the worlds laced with emotion . . . "Thank you, sire." They drank to it, and moments later both departed for individual appointments.

Roak was awaited within the large rectangular imperial court room, where all the senior magistrates from the empire sat in judgement. Now however, the appearance of the duplicate throne positioned in the middle of the arc stirred more than just curiosity . . . . some concern over what the emperor would say or do was evident. Normally the court's function was to arbitrate the existing laws and make recommendations to the emperor for new laws. Several of the judges were discussing a case in point when the imperial chime sounded. Standing quickly the judges waited as Roak walked in crisp and business-like and sat down, giving every indication of being ready to begin. And almost immediately told them why he decided to appear and exactly what they were to do.

"And in addition to your other responsibilities . . . you . . . each of you, will review all laws pertaining to the empire as a whole, and recommendations to change or discard them; or in what way they may be altered to serve the greater good." Roak went on to say more. "But more important all our laws must keep pace with the empire, and its people. They must all go through a process of re-evaluation and if necessary . . . revised. If that does not prove practical . . . the individual law must be discarded and re-written."

"I full well realize the enormity of the task. Therefore, each of you shall submit a list of knowledgeable, quality persons . . . who of course must already sit on a regional court. I shall listen to your opinions in each case, and assistants will be appointed to handle your normal caseloads. And henceforth the only individual cases you'll hear directly, other than arbitrate an unusual case from some lower court, shall be those involving the throne." Roak finished and sat looking at each of the nine judges, as a few seconds passed each of them bowed toward Roak while, still seated . . . . then stood and applauded.

Remaining on the agenda were a number of cases involving the subject of trade, and how there was conflict of law. Roak decided to stay.

In front of the wide arc, as if one long white counter solid in the front and on top with a one foot high rim around the front edge, the floor dropped away seven feet. And centered twelve feet in front of the judge's bench is located the legal C'pter, ensconced permanently within a small island loaded with sensors and other paraphernalia. Again another twelve feet beyond that is located two rows of triangular shaped desks, where participants and legist's, acting as adviser or legal agent. Each row held twenty such triangles, with each "desk" containing voice enhancer equipment and recess's for belongings et-cetera.

Only moments before entering, the participants and legist's, and all those who would be in court, were told they would see the new emperor, and were instructed in the proper forms of address and proper conduct.

The thick two story metal doors disappeared into the walls, and in walked the participants, their legists and witnesses for each group . . . all under the watchful eyes of four armed marshalls. Standing by the desks they bowed en'masse to the emperor . . . and only when Roak nodded did they sit down. And almost immediately the legist for each side carried their evidence to the C'pter. Laying the material on each side of the center sensor displays, each inserted a plick into each of the appropriate slot for assimilation.

Inasmuch as the citizens came from the close system of Sa-gor, the judge on the panel who held jurisdiction over that system opened the proceedings. "With permission sire." Roak nodded with a smile, and the judge had C'pter read the case . . . plaintiff, defendant, and the basis for the action and other particulars. The judge then had each side present any last minute statements they might wish to make in their behalf. Some moments went by while the judge thought and considered his decision. But instead of voicing any decision, he spent some seconds writing then signaled to his aide standing a yard or so behind him . . . . to take the note to the emperor.

Roak opened and read the note . . . . "In this case it is the law which is more at fault, hence the reason why hereafter all laws will be scrutinized carefully, and revised where necessary.

The court has reviewed the case and find both participants equally responsible, and because much time and effort has been wasted in argument and fued . . . it stops here!! During your struggle you've lost sight of the fundamental point. That is . . . trade, the business, the art of exchanging commodities for other commodities or for money. And or the art of the "barter" for profitable gain." Roak let his words hang in the air for a few seconds then continued.

"Therefore, in as much as neither of you can afford the opening and stabilization costs necessary, the court has decided the cost is to be divided three ways. Each of you will assume a third of the burden, while the empire will assume the remaining third. In fairness you together will reimburse the empire for, after an agreed upon interval, its share, at which time the route will be yours jointly. Understand, . . . at no time will the empire actually be an active partner." Roak stated.

"We assume this agreement meets with your approval?" Both participants nodded smiling broadly. "Yes, thank you sire." They said almost in unison. All the participants were ushered out to sign required documents, et-cetera. Of course those outside waiting patiently, perhaps a little apprehensive were calmed at news of the emperor's decision. Indeed, the court, all the judges felt it was eminently fair, practical and greeted with much enthusiasm, . . . as it meant work for more people in that area of the empire.

Other cases were heard, and decisions handed down, and in each . . . . the tone and substance was similar.

After adjourning for the day, the court retired for their meal. However, Roak instead of taking time to eat spent the period in his formal office reviewing certain mining treaties and commercial contracts, deeds, surveys all belonging to the family. About fourty-five minutes later, Barith was a step or so behind Roak as he walked from his office toward the private dining hall, followed by newly appointed ministers and secretarys. Roak silently signaled to one seneschal . . . he would be dining with his military aides, and other staff members.

The short meeting hadn't even accounted for an hour, when over half departed for their own departments and staff. Meanwhile, Roak signaled his key aides to join for the meal, as gradually the palace staff was becoming accustomed to the emperor's "working meals."

CHAP. 56

Hours later, exhausted from prolonged lovemaking, Marcel drove Aquina back to her car.

The summer semester began as always, hot and humid. And Aquina acted the same way toward Marcal, no-one would suspect he was her lover, or that she was capable of the metamorphises . . . . from one of refined patrician behavior to a total sexually uninhibited female interested-obsessed with the acquiring and giving of sensual pleasure.

In june the club experienced a surge of growth and instead of meeting twice a week, Aquina and Marcel tentatively arranged a third meeting. With Laura and Dave doubling with them so often, they joined the discussion periods at various places including Marcel's apartment, Laura's apartment, and or Aquina's brownstone. During the course of several evenings they revamped the club's schedule for a firm three days. And as a general rule both women dressed a little on the conservative side, which did nothing to reduce the men's blood pressure.

It wasn't long before each couple retired to different areas of whichever apartment they were in and made love.

This went on all summer heating up their friendship, until the two couples happened upon circumstances that changed everything.

It chanced to be the first saturday after Aquina's summer semester exams, in which she again maintained solid four-o's. An overcast morning and all four went shopping, and the humidity and heat was oppressive. All four wore shorts, of course the girls . . . . theirs were tight and both wore loose blouses. The men had on T-shirts in complimentary colors, and commented on the skimpy bathing suits bought on sale, in fact they made many such purchases. Early their men went off on their own visiting a shop which specialized in custom sporting equipment, and made several purchases planning on using them at some later date. And after they bought several bottles of liquor, each were on their way to the car when the heavens opened up catching the men, the ladies in the open drenching them to the skin. Once in Dave's van the bundles in the far back corner . . . . Marcel bent over kissing one of Aquina's nipples through the now transparent blouse. With one hand, Aquina pulled his head in hard telling him to nibble hard as she undid the bottom buttons, and the rest, opening the blouse, and then opened her shorts. Dave and Laura looked in the back hot and got turned-on. "God, look at those breasts." He went in the back through the space inbetween the seats, and with both hands on one breast began sucking and lightly biting the nipple. Laura had in the meantime stripped and went in the back.

Dave and Marcel stopped what they were doing and quickly got out the sleeping bags, blankets, and a few pillows from the lockers built into the sides. The plush carpeting throughout lent an air of comfort as the torrential rain continued. Laura was still oblivious to everything. With the doors locked, drapes pulled in the back . . . they continued.

The rain continued and so to did the couples for several more hours as they exchanged partners and positions. When they finally drove out of the parking lot, Aquina and Marcel were dropped off and each couple went off in pursuit of their own fun. Their open sexual get-togethers continued well into the winter, until . . . Laura became pregnant; But although she and Dave were married . . . it still continued much as it had before with only slight variations.

The christmas party was a rousing success and coupled with consistently excellent grades made Aquina breath easier. But, Aquina knew the upcoming courses this year would be more difficult, especially back-to-back, and the lab courses were absorbing many hours of study. And decided during the holiday to begin shopping whenever possible through alternative means. It was not to many weeks later that catalogs of all types started arriving. At the same time Marcel showed her some very risqué, and hot sexual ads, and catalogs he acquired, dealing with marital aides of all sorts. He took out some of the many "toys" in his collection and showed her how good they felt. Marcel gave her ten of them varying in size and shape, some battery powered, while others were not. Aquina took them home with her and began using them each evening. Several days passed and while cleaning the princess's bedroom the young svelte upstairs maid happened to find one. She is young with well rounded hips, long legs, narrow waist and "C" cup breasts. Too some extent the girl is a small version of her mistress, but highly over-sexed.

That very afternoon, Aquina came home at the normal time and went upstairs after looking at the mail. Feeling horny, she prepared for a workout. She had been exercising for well over an hour, and decided to use one of the vibrators before her shower. Climbing out of the damp sweaty workout clothes, Aquina paused at the light knock on the door . . . and said "come in." The maid entered with a large towel and stopped, staring at her nude mistress.

Dressed in a traditional french maid's uniform with tiny skirt and black mesh pantyhose, Miriam was definitely not going to pass-up this opportunity. Aquina knew all to well what was whirling through Miriam's mind, and didn't overly mind the thought as she saw the maid lick her full lips.

Aquina was sitting on an upholstered bench seat with storage area underneath, and the large vibrator laid next to her. "Come sit next to me." Miriam with a small curtsy, smiled, and didn't take her eyes from the large melon-like breasts as she almost sat on the vibrator. The maid jumped up, Aquina stood with the vibrator in hand and bent over the open seat putting it back with the other toys. Having discarded her uniform the maid sat up and moved laying down next to Aquina and began kissing the seemingly delicate rib cage. Miriam went slow with both hands and stroked the sides of the tantalizing breasts. They continued to play for another hour until Aquina called a halt. Miriam got dressed then knelt in front of her mistress and kissed the slightly recessed belly button then scampered off to attend to chores. Aquina showered and dressed going down to the dining room and kitchen for coffee.

The new year, '66, progressed much like '65, except more demands were made for her time, from the club and elsewhere. At least at the club there was Marcel to help, but the other request made recently was such, she could not refuse. It was a natural chain of events really, the more contests in which the club participated, the more widely known she became. She supposed it was normal someone in the asian community would take notice. But between three club meetings a week and the extra labs, her available daylight hours were at a premium. It was at a wednesday club meeting when the two korean gentlemen appeared.

One is clearly middle age and the younger perhaps twenty, and standing in the doorway, the older man clutched the younger one's arm. "There, there . . . . is Little Star exactly as I remember her." But the younger man objected, whispering, . . . "it is not possible father. She is but a young woman, younger than I . . ." "Fool! You have learned nothing. She is immortal compared to us." Without turning, Aquina called over. "Wou Lee, I will be with you in a moment." He bowed, and smiling moved over to a wooden bench and sat down. The son was a little intrigued as to how she could know they were there and know their names.

She finished with a lesson and walked with cat-like strides to stand a few feet away, and as she approached . . . the two men got up and bowed deeply from the waist. Speaking first, Aquina recognized and addressed the elder. "Always am I glad to see a friend . . . Wou Lee, and your son, you have done well. It is good to see he no longer torments the oxen." The older man smiled as the younger showed some discomfort. In the interim she gently looked into the minds of both men, and each experienced a slight warm feeling in their heads . . . an instant later it was gone.

Wou Lee was going to speak. "No need my friend, I know the errand that brings you to me. And, I look forward to officiating at the temple's opening. And as for the gang who desecrated the first temple . . . they will not escape, nor will they interfere." The young man felt the malevolent words, more . . . than he heard them. As the enormous surge of energy hit him and his father. Indeed, all the people in the room winced from an unseen pressure. For the first time in his life . . . the young man experienced the cold steel hands of fear. He looked, silently . . . eyes closed to Buddha. This he did for guidance . . . too do nothing, nor speak out of turn . . . or do anything that might incur the wrath of his "priestess."

Aquina sensed the change in the young man and smiled inwardly. She had them sit and relax, and explained they will be leaving with her immediately after the class. Between that moment and the end of the class, she spoke to Marcel giving a partial reason for asking him to take the entire class on friday. It was only for the weekend, and she would be back sunday night. When they did leave the young man was relieved the ride was brief, being cramped in the small rear area behind the seats.

With the father and son comfortable in the guest rooms, she made two calls . . . both for reservations. One for a hotel suite in manhattan, and the second for airline seats, specifying in each case the number of people involved. The intervening period went quickly and for Aquina, it was just as well. Late friday afternoon the five arrived in manhattan, checked into the hotel and was glad she had decided to bring the upstairs maid and the houseman with her. It was much easier handling their bags, and her wooden weapon's case, which Bill carried. That evening was spent in the two bedroom suite, with both dinner and breakfast provided by room service. The father and son shared one room, Miriam slept in the other, while Bill tried to sit-up on the plush sofa watching Aquina. She stayed for hours sitting in the same lotus position meditating and praying. When the father and son came into the large living room they shook him awake, . . . trying hard to be quiet not wishing to disturb . . . "Little Star."

The four sat around the breakfast nook, with coffee and toast asking questions of Wou Lee about Aquina. "Why did they come to her?" "And what was this business about a temple? And how did she know Wou Lee?" Neither of them believed what Wou Lee had to say, except Miriam, remarked witnessing Aquina doing a kind of breathtaking exercise. Each of them contributed to the discussion, the reluctance on the part of Bill was slowly eroding. For Miriam's part, she half believed Wou Lee's answers without any additional coaxing. Bill tried to understand, but found it too fantastic. He needed to see with his own eyes and to some extent Miriam was of the same mind.

Aquina walked into the nook during a lull in the conversation and filled a cup with steaming coffee from the pot provided from room service, sat down and began to sip slowly. Handing Miriam a piece of paper, "you and Bill do some shopping. Pick up this list of things and here is some money. I expect to return some time this evening." Miriam nodded, "yes ma-dam."

It was a partly sunny day, in point of fact, whatever type of day it was . . . it would not have altered the scene or what is about to happen. The participants caught up in the business of opening the new temple are part of the drama, . . . as well as those responsible for ruining the first attempt and desecrating the first building. Miriam and Bill left early, but not before Wou Lee slipped them the address of the temple, and the time the ceremony was to start. And two and-a-half hours before the ceremony was to begin, Aquina changed into a black turtleneck, black slacks and a nondescript jacket. Just before stepping out the door, she slipped into a pair of canvas mocs. She swung the large shoulder bag containing the light blue hooded robe, one ornate candle, plus the normal sundries found in any elegant woman's pocketbook or shoulder bag . . . on her shoulder.

There was still an hour and fifty minutes before the simple ceremony, as they got out of the taxi about three blocks away from their destination. Aquina wanted an opportunity to walk through a portion of the Asian community . . . get a sample of the feelings and prevailing sentiment. This she did, occasionally to chat with vendors, shop owners and people on the street. But she listened, talking little except to answer a question. And the street toughs gave way when she approached or at least most of them. Those that did not happen to see her received a rude awakening. For in those instances, Aquina doled out justice befitting the crime encountered whether it was robbing and old person, extortion, assault or some other offense.

The appointed hour for the ceremony was close, and in spite of her wanting to continue the walk, she returned to the new temple with Wou Lee and son in tow. She quickly changed and turned the waves of hair pinning it up on top, and hiding the candle in an inside pocket . . . was ready. And already people gathered inside kneeling in rows filling all the floor area, save an aisle in the center, and that aisle is covered by an ornate carpet. It measured five by nine feet and laid upon the floor evenly on either side of the small alter. The floor is occupied now on either side with people kneeling. Wou Lee positioned Miriam and Bill in the far rear corner, where they have an excellent view.

On either side of the small alter were double rows of white candles casting a soft glow beginning at six feet on down to waist high, with scrolls hanging on the wall. With a soft melodic chime of a diminutive gong . . . the whispering ceased instantly. A door opened, and through a curtain came a hooded figure bare foot carrying a two foot high bronze Buddha. Bill was astonished, estimating the statue's weight at least several hundred pounds, if it was an ounce. He watched as the figure turned to stand in front of the alter. The figure raised the statue and placed it gently on the white silk drape covering the alter. The robed figure backed a step and bowed respectfully, stood and with hands and arms folded in front lowered with smooth flowing grace into a lotus position.

Immediately apparent to everyone the figure was a woman, not only because of the curves underneath the robe, but the prayer was in a woman's voice. It lasted for about eight minutes, after which the figure produced a lighted candle. Having quickly lit it while the robe blocked everyone's view, and bending forward . . . she placed it in the waiting receptacle. The candle wasn't in place more than a few seconds when sounds of a disturbance outside suddenly became much louder as three asian gang members pushed and shoved until they stood just inside the front door. The people cowered from the three intruders, but nothing serious happened until two of them pulled hand guns out from under their jackets.

Suddenly the unexpected, all three were seized by an unseen and unyielding force. They were yanked up virtually off their feet hanging like rag dolls holding their heads, the guns still held by two of them. In fear and awe the people tried to move back from the horror. People looked at the robed figure still praying and back to the three men being shoved out the door. Once outside . . . whatever had been holding them . . . let go to collapse in silent death. Their faces . . . grotesque masks mirroring unimagineable pain and agony . . . laid motionless. In scant seconds every person in the temple was told what happened. Wou Lee, although shaken, smiled bowing repeatedly . . . while his son shook from fear . . . bowed as did his father.

Miriam and Bill stared in awe, speechless with their mouths open, and as if one they knelt and prayed in ernest.

Wou Lee felt something warm and gentle in his brain and looking up . . . saw the robed figure point with the right hand to a spot on the carpet next to her. Still bowing, he took careful steps kneeling next to her joining in the prayer. When his father moved, the son looked up and tears welled up inside spilling over to run down the youthful face, for he knew of no greater honor that could be bestowed on his father . . . a lay priest.

Meanwhile outside, some people had taken the three bodies and carried them into a nearby alley. It was already dusk when the robed figure finished the long prayer, bowed once and stood followed almost instantly by Wou Lee. He moved and stood on the robed figure's left side as she made a hand gesture meaning the people should present themselves and offer prayer.

While they did this, she moved slowly gravitating toward the door, in time to hear shouts and threats directed toward the temple and its followers. And before those gathered outside could react, she walked calmly through the door and stood among them moving to the front of the group. Standing on the sidewalk close to the curb, she is confronted by eleven gang members forming an arc in front armed with a wide variety of hand weapons. The hood still partially hid the face, and the face changed. The darker it became the more effective the hood, until virtually no-one could see her face unless . . . very close.

She noticed a large luxurious sedan parked at the curb across and down the street some thirty yards. There, she concentrated . . . the gang leader stood next to the street side rear door, while inside a crime overlord and two lieutenants lounging eagerly . . . waiting the temple's destruction. Seconds ticked by . . . the one standing next to the car grabbed his head, as did the three inside. The air is filled with blood curdling screams and shrieking. It stopped, four dead bodies . . . one next to the car and three inside. Instantly some in the gang voiced threats and began marching forward brandishing their weapons.

Those thugs on the flanks, five in all, clutched and pawed at their heads screaming . . . and in a matter of six seconds the eleven became six. Their fear caused the remaining gang members to charge.

In the interim, Miriam and Wou Lee's son had come out on the sidewalk, and saw bodies laying in the street. They watched as the first two attacked with a machete and a wrecking bar. By now both sides of the street was crowded with on-lookers, the poor and down-trodden wanting revenge. But this . . . nothing could have prepared the crowd for what they had witnessed, and it wasn't finished, and they trembled in spite of self-control.

The first pair went down quickly in a blur of movement, and a third from a power kick to the sternum. And with similar grace, she destroyed the remaining three . . . and without uttering a single sound the entire time turned, walking back toward the temple entrance. Bowing, the people backed forming an aisle to the entrance, as she walked slowly to the door and went inside. And in so doing afforded Wou Lee the opportunity for a chat. Both heard the persistent wail of police sirens, until five cars with screeching tires came to a halt in the vicinity of the bodies, and seconds later more cars arrived disgorging grim-faced men.

Ending their brief talk, Wou Lee went outside to confront the police and tell them . . . "he knew nothing." Aquina changed from the blue robe to her street clothes, and by way of a side door walked with an easy stride to the front sidewalk. As she did more ambulances began arriving and news trucks with reporters. She tapped Bill and Miriam on the arm, "come." They did so with alacrity falling into step on either side and walked a block away from the scene, across the street and north three blocks before hailing a cab.

Still not a word was exchanged between them until reaching the hotel. And again, no-one took notice of the three entering the elevator. And once in the suite they relaxed for hours. Bill officiated at the bar, repeatedly mixing the drinks stronger and stronger, until they drank the liquor straight. During which Miriam showed Aquina the items she purchased according to the list given to her earlier. Aquina liked all of the black lace lingerie, fishnet stockings and other articles. Although the evening ended with Miriam and Bill making mad love together, Aquina was content to strip down to her panties and go to bed alone.

Mid morning sunday, with all of the luggage and baggage in tow, the three boarded a return flight to Logan. Marcel was prompt and picked them up spending the entire balance of the day at the brownstone. Still no-one spoke of the happenings they witnessed in manhattan.

That monday, Aquina resumed her schedule, and march slipped away as did april, and almost all of may.

The semester ended successfully as had the others. Summer followed and winter with cumulative grades reinforced her four-o average. Immensely popular and the club doing well . . . she was happy, or at least as happy as she thought it possible too be, but certain doubts remained. Doubts about her sexuality and the affair with Marcel, or the pleasant interlude with Laura and Dave, Miriam. It wasn't that she didn't enjoy the sex . . . she did, but didn't feel that star shaking ectasy, the raptures, elation that she knew the others experienced. Aquina didn't let on not wishing to hurt Marcel, and continued with the sexual get-togethers. The more Aquina pondered the problem, the more perplexed she became, and finally well into the '67 spring semester passed it off. "It was because she is different, odd . . . not like a normal woman." The pain, it was a dreadful period of absorption and logic. Aquina could not change what she was or had become, only grow and through meditation accepted the pain, marked it . . . and used it to strengthen herself.

CHAP. 57

Her aura increased, a thing so subtle as to be indiscernible by the average person, but others detected it and so did the animals.

In may she graduated, valedictorian, but didn't really enjoy giving the traditional speech. Aside from sending a cable home and gifts, there wasn't to much she had to do immediately and postponed reading the mail. Most of it, aside from catalogs and sales notices, constituted job offers, but not a single envelope was opened. And when she did open them, read and answered thanking the person and or company explaining her decision to pursue the master's program in both disciplines. And the very next day she happened to catch the dean of admissions before he went on a summer vacation, explaining her decision, and asked him to arrange the paper work. And hours later, after lunch and the return of his secretary, the necessary papers were filled out and signed. That was all there was to it, she would begin in the fall.

She found most of the students had already left for the summer break, and as a consequence the club cut back to two one hour afternoon periods each week. Of course this left Aquina and Marcel more time, or at least he first thought so.

It began innocently enough, Aquina and Laura were in the city shopping and decided to have lunch at one of the posh yacht club restaurants lining the affluent area of the harbor. From a client Laura had the name of perhaps the most well known of the posh clubs, and had called early for reservations. Primarily known for its outdoor terrace which overlooked freshly painted docks and hundreds of yachts, but the cuisine was excellent and the atmosphere . . . perfect.

The sun was high and warm, and wearing only light transclucent blouses of silk and pleated mini-skirts, they drew many an admiring eye as the ladies were seated at a table directly against the terrace railing.

During lunch they chatted about styles, the war and what they were going to do for the summer. It is the first week in june, and they had to decide soon. And while discussing what to do and possible places to go . . . the head waiter brought another bottle of wine. And before either lady could object the waiter said, "excuse me ladies . . . from the midshipmen." He quickly opened the bottle after Aquina . . . "would you open it please?" "With pleasure miss." As soon as the waiter poured and withdrew . . . Aquina indicated for the midshipmen to join them.

Smiling both came over and introduced themselves, and Laura introduced her illustrious companion and herself. Aquina asked them about their uniform and the markings. Both men took turns explaining they are upper classmen at the naval academy, and came home on summer leave. After those opening statements the conversation raged for two hours more and another bottle of wine. After a time the conversation reverted back to the ladies. Aquina explained Laura is an attorney, and Laura explained Aquina had just graduated from the institute in Cambridge, and is in the master's program to begin in the fall, and she is co-instructor of the fencing club. Further, they were discussing what to do for the summer.

Before either young man could answer Aquina piped-up about looking at the boats at the dock below them, as several are for sale. She was trying to change the subject, not wanting the midshipmen to learn too much or get too close. As Laura told her later, "they were considered available because neither had an engagement ring or wedding band."

Aquina used a credit card to pay for lunch, wrote a generous tip on the form, initialed it, and signed on the appropriate line. The one midshipman sitting at her side noticed the name on the plastic card, and the two capital "H's" in front. He was curious but said nothing. The waiter bowed smiling. "Thank you mum." A term of affection used by the english toward certain titled females. And when exiting the maitre' d', bowed and touched is nose to her hand. "Thank you mum." "I enjoyed it very much especially the view." Aquina remarked.

She then inquired about the boats for sale at the dock. The maitre' d' explained it is immediately next door, across the few parking spaces . . . the sign saying, "yacht brokers." And he went on to ask permission. Aquina nodded. A quick phone call . . . and it was done. They will be expecting her. Aquina thanked him for his assistance and turned with Laura at her side.

Once outside the previous spirit of conversation seemed to dry up, the men are quiet, too quiet. Aquina was only partially successful in getting them to chat, but was satisfied for the time being and made a mental note to continue later.

They arrived, walked inside and everyone stood. The secretarys and three salesmen each with jacket and tie introduced themselves and in a minute or two are on their way down to the dock. Each man carried some information concerning the boats at the dock. One-by-one they showed them to her beginning with the smaller and working up in size and price. It didn't take long to reach the upper range in size and money. There remained three, one 48', up to 60' . . . She asked the young midshipman by putting her left arm around his right one, and into his eyes. "Steve, what do you think about them?" And she whispered, "first names please."

Indicating the larger, "there is no denying it is attractive, but it is for someone with considerable experience as a helmsman/operator. That is a lot of boat; whereas this 48' or 53' footer . . . these are more apt to suit your needs better. And one is a yacht fisherman and the other is a motoryacht, but no cockpit." Steve explained. She gave him a little squeeze. "I think your right Steve." Aquina said softly.

The senior salesman asked which one held the most appeal for her and Aquina nodded at the yacht fisherman. As the group walked over they filled in the blanks. It seemed there had been serious illness in the family and were forced to sell thereby getting out from under the hefty bank loan. "Your Highness, we can get it for at least two hundred thousand under its book value." Hinted the senior salesman. "Are you positive?" "Yes Your Highness."

"Very well, make your arrangements with the owner, while I look at it more closely, at which time with the owner's agreement, I will have a certified check delivered here by the bank." The realization of a cash deal on such a large boat practically made the salesman drool openly. Excusing themselves two of the salesmen hurried back to their office, while the third stayed to answer any questions.

"Steve, would you tell him to stay here on the dock, and we shall go take a closer look." He nodded, but didn't like this whole transaction. Oh it was good business, but the owners were being legally ripped off, and he didn't like to see these things happen. And when he finally rejoined the group . . . they were down below all smiles with mixed drinks. "Mike, what the . . ." "Here Steve . . ." And Mike poured him a generous amount of chivas in a glass, handing it to him. Smiling . . . Aquina indicated the owner's son Phillip. "Steve, Aquina is going to reimburse my folks for the equity they have in the Sea Dragon, plus give me a steady job." Steve smiled and took a healthy swallow of scotch.

"You see Steve, I simply loathe slobbering people. So by agreeing to a price that I heavily suspected was on their break-even point, the greedy idiot will actually make little on the deal. And Phillip's parents will be given their equity in cash, and he has a position with me as crew taking care of the boat."

The deal was agreed upon by the then current owners and save for the bank loan there was no liens on the boat. Inside of an hour and a-half the papers were drawn up, and of course, when the final figure was given by the bank holding the note . . . none of the salesmen were pleased. In fact when the arithmetic had been completed, their total fee or commission on the transaction amounted to little more than two thousand dollars, even the dockage fee was lost to them.

Aquina and Steve drove to the bank, and as she tooled the jag through traffic, Steve did his utmost to study her discreetly. The stop at the bank actually did not take that long, and leaving . . . Aquina carried the attache' case with a certified check tucked in her purse along with some mad money. Steve shook his head as they climbed back into the roadster for the quick trip back to the broker's office. Once everyone sat down the actual signing of the papers and the boat's re-registration papers required only a short time. She had receipts for everything, the various sets of keys and the multiple pages of neat type, listing each and every piece of inventory and equipment. Laura officiated as attorney for the buyer, i.e., and had two copies in her possession, when they left the office.

Steve and Mike stayed on the boat at Aquina's request, while she, Laura and Phillip drove to his parent's house. And at first the parents were a little hostile until phillip explained. Laura produced two copies of a statement, saying in affect the couple had been fully reimbursed for their equity in the boat; but no sum was mentioned and everyone smiled at the connotation, especially when she handed them the black case. They opened it and squealed with surprise, and consumed an hour discussing Phillip's responsibilities, and the fact Aquina should join the yacht club as a full member. They explained about that, the activities and a few other things . . . such as the idiosyncracies of the boat.

Everything was fine when they returned, and while Phillip started on the maintenance list given to him by Aquina, the four walked next door to the yacht club's main building. There sitting and talking to the secretary who politely verified the sale with the former owners and receiving a good deal of character information, while Aquina filled out all the forms, and showed her identification. She found the secretary pleasant and helpful and shortly after completing the paper work was given a nice tour of the facilities.

As it slowly moved and became mid-month, the two midshipmen became fairly regular fixures, along with her close friends and the household staff from the brownstone were usually onboard at least once a week. In due course Aquina had been welcomed into the yacht club and began fitting into the social atmosphere, with some reluctance. The green jag became a common sight in the parking lot as she usually spent a minmum of four days a week on her boat. And in the initial days of her membership, the regulars were concerned as how they should act, or how to strike up a conversation; but she let the air out of the tension with a smile and an extended hand in friendship.

Most of the time it was Laura, and Marcel, and Dave if not the midshipmen who were seen on the boat. And twice a week, she and Laura had lunch next door at their table, and always with a single red rose as a centerpiece. Plus they happily provided meals onboard, catered the parties, and in honor of her "mother," on the celebration of "D-day." The victory in europe, she catered a black tie dinner complete with muscians either on the boat or in the restaurant. Aquina reciprocated by sitting down with membership, such as attending, director and commodore, and planned a july 4th., party. Too wit, she invited all the personnel of the restaurant, and all those working next door at the boatyard, which is part of the yacht club.

And as luck would have it the party expanded covering much of the yacht club grounds. And with live music, dancing and laughter, a few small orgies went on in separate discreet areas, and on the larger powerboats. Phillip and his girlfriend were already deep in the throes of ectasy when Aquina and

Marcel came back aboard. Passing Phillip's cabin, which was immediately next to the engine space, the sound of squeals and grunts told everything. Passing the guest cabin, the door was wide open, Laura sat on Dave making animal noises, and continued on to the master stateroom. Inadvertently they left the door wide open while petting and drinking while in varied stages of undress. A little later it developed into the erotic sight and sound of group sex. The whole thing culminated in gasps and squeals, crys and grunts as the men climaxed, and the women experienced luscious multiple orgasms.

CHAP. 58

Although small compared to the other dining halls within the imposing palace, the private dining hall seated in excess of fifty, elegantly furnished and appointed with everything done to imperial standards, as indeed was the entire palace. The group ate heartily though slowly, punctuated with heavy conversation, and afterwards an amount of liquor. Their subject . . . . taxation and the financial state of the empire.

"A great deal has been squandered in the past, waste, abuses and more. All of this is going to stop . . . now!" Exclaimed the emperor, and continued. "Until such time as our combined efforts result in the repair of the tax structure, and duly investigate all suspicious expenditures, we have decided to begin mining acksathium ore, and corthium gem stones." Roak stated firmly. "But sire. Those are among your family's holding." "Very true minister. However, because of the tax roll-back and with the empire's finances in some disarray, there is no-other way. When the empire is safe and financially firm, ... it can then begin to reimburse the family for the worth involved."

"My emperor, please?" "Yes minister?"

With something of a stunned look upon her attractive face . . . . "You are buying a new empire?" His face slipped into a grin, "excellent minister, very astute." Even Barith was slightly taken-a-back. Roak continued. "In essence that is correct, but only in part; it will all become clear before too long."

They are all more than a little surprised, and perhaps some were concerned, but tried not to reveal the emotion. After-all, they reasoned, the new emperor had thus far accomplished more in a few weeks than his predecessor did during his whole reign. Several hours later, Roak bidded all the ministers and secretaries good night. And after the required protocol, rode to his wing and up one floor . . .

Disembarking from the two person slider with Barith behind him, also bid his friend good night; but instead of sleep, Roak headed for his private garden. Approximately the size of a large playing field, the emperor's garden lush with white and other rich multi-collored blossoms, blue-greens, exotic flowering shrubs, hanging crystals and numerous artful fountains with a thick resilient grass it covered all the walk and open areas. Roak walked for hours loosing himself amid the lushness, the aromas and the peace. He was almost totally alone, only occasional glimpses and sounds of tiny gray-brown long whiskered rodents, who sometimes would take a crumb or piece of something from a royal visitor. Leaving momentarily, Roak returned with small cakes and several pieces of fruit, and after cutting everything into small pieces, left his offering under different separately located shrubs and returned to his informal office.

He spent more than an hour working on his previous night's notes and then retired for the night. For a time thoughts and pictures flitted across his mind's eye, until a distinct pattern developed. It turned out to be only a short nap, but he awoke fired with purpose. Immediately . . . . Roak called Barith.

Barith stooped showing almost ancient battle scars on shoulders and arms, but the captain's uniform is clean and crisp. The second a young Jlun'or, who had been appointed a junior aide only a matter of days ago, responded promptly to Barith's late call. The old officer knew something important was afoot, else surely the emperor would have retired for sleep by this hour. With a measure of grace and agility unusual for one so old, Barith quickly prepared himself to answer his emperor's summons.

Barith answered first discreetly knocking then entered with a quick salute and . . . "my emperor." It is then the young junior officer came in and saluted, but said nothing in proper protocol to the address already given by the senior officer.

"You have served the empire faithfully Barith, without question. Now answer me as an officer with long battles behind him. Can we send a modest force with success to the rim, get our people . . . . and return?" Roak asked.

Barith straightened, smiled and said . . . "yes my emperor . . . we can; but we . . ." "Enough!" Roak said walking over and clasping Barith by the shoulders, and said . . . "good! Call all senior admirals immediately for a working meeting, bringing all pertinent star records and related information on the area. Remember old friend . . . our nephew is one of the traders marooned. We want him . . . be returned . . . safely!"

"Aha!! So that's what had been eating at him. Barith thought to himself as he signaled Jlun'or to send the summons, and who promptly vanished to the nearest vid-screen, while he would notify the proper seneschal.

By now the huge palace was more than awake. "The emperor had called military officers." That statement and rumors ran (and others as well) almost as fast as servants, attendants, and everyone who had something to do with any activity at/or connected with the palace and its attendant buildings, were at their places and jobs in case the emperor needed or should call on them for anything.

About fifty minutes later the most senior officers of the military arrived by personal and military flyers to the aerial garage adjacent to the palace, and immediately made their way to the council room. Whereupon arriving . . . Jlun'or advised them . . . . "The emperor will see them in the war room." The consternation on their faces would say a great deal had anyone taken notice of whom and to what extent.

The war room had not been used in recent memory, still the room had only moments ago been quickly cleaned and scented by select staff in preparation for the urgent meeting. With all its military headquarters command type equipment, it is very impressive, not so much its size, but what use of the room signified.

Admirals and aides filed into the cavernous room each standing at their respective places at the elongated "U" shaped table. Most of the room is in black with black metal trim. The stationery wall mural to the immediate right of the entrance is three dimensional . . . an accurate depiction of the empire. The home system, Tucana(also the name of their large blue-white star) is illustrated in gold with each of the nine systems having a separate and distinct color. Those colors corresponded to most of the C'pters, navigational and C'pters relegated to military preparedness and maneuvers. The table held voice and data controls for each area regardless of purpose, and on each small vid-screen surveillance data on any part of the home system, and for each system of the empire. However, in some systems toward the out-lying regions and all fringe areas and territories . . . the necessary sensors and transmitting equipment had been destroyed, so they are effectively blind in those areas.

The emperor's large chair dominated the relatively small side of the elongated "U" shape, or the base . . . a position of prominence. And with that the table held a similar unit as each of the admirals, but equipped with master override capability. This plus command unit communications and direct tie-ins to all the military's 'pters; plus controlling the large vid-screen occupying the opposite wall from the emperor's chair. In the six foot wide space inbetween the parallel sides of the table, is actually a hallographic area capable of projections to the most minute detail. Plus its able to have an object fully animated, change color, shape, add or subtract components and alter an object's apparent density.

All are still standing at attention quietly as Roak entered followed by Barith. Dressed in straight black tunic trimmed with black metal and the snug stirrup onavest(similar to a unitard), with shining black ankle boots . . . . the ornate scabbard of gold with the ancient sword of office, and the emperor's large medallion suspended by its gold chain thoroughly set the uniform off to eye-riveting advantage. The effect well exceeded his hopes, and as the emperor planned . . . it definitely did not go unnoticed even among the senior aides attached to each admiral. In one bold move Roak rose measureably in the esteem of all those present.

Roak removed the heavy ornate belt and scabbard and put it on the table to his left, and continued to stand looking at each admiral in turn, studying each face. And finally after some minutes formally called the meeting to order, and commenced to outline and partially explain a momentus plan of action for the future. In simplified, it was recorded as follows:

A) "Until further notice, the empire is now in a state of war!!" The officers sat stark still, and with an almost audible sigh all finally realized at long last they have an emperor worthy of "absolute power."

Attendants in the various sections of the palace knew important matters were discussed, and those close enough . . . . cast furtive glances at the doors behind which the future course of the empire was being decided.

> "War!! With those without and within . . . who consciously or unconsciously plot our destruction. We speak of those within, who practice complacency, disinterest, weakness and or protracted inactivity. Most especially with the forces without . . . . i.e., the raiders and other organized and unorganized enemies."

B.) "Before that is made public . . . . a well organized mission must be completed first. Too reiterate . . . . the fact the empire is openly at war must remain a closely held secret for now."

C.) "You will seal secret and prepare the entire moon Untey-3, the old military base, and make it battle ready. Whatever is required . . . . procure it, and for now . . . . submit everything to my aide Barith, or one of his assistants and we shall see all is provided with needed dispatch. Untey-3 will therefore always be a prime military installation for offensive and defensive operations."

The admirals who looked and perhaps acted old previous to the meeting now were as if thirty years younger, gesticulating their fellows . . . . silently and with good humor-itching to be into the fray.

D.) "In secret upgrade, repair, refurbish three vessels cruiser class immediately, for a very important mission."

Most officers were writing furiously inserting comments as they went. Each C'pter along both arms of the table, would provide a plick of the entire meeting for each admiral; but being somewhat old fashioned, enjoyed making their own notes.

E.) "While the as yet undisclosed mission is underway again upgrade, repair and refurbish every vessel possible regardless of size. All are to be equipped with guns, even scout ships should have as many as is safe to hold."

F.) "A comprehensive program: i.e. reopen and repair and recrew all of our docks, the dormant space

> yards, ground facilities that supply the yards and docks. In short fire-up the guilds in question . . . to begin getting ready to build new ships. We did it once . . . we must re-learn old skills and do it again. We must learn new things, new ways methods and with that . . . new weapons. Start as soon as you can immediately in fact. Our signed orders will be issued shortly."

"Let us take a short recess." Roak signaled for his aide. "Have refreshments brought in." Barith smiled, bowed . . . "Yes sire." Roak called for an interruption in the questions being asked. "We have ordered the only refreshment befitting honored soldiers. A smile and a nod went around the assembled officers.

After trusted attendants finished bringing in an ample supply and departed, the respective aides did the actual pouring. Roak stood, immediately followed by the assembled officers, and held his goblet high . . . "On this heavy night the first salute, I pledge to . . . . our empire."

They all drank deeply of the scathing hard beitra, the senior-most admiral stood with help from his aide, and said . . . "Sire, we here and the loyal empire have much to be thankful . . . for now we have a worthy commander . . . . a fighting emperor!" While giving no outward sign save a ghost of a smile, Roak is inwardly pleased.

An emperor wore the imperial military uniform trimmed in black and metal only during time of war, and by so doing assumed an important symbol for his people . . . absolute commander of the field. It was rare for an emperor to assume the position, to assume the risk, and had been done only once before. "We thank you." The emperor replied. "We appreciate the lateness of the hour, however, organized effort is imperative. Orders will be dispatched forthwith for all technic guilds, laboratories and manufacturing guilds to organize with the military for a single minded assault!" Roak continued. "For too long this empire of ours has been permitted to grow weak, lazy and soft, forgetful of its beginnings . . . its heritage. If we are to survive . . . the empire to survive and prosper, we must act now or loose everything. Therefore . . . . the important mission is . . . ."

A.) "It is necessary at once to re-open the search for the lost survivors of the trading vessel and the would-be rescuer. All records must be available to aid in planning, including the star plicks of the area."

A spontaneous reaction in the form of applause erupted around the room and when the admirals and aides quieted . . . the emperor continued.

> "The pilot and senior trader of the first vessel is our nephew and in place of his sire, whom we believe you know is incapacited of body, longs to see his son. We wait his return to us (Roak slams his hand palm down hard), moreover, he is a trained pilot intimately familiar with the area raiders occupy and their tactics. But above all, those are our citizens and therefore entitled to our best possible effort and support." He took another sip of the hard beitra, and continued. "Therefore, prepare

> and launch the mission with three ships heavily armed with the maximum of everything. Also a sealed envelope and a small box from us, will be given to him as quickly as is practical. Although this legally will convey upon hin "crown prince," the ceremonies will wait until you gentlemen have secured his return to us."

Roak stated, with the look of absolute determination. He had no sooner finished and regained his seat . . . . when the admirals began to ask questions. They were hard pressed not to interject to early, trying to observe protocol and keep their excitement under control. Not until each and every question had been answered did Roak adjourn the meeting. Which in itself took over fourty-five minutes . . . . but it had been necessary.

Roak stood, only then did the admirals stand and begin to file past him with the intention of "shaking hands." However, Roak brought up his left arm momentarily causing a second of confusion for the first admiral, but as each grasped the other's left forearm(the ancient shield arm, a salute of high respect), the admirals pledged themselves and that of the military vowing to begin at once. Every admiral followed Ata'pel's lead.

Alone, Roak sat in his chair, and looked around the room . . . . his room of destiny. For good or bad he . . . this fateful evening . . . forever altered the history and path of the empire. Never before had he known such power, and for the past several moments . . . . it scared him. Barith coughed slightly in his throat so as to be sure to announce his presence in case the emperor was in private thoughts. It is not, thought

Barith, wise to walk quietly up behind one's emperor. Roak smiled slightly, knowing his old friend's habits and knew he would stand there quietly all night if necessary.

"Barith?" "Yes sire." "I need more of that beitra." "Gladly sire." Barith smiled opening the bottle and carefully filled Roak's ornate goblet. "Thank you my old friend." A simple statement, yet to Barith it was akin to a youth tonic. "Barith sit down and drink with me." "Yes sire." And filling another goblet, he sat down very self-concious. The fact of the emperor should ask him to sit and drink with him is unheard of. "Barith we wish you to do us a favor, an important one." "You have only to say it, sire." Barith replied. "There will no doubt be periods of heavy fighting in the future, and you will be going with me." "Yes sire, he said with pride. "I know old friend, but, . . . if I am mortally wounded . . . . you will leave us where we fall and tend to the others." "Yes sire." He said softly. He knew exactly what the emperor meant.

CHAP. 59

The very next morning promised to be very warm so everyone dressed in brief garments. Men wore shorts and sneakers, Aquina wore shorts and a silk skimpy halter, and the other ladies put on bathing suits. They stopped for fuel, taking on over a thousand gallons which she paid for by merely signing the receipt. Aquina was the only person in the general membership afforded such priveleges other than the commodore. Afterwards it is fresh water from the dock, and another stop . . . for food from the restaurant.

A mixture of days out on the bay fishing, erotic adventures, week-end cruises, and gatherings at dockside constituted the large portion of the summer and early fall. And aside from the fencing club and some reading done at the brownstone, she spent considerable time with the midshipmen satisfying a curiosity about naval ships, battles during the last war, and the tactics used. More specifically the role of each ship, position and scope of operation. A good deal of it she could easily have found from any decent library; but the explaination and description plus feedback from the midshipmen enhanced the information. It also filled in some blanks in her knowledge of the ships. As a consequence, Aquina spent many hundreds of dollars on available books relating to naval aviation, strategic deployment, proven tactics, types and duties of various fleet units and with the coming of fall, she continued her new "hobby."

Between '67 and '70, little changed insofar as basic routine and the summers prevailed as they had in '67 . . . There were some changes although her participation in the fencing club continued, she was approached by the athletic director in the beginning of the '68 fall semester. At first, Aquina thought it had to do with her use of the pool, but it proved to be about a totally different subject. She could have "looked into" his mind, but stopped doing it indescriminantly and schooled herself to use the ability only when absolutely necessary. Therefore, she let him explain his purpose with few interruptions.

It seemed a number of female students in the area had been sexually molested, some were attacked, and a few were even beaten. The upshot was, he and the institute's administration considered bringing in an outside instructor to teach a class in self-defense. That is, until the board mentioned Aquina's prowess as so clearly demonstrated earlier during the scuffle in the school store. She pointed out the rather cramped schedule of work and classes, and the few extra curricular activities. He pointed out the chief reason for his asking her . . . "The girls would be more apt to trust you because of being a classmate." She thought about it and moments later agreed on that basis, that premiss and after appropriate meetings with members of the administration, agreed to teach a 90 minute class each late thursday afternoon until further notice. A good number of flyers were printed and posted in almost every practical vantage point around the campus. Thus informing the ever growing female portion of the student body as to the class and its purpose.

It began with an initial enrollment of 35 girls, and faired well during the winter months of '68 . . . Aquina's schedule was tight, but she still found opportunities to drive through sometimes bad weather and check on the boat. Which as in the case of the other large power and sailboats, were brought close into the large docks running parallel to the bulkheaded parking lot, and buildings. The electric hot water heating system worked well, and often she spent hours lounging and reading. And in spite of the additional draw on her time and energy, Aquina's course and grade performance continued to well exceed the administration's expectations.

CHAP. 60

Beginning with the spring semester, January '69, the enrollment in her defense class grew to almost one hundred. So instead of one class during the week there was now two. This partly because of the war in south-east asia. The popularity of martial arts increased dramatically becoming "in vogue." In early may, when the size and complexity in the classes increased the institute found it necessary to have it listed with the national association; thereby making it easier to obtain necessary insurance coverage. And for that to happen, she had to be licensed by the sanctioning organization. That meant flying to the city of the golden gate for testing.

Aquina was excused from the appropriate classes, and Marcel took up the slack with the fencing club, while the defense class had the time off. She packed a few pieces of luggage, her weapon's case and considered herself ready. She had Miriam pack a bag or two, and the two boarded a plane at

Logan for the coast. They arrived late afternoon and with the appointment not until ten a.m., the following morning, decided to check into the hotel suite, and then did some sightseeing. By 6 p.m., they had checked in, changed clothes and went out to dinner at one of the city's best restaurants. Afterwards it is a little late shopping until the stores began closing, then the return trip to the hotel laden with packages.

With Miriam holding the weapon's case they arrived by cab twenty minutes early. Aquina gave her name to the secretary, verifying the appointment and time. She was directed to a side room to change, and prepare for the tests, and Miriam tagged along. It is the first time in nineteen years, she thought, as hands quickly pulled snug the drawstrings to the pants. Only the panties did she keep on . . . . then the top, buttoning it closed. The black silk provided a cool and slinky feeling on her bare breasts. Miriam sucked in her breath at sight of the uniform as she wound her mistress's long hair into a bun at the nape of the neck pinning it together so it wouldn't fall. She couldn't help but stare at the tiger-dragon emblazed/embroided in gold thread across Aquina's entire back. And she stared at the black belt with blue and red stitching.

Aquina exited the room slowly with accustomed feline grace, and walked toward the hall. All those sitting and standing around the reception room including the secretary stared. Walking in she turned to a panel of seven men, they didn't see the emblem on her back, but seemed annoyed at sight of the belt and its obvious connotation. One was an older Korean, and spoke in his native tongue. Aquina answered in kind, giving her name and temple affiliation. He got up bowed to her, and came around from behind the tables and stood before her. And again spoke. "May I see your right shoulder?"

Aquina nodded, and pulled up the semi-dolman sleeve. The man stood at her side moving the silk back exposing the upper portion of her shoulder. The change in his manner was instantaneous. Smoothing the material he apologized, and standing before her bowed low in subservience retreating to his place. "This person is genuine." He said to the panel. The others did not share his opinion and stated as much. "In all the world few if any are comparable to those of Kodo'Kun Temple, . . . supreme scholars of wou shu, and she is "Little Star" . . . . Kodo'Kun nunueichi." He said in english. However, the Japanese gentleman was a bit younger and was not going to be put off. Coming out onto the mats, he bowed and began to move.

Like poetry in motion, wherever he struck . . . she was elsewhere not even bothering to block or deflect his moves. Then she easily struck like lightning . . . a blur of motion . . . a foot stopped within a half-inch of his sternum. Her hand likewise a half-inch from his throat, both killing strokes. It simply was no contest, but more akin to an adult sparing with a child. The man was stunned . . . shaken badly, he regained his seat with both hands shaking. And during the entire time Miriam stood as the other onlookers, entranced most with their mouths hanging open, and taking pictures . . .

Quickly they filled out the register forms and in the space for school was written . . . Kodo'Kun Temple Monastery, Korea. The next space was for rank, and each looked at each other unsure as to what should be filled in. Smiling the Korean whispered to the others, they in turn looked to Aquina, who only nodded yes. They inserted . . . Priestess, Khan Master, and where it said belt . . . was written . . . black, with red and blue. Where it said Dan . . . they put down one word . . . unlimited.

All the men stood bowed to her and asked if she would sit with them. Aquina in turn bowed her head just as Miriam came in handing the black mocs to her. She walked around and accepted a stool and sat in the middle. The Korean got up bowed to her, and carried the papers to the secretary, then walked the hall leading to the building's rear. In his absence, Miriam handed Aquina's i.d., to the secretary who in turn typed in the correct spelling of name and address, with a double take at the name, and returned the wallet to Miriam. She stayed in the reception area answering polite questions about her mistress.

It became apparent to Miriam her mistress was being made a director of the national organization, and found out from the secretary there is a restaurant attached to the building; and that they will probably be eating lunch there because of it being and important occasion. She also found out the Korean instructor owned the restaurant.

The Korean gentleman returned and a short while later Miriam tucked the typed documents and the i.d. card back into Aquina's bag. Minutes later the panel, now eight filed out and walked down the corridor toward the restaurant. Miriam and the secretary brought up the rear, leaving the two receptionists to hold down the fort.

Next door the private dining room was glowing from dozens upon dozens of candles and the long ornate table surrounded by cushions. All the personnel had formed two lines and bowed when Aquina entered. She slightly bowed her head and sat at the table's center, on the one black cushion. Miriam and the secretary sat next to each other with the secretary whispering quick points on ediquette. She watched as Aquina speaking only korean, was always served first and they all waited until she began with the tea, soup, or the main dishes. If involved in a discussion and she paused for tea . . . the conversation ceased until she had finished, then continued.

Its an hour and fourty-five minutes later, lunch over, Aquina had changed once again into her chic white suit, and had no sooner entered a cab with Miriam carrying the weapons box, when the secretary entered a camera store with two rools of 35mm. film. Arriving at the hotel they paused at the information and travel desk inquiring about flights to the east coast. The clerk discovered a flight to Logan was leaving in a hair less than two hours. Leaving instructions for the clerk to reserve two first class seats, Aquina and Miriam hurried upstairs and quickly packed. With little time to waste everything was thrown and squeezed into their luggage checking quickly to be sure they indeed had everything . . . gave the nod to the bellman. Miriam carried the weapons case and as the cab waited, Aquina paid the bill and a moment later settled into the back seat.

It wasn't too long and each buckled their seat belt relaxing . . . waiting for the flight crew to do their thing. The captain finally did, after waiting for what seemed forever to Miriam, but was no more than half-way when a complete set of pictures went to the publisher by bonded messenger. Several sets of copies had been made with the headquarters of the national organization holding them for later use, plus enlargements planned for framing. And by the time the plane touched down at Logan the story and art work were in progress to accompany the best pictures.

Life returned to normal, at least for the most part, Aquina did well on the few exams she had to take and concentrated on the class, fencing club, and the few requirements for her boat.

June arrived, and Aquina made a point of acquiring a copy of the leading magazine devoted to martial arts. And breathed a sigh of relief, when she found nothing, no mention of her whatsoever. But she worried about net month's issue. But aside from the defense classes each week, even during the summer there was a need to keep the second class. The summer was much as it had been last year. That is until the july issue of the same magazine came out on the stands.

Aquina is featured on the cover, accompanied by a feature article complete with pictures. Laura reached her on the boat by phone telling her all about it. "Laura, don't divulge my whereabouts to anyone. Tell David and call Marcel for me." Aquina said, trying to head off and minimize her expected loss of privacy. She quickly told Phillip and called the house to let the staff know, and quickly called the administration building on campus. They are sympathetic and definitely on her side, and agreed to post a security guard at the hall's entrance. However, short of that there wasn't too much they could do to help. She thanked them for their aid and put the phone down. Phillip poured a chilled glass of white wine and handed to her, as she mumbled "thank you," and watched as she sat thinking.

Sure enough, the very next time the class met every person had a copy of the magazine. She was surprised . . . there had been no interruptions during the class and little conversation. However, after the class was finished they did start conversations and that was mostly by whisper. Each bowed asking her to autograph their copy, and when she had done so, . . . they left quietly unlike other days. With the exception of the class, a few campus security guards, the summer went by much as the previous one although the party on the 4th., was smaller.

The fall semester started with a notice from the national board stating any person wishing to qualify or improve their standing must participate in competition. The schedule was included with the envelope, and there was other mail from the west coast headquarters addressed to her. Mostly it dealt with organization business asking how she felt about certain things, and thoughts and wishes on other topics. The list of dates also included the addresses, and the city of each competition for the balance of '69, and the first half of '70 . . . And of course as instructor and director, she had to be present. This was true for all the national "meets," and regional events.

Her hopes of largely remaining obscure were dashed. She was disappointed, but didn't allow it to disrupt the class or anything else. And in due course selected those of each class she thought should go to their first regional . . . manhattan in october. Aquina filled out the forms to register her pupils for competition and the papers, plus money from each participant, for hotel reservations, and meals. The subject of transportation she decided to organize herself.

The day in question was a saturday in mid october, and because of her position had to be there at least 12 hours early. Miriam, who was quite familiar with manhattan drove Marcel's large station wagon. Laura and Dave used their new extended club van. As a consequence, they arrived in good time with no baggage problem, and were able to park in the hotel's underground garage. Their rooms were ready all in sequential number, four of them, and unpacked, and relaxed. With everyone armed as to the floor number and address of the coliseum, Aquina and Miriam left for the coliseum via a taxi . . . which they would all use leaving the two private vehicles underground.

Around a portion of the park, across the wide avenue the cab entered the semi-circular entrance discharging the ladies directly in front. The flat marquee announced the national organization regional "meet" as they walked through the outside entrance. Both wore black suits however, Aquina's a-line skirt was a bit more snug than Miriam's and where Aquina wore a blouse of irredescent pearl, Miriam wore a light pink. They are beautiful women each stunning in their own right, but as the manager walked over he instinctively knew which was which. He interrupted them introducing himself then walked with them to the windows identified by floor signs as offering tickets to the regional martial art meet. Explaining about principals and participants having to have a badge. He talked to one cashier-ticket person and was handed two plastic badges asking if he might affix them to their lapels. Aquina nodded, and with the I.D., badges in plain sight nodded to the manager and walked past the guard and attendant, and around the corner to the elevators.

Exiting from the elevator, Aquina stood for some minutes observing the activity on the floor, i.e., the coliseum workmen setting up bleachers, arranging floor mats, tables, sound and other related activities. The korean, nippon and others of the panel dropped what they were doing and came over to them, bowed and immediately began bringing her up-to-date.

It was after eight p.m., when Aquina walked through the door of her room with an exhausted Miriam in tow. Much of the evening was spent eating and drinking mixed with a good deal of conversation. Mindful of the hour, she thought it best everyone go to bed early.

Aquina wanted to be early, and she was . . . . stepping off the elevator with uniform and mocs in the large shoulder bag. It is 8:10 a.m., and slipping out of her suit jacket, layed it over the chair, she went back to work. The food concessions were open and setting up for the day's expected customers. The other panel members arrived and observed a traditional greeting, then retired to the side room reserved for the directors. And as the time crept from 8:30 to 8:50, and then 9:00 . . . the room became a hive of activity. She was the last panel member to change, and by 9:15, . . . the two TV crews were ready to go. Plus all the participants had arrived, and the numerous reporters were in place. Most of the contestants had changed and were taking their places at various benches around the large mat area.

At 9:18, Aquina exited the clothing room and told the guard to admit no-one. He nodded. "Yes Your Highness." He stared at the large nipples pushing against the black silk and the way the breasts jutted out and swayed to her body movements. Walking around the curtain, she approached the long table, and instantly seven men stood and bowed, and didn't sit until she assumed her place . . . . the center position of the table. She was busy with the schedule, scoring forms and didn't appear to notice cameras and the like. Positioned on the table at intervals are microphones and scratch paper.

Time . . . 9:30, the public began filling the seats rapidly and with the clock moving closer to 10:00, people stood in hastily roped-in areas. A moment later the competition started. Aquina's class was the third group in the first classification, and it was the most numerous. Each group fought, with the odd group fighting the previous winners. Several times two contestants were so evenly matched, each was awarded their next higher belt . . . yellow. But in the final analysis very few were scored below acceptance.

The printed schedule allowed for an hour's intermission at noon, with the last two classifications beginning immediately at 1:00 p.m. People used the hour to visit the concession stands and browse through the ample number of booths handling all manner of martial art paraphernalia, except weapons. There were pictures of the weapons and books, but no actual weapons could be sold. It didn't appear to matter as books and pamphlets did very well. By all appearances the general public, or at least certain types, were curious and intriqued by the sport.

One p.m., the first contestants for brown began, after their bow of respect to the panel, their portion of the program. And with it the excitement grew . . . This is what the people had come to see and the feeling, the excitement heightened because there was still the black belt class. During which the crowds roared with approval as contestants maneuvered struck and went through various movements in an effort to gain advantage. It was difficult and frustrating for both men with each unable to press an advantage. And they well knew all to well the clock was against them. One, of Japanese descent attached to the club known to train street gang members in militaristic fighting, used a trick clearly in violation of sport and organization rules, resulting in the opponent suffering a broken shoulder.

"Foul!!" Stated the nippon panel member. All seven waited . . . . Aquina said in a clear voice everyone heard . . . "Expelled!!" The contestant began objecting, thereby breaking further rules of conduct and ediquette. Something that just wasn't done. Another man, older, stood and added his protest to that of the contestant. Slowly her face became the malevolent mask as she repeated . . . "expelled!!" The older men obviously the instructor, a black belt of multiple rank lost control, but for only a second. He shouted an insult in korean, and challenged.

The tension throughout the entire floor is palpable, deathly quiet . . . not a sound as the cameras and people waited. Aquina slowly stood, backed a half step and vaulted over the table . . . a somersault landing without sound catlike, and nonchalantly kicked off her canvas mocs. While walking onto the mat, other affiliated TV stations began patching-in quickly bringing viewers in neighboring areas up-to-date with explainations et-cetera. She is within a few yards of the contestant, who feeling bold with his mentor only a yard or so away launched into a double movement. Done to force her into an ideal position from which the instructor could effectively finish the job, but it was not too be. Her body was not there, . . . instead she occupied the oblique, and struck both simultaneously. The contestant was struck in the hip area of the spine and lay parallized . . . whimpering. The instructor in the hip effectively breaking it . . . plaintively wailing, she wasn't human. Reaching down still not uttering a word . . . and reaching with her left hand picked him up just barely at arm's length . . . and clamped her right hand thumb on one side of his forehead, the fingers on the other, and said, "you are the evil. But where there is no mind . . . there is no evil." An instant later he screamed, then started babbling like an infant. Opening her hands, she allowed the miscreant to collapse in a heap, great pain racking the once formidable body.

Silence still reigned as medical personnel carried the two off, only an occasional whimper disturbed the surprised and shocked audience.

The malevolence gone from her face, it once again assumed the youthful mask of wisdom and patience. While making her way slowly back across the mats . . . all classes and clubs ringing the mat area on three sides, stood and bowed deeply, and stayed thus until she had sat down. The audience began to vigorously applaud. When the audience began calming down, the referee proclaimed the competition continue, but reminded them everything would remain open until 6 p.m. The competition continued with the black belts.

Reporters, many of whom came in late because of the unusual circumstances moved forward each trying to out-do the other. Their targets were any and all panel members, most especially the woman in black silk. However, none succeeded in getting close, adding measureably to her appeal. She remained aloof and distant. Of course it did nothing to detract from her image. Most if not all the contestants had left by 5:30 . . . and the panel members a half hour later. Slipping past the reporters and the curious, she arrived at the hotel only a short time later after the others.

Dinner that evening was kept light mostly because the girls, Laura, David and Miriam were exhausted. Finishing her salad, Aquina decided to enjoy a nap admitting she was a little tired. As it turned out Miriam went in to wake her at 7 a.m. And within the hour had checked out and on the way back to Cambridge. The traffic was normal for a sunday morning, but still required a bit over three hours before reaching the brownstone.

With the exception of reporters occasionally nosing around, life returned to normal. That is, as far as routine, but the addition of warrior fame was a consistently annoying ingredient in her life, thus far. Despite her longevity and the well-deserved credit and fame, Aquina had never in the past and certainly not then . . . at that moment, with feelings of annoyance understood the fame. As far as she was concerned it represented invasion of privacy. And . . . if she was not careful could destroy her and Dien. For Aquina knew all to well how their thin veneer of sophistication and civilization actually was, and how close they really are to the jungle beast. No, if for any reason the well guarded secret was discovered . . . the primitives would likely kill her and Dien out of fear and superstition, if nothing else. All that it required was for someone to dig back far enough and deep enough, then assemble the puzzle.

Meanwhile, Dien with similar thoughts moved the entire office and business headquarters into the city.

She used the business name and acquired two buildings in the city; plus another large building to house the garage and serve as a depot for the trucks. Thereafter, she closed up those portions of the compound now unused and kept a lower profile.

May '70 arrived without serious difficulty, partly due to her eluding reporters and curiousity seekers. But the concern and need for caution stayed uppermost in her mind. So to that end, Aquina formulated her plans carefully and chose of the substantial number of job offers one she found strongly appealing. Partly because it is related to the space industry and to R&D, and partly due to the company being located only a state away. Thereby being close enough, she could effectively move everything herself. She didn't want the necessity to have friends know or freight receipts showing her final destination.

For that, Aquina prepared a letter of acceptance and mailed it the evening of her graduation. The following day she mailed a letter to the national martial arts organization announcing she was going on a sabbatical, and would be out of touch approximately a year. During the same time she contacted Laura and Dave who agreed to buy the boat and arranged a down payment plus an easy payment schedule through the bank. She was pleased over the sale . . . . another item disposed of in her plan. The next stop was to close out all her accounts. However, she had to wait till the following morning . . . at 10 a.m. Aquina insisted on cash, and due to the overall amount . . . the bank didn't have it ready until 10:20 . . . that morning; all together in a large aluminum attaché-like carrying case with several locks. What with the sale of the boat, the total is enormous. And once back in her room repacked the cash into small bundles. She used # 10 envelopes, and salted them away into the various pieces of luggage . . . except one. The last one she put into the shoulder bag.

At the end of that week, she received a reply from her initial letter welcoming her to the firm, and requested an informal meeting two days hence. She sighed with a small measure of relief, and while smiling went out to retrieve a needed road map from the jag's glove compartment. Returning to her bedroom, Aquina avoided the staff and began planning the best route. "Oh . . . well that's not bad at all. It's onlyyy, about a hundred miles or there-abouts." She saw how route I-90 west to I-86 gradually curved southwest making it essentially an easy trip. Once on that turnpike it would leave her off only a comparatively short distance from the company.

The very next morning, she obtained a complete transcript of all records and activities from the institute. With that and the map, Aquina began to relax spending much of the day reading.

She was on the road bright and early crossing the Charles river at 7:20 a.m . . . Leaving the bridge behind, she was behind a scrap truck heading for I-90 . . . when some twisted sheet metal fell off the truck. With cars on her left and the guard rail to the right, there was no place for her to go. Realizing all this in an instant, she stomped on her brakes down shifting at the same time, but not in time. Her jaw clenched and nerves jumped at the grinding and scraping sounds. When the jag rolled over and jumped . . . the metal junk carving open the oil pan and jamming into the suspension creating substantial damage. The car came to a sickening halt.

The car directly behind her barely managed to stop in time and the officer driving the police car waved to Aquina as he tore-off after the offending scrap truck at high speed.

CHAP. 61

Immediately after the military's old guard exited from the war room with the emperor's blessing and lengthy instructions, they quickly retired to their own headquarters high council room for another meeting. Within the sophisticated technocratic tucanan society, the circle of admirals held substantial influence over many of the guilds. These men are tough campaigners in their own right, although only one amongst the circle has any actual combat experience. And that was as a young up-an-coming officer engaged in fringe and territory boundary wars. Nonetheless, they knew how to begin preparations, how to marshall the energies of tens of millions toward a single goal.

They are matchless in every area, but one . . . . tactics. One junior admiral possessed marginal skills, a dozen or so captains and an equal handful of commanders all possessed some skill, some to a greater degree than others.

Eleven senior admirals occupied the large obloid shaped table, with aides sitting behind them. Their unanimous decision regarding the new emperor is one of respect and praise, and the outline he ordered . . . . would be implemented with hard careful planning. So to that end, one of the senior admirals interjected an important fact. "While the old hated emperor was alive there was no need to choose amongst the circle for a chairman, or chief; but now with this new dynamic person as emperor . . . it is necessary." And so, within thirty minutes . . . . a criteria had been established and the voting done by written ballot. A few seconds to count . . . and Ata'pel was dubbed "chief."

The old distinquished admiral graciously accepted the post and sent an official message . . . a matter of protocol, by military messenger to the emperor. It explained in detail the decision of his peers and asked for the emperor's blessing.

It didn't require much more than a few moments for the messenger to reach his destination. Once passed through security, the messenger was escorted through the palace to Barith's office. The messenger relinquished the note to Barith and waited for a possible answer while the old captain walked to a black heavy wood door and waved his left palm over a sensor and instantly rapped once gently on the door . . . then opened it and entered. Barith smiled, instantly saluting when Roak looked up . . . immediately handed him the note. As he stood waiting, Roak read the note and began chuckling to himself. He quickly penned an answer, and asked Barith to include with the return note . . . a large bottle of hard beitra.

The messenger departed quickly making good speed back to the headquarters building; and with alacrity and in excellent time once again entered the high council room. Both note and the formidable size bottle was put on the table in front of Ata'pel, who immediately began reading the note aloud.

> "We extend to you our blessing, and also a large bottle of that fitting soldiers brew, as it should be opened and shared by those of your peers responsible for making such an excellent choice." Signed with the emperor's name and signet.

Each and all of them laughed good-naturedly, and as loyal subjects complied with the emperor's wishs. The meeting is well underway and the hard effective plan of action outlined by the emperor was being broken down to the bare essentials. And while they refilled empty goblets, each segment, each broad point of the outline was discussed thoroughly . . . until new lists began appearing. Those lists were in time replaced by other more complex outlines.

Hours passed as the outlines matured and each one complimented the other . . . each department's outline became an integral portion of an immense logistical complex definitive plan of action. Each portion, by department had its own timetable, in itself a plan of attack for each department. All calculated together, achieving the desired initiative.

Ata'pel adjourned the meeting. Every admiral armed with their segment of the plan had in turn an outline for each branch of their department; and a brief outline for each of the small varied functionary staffs, running offices seeing to and controlling thousands of tiny functions, which would normally fall through the cracks between one department and another. Altogether the eleven departments controlled a fair number of branchs. And of course these in turn held sway over a myriad of other functions, all contributing to the enormous military machine.

With dawn of the same fateful day each of the senior admirals, armed with various outlines, descended like angry gods on their respective department heads. Each held hurried meetings with department chiefs, branch officers et-cetera, and started giving orders . . . and building fires under each segment of each branch of their command.

One of the problems was inefficiency, and then lack of personnel in many places. Department chiefs and branch officers immediately after their meeting began attacking these and other problems by first streamlining their departments, promoting where necessary and putting things into proper motion. Several days followed where the over-all number of staff members were increased, and all off-duty status was cancelled. Plus personnel began contacting the tens upon tens of thousands of past military personnel; that had left because of the old emperor encouraging them to return for reasons of loyalty, and the new pay scales. And along with those points, each was informed about the new intermediate ranks which were created to help administer activity and make the military more effective. Both former fleet personnel and ground troopers began arriving in droves, and were beginning their processing and re-training. Once empty barracks . . . . now resounding to the stomp of boots, the sound of voices and laughter, officers shouting orders . . . . and in the air mixed with the scent of various species . . . the feeling of expectancy. All of them could smell a war, and the excitement was like a fuel for their bodies as they went through re-training. All their uniforms were brought up-to-date and cleaned then packed away into a space bag or trunk.

Of course the sudden surge in military activity so soon after the rumored late evening meeting in the palace war room, caused hundreds of wild rumors. And as more days passed the rumors were rampant through the city. The spatial information news guild, or spa-inf., running hither and back valiantly trying to gather interviews with no success. No-one was talking especially not the "chips,"(elite messengers created during a time of incessant evesdropping, where no secret or confidential information could be sent by C'pter, or other means without it being intercepted, or overheard) and no officers spoke of anything amiss . . . . thus adding fuel to hundreds of additional rumors.

In a very short amount of time all over the surface of Tucana (homeworld) citizens and nobility alike were discussing the rumors, and the unprecedented level of military activity was within recorded memory, to say the least, newsworthy. And in only minutes began spreading to the other three planets of the home system via the normal communications net. But when the chips and other couriers began carrying personal blasters with published orders to shoot anyone attempting to delay them or steal a plick, well . . . . that quickly brought the citizenry out of their rumor induced reverie.

On the industry side various officials, not only on Tucana, but throughout the home system, were contacted and meetings held at the palace. During the protracted meetings, a great many points had been examined all culminating in orders for new fields of research, dozens of ambitious projects related to the military, production of new materials, plus the "ok" for a new innovativeness in weaponry. Roak was totally successful. And as each industrialist departed with a signed order from Roak, . . . they are to contact other smaller factory owners and incorporate, include or sub-contract to as many as possible in an effort to boost production.

All of this occurred during the first star week.

The second week proved far more hectic than the first, Roak had received a message plick from the military's personnel headquarters, with the disturbing news, "though many tens of thousands have returned to active duty, it is clearly not enough. A serious shortage of both planetary soldiers, and fleet personnel will result . . . if something is not done." Reading it again changed nothing. So Roak sent by return plick . . . . orders for a comprehensive recruiting campaign be initiated without delay.

Reading the recently delivered plick, a smile of relief brightened the admiral's features, and within minutes regional military offices were beginning to spread the news and within hours the campaign was well on its way all over the home system's four planets. And by the following day was allowed to go to Sa-gor, the first system of the empire.

By the end of the first day a similar order was issued to each and every guild, which up to this point because of a near dormant economy many guilds had accepted no-one. However, those previously closed to new applicants suddenly began taking all those sincerely wishing to join, who had no other guild affiliation. Most though joined to learn or simply work at their vocations. The others were simply trying to avoid the military, or they were of the nobility attempting to arrange a cushy situation for themselves.

And very soon other changes were taking place, such as the replacement of ceremonial guards with better combat-ready troops. At first, only military and government buildings were guarded this way, and of course the palace;

but very quickly expanded to include data central, power generating complexs and power distributing centers, and the civilian and commercial spaceports. All the troops are armed with conventional weapons including personal blasters, but those outside guarding perimeters also have the much more powerful blaster rifles.

For the military the next item on the agenda is Tucana's three moons. On both Untey-1, and Untey-2, the military landed in sufficient strength to guarantee martial law. Troops immediately began inspecting I.D. insignia against lists of suspected raider sympathizers and possible spies, and such. Anyone suspected of questionable loyalties or affiliations were watched or put into detention, until their loyalties could be verified . . . one way or another.

In the interim, the overall economic condition of the empire being what it was, all those unemployed for whatever reason found work immediately, usually in either one of several guilds. If they sought work in some capacity for military employment . . . proper information was given and backgrounds were carefully scrutinized.

But by the end of that week, enough people were employed so as to provide full shifts in a few of the guilds. They covered every hour of everyday . . . . and there were no exceptions. More important, salaries had certain criteria according to job classification, but the overriding factor was what one does, and most especially . . . how well the person performs the task. And as the average citizen routinely discovered . . . it was a blanket order issued by the emperor. For most citizens, they couldn't remember a time when an entire family didn't have to work. This was every member, even older children had to help. Each person began believing the things the new emperor said.

And they started looking to the palace with respect, and new pride. It didn't take long for the shifting of energies, programs enacted, the increase in tempo on and all over the Homeworld system; and gradually throughout the loyal empire . . . it is fast becoming felt . . . and citizens realized this emperor meant business.

Quick and decisively the military descended upon Untey-3 . . . And with the impenetrable cordon of small and medium sized armed ships, no vessel could escape, as the military astonished the inhabitants by landing troops. The general citizen could only watch in fascination as hundreds of troops landed at various locations around the moon. In short the word had "gone out" to cities and the intermeshing suburbs, informing the entire population of the state of martial law. They were told what the restrictions are, and there was a considerable list of them. Everything remained fairly well contained until the news . . . . that they had to work. It didn't last long when realization settled-in . . . "they would indeed be paid." And just as quickly they learned it is the old near decrepit military base that was the military's objective.

Of course by this time, what few spies still lived or were still free had already reported to their masters, the substantial military and guild activity. Though it did not bode well for them . . . it was decided amongst the raider leadership to keep a careful watch, and to be on the safe side . . . decided to accelerate their own preparations.

CHAP. 62

While pulling away from the scene, the cop called in for a tow truck and another squad car to direct traffic. And by the time the tow truck picked-up the damaged jag, and brought it and its fuming driver to the dealer . . . she had lost an hour and fifteen minutes. At least there . . . activity sped up a bit, and perhaps ten or eleven minutes later the service manager walked into the owner's office and broke the news.

When she had digested the service manager's words, Aquina reiterated the need to be at her scheduled meeting on time. But there was no possible way her jag could be ready inside of three days. And to make matters worse, they had no loaners available.

"What do you have?" Aquina asked with a sense of urgency. "Nothing, really, I have two demo cars and they are out, and the loaners are out. None of the used cars are prepped." The owner said trying to think, as he saw the princess look at her watch . . . again. "Well, there are two cars available, but only one is prepped and ready to go. But these are exotic thoroughbreds, and I'm not sure you would wish to own them."

"Quickly show me. I'm in a dreadful hurry," she exclaimed.

The owner nodded, and looking to the assistant manager... told him what he is to do, handed him the registration from his billfold and explained to the manager to fill out the papers, and a quick bill of sale. Outside, off to the side of the service area more-or-less a separate building, the owner opened one of the garage doors and stood back so his favorite customer might admire the two cars. "The Maserati is a '67, but is not immediately ready for the road. However, this Ferrari is ready. This is a '67, 330 gt., and is a superb machine with very low miles, wire wheels, a.c., and the blaupunkt is breathtaking." The owner said beaming with pride. Aquina groaned inwardly. She had given serious thought to trading-in the jag, but for something less conspicuous. In this blood red exotic . . . . she might just as well take out an ad in the local papers. But, she looked at her watch for the time, and . . . "very well. I'll take it, but we must hurry."

It was, and he did. By the time all the fluid levels were checked, full gas, et-cetera, and she signed the papers plus signing over the registration to the jag . . . The assistant manager had returned from the commissioner's office with the new registration, title and plates. With a sizeable cash payment up front, the owner was quite happy to wait until the following day for the adjusted balance.

Aquina quickly transferred all of her personal belongings and nick-knacks to the blood red thoroughbred, and was off. She knew the margin will be close, and settled back to the business of driving. Smiling with pleasure at the spirited response, she began to enjoy herself in spite of the time. The V-12 performed flawlessly rapidly eating up the miles. Almost before she knew it, she turned off onto I-86, and crossed the state line. About fourty minutes later, Aquina pulled into a gas station for directions and filled the fuel tank at the same time.

When she pulled into the outside drive and stopped at the guard booth there is but twenty minutes until her appointment. She parked in the visitor's area located the width of a narrow drive, about ten feet directly in front of the main office building. Scooping up her bag and the leather folder containing her papers, she locked the car and walked into the spacious reception room. Giving her name and the person's name with whom she has an appointment, the receptionist handed her a clipboard on which is fastened a multi-page employment application. Though explained as a formality, it was still vaguely annoying. Aquina was pleased at the effort put forth earlier, when she carefully omitted any information alluding to being foreign born. Thereby allowing her to work in areas of "interest" without a heavy background and security check, which she had to avoid at any cost.

Among other things, she indicated an age of twenty-three on the form, and current address, plus filling-in the other spaces. And filling in the balance in all sections didn't prove worrisome, but she was inwardly relieved when it was completed. Almost immediately after returning the clipboard to the counter, a young woman wearing a clip-on I.D. tag came-in, picked up the clipboard and asked Aquina to follow her. A short walk down the wide corridor exposed her to the hustle-n-bustle of the company. The slight aroma of pine assailed her as the young woman ushered her into the personnel manager's office.

For the manager it is but a formality, admitting to himself his decision to hire Aquina sight unseen. But meeting and talking with her was much more satisfying than conversations with other women. He recognized her intelligence, after only a few heartbeats, but her ripe sensuousness madly assaulted every hormone and sensory organ in his body. There was no question she has the job, they merely discussed salary, benefits and choice of three openings. Two of which were in R&D, and the third . . . a slot in the special projects design shop. She opted for the third position pleasing the manager. This is because it had proved in the past difficult to fill.

Aquina handed him the copy of her curriculum and course descriptions and degrees. The application he stamped approved and put everything in a file folder, and buzzed his secretary. When the attractive brunette came in he told her his decision handing over the folder, and asked an I.D. badge and card be made out quickly. And during the next fifteen minutes they enjoyed a cup of coffee and chatted. She responded to his question . . . saying yes she will relocate. "In fact, I will spend time today looking for a house, preferably in the suburbs."

The manager was just about to show Aquina around the office area, and then the special projects set of offices, which actually is a separate building; when through the door came the brunette with a clip-on I.D., and a plastic I.D., card for wallet or purse. The I.D., she affixed to the suit jacket upper lapel instead of the upper breast pocket, which is canted on an angle because of her very ample bossom. She signed the required papers relating to the secrets act, and that of confidentiality. With those signed the manager spent the next hour and-a-half showing her around and introducing her to the immediate superiors of the special projects section. And in turn spent some twenty minutes being shown around and through the offices, engineering section, and the design office, and drawing and layout room.

While she was being given the grand tour the secretary made out the corrected personnel roster for the security section, and those at the guard house taking care of the main entrance. She was assigned a parking space in front of that particular building and security was given the parking space number, license plate, year and make of car.

Walking through the front door at three p.m., the afternoon sun was warm and the air fragrant with the scent of lilac, and freshly cut grass. Once in the car, and on the main road, she unfolded the piece of steno paper and read the names of the realtors provided by the personnel manager. Stopping at the gas station across and down a-bit from the company's entrance, she obtained directions for each of the realtors. And without delay began making the rounds. At each, there seemed to be a lot of pictures of homes for sale replete with description and such noteworthy information as deemed necessary by the individual agent. The first realtor had nothing that interested her, and she immediately drove to the second realtor where she began having some luck.

She narrowed it two specific homes, and with a smile the realtor was happy to show the homes. Aquina declined the offer to use the agent's car not wishing to leave the ferrari until she was more acquainted with the area. The agent clearly raised his eyebrows and instantly reappraised the young woman. Giving directions, he also explained in detail about the first house. As it turned out she did like it for a variety of reasons. Not the least of which is its reasonable distance from the company. Its within twenty minutes and its location is on a nice quiet tree-lined lane in a reasonably affluent section. She noticed several lower echelon and domestic sports cars and lots of children.

However, they still had one other house to see, and drove to that one without delay. It didn't take long to make a decision. "No, this won't do. I will take the first one we looked at. However, because my schedule is tight, I must have the closing on friday." Aquina said. He began to object, explaining about time to arrange financing, title search, and give the attorneys time to prepare. "First, the title search doesn't require that much time. And second if the bank is the sole owner because of someone's previous difficulty, well then their attorney should jump at the chance for a cash deal." His eyes blinked once . . . twice. And a broad smile brightened his features. "Cash?" Aquina nodded. "Ahhh. Well then yes it is possible. Let us return to the office, and I'll begin the paperwork." The agent said, already opening the right-hand door.

During the ride back, Aquina gave him a list of a few small things she wanted done between then and friday. Once back at his office, she handed him two one hundred dollar bills as a binder, waited for the receipt, and to sign the other forms. With the receipt and several other copies in her possession, Aquina told him she would be back sometime tomorrow morning with half of the remainder as a down payment. And declining his invitation to dinner, Aquina explained . . . she has a long drive and should be going.

She pulled into the driveway at the brownstone and it seemed only minutes later . . . she sat down to dinner. She answered polite inquires about the accident having heard about it from the police, who had come by to ask some questions, and finish their report. Everyone on the staff knew she was leaving, they already had a month's notice and everyone but Miriam found new positions. And that very evening, Aquina gave each three months salary, except Miriam. Aquina's compassion reached out to her as Miriam seemed lost and so insecure . . . . almost to the point of tears.

"Don't give it another thought." She touched Miriam on the arm. "You will come with me, Miriam." The others were happy with the arrangement especially Bill, she had given him the truck. So, while Aquina put several fat envelopes in her bag, and left on her errands, . . . Miriam packed her things, and the few things her mistress hadn't packed. It included the rifle, weapon's box, and other sundries all of which easily consumed more than one day.

Meanwhile, Aquina stopped at the dealer and paid the balance owed on the car, then immediately got back on the road. But only after the now previous owner had agreed to box up all the spare parts and supplies. She felt better with the pink slip in her possession, and smiled knowing the second part of her little "move" would be finalized soon. The V-12 sang its throaty roar as exhaust pushed through individually tuned pipes and collector-resonators exciting her in a crescendo of power announcing its thoroughbred heritage. Nothing can quite match the feel of power exuded by a racing machine, except another like thoroughbred.

Aquina ignored the car phone, and turned on the radio, but didn't find anything, and instead tried one of the many cassettes. It was Beethoven . . . and with a sigh she smiled and tried to sing to the music. The music lifted her spirits considerably, and helped to shorten the trip. And arriving a bit before twelve, she roared into the parking lot with a screech of gravel. The sun glistened off the pearl studded blouse and mini a-line skirt. The shoulder bag was on her shoulder . . . in the left hand a black leather monogramed diskette portfolio. Walking in, she was about to give the receptionist her name, but was interrupted by the agent.

It really only required a few minutes for her to hand him the envelope containing over half the sale price in cash. He in turn made out a receipt in triplicate, then spent fifteen minutes bringing Aquina up-to-date. A bonded cleaning company had been hired to clean the entire house and the two car garage. Aquina asked him to hire a house painter, and repaint the shake shingle and exterior trim. And to help him she handed over two pieces of cloth one a nice soft celery green, and the second a light sand color. Finishing the business at hand, the agent invited her to lunch. She smiled and accepted.

An hour and-a-half passed to the soft sound of a live combo, and quiet conversation. Aquina was only partially successful in keeping the tone light and skillfully changed the subject whenever he attempted to probe her or draw her out about personal likes or dislikes.

For the agent lunch was over much to soon, but to Aquina it was already too long. After-all the house was only sparsely furnished, a situation she intended to rectify that afternoon before beginning the long return trip to Cambridge. And she did, by going to the better stores. One after another, she went in and browsed sometimes not buying anything, while in other instances purchases were made . . . . and heavily. In each store, where she made purchases, Aquina arranged for delivery on saturday of that week. With all receipts . . . furniture for fifteen rooms, in the billfold, she headed for the turnpike stopping for gas on the way.

She arrived at the brownstone slightly earlier than the night before pleased to see sometime . . . someone had picked up the boxes of spare parts and supplies for the car.

Early the next morning, thursday, Aquina reserved a rental truck and a large trailer for the car, to be picked up on friday. And for the balance of the day, she and Miriam continued to pack odds-n-ends, while the staff packed for themselves. Everyone opted for a quick take-out dinner and so, while Bill went to pick it up at the restaurant . . . the staff packed all the food, vegetables, liquor and staples. They would leave in the morning so it was their last evening together.

Bright and early the next morning, Aquina and Miriam drove into town with Bill and picked up the truck and trailer. And returning instead of leaving as the other maid and cook had, Bill stayed and loaded the truck insisting on carrying all the heavy bulky items. It all went rather smoothly, the only tricky part was Aquina driving up on the trailer. Bill guided her every foot of the way trying to do it right the first time. Once on the trailer, Bill pulled up the ramp-gate and secured the ferrari down with chain and binders into the chassis provided by the rental company. With that completed, Bill covered it with its own custom made cover and secured the zipper and elastic cords.

By 11:30, the loading was finished, and again Bill went out for something. Good to his word the attorney, who met her at the airport years earlier arrived to say goodby, and pick up the keys. Bill returned and the four of them ate and said their goodbys.

At 12:40, Aquina behind the wheel took one more glance at the brownstone and pulled away for the last time. Miriam had custody of the food and thermos's, and the radio. Because she was only doing a maximum of fifty m.p.h., what with the trailer, they arrived only twenty minutes early for the scheduled closing on the house. They barely had time for coffee, and the restroom before sitting down to business. During the next hour they discussed such things as reimbursement to the realty for the cleaning crew, painting crew both of which presented bills, and the deposit to the electric company as power had been on since that morning. Aquina paid each bill careful to obtain the receipts "paid in full." The plumber had inspected, adjusted, replaced a few things, and tested the furnace, and air conditioning throughout the house; also the electrician who provided a similar service. She paid all the bills and the fuel oil adjusted amount, plus handing over in a business envelope . . . 75-one thousand dollar bills as the balance owed. Both the banker and attorney had expected a certified check, but actual cash . . . they provided Aquina with a separate receipt which both signed.

With everyone's signature on the papers . . . the banker handed over the notarized papers and the title, and deed to the house and land, . . . and of course the two sets of keys.

Just barely six-thirty p.m., they pulled-up in front of the house, and while Miriam opened up the house a bit, and the garage, Aquina had the cover and chains off the car. In minutes she has it off the trailer and into one section of the large deep garage. Then disconnecting the troublesome trailer, she backed the truck into the driveway stopping just by the front walk. Even though the perishable food was packed in ice coolers, they carried all of that into the kitchen first. And while Miriam began packing it into the spotless refrigerator and pantry freezer . . . Aquina started bringing in the first items she came to on the truck. There were a few voices coming up the walk as she was on her way out for another trip. There, at the front door, she confronted about a dozen people . . . three married couples of varying ages, and five young people between nineteen and twenty-one, four young men and one young lady. Each couple has food of some sort . . . a tray of sandwiches, casseroles, salads et-cetera, while the men had the responsibility of carrying the wine, champagne and other bottles of a similar kind.

The husbands let their eyes roam over Aquina's mouth watering body curves and the young men were doing the same. While on the other hand, the wives were not only jealous, but worried, the teenage girl was just mildly anxious. Aquina called Miriam and introductions went around the circle. She said, Miriam is her friend and secretary, and when Aquina said . . . she wasn't married . . . the women became more, more worried feeling threatened . . . more than ever.

While the teenage girl helped Miriam, the wives chatted and helped Aquina with the food, unpacking glassware and other similar items. The young men in a comparatively short time had the truck unloaded and the boxes distributed in the proper rooms, the luggage, bags and trunk in the bedroom section of the house. With the house forming a massive "T" the bedrooms were located in the large two-story head of the "T." The large deep garage is at the opposite end. By eight-fifteen . . . everything was pretty much put away though the dishwasher was full, while she and Miriam sat with the couples on what was available. And that is two couches, and a number of chairs . . . a repore' began, understanding . . . a basis for friendship.

The conversation was open, friendly each getting to know each other better. They were progressing nicely, with Aquina carefully relating some things about herself. For most of the evening, Aquina talked they listened, then it was their turn. The younger people had been looking at the ferrari, so when they came in it became the subject of a number of questions. And of course the subject of furniture came up, natural as there is so pitifully little of it in the house. Aquina explained the stores were delivering everything the following morning and day; but didn't have any idea as to time, or what would be delivered first. They began to leave at about eleven p.m., with promises to return at 9 a.m. in the morning. Well at least the windows had drapes or curtains, so after locking all the doors they pushed the couches together and slept.

Actually it is a little after nine when the young men began to arrive. There was plenty of hot coffee, and Miriam had them sit down to that and toast. Miriam had just poured the third cup for the young men when a large van pulled up and backed into the driveway. Aquina told the driver they were at the correct address and immediately he and two more men began carrying in dining room furniture. Before those three men finished two more trucks arrived . . . big ones. Each driver followed the same procedure, but handed Aquina an itemized list; and as each piece was carried in, she and the drivers checked the items off as delivered. Afterwards, she quickly checked the condition of each piece. Then, and only then, did she sign for each delivery. After which the four young men began carefully moving the furniture around according to Aquina's directions.

Soon after the large vans arrived so did the three couples to pitch-in, but counting lunch, coffee breaks there still remained much more to accomplish. But of those rooms that were finished . . . it is gorgeous. Some of the neighbors had curious glances at some of the motif, especially the master bedroom and bath . . . as it is done in an oriental décor. In fact each room had its own subtle hint or oriental feel to it, but this was skillfully mixed with mediterranean style. The "boys" thought it was "cool" especially when they stumbled onto the weapon's cases, swords and the rifle.

One of the cases was modern and long, and when she opened it the young men showed their appreciation by the way they handed each sword to her. Once on the rack, and the rifle below them, they were beautiful in a sense and menacing in another. Aquina would not open the old wooden case and put it safely in one of two walk-in closets located in the master bedroom.

CHAP. 63

Freighter after freighter began ferrying supplies to a temporary storage area as troops continued to land . . . hundreds soon became many thousands. The on site skeleton crew was joined by additional staff, while troops began erecting new plaste's in both large and small sizes.

In the interim, every unemployed person was in the process of being assigned to various work crews. But the big numbers came from that portion of the population which had only split-shift type of normal jobs. They numbered in the tens of thousands, and when they had been organized into teams things went into high gear.

Initially it was cleaning and repair work to the small headquarters building, the two small barracks and one remaining repair facility. While troops gave way to the landing of construction guild personnel and their huge equipment. But once the huge robotic caterpillar-tread equipped unloaders were readied and put into action, the overall pace of unloading skyrocketed. Each colossal machine extracted hundreds of tons of equipment and supplies, from close hovering freighters, every few minutes conveying it quickly to newly erected plastes.

Equally large ground machines, complex C'pter controlled, needing only the few essential raw materials and supplies . . . to create a flawlessly hard surface. With a maw just over fourty meters wide, it sliced . . . cut and gouged the ground to preset depth. In this particular instance five foot depth using low power energy beams. Whatever it digested was immediately pulverized into a uniform bedding material. And with a height of ten and-a-half meters and a length of fourty-five meters, it is able to put down the bedding material in a precise thickness and crushed it down under enormous pressure. While simultaneously mixing, processing and laying a fourty meter wide ribbon of thermoplastic type of indurate.

As the mechanical "sloth" progressed at its sedate ground speed of one and three quarters feet per minute, the supervisor of each "sloth" team resigned himself to doing fourty-nine hours for each ribbon. He well knew it could easily be done faster, but headquarters ordered the rather odd depth-thickness requirements, and all he could do was shrug and obey the construction order. But it intrigued the supervisor, that the indurate should be so thick knowing full well its incredible strength and toughness. At a few inches less than a third of a meter in uniform thickness generated strength readings astronomical in size . . . so then . . . why? He didn't have time to complete the thought as several small supply shuttles arrived, hovered replenishing the materials for the moldable indurate.

In six and-a-half star weeks, just shy of a month, the once decrepit base underwent a remarkable transformation. Though still unfinished the overall size had been easily trebled, and the surface capacity quadrupled. And still tremendous amounts of equipment of every conceiveable kind arrived, ferried and unloaded to the surface. Part of the unending flow consisted of supplies in raw materials for still more indurate. And still more supplies for the troops and those still to arrive, control equipment and various C'pters and other similar devices, sensors and scanners with and without transmitters. And still other supplies and equipment . . . military ordinance of all types, massive battle guns represented only one type. Much had arrived and the convoy of ships kept coming . . . unabated.

Of course the "sloth" supervisor wasn't told, but after the three "sloths" finished a good third of the eighty-seven hundred yard field, and the "ribbons" heat bonded together, excavation was started on a large subterranean cavern. The entrance of which alone is to measure one hundred-eighty meters wide by more than two hundred plus meters long. It is too be totally complete onto itself, even to incorporating its own power supply.

In the interim the massive and complex industry necessary to produce military type ships was receiving a total facelift of its own. From small fabers, fabricators, to the larger material mills, speciality houses, and C'pter industries and other related industries, munitions-ordinance houses, warehousing and shipping . . . . to the huge space docks where actual construction took place . . . . all sections underwent re-organization and re-furbishment or replacement of equipment. The many, many guilds involved all sent their best experienced people first. Those that followed weeks later had some experience, but needed those weeks as retraining. They followed and were in due course added to the labor force fattening it out to one solid shift and a-third needed for a second shift.

Two and-a-half star months later only a portion of the base is functional, as construction was still being carried out . . . on extending the "field" and aprons; although everything necessary to have a first rate or prime base is there, in storage. The ordinance technicians were doing their thing, while permanent barracks were being built, and prepared at various locations around the giant octagon shaped base. Located at strategic points, plaste storage buildings held equipment and supplies ready too be used or installed within short notice.

And throughout all the weeks of military movement, preparation and all the other extroadinary activity Spa/ inf. ran frantic, frustrated in their methods to get the news. For instance, they reported martial law on the three moons, and the fact the military was building on Untey-3, . . . but were stonewalled from that point forward. They could get no information, so they descended on the ship building facilities only to be turned away by small military ships.

Finally, in desperation they congregated at the palace pleading, badgering the public secretaries, located around the spacious and open public viewing and information hall, trying to get a quote or statement.

The emperor took brief notice of the hubbub, while on his way to a meeting with the court. Having discussed the very problem of periodic information releases to guild members, and the value such releases would have if timed properly. Barith filled his lungs . . . then exhaled slowly. He cut a very distinguished figure in uniform, the full scarlet cape hanging just right . . . automatically marked him as a senior ranking officer. The brownish uniform also marked him as a ground soldier, and there were few such officers entitled the scarlet cape. Barith automatically drew the gaze of many in the hall.

Barith stood well into the main rotunda, considered inner palace and therefore off limits to everyone, unless by appointment or invitation. Those out in the hall were expected to keep their voices at a moderate level and all shouting was strictly forbidden. Nor could they call to him, but when he turned and they saw his sword and blaster, well it meant he is on duty. Most in the crowd inquired of the officer with the scarlet cape to the secretaries.

"Oh yes . . . the officer is Capt. Barith, chief of the emperor's military aides."

Their heads snapped up at the name and position, and he is quickly walking back to the archway. While still a few yards away they heard one of the guards say, . . . "nothing unusual captain." Barith nodded as both guards saluted and continued through the archway confronting the large crowd. After a few minutes he gave them a statement. Barith chose his words very carefully, indicating the military was indeed cleaning and refurbishing the old base on Untey-3; but he omitted the other pertinent information believing it unwise to divulge too much at one time. The crowd pressed for more information, but Barith was able to successfully dance around their questions. And as Barith turned walking back through the archway the crowd reluctantly began to leave.

With the base virtually completed, insofar as repair and refurbishing facilities were concerned . . . although several more months would be needed to finish . . . three medium unused-retired cruisers are ferried to Untey-3 . . . An inter-connecting pair-set of overly large plastes are waiting to receive the three ships. And much like a well practiced drill, the ships after touching down are immediately moved into the waiting structures. As the doors closed, a cordon of tight-lipped, grim faced troops encircled the mini-complex . . . alert and ready. They knew the success of whatever the mission would be for those ships may ride on their shoulders, . . . and their attitude and behavior reflected their dedication. The perimeter was not walked with weapons at rest, they prowled, angry, with their rifles ready to kill at an instant's notice.

The lead sergeant's name is Gal'pr-Snz, a young soldier of some repute, personally chosen by Barith for the coveted assignment. A man who led his men by example not by orders, as he was not one to say much; but . . . his detachment of a hundred men followed him without complaint.

Multiple crews inside the huge buildings attacked the ships like army ants, beginning the laborious task of stripping equipment and components. It is almost a week before the ships were gutted on the inside, at which time the crews began on the hull of each ship, stripping and cutting until only the bare frame and inside decks remained. In some cases entire frames were replaced by new ones made of new harder materials and the decks as well. All integral bulkheads are replaced, as well as secondary walls and others.

Now the transformation started in ernest. Usable room is added by making the ships longer for additional crew plus troops and supplies. Once each ship had been up-dated structurally and multiple electro-bio decks installed, many more gun positions had been specially fabricated and installed.

And with many weeks already gone and the extent of structural rebuilding and lengthening accomplished, each set of crews began replacing the main and auxiliary engines in each ship. As an additional safeguard, three totally separate life support systems are incorporated. Each with twin generators was located in a totally different part of the ship, along with standby power cells. In every area the level of redundancy is unprecedented. Only the very latest of equipment is incorporated reflecting the latest technology, especially with respect to the guns.

Using the latest innovations the new battle guns are much more powerful, incorporating twin barrels or projectors. In addition, each gun had coupled to it standby power cells which could be used in the advent of a crippling hit to the ship's main energy source.

More weeks went by while control systems are installed and tested, and most eye opening was the installation of the "spatial navigational cube." A total reproduction in miniature of a half parsec of space around each ship. With the ship occupying the center of the "cube," and whatever other ships with it are positioned accurately, and objects or planets, or approaching ships . . . whatever . . . are faithfully positioned. At the same time, whatever is picked up by sensors and scanners is displayed, such as relative position and speed, inside the cube and accompanying vid screens around the control room. Everything is depicted with the help of color and size point of light designation.

Choices for commander and aux. commander for each of the three vessels proved tremendously difficult. But to make matters worse . . . one of them must be professional enough to command not only his own ship, but be overall mission commander. And there layed the crux of the problem. Several possibles were considered each possessed current battle experience, meaning of course with raiders.

The presiding senior admiral, sitting in the center, looked over his subordinates . . . cleared his throat and began to speak. Inserting an identity plick into his C'pter, and simultaneously on all screens. "I refer you to this young officer, promoted to commander seven star months ago. Notice the conspicuous record . . . we of the circle consider this officer highly promising."

Member officers of the committee looked knowingly at one-another as the chairman continued.

"Having only hours previously engaged three enemy ships, was successful in destroying them but not before sustaining heavy damage to his own ship. The commander did not return or call for aid, but continued to patrol his sector. Whereupon he received a distress call from a fully loaded passenger ship."

"Answering the call, he arrived on the scene to find it under attack from four raiders, one of which was clumsily trying to lock-onto the passenger ship's air and boarding lock. He immediately attacked, successfully disabling the raider trying to lock-on to the passenger ship. Pressing the attack his ship was hit repeatedly with expected consequences. He was able nonetheless to destroy the remaining three, but not before absorbing more crippling hits, virtually incapacitating his own ship." The admiral continued.

"Beginning to drift . . . the little cruiser is twisted and ragged, ripped with damage, looking to all on board the rapidly approaching passenger ship as a lifeless mass of junk. The captain of the approaching ship called repeatedly without hearing anything, However, some minutes later static from the wrecked ship, then . . . a strong voice coughed a few times and spoke. Through open connecting doors passengers on the first deck, reserved for the nobility, and the lower decks heard the cheering going on in the control room. They passed the word as the captain spoke to everyone by intercom, informing them that there indeed are survivors."

With quick skillful maneuvering the captain matched the air-locks and although they had problems opening the hatch on the crippled ship, they finally managed to get it open. Of the nine crew, four were dead and the five remaining all suffered various wounds including the commander. Dozens of willing hands evacuated the dead, and wounded; but, as his arm is dressed and covered . . . the commander notified the grateful captain; and overheard by many, he would leave aboard his own ship, and if he could leave his remaining crew onboard the passenger vessel."

"Before the captain could object the commander quickly returned to his ship followed by his long-time friend, who also is second-in-command. Almost immediately the ships separated. The captain waited hours until close to his destination before contacting the military advising them about the commander's intention. Meanwhile the two officers managed to eke out a miniscule amount of auxiliary power and notified headquarters their intention; but did not reveal their position in case "others" were listening." The admiral continued.

"Just over two star weeks, ship's time, our long understaffed small base on the fringe of the Sa-gor system detected the ship on their scanners. But, they waited anxiously to see if the ship was being used as bait for a raider ambush. However, as events proved the ship was quite alone, and in due course two small ships went out to meet and escort the commander and his shipmate to safety. As the two ships brought the derelict in close, two space tugs went out to gently bring the crippled ship into the space dock."

"I wish you, the committee, to consider the enormous odds, the almost overwhelming problems encountered in bringing that ship back." Pausing to allow his words time to sink-in. He held up another plick . . . .

"This is a recording of the commander's actions at the space dock. He is gaunt, ragged and weak from too little food, as is his companion. But his pride and the need to keep his ship lend him energy." The admiral replied.

In went the plick. The vid screen showed the wharf snaking out to the battered hulk . . . then the hatch was opened by workmen, and the waiting bio-techs rushed in with their bags and supplies. Muffled sounds from the technicians giving nutrient injections and vitamin liquids. A large man leaned against the open hatch holding an injured arm. With stubble on his face and bleary-eyed, torn and dirty uniform, a small cut on his high forehead, but a grim determined face as he straightened walking slowly up the wharf. Though a little unsteady, he made his way past staring people who applauded, smiled as the commander rested momentarily against the wall, only inches from the yard manager's door.

Minutes later he waved at the panel and walked in as the door whooshed open. Going on into the inner office, he faced the yard manager across the desk littered with papers, and other such similar items. The commander slammed his hand down hard demanding to know when his ship would be repaired.

"Commander Dra'lr, did you say repaired?" "Yes," replied Dra'lr patient but intense. "First of all . . . . even if it was possible, which it isn't and assuming . . . I had the time . . . . I don't . . .

I could not repair space junk." The yard manager replied . . . patiently

"Space junk!" Dra'lr almost choked, his face red his fists clenching. "Here commander is the C'pter's list of damage to your ship." Dra'lr took the many sheets . . . . and by the time he finished reading, his mood changed considerably. Gazing through the view port, he looked out upon his once beautiful ship, and one solitary tear cascaded down his cheek. Turning slowly to the yard manager . . . "I will go aboard and remove my flag." "Of course commander." Said the yard manager softly, understanding the commander's feelings.

As Dra'lr walked solemnly back to his ship, people he passed offered quiet gradulations and praised his efforts, and those of his crew. Arriving at the wharf, he walked out to his ship and retrieved his flag and belongings. The flag was his father's and his father's before him, and wherever he served the emperor, there also was his flag announcing a member of the house . . . Dra'lr. Only when a soldier rose to command rank could his flag be displayed. Otherwise the emblem was worn proudly on the right sleeve of the tunic, and usually on all personal equipment. It had long been established thus allowing the soldier to wear the uniform of his emperor, and still carry the identity of his house.

The vid screen in front of each committee member went blank. The admiral immediately asked for any further comments before the vote. Meanwhile sitting in the admiral's office in a new uniform, the blue commander's cape folded over the seat, Dra'lr vividly recalled some of the events of the past few days.

He stood waiting for the one other officer, his trusted shipmate, and by the look on his face the lieutenant knew the ship was at an end. Both went aboard one last time. It was at this point the official messenger caught up to them. "Commander Dra'lr?" "Yes." I have been ordered to give you this . . . . sir." "Thank you." "Yes sir." The messenger said with a snappy salute smiling broadly and rode off on her miniscule scooter.

He read: "Commander Dra'lr, with the below named officer report immediately to Untey-3, base commander's office for command reassignment." "Well, it seems we are wanted or rather someone wants us." The lieutenant replied. Jovialities over the two boarded a military transport heading for Untey-3.

In the interim the vote was taken and much to the admiral's pleasure and relief, it had been unanimous in the commander's favor. And with there being no further billets to fill, he adjourned the meeting and returned to his office, and Dra'lr. When the admiral entered the commander was already standing, and sat only after the admiral had regained his seat. And without being told an aide filled two goblets with soft beitra handing one to the admiral, and the second to the now famous commander. Both drank deeply enjoying the beitra . . . the admiral spoke first.

"Concerning our previous conversation . . . the committee voted unanimously in your favor. This plick makes it official. You're now overall mission commander. Your orders are contained in this as well, and I'm also giving you command of the lead ship. The command ship has been fitted out differently than that of the other two, as it has a large cabin prepared specially for one of the survivors." The admiral had withdrawn from his desk a pouch approximately one foot long, four inches thick and five inches wide bearing the emperor's seal.

"As part of your orders, you will hand that pouch to the survivor who you'll know after listening to the plick. Put that in your personal closet or some other equally safe place divulging nothing about the person prior to arrival on the rim planet." "Yes sir." Dra'lr said.

They both checked over their equipment and as a consequence drew a number of items from officer supply. Still with time to spare both entered the officer's briefing room and waited. And while doing so the crews for all three ships gathered in the large new crew briefing room, where after a thirty minute period, giving the crews time to meet each other, the briefing was called to order. The base aux. commander explained the mission, their new ships and most especially the officer as mission commander.

Following the crew briefing all selected officers began filing into the new officer's briefing room, and acknowledged the two officers already present sitting against the rear wall. Quickly they began saluting, and as recognition hit them, whispering, smiles and all nodded with respect. Within minutes the base commander entered as all stood . . . and quickly sat again at the admiral's command. He went to some length in his explaination of the mission and substantial detail about their new ships. The admiral's last few words concerned their mission commander, after which he introduced Dra'lr to them.

"I believe you all recognize the commander and his shipmate. Commander Dra'lr is in command of this mission. Take over commander." "Thank you admiral." Walking to the front of the room . . . Dra'lr faced the group of officers for a few seconds before speaking.

"Our mission is very simple; we stay on signal and bring our people home! Whoever or whatever gets in our way will be destroyed. Understand me, there is no time to run or chase, but if attacked we will destroy the attackers. I will divulge further plans after we are underway." Dra'lr said, and then a pause continued. "All senior lieutenants and up stay. The rest of you return to your ships, make your crew assignments and make ready for departure." Instructed Dra'lr. After most of the group had exited Dra'lr continued. "During our warp to the Ceti system, we will hold drills constantly until we're ready. I will explain our battle strategy on board. All right go to your ships." Filing out many exchanged knowing glances with one-another.

Dra'lr and his shipmate . . . . lieutenant Gri'ry, each inhaled letting it out as a sigh, and with a pause followed the last members of the group leaving for their ships. It wasn't a long walk to the three ships, but the first faint rays of dawn were just beginning to cut the darkness giving the three ships a surrealistic aura, highlighted by the corden of troops checking crew members. In that brief pause the rush of adrenalin is sweet. He has three new vessels at his command on a trusted mission for his emperor. His father would be proud, and his sister, and mother . . . her memory still fresh and sweet. He is in rank equal to his father, and closing his eyes . . . gave thanks to the universe for granting his career. There was nothing more he wanted.

> [On a plane of reality, in a dimension as removed from this universe as black is to white, an awesome super omnipotent being held court over far lesser omnipotent beings of worth. A place where time and

> the only physical laws were those of the supreme being's own making. Several lesser beings drew pleasure from a play already in motion, where one being was not above causing mischief to increase its own pleasure. The supreme being drew a measure of pleasure as well from an occasional play . . . the course of which . . . . it detected a low lifeform's prayer of gratitude for granting its career. It pleased the supreme being and as a consequence introduced a nuance into the play . . . so subtlely the lesser ones could not ever detect the shift in the play's pattern.

Within ten minutes Dra'lr stood on the control deck, set up his flag in its proper receptacle and began a quick tour of his ship. He knew the first ship would always remain in his heart, but this one is a beauty also, and smiled as he looked and learned about "her." The crew watched him with growing respect, and when he came close spoke a traditional greeting. He answered with a grin or patient smile and a customary word or two. There wasn't a place or area on board that he didn't visit, and immediately came to love the new ship. Returning to the control room, Dra'lr quickly reviewed fuel reports, and matters pertaining to navigation. Above all the secret code identification for the pulsar signal, which would lead them to the marooned survivors . . . "that" he committed to memory. Needed preparations were being made while the crew brought additional stores and supplies onboard.

Prior to departure, Dra'lr convened a meeting in his cabin attended by the junior commanders and aides second in command from the other two ships, and proceeded to outline tactics with likelihood of attack from raiders and pirates. A discussion of course to follow for consideration of speed and possible avoidance of attack from raider groups was the only topic.

CHAP. 64

For the most part the house was completed around noon the next day, sunday. That night, Aquina invited all of her neighbors for a party. It was a spontaneous fun filled evening in which she learned a great deal about them . . . but, they learned nothing more about her until many more months went by the wayside.

As time went by little things were noticed by the neighbors, which on the surface seemed unimportant, and trivial, but when scrutinized carefully, and put together . . . . caused them to wonder. A good portion of the curiosity began when the teenage girl occasionally saw Aquina clad in halter and shorts instructing Miriam in moves the nineteen year old recognized as martial arts. And the fact she had seen the tattoo on Aquina's right shoulder. Soon after, several of the young men using binoculars confirmed what the young lady had seen.

They dug into the library section of the college library seeking books on oriental logos and tattoos; But they found nothing even remotely similar to the tattoo they'd drawn after looking at Aquina's lovely back. On the faculty of the school there are a number of orientals. The young men went from one to the other asking the same questions, but in each case came up empty until they spoke to a man of Japanese ancestry. He identified it as being korean and suggested they speak to a certain professor whose family immigrated recently from korea. The professor was amiable enough even though they interrupted his concentration. The professor didn't hesitate but identified the logo as old korean, . . . that of the Kodo'Kun Temple Monastery. He answered one question and then elaborated on what he knew of the monastery, and its masters. The young men urged him on further to say what he remembered of the masters. Explaining about how the communists feared the masters and why, and that until the latter half of the 40's, the temple had alsways been a male stronghold. "But then a young teenage woman, rumored to be european, was hailed as the object of an ancient confucian legend and admitted to the temple. She is said to possess extroadinary power and excelled in all aspects of her training, until she far surpassed the masters. It's said she departed the temple grounds with a weapon's case, the ancient wood staff and always wore the light blue robe. The robe could not hide her figure, as not many saw her face, it was not important. Many more, untold thousands more of my people would have perished from lack of supplies, exposure and the hated communists were it not for Little Star."

The young men asked what the name meant. Becoming more and more suspicious as to their motives . . . he explained only the bare facts. "It is her temple and Confucian name." The professor replied politely refusing to answer any further questions. In spite of the information they were stymied, their curiosity flamed hot; but there was nothing they could do . . . and knew it.

Meanwhile, Aquina made a consistent contribution to the office and layout room. Initially the superviser assigned some support equipment and shop problems, and with the smooth competent manner in which Aquina solved them came more difficult and trustworthy work. The two men directly above her, in the chain of command, cited the appropriate instances to coincide with the excellent performance reports. That is not to say she didn't experience some difficult moments . . . she did. But these were of a personal kind having to do with dating, et-cetera; However, she had few problems concerning her position or work. And those were of a kind to enhance rather than detract from her reputation.

As '70 became '71, she and Miriam attended the normal x-mas functions and became cemented into the corporate family. Time went by, she became consistently more popular. Only her neighbors, that is the adults, half suspected something was not what it should be; however, the young men and young lady knew she was more than she let on.

Miriam was popular as well but of course much closer to home. She dated in the evenings and remained at the house all day. While the only dates Aquina accepted were for lunch only. Reason, was she didn't believe in dating co-workers. And as hard and as persuasive as the men were . . . she would not compromise her position. She did however take part in gatherings around the neighborhood and in turn entertained her neighbors. And during the last week of the year, both she and Miriam joined a new health spa located only a short distance from the company's main entrance. The "club" advertised a large pool, plus other attractive attributes, but the pool was their prime reason for joining.

The beginning of '72, Aquina notified the national panel of her return, new address, and that because of career obligations was forced to scale down her participation. Which meant activities in the general area, and New York, unless time permitted otherwise.

A week later the seven panel members arrived on her doorstep with smiles and good news. They were fairly impressed with the house and spent the entire weekend. Aquina found she indeed . . . missed each and everyone of them. Divided organization business, prayer and workouts . . . the weekend sped by all too quickly.

With assurance she will attend the national meet . . . their Olympics, her picture and name once again appeared extensively within the tabloids. The meet was on a friday and saturday, and the panel understood she would not arrive at the hotel until friday evening. Not withstanding the three month wait until the nationals, the martial art tabloids ran pictures of her sitting on the panel, and shots taken during the trouble at the previous meet she attended in New York. But this . . . . the nationals, would be held at the garden. In spite of her self-control, Aquina was excited and concerned, a good number of people would see her there. It was obvious in the weeks that followed, some of her co-workers were afficionado's of martial arts. Aquina felt it more than anything else . . . . the subtle change in many attitudes, the degree of respect accorded her substantially increased. Even the occasional joking and bantering was mollified. Then, as to their curiosity . . . . it increased more . . . much more.

Although, she tried to minimize the effect wrought by the magazine articles, her very nature and reserve, and the way she walked, and carried herself helped to influence them.

The weeks went by smoothly, month by month fell by the wayside, until two weeks before the event one of the company's senior vice presidents who happened to head public relations and advertising sent for her. And when she entered he stood offering a comfortable chair next to his desk. And immediately broached the subject of the interview. In short, the company felt because of her leadership position in a unique organization, and the company's constant wish to appear in a strong community service position, and there was one or two more reasons, but the upshot . . . was the company gave her that particular friday off with pay. She thanked him and after leaving placed a call to the organization, and informed them of her change in plans. They in turn made the necessary changes in schedule and hotel reservations. The organization's secretary then notified the "garden" to have a separate dressing room available starting on friday rather than saturday, for the same person.

Unbeknownst to Aquina, many of the corporation's top officers and managers purchased tickets for the national event.

The friday arrived, and with Miriam carrying the large shoulder bag they were driven to the airport by a few of the young men of the neighborhood. A short hop later both hailed a cab for the ride into the city, and the hotel. Although the meet didn't begin until 7 p.m., both ladies departed for the garden after checking into the hotel, and deposited their bags in the suite.

At the garden, she oversaw, with help from the other panel members preparations already well advanced. Aquina looked at the large open expanse of the garden, plus the dressing rooms, back and equipment rooms. She noticed tv crews setting up equipment, and the press box filling up with the professional "snoopers." And during the entire afternoon Miriam ran interference between her and the reporters. She successfully ducked out at 5:45, the preparations finished, and only the last minute details had to be done.

It is 6:15 p.m., the entire center and side floor areas are in total darkness as the public began pouring in locating their seats and assuming them, and made themselves comfortable. Aquina exited the dressing room and walked to where the other panel members waited peering through the curtains. At 7 p.m., ceiling lights came on bathing the entire floor area, showing two distinct combat areas covered with gymnastic mats. While the announcer went into his normal oratory. Some referees came out with their people with towels, and sundry other items, and occupied each area covered by the straw mats. At the opposite end . . . the access-way, are located the long tables with eight microphones and pitchers of water. All the chairs are in black except the center chair which is covered in blue.

Groups of contestants filed out wearing basic white with various color belts, but all are below brown; and virtually no insignia unless the person belonged to a club. There is quite a few of them, and when all were sitting on their mats, the announcer drew attention to the tables. As soon as he announced the organization's governing board, they began walking out. All the contestants stood as if at attention, and the short line walked slowly . . . the emcee identified each. But when he called Aquina's name every oriental in the audience stood-up. When she sat . . . the entire panel sat, and so did the contestants and those people in the audience.

The competition began. For a little over two hours the contestants battled, three sets or rounds for each pair. And by 9:20 p.m., the first half of the competition was fini. After Aquina had changed and eluded the "snoopers," she and Miriam joined the panel members for dinner at a fashionable korean restaurant downtown.

Two hours later they unlocked the door and walked into their suite. While Miriam slept like the dead, Aquina intended only a cat-nap, but instead drifted deeper and deeper until she entered rem sleep. Her mind's eye saw spacecraft, sleek and shiny, elegant and a deep dark black edifice . . . . a building, but of awesome proportions. And in front . . . a monstrous door. She tried to see more, but it remained fuzzy. A bit later she woke, a fine layer of perspiration covered her entire body. After a hot shower, Aquina put on panties and a black blouse. She then padded out into the next room and filled a wine glass with an adequate vintage white wine. Sitting on the couch she tried to analyze the dream, but found more questions than answers.

Between breakfast and shopping most of the day was gone when they returned to the suite. And with little time to waste caught a cab to the garden. It dropped them off at the performer's entrance; and as she did the night before set about helping the other panel members with the schedule.

Everything progressed normally, the only deviation was the level of proficiency of the contestants and the size of the crowd. First, the second half of the competition was restricted to brown and black belt contestants and second, the crowd swelled filling the entire building plus many aisles.

With the announcer the meet began just as it had the night before, except there were more injuries and fouls. The large difference occurred when not one person risked . . . . challenging Aquina. Which of course was exactly what the audience was waiting for . . . a serious confrontation. But everything concluded on an up-beat note.

After a lingering dinner, Aquina called and found there was a shuttle heading to Bradley from JFK . . . A quick checkout at the hotel and a rapid and borderline illegal speed run by the cabbie, put them within minutes of the plane's departure time. They just made it, barely and were allowed on board. From their destination . . . another cab, and then home. The next day was sunday, just right for lounging, relaxing and they did . . . doing very little of anything.

The following morning, Aquina walked into the same building, through the very same door while guards touched their caps with the right hand . . . . a smile and a hearty "good morning." Although the coffee and her desk and drawing table, and instrument caddy was the same . . . co-workers treated her as something of a celebrity. She tried to accept it in good humor assuming it would cease in time. Which it did of course, but there remained with them the memory of Aquina's obvious prowess as a deadly fighter. The one thing associated with the recognition she appreciated, the singular blossom found on her desk each and every morning. Sometimes a rose of one color, then a different color on another day, a tulip, primrose, mums, iris, daffodil, aster, oriental poppy and many others. The array was both extensive and highly colorful and succeeded in brightening the office.

Shortly thereafter, Miriam met a young man who became a steady visitor to the house, and an important person in her life. And as '72 dragged to a close, the two began to get serious.

In the meantime, Aquina became better and much more proficient in airframe design and propulsion techniques. Both of which caused her work to be noticed more frequently, especially when she included mathematical equations and proofs with her concepts, and work sheets with necessary drawings. She had early on developed a real passion for the calculus, hence one reason for her excellence at the institute. That ability matured to the point where much time was saved on a continuous basis because of her "notes."

During the spring of '73, Miriam accepted an engagement ring, and as Aquina continued to officiate at various meets, she became progressively more well known. At more or less the same time, she is given a promotion from assistant to full engineer, and thereafter proceeded rapid advancement. It was long established company policy to review each person's performance, and other factors in their record, quarterly. In june, and again in september, she had reviews, and in each case it is significantly better than the one previous. December of that year, after all the new construction had been completed, and new companion design facilities were ready to occupy, a senior engineer had been chosen as chief. After looking over Aquina's recent quarterly . . . . he chose her for assistant.

While the chief has the formal office, Aquina has the informal office directly outside but connected, in which two walls are transparent on the top half. The secretary's little cubicle and desk is directly across from her. While the other desks and tables are directly down from her office, and the secretary's forming parallel lines. There are a total of four engineers, eight assistant engineers and one copy machine . . .

a diazalid operator for Aquina to oversee with the secretary. A friendship soon developed with the secretary, which Aquina kept in the proper tone, and overall most everything ran smoothly. She is happy because now there is actual space hardware and systems to work on . . . she is very happy.

Year '73 turned to '74, and the dream continued. On occasion she would see more, learn a little more . . . see something new. Aquina did her best to analyze why she dreamt the same thing so often.

It wasn't because of pressure at work, it wasn't that bad, and her diet was reasonable, and she ruled out anxiety and that sort of thing, Again, she has far more questions than answers.

In june, Miriam and her fiancé were married in a local church, and Aquina gave the reception at the house and backyard. A nice size party with virtually all of the neighbors, Miriam and the groom's family were present and select friends.

The weeks that followed are mainly of adjustment, not only at work but at home as well. Aquina obtained the services of a bonded cleaning outfit for three days a week, and did for herself the other four days. She enjoyed doing for herself. One of the noteworthy steps was re-arranging her den into a design office, and often spent most of a weekend working on avante-garde concepts. Or in some instances, she spent an enjoyable few hours of an afternoon checking the ferrari's fluid lavels, washing it or vacuuming out the inside . . . In which case almost always the young adults would congregate . . . around her casually helping or doing other things.

More and more the dream began to influence her, intruding on her thoughts to the extent she became genuinely concerned for her health. As a precaution, she made out a will, had it notorized and brought other business matters up to date, and lumped them all together in a large safety deposit box at the bank.

Meanwhile, Dien had weeks earlier been forced to enter the generator compartment in the unused "ship." The wave had fluctuated and lost power so Dien brought the second and remaining generator up to power, but not before receiving a serious dose of radiation. Slowly the greater portion of her strength ebbed away, and with the supply of serum so low . . . Dien didn't succumb, but the serum wasn't sufficient to restore the full measure of health. Therefore much of the time Dien spent in her bed too weak to do much of anything, but take medicine which she knew would only prolong her agony. It was because of this she saw no-one, and soon those that revered the family realized grave sickness had befallen Dien . . . . and there were no visitors. Dien continued as she was, not getting any better, but then, not getting any worse either.

CHAP. 65

Departure was of course not announced, only the mission commander and base commander knew the scheduled time. Using newly formed codes, the admiral contacted Dra'lr with a last minute word.

In the first rays of dawn, the ships lifted off effortlessly and silently to assume their rightful place in empire history. As the three reached optimum distance from Untey-3 . . . all three formed up and went into warp as a unit. While in warp phase because of certain physical laws of the continuum sensors and scanners were alright, but communications could and usually were troublesome. Each of the other two ships took their cue's from the command ship.

The commander immediately after jumping went to his cabin, and relaxed, trying to think. For the better part of an hour . . . he worked to formulate a comprehensive list of drills and exercises. All of which to be practiced individually and in tandum with others. Pleased with himself, Dra'lr walked quickly back to the control room handing the plick to the communications officer. "Put this into our main C'pter, and send it repeatedly until they acknowledge its reception." "Yes sir." She said alert and ready. She managed although it required for more time than it should have, before each ship understood what it was to do, as far as holding drills. Dra'lr immediately spoke to the crew by main channel intercom explaining the various gunnery position drills, warming the guns, damage containment teams, loss of power drills, battle readiness and repelling borders.

He commenced with gunnery drills that very morning and ran through the entire list of drills. Straight through with no let-up, not even for food, but did almost seventeen hours later for a two hour rest period. They didn't leave Untey-3 until before five in the morning, ship's time, and therefore Dra'lr considered those hours wasted. With twenty hours remaining of the day, he instructed the schedule of drills be shuffled like cards, thoroughly mixing up the sequence. And continued with that phase until late in the evening when his crew were literally dropping or already fallen in a stupor at their guns, in passageways, the control deck . . . . all over the ship . . . and the other two the situation was practically the same.

Dra'lr nodded to the communications officer to halt the C'pter call and had her pass the word to the other ships . . . . to stand down from drills. For five blissful hours the crews slept where they were, not caring, but savoring the peace and tried to work out the aches and kinks in their sore bodies. However, when the five hours had expired . . . Dra'lr and Gri'ry awakened the control room personnel, and again gave the comm. officer the high sign. She immediately established contact with the other ships bringing her counterparts up-to-date.

Not until eighteen hours later, there were several breaks inbetween, did Dra'lr finally call a halt. By that time, when drill after drill exercise after exercise was completed in good time and his crew much leaner and definitely meaner . . . . did he indicate his satisfaction with a smile. He had comm. pass the word . . . every crew member on all three ships to stand down with a cup of soft beitra. Their education into the nature of the commander had begun.

With both short and long range scanners showing zilch, he ordered the ships to de-warp, or decelerate back to normal space, which was accomplished without incident. By their best warp speed the Ceti system is still some ten hours distant. The three ships linked-up in answer to Dra'lr's call for a meeting of the commanders. A bit later two sat comfortably in Dra'lr's cabin chatting about the drills and their effectiveness. And it bore out his feeling when each commander gave somewhat different answers, as the percentage fluctuated . . . . but all agreed they are far more ready, better prepared then they had been.

"Good, the drills just might save some lives." Dra'lr remarked with a wry grin. He nodded and then handed to each man a plick, a copy of the raider's many favorite and most used tactics. "Study this in detail, then pass out further copies to your gunners and helmsman. We will stay and hold this relative position for the balance of today. By six tomorrow morning, ship's time, we must warp for Ceti . . . . there is simply not more time." Dra'lr explained. Each officer stood and offered their left arm . . . Dra'lr clasped each warmly. But not a word was spoken . . . it wasn't necessary.

Although each crew was winded and tired, their respective commander is relentless with seminars and exercises for gunners and helmsman. And each ship had made strides, each commander recognized the need for more work; so even though the appointed hour arrived for their departure the exercises continued, while they were in warp speed.

Two hours shy of mid-day, ship's time, the three ships slowed re-entering normal space. Continuing on in maximum space drive Arbus-Ceti filled the main view screen on each ship. Possibly the only person exempt from the exercises was the senior operator, who had to pay constant attention to his equipment. It had been explained to them the characteristics about the energy spectrum permeating the entire area. They could not warp through the system with assurance of picking up the signal on the reverse side; nor could they warp around the system with enough assurance of finding the tight signal. Therefore the ships were forced to proceed through the system making them susceptible to attack.

Assuming a modified "V" formation, they pushed for maximum speed. While doing so, gunners continued having repetitive briefings on the known plans of attack most used by the raiders, and became quite good in the simulations. But then simulations do not fire back with sometimes devastating results. Of course those of a military mind understand this concept, but unfortunately there exists a great difference between simulation and the real thing.

One may also say with an equal feeling of confidence, unless you are very lucky with hindsight . . . does an actual battle go as one thinks or predicts.

Everyone expected to be attacked, it is the "when" that bothered most, though the gunners are itching for a fight. So it was . . . when the word came through . . . . they had entered Ceti, the gunners quickly manned their guns warming them and reported in to the control deck. For an hour things continued peacefully, but having covered less than a-third of the way through the system the expected attack occurred in the form of three small raiders. Using nothing more than reworked scout ships, they found themselves up-against much larger and superior vessels. And were no match for the superior firepower of the small empire cruisers. Thus were quickly destroyed, while the empire ships suffered no damage whatsoever. The combined crews were jubilant.

Dra'lr of course, knew instantly what was happening. "Mind your guns positions, we were only being tested. Continue to scan and stay alert!" For the rest of the day primary gunners took turns with the station two gunners allowing each to stand down enabling them to eat and relax . . . or at least to attempt to sooth their anxieties. It was all a sobering truth, and each admitted it to themselves . . . it had been too easy. And as the commander hinted . . . there will be more. The night was spent quietly, but few of any slept including Dra'lr. With the first moment of the new day he walked onto the control deck and relieved Gri'ry. At the same time first station gunners began slowly relieving their counterparts, and by the second hour every gun was occupied . . . ready.

Not quite an hour later scanners picked up incoming ships and the alarm automatically sounded. Instantaneously the information went to the spatial cube, number, course and speed, and the pinpoints of light . . . one for each enemy ship. Once the raiders passed a certain distance a low level alarm sounded in each gun cell. And corresponding action took place in the cube . . . the pinpoints of light turned to red, making it easier to distinquish friend from foe.

Dra'lr informed all three crews what formation the raiders were using and notified those gunners in certain positions . . . to make ready. All of this while having approximately fourty-five percent of the Ceti system to travel.

Closing the distance rapidly, the raiders began firing and as luck would have it . . . a serious hit was sustained aft by the command ship slightly wounding Dra'lr. But all guns continued to function valiantly. Troops on each ship quickly began helping the regular crew clear away debris and repair the damage, while the guns began to take a toll. With the imperial ships using entirely new formation and evasive tactics it was successful in taking the edge from the numerical superior numbers enjoyed by the raiders.

Immediately after the hit was scored on the command ship, one cruiser scored a direct hit on one raider destroying it utterly. During subsequent action . . . . four more raiders were crippled and later one exploded, while the lead raider received two hits and retired. Only two raiders remained and they both are seriously hit following the apparent leader from the scene. Whether or not the withdrawl was to rescue the wounded from the crippled ships, or realizing the superior firepower and having lost most of their force withdrew . . . . Dra'lr didn't know or care.

Looking over the damage done to his ship, Dra'lr gave the crew encouragement and felt relief it wasn't any worse. Returning to the control room, he learned the other two ships sustained only superficial damage and are still very battle ready and worthy. And while repairs were being carried out, all three ships proceeded at best possible speed out of the Ceti system. Once beyond Ceti, Dra'lr on course, on signal intended to warp as soon as possible. But with their present speed the navigation officer said . . . "Commander, point eight days before exiting this system." Dra'lr nodded to her and went back to his thoughts.

All the gunners stayed at their posts, while the available crew were making excellent use of the time. Repairs continued at a lively pace as the wounded were tended to with care, and attention to comfort. And by the time they reached the edge of Ceti, the repairs had been completed using spare parts whenever possible; and once the debris was disposed of . . . cleaning the ship was given priority.

Just past the edge of Ceti, Dra'lr instructed the ships to slow . . . then stop and maintain their position. He passed the word for the gunners to stand down with refreshments passed around and food. On all three ships during which the other commanders followed Dra'lr's lead, and concentrated on long range and short range scanners. When more than an hour passed and nothing registered . . . "alright full ahead max drive."

The squadron, such as it is . . . really a "group" being only three ships was in high spirits. They destroyed or crippled eleven raiders, ultimately repelling two attacks, and are still very much in action. That was in essence the substance of the coded message flashed back to the empire. Actually Untey-3, base comm. section which received the message relaying it to the palace and military headquarters. In turn, Barith was quickly asked to the comm. room where he looked at the letters and symbols of the message, and with his back turned to the others quickly deciphered the message. Leaving the room at a quick walk, he went directly to the emperor in his private office.

Barith saluted and bowed then put the message in Roak's outstretched hand eight and-a-half hours after it had been sent. After reading it, Roak is elated, but pointed out the need for caution. "We cannot as yet make this public. An organized effort must be made to clamp down on any potential leaks." The emperor explained to Barith. "Our people have yet to make the return trip, and now the raiders know the strength and position of our ships."

"I understand sire, and it shall be as you wish." Barith said bowing as he exited the office. He first visited the comm. room beginning his task.

Dra'lr, after sending the message, ordered the group to warp. It is just over two days, ship;s time, until reaching the general area known as the rim.

CHAP. 66

The office wall clock showed 5:05 p.m., and Aquina leaned over her office layout table changing part of a view, adding a line and changed the dimension putting in the new one. Straightening, she sighed and looked at the clock, and hurriedly picked-up some personal things from the desk dumping them in her purse. Closing it, she leaned over for the suit jacket searching for a handkerchief.

"Working late Miss Aquina?" "Hi Hal, no. I didn't realize the time, but I'm just leaving." She replied. "Date?" "Not tonight. This is one of my work-out nights at the club." "Oh. Well good night then." "Good night Hal." She said with a smile.

Putting on her jacket, her long hair out from underneath, picked up the shoulder bag and attaché case, turned the lamp off and walked out of the office. She walked around the corner and in seconds opened the door leading to the corridor. Closing it behind her, Aquina headed down the main hallway toward the exit, saying goodnight to two more guards as one opened and held the door. Aquina squinted from the late afternoon sun. It was still quite high, and during that part of the year evening didn't begin until around eight p.m.

The fresh breeze felt good during her short walk to the car. Getting in the molded seat felt good and cool, and luxurious as she put the attaché case on the floor, and jacket on the passenger side. She left the shoulder strap off using only the seat belt, buckled it and put the key into the ignition. The previous owner of the ferrari, the jag dealer, had put an ignition cut off into the system . . . she flipped that toggle switch first, then turned the key to on. She waited a few seconds then turned the key. The starter sounded identical to that of a small turbine, and suddenly the twelve cylinder cat erupted into life with a healthy roar, announcing to the countryside it is awake.

It didn't take long to cover the distance to the club, being only minutes from the company's parking lot. Parking directly in front, she reached for the bag behind the seat. She locked the car and walked past the fountain and entered the vestibule thence to the reception desk to check-in. Walking down the center hallway, she entered the women's locker area, and unlocked the tall rented locker. Hanging up her jacket, she began to strip, and in a moment stood in the buff. And just as quickly donned dancer's nylon tights and a leotard over them in a contrasting color. Pausing momentarily to adjust her full bosom, she grabbed her slippers, closing and locked the door, and moved through the double doors to the exercise area.

Many of the other women watched as she began tumbling and doing somersaults across the mats. The display continued for awhile as they looked on envious of Aquina's youth and vigor. She would pause for a few seconds in between routines to adjust the leotard only to begin again, and again. While doing so was the object of many of the men's stares, and desires. For the exercise area was one of the few co-ed places in the club, and the men appreciated her "very" much.

The small group of ladies continued to watch for a few more minutes then went about their own exercises; but the men . . . . ahhh, well they could do little except watch and stare. Many were helpless and others near helpless because of her unconscious display of uninhibited sensuousness . . . their own hormones made them virtual slaves. If for any reason Aquina had encountered them . . . welllll, she didn't have to . . . she already had their undivided attention and devotion. Finishing her set, Aquina went over to various pieces of floor equipment.

Almost an hour and ten minutes later, Aquina smiled to the men and said, "Hi" to the girls as she returned to the locker room. Skimming off the perspiration soaked leotard and tights, she shoved them in the bag and quickly donned the halter top swim suit with plunging back and high cut legs, a French creation she liked very much and has several in different colors. With towel in hand, she headed for the pool, and spent something like fourty minutes swimming back and forth. Aquina appealed to many, but her affiliation, position with the much publicized national martial arts organization and her prowess discouraged almost everyone. If that wasn't sufficient enough, they heard accounts about the few unlucky men who tried to get physical . . . and wound up hurt physically with their ego's severly bruised.

Men found her perplexing and different. Fairly often Aquina found herself having lunch with her immediate boss, usually discussing some portion of a current project, or one of the junior engineers . . . or assistants. Though before to long the frequency of their lunch meetings increased and he, the chief engineer in charge of the entire section, would discuss everything with her. Not only office and project business, but his feelings about other matters, and more often than not . . . asked her advice. Aquina compensated by arranging appointments such as taking the car in for lubrication, having her hair quickly washed and set, shopping and numerous other tasks. She did it gradually and before another month (planet time) had passed, the former status quo was again re-established.

In her position as assist. section chief, Aquina exhibited little else but hard professionalism, imagination fueled by an almost fanatical zeal for a project well done. She won respect because of work done well and on time. On those occasions when she handed in mathematical notes and/or drawings to question a master drawing, problem or process . . . she had been correct in every instance. This always made the subsequent work for the other higher managers within the "special projects" chain of command, easier . . . and virtually nothing guarantees a promotion quicker.

The few full engineers and the many assistants in her department knew she is all business, but never failed to appreciate her. Of course . . . of those three of the men were a little infatuated, three others perhaps a little more, and two or so had it bad. While one poor soul was actually willing to be her slave . . . he is so totally captivated. It wasn't that she showed off, but is pleased with the effect her body elicited from men and some women. Every woman appreciated attention and flattery, compliments on their looks. There is nothing new in that, though for her it was sometimes subtle, and other instances verbal, but always sincere.

Only the weekends she reserved for herself. And usually it is Beethoven on saturday morning filling the house with waves of sound she found pleasing . . . coffee and breakfast was sometimes forgotten. But not for long, and would change the tape to Bach, or something from Tchaikovsky and drink her second cup of coffee. Aquina would take a quick shower and into halter and short-shorts or old "cut-offs," after which she would normally open up the windows in various parts of the house. Aquina has a thing for fresh air, and from there to the few inescapable chores that can be found to do in any house. And by 10a.m., she was singing to Gershwin, while working in the den. During each weekend at least eight or nine hours would be spent working on certain design concepts, private sketches and drawings.

Her other activity was the planting and nurturing of flower beds around the front walk, and the front of the house trying to balance it with the evergreens. And the neighboring wives would come over and help, because try as hard as she did, . . . Aquina simply did not have a green thumb. Very often over coffee or tea, she and a few neighbors talked about it and still she found it difficult.

The weeks varied only in that she occasionally was the guest at a neighbors for dinner, or Aquina would invite them over for dinner, or an informal party. She is a much better cook than a gardner, to the relief of her dinner guests, There was of course the country club for occasional dancing, which she enjoyed, or the movies.

In warp drive, routine had set in rapidly. Some of the wounded were already up and around helping other crew with fine repair work. The more they progressed on their present course the stronger it became . . . ever stronger. And at the appointed time the three imperial ships re-entered normal space, and entered the system belonging to the small yellow star. And as did the ships before them, they used a large polar trajectory enabling them to quickly intersect the third planet's orbit. Drawing closer, Dra'lr gave orders to take up positions behind the one natural satellite. Giving orders for the other two ships to remain, Dra'lr inched out to employ sensors and scanners.

Completing the soft probe, Dra'lr returned to his position behind the satellite and waited patiently, His officers looked on more or less waiting for him to explain. But he waited the extra minute or two until the master C'pter had processed the information fed it by the sensors and scanners. When it did, the information corroborated the commander's suspicions. "We have failed to consider the time dilation between Tucana and this particular system. Also it appears very likely they still retain their primitiveness, but more important . . . should be considered very dangerous."

"How commander?" Asked the first aux. officer.

"The scanners show artificial satellites in varied orbits about the planet. Worse is the detection of substantial amounts of mutated atoms in the atmosphere, indicating a crude fission capability. In addition tremendous levels of altered carbons and ozone quantities have been detected! Irrespective of the mission's outcome, this information must reach the emperor. Should the raiders ever discover this system and subjugate these people . . . I feel quite sure you can see the logical conclusion." Dra'lr explained firmly, his jaw set then continued.

And of course these indicators do not bode well for the survivors, who if alive are probably in hiding, making our mission that more difficult. Remember . . . interfering with primitive cultures is always unsettling and always dangerous!" Dra'lr intoned.

He immediately convened a meeting of all senior officers. Whereupon the available information was discussed at length. Many suggestions were brought forth only to be discarded later. After more than an hour . . . and no-one could agree on . . . or formulate any hard plan, Dra'lr put forth his own. This was also discussed at length, but regardless thought Dra'lr . . . "we'll follow this one." Soon after adjourning the meeting, he returned to the control deck.

Allowing time for his officers to return to their ships and report in . . . he was about to implement his plan.

CHAP. 67

Moving out from behind the satellite, carefully inching out, using only auxiliary power with sensors and scanners on full . . . Dra'lr was ready should there be any outward sign of alarm. Thankful there wasn't, his ship crept closer . . . and closer. Obvious to Dra'lr, whatever primitive detection devices they had could not cope with his scanners. He ordered one-quarter power from main engines and almost instantly closed the intervening distance. Establishing a tight orbit with the ship on full alert status, Dra'lr systematically covered the surface obtaining as much data as he felt possible.

He continued until the full scope of the planet's inhabitants, culture, technology, languages and military capability was fully understood. Of course most important was finding the exact location of the pulsar signal, but he knew they would find it as soon as they completed one orbit. Dra'lr felt they could either be there or at least their location and movements would have been recorded, and left for rescuers to locate.

The ship was seconds from completing its first orbit when sensors pinpointed the precise location of the two marooned ships, and not wishing to approach over any population centers decided to spiral down from the northern pole. Just after beginning the spiral, Dra'lr had the helmsman slow the ship, and the lower their altitude became, the wider the spiral and the slower the speed. Their speed though vastly reduced still had to be lowered, but especially so once below fourty thousand feet. Dra'lr and Gri'ry found it necessary to practice avoidance maneuvers trying to keep a healthy distance between themselves and the many primitive atmospheric craft. Because of this need to avoid the frail craft, they arrived over the signal's origin later than anticipated.

Waiting until he is within a few hundred feet of the surface, Dra'lr ordered the appropriate gunners, with battle guns on minimal power, too burn out a crater prior to landing. Once a fairly deep "dish" had been cut the helmsman and the aux. commander brought the ship down. They actually made planetfall just after darkness enveloped the area. Orders are given to have sensors on full alert at all times, while the four soldiers assumed guard positions around the crater's perimeter.

While affording them temporary cover from potentially curious onlookers, the crater only a short distance from the signal's apparent source also allowed easy access. Dra'lr chose who stayed with the ship and who would come with him to investigate the signal. Once outside a technic reported energy readings emanating from apparently within the rambling structure only some yards away. Walking up the incline, which also led to a number of hills and a ravine on the right, required only moments to cover the distance between the structure and Dra'lr's ship. The readings were confirmed, work is immediately started to negate the energy shield surrounding the building.

Quickly neutralized they entered the compound, and were confronted by two ordinary plain doors flanked by shrubs overgrown weeds and other signs of neglect. Dra'lr looked carefully in the light provided by lamps and decided the material around the doors was nothing more than very clever camouflaging.

In the interim, Dien heard the trilling sound from the sensors signaling an incoming ship. So intense was the feeling of relief, she wept for a brief few seconds, a rare act of emotion for her. While the C'pter turned up the lights and unlocked the front door, Dien tried to rise, but is simply to weak.

While shrubs and debris were cleared away from the two doors, Dra'lr and two other officers kept urging the varied crew people to greater effort in their investigation of the other wings of the crude house. After some fifteen minutes it is possible to gain entry to the two ship's hidden underneath. In mere seconds Dra'lr, one of the ship's bio-techs and an aux. lieutenant entered the first ship, which happened to be the trader. Other crew aided in searching the small ship and almost immediately they found Dien. It is an emotional few minutes, while she instructed the ship's bio-tech in what serum to administer, but first she drank the potent greenish liquid. The surge from the liquid was like electricity to a dead battery.

A few minutes later some color came back, and propped up by cushions she began answering Dra'lr's questions. She explained in detail how the others died, but kept referring to herjournals, and the C'pter records. However, before Dien could continue after a pause, Dra'lr began bringing her up-to-date about the emperor, and most especially the new emperor, and ruling family. Dien saw the sadness in Dra'lr about the death of the emperor's nephew, and interrupted him.

"Commander, please listen carefully. There is yet another you must find. She is the child of Roak and a Val'py look-alike, but was not Val'py." Dien slowly touched his sleeve . . . "read, read my journals and this C'pter records." Not quite up to normal strength, she gestured behind him. "The small drawer, in the skin bag . . . part of her father's legacy to the princess. Aquina must be told who, and what she is. The princess uses my last name, and there is her last written communcae received a short time ago."

Dra'lr looked in the drawer, found the bag immediately spilling a portion of its contents into his hand. He sucked in his breath a little at sight of the precious stones, and returned them to the bag, then looked at the letter asking Dien to explain the address. She was helpful only to a point, explaining the princess had moved to an area a short distance from the school, but didn't know where it was located.

Meanwhile, an officer and several crewmembers working feverishly succeeded in opening the hatch to find the larger ship in surprisingly good order, but also found three bodies including that of the emperor's nephew . . . all in stasus chambers. The officer sent for the commander who came running seconds later. Using great care and the trader/prince's own flag as a drape, carried the prince back to the command ship where it received proper honors. Then followed Aor'tiaws, his partner, again with care and laid the chamber beside the prince. The third was that of Coss'ar, pilot of the first rescue ship, and as with his comrades was laid beside them with his flag as a drape.

Dra'lr felt let down and deflated. "All this anxiety and pain, and still we arrive too late." All the stasus chambers had been put into a cargo hold for the trip home.

The commander returned to Dien, and talked about the princess, while crew members were packing all of Dien's belongings, and next compartment . . . Aquina's room. Dra'lr was interrupted by an aux. officer and informed about the two large black vehicles . . . "primitive weapons commander, but frightening at the same time." Dien interrupted, and explained about the "tiger tank and half-track" pointing out her recorder and the numerous cartridge plicks depicting the princess. Dien saw a look of interest and respect on the commander's face as he got up and excused himself.

A moment later Dra'lr stood gawking at the black engine of destruction bathed in bright light. Though covered in a light film of dust, it is menacing, cold, brutal its force and purpose crystal clear to everyone of the crew looking at the two machines. And for the first time he voiced her name with undisquised respect.

While he was looking at the primitive machines, Dien was carried to the command ship, where she is made comfortable in a quiet cabin, and fussed over by crew and bio-techs alike. For many Dien had become a celebrity, especially to the bio-techs. Along with her came a caravan of anti-grav carriers, personal size, filled with everything of value from the two ships including weapons, all personal effects, C'pters, loose equipment, food stuffs, liquor, and other miscellaneous items all carefully stacked in the small cargo hold. Dra'lr and an aux. officer carried a container each filled with journals, and logs plus the recorders, and the many, many cartridge plicks. The generators were also stacked in the small hold after the pulsar was disconnected.

While the crew is hard at work, Dra'lr read the journals. Engrossed in his reading the officers did not wish to disturb him, and Gri'ry directed the continued loading, and loading the two heavy machines. One of the crew, an aux. officer, is also a technic, and Gri'ry left it to the young officer to run tests on the machines, and the contents of what obviously is a warehouse. In less than twenty minutes the officer reported the results of his instrument analysis. And to that end pointed out to Gri'ry, after the latter walked into the warehouse, which was fuel, lubricant, and what the officer thought was ammunition. Unsure of what to load and perhaps not to load . . . he told the officer to bring everything to the edge of the crater. And armed with large and medium anti-gravs plus heavy carriers did exactly that. When the crew had finished there is nothing remaining in either of the small ships, warehouses, garages, and the offices. The mercedes and two trucks sat next to the tank, half-track and the many, many tens of dozens of drums of fuel and other supplies.

A meeting is convened, as dawn is well advanced, whereupon the commander explained the revealing contents of the journals. "We are on a hostile planet inhabited by dangerous primitives and have retrieved our people; however, according to these journals faithfully kept by the bio-tech, Dien . . . the prince and his companion Aor'tiaws had a joining." A murmur of assent went up amongst the crew. It is further written that soon after Aor'tiaws died from some poisonous life form. Shortly thereafter, the prince met the supposed descendant of Val'py . . . or facsimile because Dien is positive the person was actually something else . . . it is unclear the meaning. This particular joining, as it is written, brought forth a female offspring. Dien wrote." "There occurred complications and the person died soon after childbirth relinquishing the infant to me, to care for and raise." Dra'lr continued.

"However, minutes after Dien carried the infant to its father and returned to the compartment . . . the body had disappeared, and was not to be found, nor was there any indication from their instruments of any person entering or leaving." Every person looked at one-another strangely.

"Therefore our mission is not completed. We must find this child who by now, according to the time dilation, even so her genes would keep her young." Dra'lr explained. A murmur like groan from the crew. Dra'lr waved that off. "Thanks to Dien we know the approximate area to look." He knew the hereditary birthmark was all they had to work on/with, and Dra'lr knew it would have to do, it must be sufficient.

As it turned out Dien's input saved them much time and effort, because at least now they have an excellent idea of "her" location. To further reduce the probabilities, Dra'lr decided to use a harmless ruse.

The recent letter sent to Dien, Dra'lr noted is in a flowing script with precise character traits showing through, aside from the obvious fact it being female. Pinpointing the area from whence the letter came showed it to be from the city bordering a northern area, and was relieved to note its outlying districts residential and rather uncongested. Dra'lr decided to use the ship's shuttle and take his best seven people plus himself, leaving aux. commander Gri'ry in control during his absence, made eight. His plan called for three to accompany him leaving four to properly guard the shuttle, and provide logistic support should it be necessary.

The optimum number of weapons are carried and all had the tiny palm blaster which of course can be hidden almost anywhere. Seven crewmembers gathered around the commander for last minute instructions, and checking of equipment, boarded and lifted off slowly. Dra'lr immediately switched on full sensors and scanners, such as could be carried aboard the shuttle, and hugging the ground where possible then gained altitude over the ocean.

Less than twenty minutes later, planetary time, Dra'lr slowed hovering over the area. Reviewing it thoroughly upon arriving, he selected a thickly wooded area and gently settled the shuttle down amongst trees and scrub. Dra'lr split his party with himself and three, leaving four to camouflage and guard the little ship. They had set out in the direction of the city, and had covered a good half a mile when Dra'lr realized the wooded area is far larger than he presupposed. But they kept going and came upon a narrow dirt road some minutes later. Following the road was much easier, and while walking, the four, with the commander in front began hearing voices.

Prior to leaving the command ship, Dra'lr had everyone disguise themselves appropriately. Realizing they weren't to dis-similar to the natives, it came down to facial masks, crème tinting, hands wearing light gloves and suitable clothing to carry out the charade.

The voices came from two males and a female, all of adult stature and apparent age standing next to a good size multi-colored van/ground vehicle. Going back to the front, she climbed in and backed it up a few more yards and stopped when one male held up his hand and said something out loud. Dra'lr just barely understood what was said. He motioned to aux. one to just stun the male native, and he would take the other.

Both men are on the far side of the van and female . . . when both blasters fired. Hearing nothing the female kept talking not noticing the four walking up behind her. The bio-tech was ready . . . the woman turned and in that split second of surprise received the bio-shot. A combination of mild relaxant and a hypno-will suppressant made the woman calm and very agreeable. While two aux. officers chatted with the native woman, Dra'lr and aux. one rolled-carried the two males into the singular tent. In seconds the five were seated comfortably in the van tooling down the road at a modest pace.

With phase one completed, Dra'lr began the second phase. He instructed the woman to head for the more affluent part of the city, and the woman complied with a broad smile. And in a few minutes found themselves going slowly along a wide avenue with restaurants and a few nightspots. Dra'lr told the native to pull to the side and stopped across from a somewhat glitsy nightspot. There is a phone on their side, several yards away close to the street intersection. Dra'lr directed the native out of the van and walked with her over to the phone.

Not many miles away, Aquina is spending a normal saturday at home working in the den. Having just finished dinner, she thought instead of doing the dishes, she would do her hair, or the nightly exercise routine.

Dra'lr produced the envelope from the inside pocket of his jacket and showed the native the name and return address, saying he needed to speak to that person. Smiling, the native dug into her jeans and pulled out some coins and began dialing the operator. Dra'lr managed to find a pencil on the ground and handed it to her . . . . and watched with satisfaction as the native wrote the phone number on the envelope. And without a word hung up and dialed again, this time the number she herself put on the envelope.

Aquina finished the customary nightly exercises, and was in the act of finishing her glass of wine when the phone rang. She answered it on the third ring with a pleasantly sexy voice . . . "hello." The commander spent a second before mastering the quaint "telephone," and proceeded to talk. Dra'lr gave his carefully prepared "talk," explaining to Aquina, he represented Dien, and must speak to her concerning important developments and it is somewhat urgent. She had become alarmed, concerned something happened to Dien, and immediately agreed to a meeting for one hour hence at the avant-garde club. A singles disco directly across from his position. She surmised the man was a stranger in the city, and probably the club was the only place known to him. Agreeing further, she gave the commander a description of her car, and a brief description of what she would be wearing.

Dra'lr returned to their rather large vehicle and directed the native to put the vehicle into the parking lot, and back it into the far side. As soon as the van stopped, he nodded to the bio-tech. She nudged the native out of the driver's seat and administered a mild sedative. Assured by the bio-tech, Dra'lr brought them up-to-date. The four referred to the pile of small journals sitting on the carpeted engine cover with a fair degree of fascination. He told the aux. officers some of the things Dien had said about the elusive princess, and soon they each sat quietly . . . thinking. Each wondered about the supposedly young woman they were going to meet. Their orders were to act nonchalant until the expected ceremony aboard ship. Still, the feeling . . . the expectation was building in each of them. And Dra'lr . . . they looked at him sitting silently thinking. He thought how strange the mission had become, and Dien's reactions. How she felt nothing was important, only the princess mattered. Her intense look and attitude made him unsettled, curious . . . finding himself very much wanting to meet this princess.

Aquina had heard this particular club was risque' sometimes fast or slow depending on the evening. She had decided, at time of the phone call, on a dolman sleeve pantsuit of black chiffon-like material with small areas opaque, and the balance near transparent, wearing only matching panty and pantyhose underneath. For some finishing touches . . . one inch patent leather heels with black sequin jacket and purse. Pleased with her appearance, she exited the house and drove to the club.

All the windows in the van were open and the powerful throaty roar was grabbing their attention . . . then he saw the source of the growl.

She arrived only a few minutes early, parked, and locked the blood red roadster, and gracefully walked in the direction of the club's front door. It was probably her fluid body motion, but Dra'lr noticed her and exited. "I believe this may be the person we seek." He and one of the female aux. officers, an aux. two, left the van and walked in Aquina's direction as quickly as possible without attracting attention.

Passing the corner of the building, on the way to the front door, she had to pass four wild looking surly males sitting on what the commander thought were totally weird looking ground machines. They began an intense verbal harassment, she was getting angry, but said nothing. Almost abreast of them, two moved to block her path, and nothing happened . . . until one tried to "touch her."

Without seeming effort, she grasped the wrist, turned and twisted into the man's left side breaking the wrist, and the arm at the shoulder throwing the person to the ground hard. The other three attacked and with well practiced movements, she disarmed one attacker by breaking the wrist as she spun him into the remaining males. Another one attacked with a chain fainting to one side, she turned in with a power kick . . . breaking the sternum propelling him head first into the newspaper vending machine with substantial force. The last surly male cursing non-stop brandished a knife fainted . . . then thrust, she deflected the thrust . . . stepped in and used the edge palm to the lyrnx, an elbow to the diaphragm, and the attacker fell choking terribly.

During this episode Dra'lr and aux. two had walked up to the crowd and witnessed the whole thing from beginning to end. A display which did much toward Dra'lr's opinion and respect. Aux. two was more than just impressed, and the few yards that separated the large ground vehicle did not alter the scene the two other officers witnessed.

Sirens are fast approaching and another second or so two city patrol cars drove up with police out on the run. Dra'lr and the aux. two held their positions. A sergeant questioned Aquina, incredulous as her hair is just barely in disarray, and took her statement. Some of the people in the crowd also gave statements verifying Aquina;s statement. She looked around and down at her would-be assailants with distain and smiled.

The police, very polite . . . . recognized her and said as much . . . "yes maaming her crazy," were in the act of arresting the four men two of which were taken off by ambulance. Some of the officers were still writing, and when finished bid her goodnight handing the sequin handbag to her. The sergeant touched his hat smiling and entered the patrol car leaving the scene clearly feeling less than adequate.

She adjusted her bodice, straightened her jacket and picked her way through the crowd. Men and women congradulating her as she gradually made her way to the front door of the club. Although the ruckus was over Aquina hesitated . . . should she go into the club or go home convinced the evening ruined. Not knowing if the person she was to meet was still here, or not . . . she turned for the door. The commander walked up slowly not wanting to provoke a bad response and said . . . "hello" in the local tongue. Aquina turned and said hello, in return. She assumed he was a foreigner, and said . . . "may I help you?" "Yes, I hope so. I asked for the meeting." "Well after this commotion, I would appreciate a drink. If you feel it is to loud or distracting inside, we can go elsewhere." "That will be fine." Dra'Ir said.

Aquina opened the door and stepped in with Dra'Ir following close behind. Their eyes quickly adjusted to the dim light, bright light and strobes. Aquina found a table and Dra'Ir followed marveling at the noise level. Word of the "fight" outside of course drifted around patron to patron . . . . so there are many people looking, staring and occasionally pointing. The waitress took their order and returned. "The manager wishes to thank you, and your drinks are taken care of for this evening . . . enjoy yourselves." "That is very nice, thank you." Aquina replied smiling, eyes still bright from the fight.

With most of the small talk finished, the commander stared for a few seconds . . . then in halting english, he asked to see the "birthmark." Aquina smiled. "I suppose you must be careful," and moved over in the booth closer to Dra'lr. With her hand holding back the waves of hair to show him the right side bottom . . . the nape area of the neck. And there the three five-point stars . . . mark of the Tywr family prominently visible. Examining the birthmark carefully, Dra'lr saw it is totally genuine.

Dra'lr sat back and smiled. "That is good, you are the one I have searched for . . ." While still sitting in the booth, the commander asked if she had children. She smiled. "No. I've never married. Why is this so important?" "Please you have nothing to worry about. I will divulge everything when necessary." Dra'lr replied smiling reassuredly.

"But, what of my Aunt Dien?" "Dien is ill, but recovering nicely and that is partially why I'm here." He replied, then pointed to the empty glass in front of her. "I've had enough, thank you." "Ready?" "Yes ahaa," Aquina replied. "Let us go, there are journals for you to read and people who wish to meet you." Dra'lr explained, with a slight show of self-conciousness.

Leaving the club aux. two, who had been waiting outside, fell into step next to Aquina and said "hello." Aquina answered noticing the nervousness only partially hidden, and wondered why? Walking at a normal pace back to the van, two people both women got out virtually standing at attention. All of these little things began to bother Aquina. She took special notice of how all three seemed subordinate to the tall man next to her. Aquina sensed his strength, the unquestioned authority and aura of command. The two women who had just got out began shaking hands with her, momentarily breaking the train of thought, which would have led to a pointed question.

Dra'lr motioned for everyone to get in and resume their seats. Aquina was feeling a bit uneasy. There had been no actual introductions, no names in fact, she realized . . . she didn't even know the name of the tall "foreigner." Getting in she sat on the middle of three bench seats, and looking around began to really look at the people for the first time. A question is on the tip of her tongue, and was about to speak . . . when the tall man spoke first.

With the journals in his hand . . . "Miss Aquina, these are the journals I spoke of . . . please, read them. They are the faithful account in Aor'tiaws and Dien's own hand. When finished, we will answer all your questions." "Alright," responded Aquina accepting the journals from him. She opened the top one. "They were just translated before arriving here." Dra'Ir said watching her. Aquina smiled and started reading.

During the first eighty minutes, she read the first two thick journals kept by Aor'tiaws, with intense interest, but sadness crept in at the ordeals, and sense of hopelessness. Occasionally she frowned and moments later giggled, and still later frowned again. Soon she began the first journal kept by Dien, and again the look of intense interest. Then she looked up for a minute. "How could a body simply vanish?" Aquina asked the commander. "I do not know, except . . . only the great one of the universe could accomplish it without their knowledge." Dra'Ir replied, looking at the others . . . they looked askance at one-another.

A few paragraphs and she looked up . . . her hands trembling and tears cascaded down over the beautiful sculpted features. Slowly Aquina looked around at each of the four. "This child . . . it . . . it." She could not say the words. Dra'Ir said softly. "It is you. The balance is a faithful biography, only that period spent within the temple is vague, blank. And of Dien? She is ill, but will recover and is even now gaining strength."

She nodded and smiled showing only a hint of uncertainty. Her reactions had a degree of effect on the four officers sitting around front and back. She layed the journals on her lap and dabbed at her eyes with a hankerchief.

"It is still conjecture, but we don't believe your mother was from this planet, but are still investigating. Your father was the trader Roak Tywr, a Tucanan nobleman and for a time . . . a warrior."

She let out a loud sigh, and tried to understand. "Some time ago, I resigned myself to the fact of being different, odd, my abilities or talent with animals had set me apart, and my longevity. I've been able to live and work, constantly worried mine and Dien's secret would be discovered by the general population. But this . . . on top of everything, to find this isn't even my native planet, ohhh God!" Dra'lr and the others watched with some pain and concern as Aquina held her hands and wept a little.

In a moment or two, she dried puffy eyes, and looked around. "Crying won't help me. Please, tell me your not sure . . . that there is room for an error." She said, almost pleading. "There is no error, and we have proof positive. You carry the hereditary Tywr birthmark. And there is Dien, a highly reputable witness." Dra'lr remarked, as he began taking off the mask and other parts of his disguise. The others followed suit.

"Ohhh! You are different, but similar and the differences are interesting." Aquina remarked. "Yes, we are many different races." Dra'lr answered pleased with her reaction. "Are you afraid?" Asked Dra'lr. "I don't think so." Aquina said looking at Dra'lr, and slowly smiled. "That is good. I am commander Dra'lr." And beginning the introductions, they went around each in turn giving their name and the house in which they belonged. Smiling, each shook hands with her as she gave her name, but slightly stumbled over the name Tywr. "It feels so wonderful to finally belong." She said with a contented sigh. "You belong to much, much more than you think, but that will wait for later." Dra'lr quipped. Dra'lr nodded to the aux. officers one, two and three. "These are aux. officers one, two and three, and as women will be able to help you get acclamated." "Thank you commander." And he smiled . . .

In the interim the young woman "native" was awake, and Dra'lr motioned for her to continue driving. Aquina nodded to herself the necessity for the "native's" presence, as Dra'lr referred to the driver. "Commander, it is getting late, and I do want to leave my car at home. Would you follow me there, it isn't far, and I think it important you know where I live." Dra'lr smiled and agreed. As she got out of the van . . . "I won't be going fast, and its only a few miles." He nodded, thinking a variety of thoughts while watching the hips and her back. She took something out of the small bag and he watched as she un-locked the door and get in. In seconds the red vehicle backed up and pulled forward slowly . . . then Dra'lr told the native woman to follow the red vehicle.

Through several lights and around various corners they followed the small red vehicle, until some twenty minutes later Dra'lr noticed it is a suburb-residential area, and the vehicle pull into a small drive to one side of a dwelling of respectable size. He watched as the large white door opened and Aquina drive into the structure. Seconds later she reappeared, closing the door, and walked toward the van. Dra'lr decided it was her body, or the walk, but realized he is in trouble. Just the sight of her aroused "things" and that fact surprised and worried him. In a flurry of heartbeats, she was again sitting in the middle seat.

CHAP. 68

On the way back to the shuttle, Dra'lr explained what they had encountered thus far in the effort to rescue their people. He gave the highlights only, especially the attacks, and how they were repelled. And by that time the native had maneuvered the van to within a few yards of the shuttle.

Everyone got out of the van, including the native driver, but was kept close to the vehicle by the bio-tech, and walked to the partially camouflaged shuttle. Whereupon the remaining four crew came out from concealment, and introduced themselves in the same manner as those previously. Aquina is excited over the shuttle, and asked many pointed questions. She held the large bag which is holding all of the journals, while looking at the shuttle. Dra'lr nodded to the bio-tech, who gave the "native driver" instructions to drive slowly, and return to her two companions." As he answered most but not all of her questions, explaining he wished to leave before next planetary dawn.

Aquina stood much in thought about her situation, as versus a new family, new home and about responsibilities. Aux. one Abn'te walked up to her, and touching Aquina's hand . . . "our hope is you will want to return with us, even if for only a short period." Abn'te explained, then continued. "We understand your inner turmoil. You can certainly come back later, if that is what you desire." They were all standing around her listening as Aquina quipped. "It is as if . . . I've been dreaming, and am now waking."

"Commander, are you sure about all this?"

"Quite sure. You are as much a part of my people and an interstellar empire, as you are part of this planet, and well . . . . perhaps more." Dra'lr remarked.

"Commander, is it permissible for me to have my things . . . please?" "Of course." Dra'lr said, pleased she decided to accompany them willingly. "However, first we must return to the command ship." And on that note each and every person began boarding the shuttle, and in only a moment it lifted off silently with sensors and scanners on full. Aquina was amazed at their speed, the guidance systems and tried to realize the level of technology enjoyed by these people . . . her people . . . but couldn't. It seemed they had just lifted off, when her stomach said they were descending rapidly. And as soft as a cushion the shuttle settled to a halt. The door opened, and Dra'lr got out first motioning for Aquina to join him. With the others getting out quickly . . . and all the available crew began to congregate from the ship, many from looking and listening to the filch recorder.

Dra'lr spoke to his crew for several minutes, and while he did Aquina noticed one person held what she thought was a camera of some sort. And she was right . . . in a way. The spatial camera immediately transmitted video and sound to the command ship and simultaneously to the two other ships now sitting to one side of the natural satellite. They are receiving excellent reception.

He finished his little speech and indicated Aquina. Buckling on a belt tranalator, he looked at Aquina while being handed another and asked if she would like to wear one. She said yes and smiled. With slightly trembling fingers, he put it around her waist cinching it up until snug and fastened it, rolling up the foot and-a-half left over belt material. It served to accent Aquina's small waist and thereby draw attention to her other measurements.

The crew had mixed feelings, all good, but unsure of themselves of what to say. She dispelled this feeling to a high degree with an open attitude and an infectous smile, plus a warm solid handshake. Dra'lr officiated, introducing Gri'ry first then the other crew by rank. First he said their name, house, then planet and system. Dra'lr quickly had those standing watch relieved, to come and be introduced. It wasn't until she had walked to one side of the group, that the ship came into view. And then she realized a sizeable portion was hidden from view. But what is visible standing above the crater made her stand . . . staring at it mouth slightly open. All Aquina could manage was . . . "ohhh." Said along with a deep sigh, which conveyed a great deal to Dra'lr, who is perhaps only one pace behind her.

While the commander explained to Gri'ry about picking up all of Aquina's belongings, and the number of crew necessary, and the size and number of yid containers. Aquina walked over to that part of the ship extending above the crater. Many of the crew went back to the loading, but a dozen or so, including the one still holding the spatial camera, stood about watching. Still marveling at it . . . she touched a portion . . . then touched it again. "It's so . . . so beautiful. Oh, I love it . . . it's so fantastic, just like my dreams." She looked thoughtful as if in a light trance, and slowly with fingers splayed wide open . . . touched the ship. A blatant sensual touch, a caress and murmured . . . "am here and you feel warm to me. We will do very well together."

Those that watched were between surprise and incredulous realizing they witnessed something mystical. Hitherto only various head priestesses of certain sects had a smattering of "the power," so all knew this indeed is a special person . . . very special.

When she came away from the ship and noticed crew people boarding the shuttle, Aquina quickly asked Dra'lr, if she could go along to help facilitate the packing. He readily agreed, knowing his crew, and himself, would need to digest what they had just experienced, and it would be easier if she were not immediately around. At the last minute three more crew boarded carrying small and medium anti-gravs, and one small carrier. She made twelve aboard the shuttle as it departed quietly.

Mere minutes and they are slowing drastically, following a main artery until Aquina pointed. "There, that one . . . third on the right." With lights out they slid in sideways landing only a yard or so from the rear door. Unlocking the door she flipped on the lights and in each room explained what is to go. The belt translator made things much easier, as she literally ran upstairs and pulled out every trunk and piece of luggage she has.

She grabbed the two proper cases and ran downstairs pulling the swords and mauser off the wall putting them in the cases. As she put those, the other sword case, weapon's case and wood staff, plus the two bows and multiple full quivers into the shuttle . . . two rooms had already been emptied according to her instructions. But most of the time is spent packing her clothes. Soon she merely threw things into the bags, and trunks until all the drawers, closets, and storage rooms are bare.

In the interim contents of five rooms, less the furniture, had been ferried to the command ship and returned. When the shuttle doors opened various containers were immediately loaded. All of her personal affects, the entire music system, paintings, the entire contents of the den et-cetera are loaded. The only item remaining is her car. And before leaving she called Miriam, and after several minutes of chit-chat, telling her she was leaving, and they would have the house free and clear. She told Miriam the number for the safety deposit box, some other information and wished them well hanging up the receiver before her friend could say much, or object.

She went out to the mailbox and put a letter addressed to her employer inside with the little flag standing up. Aquina explained a distant relative is in dire circumstances and she must leave. Aside from expressing her gratitude and thanks . . . she was finished. It is far more true than she realized.

As before the return trip is disconcertingly quick, and no-sooner landed when crew members emptied what is inside transferring everything to proper containers and receptacles in the storage holds. When she inquired about the car . . . Gri'ry explained the command ship would pick that up because of its size. Aquina nodded with a smile, then walked the twenty or so yards to where the tiger tank and half-track sat shrouded in dew. The eastern sky was brightening slightly and Aquina watched as the last few drums are loaded into the half-track. All the other drums and cans, cases and boxes were in large odd looking shiny containers.

Dra'lr spoke into his tiny communicator giving the comm. officer instructions. Almost all the crew is outside, when from a distance . . . the lone howl of a wolf. It is joined by another on the opposite side of the ship, and still another to the north. Immediately, she walked over to Dra'lr. "Commander, please tell our people no matter what happens, they are not to make any overt move especially with a weapon, or run, and no loud talking. These animals are very dangerous, please?" He nodded. "As you wish." Dra'lr said looking thoughtfully. He started passing the word, and the person with the spatial camera and operator was still doing his job.

She picked up a two foot octahedron, which was empty, and walked about ten yards away putting it down. Cupping hands to her mouth, she called out loud one word. Almost instantly the surrounding forest echoed to many wolves howling, then as if hundreds were barking from varied parts of the wood . . . they came. Noises from other animals mixed until a crescendo of sound emanated from all directions. Every crewperson was told, but it didn't stop them from being afraid, though some were more fearful than others.

From the customary place across from the compound, the first pack burst from the tree line running pell mell for Aquina. Barking, yelping through a slight early morning mist, the wolf pack has the appearance of individual spectors of doom. The leaders are large animals healthy and lean, eyes bright, as only a few yards from her they began braking . . . trying to stop. Some couldn't . . . and they stumbled and fell, instantly up again prancing around her . . . as she held out arms and hands to greet them. They mobbed her trying to lick face, hands until she began to hum and sing. The effect was almost instantaneous as they quieted, forming an arc in front and a little to each side about four feet in front and sat on their hind quarters. Aquina spoke, and the leader came forward putting his head and forehead against her right palm. She leaned over and kissed his forehead, petted the animal and continued to hum softly. This went on from wolf to wolf, through the entire pack on down to the wee cubs. And it wasn't limited to one, but four packs came, one would leave . . . there is another to take its place.

The Tucanans stood amazed, watching the almost endless parade of carnivores. Some are similar to beasts they knew, while others are not. They looked-on as large bears came with their young, deer and others, small cats . . . but the horses really caught their imagination. About fourty of them came out of a dip, not really a valley, or large gulley inbetween a hill and a plateau . . . at a full gallop. With a lot of whinnying they came, fast . . . the earth resounding to the galloping hooves.

Aquina is on her feet clapping her hands and began calling names. The small herd crowded around and with heads lowered, gently rubbed the forehead against her. Each one she petted gently and kissed them above the muzzle.

Meanwhile, the second cruiser arrived sitting on the open ground on a network of five pod extensions, similar to elephant legs. Most of the crew exited around to mingle with Dra'Ir and his crew. Thanks to the spatial camera, and operator, they had seen and heard everything, as had all those on the third ship now orbiting at a mere height of one hundred miles.

Soon, with the dawn becoming much brighter all the animals ran off in groups, some gingerly, but all returned to the hills and forest. She was able to say good by and was grateful. As the second ship lifted off slowly and hovered, a tracter beam extended down . . . enveloped the tank drawing it up into the ship. Perhaps a minute later the half-track followed, the benz, loaded truck and all the "odd" containers also were drawn up inside. Before the ship sped off to rendezvous with the third ship. Aquina turned continuing past the compound up the slope of a nearby hill. There she dropped to her knees beside what Dra'lr realized is a grave. His mini palm stereoptic unit enabled a close view of Aquina. "This must be the person Dien refered too . . . . I envy him." Dra'lr thought to himself, as he watched her weep. He walked away putting the mini unit back in its belt holder.

Using the small communicator Dra'lr gave orders to prepare for departure. He waited on the crater's rim, watching Aquina as she came closer. She saw him watching her, and being alone guessed their departure is at hand. Increasing the pace, it required only a moment before she accepted his hand, and descended into the crater to the ramp. Two crewmen inside the small air-lock saluted smartly as Dra'lr and Aquina entered, and secured the outer and inner doors behind them.

She went with him to what was apparently the control deck and stood to one side as he started issueing orders. It was a fairly large room crammed with equipment that used light in shapes, patterns and shades of color. There are five people sitting while the commander stood as did his second in command.

Dra'lr stood by what she assumed was the command console, as it has a padded recess that enabled him to lean . . . . and it molded itself to his form, not unlike a living thing. But in front of him is a lighted cube surrounded by what she guessed was some type of super computers.

"Alright Tha' clear your crater." "Yes commander." Without any effort the ship rose and hovered . . . . not attempting to mask their departure except where necessary. Dra'lr gave Tha' Gri'ry planetary co-ordinates. "We must stop at those co-ordinates, to pick up Aquina's vehicle." "Yes commander." "Full scanning Tha'." "Yes commander."

They sped at what she knew had to be incredible speed across the ocean to the same area, same city, and within moments found the proper street. "notify cargo hold to put a tracter on the vehicle and bring it onboard." "Yes commander." It was a good thing the hour had been so close to dawn . . . no-one was around, though for the few minutes the ship hovered, and brought the car onboard there existed a blackout of local electric power, no street lights and no traffic lights.

Safely in the cargo hold, pressurized with ambient temperature of 65 degrees. "Depart planetary atmosphere Tha'." "Yes commander." Aquina stood enthralled, her foster home shimmering, bright from the sunshine reflecting off massive cloud formations as it revolved. With orders from the command ship, the other two ships extended their orbit to three hundred miles, meeting the command ship and linked-up main air locks. In all, no attempt is made to mask or hide their presence.

In the interim, Aquina is being instructed by aux. one Abn'te, in the use of the bio-compartment. The aux. officer explained and showed her how it functioned until she caught on, and marveled at the rad enclosure. A shower-like section which cleansed the body and hair by soft rad. light, and then not unlike a seductive vacuum system cleansed the residual particles from the body. Aquina found it fascinating.

Abn'te began showing Aquina through the now almost totally repaired command ship, where she looked at everything and everyone. She asked questions about the crew, with Abn'te's help, and where each came from, and asked each a little about themselves. Aquina especially looked at the tell-tale signs of damage, and the guns fascinated her. There were many parts of the ship she had not seen, but what she did see illicited many more questions. So much had to be explained, and patiently because most of it she simply did not understand. But after what seemed like only a few minutes, she heard her name spoken over the ship's internal communications system. Aquina heard the commander ask her to report to the control area.

Still wearing the black jump suit, she walked onto the now crowded control deck. Crew people from other parts of the ship crowded in close including senior officers from the two other ships. Dra'lr indicated where she should stand, and Aquina moved over to stand within a pace of him. He called behind him for the ship's recorders to be engaged and instantly logged into the SH'pter, and beamed to the two other ships. She still wore the belt translator around the waist, which provided a great deal of help with the language.

It is so quiet, she could hear her own heartbeat. Dra'lr turned to face her. "There are many things of which you have not been told. Only recently the old vile emperor died leaving no heir, that is, his house died with him. Immediately there ensued a power struggle amongst the more powerful noble families. Your family, the Tywr's was among them. Because your family won the struggle marshaling the required support, . . . your uncle assumed the throne. From this your father Roak Tywr died a crown prince." Dra'Ir paused then continued.

"More specifically the eldest is actually emperor and is passed to each family member in turn." Aquina's head is buzzing. "Your uncle is emperor, and absolute monarch. Your father as I said was a crown prince, and is now on another plane only partially removed . . . for he will be remembered. The father of your father is incapacitated and therefore by law is passed over . . . which puts you next in line from your uncle. Already the emperor has been many times the monarch than his predecessor. And because of this the loyal empire feels much attachment for the new royal family." Dra'Ir paused . . . then continued.

"We did not have the opportunity to know your father . . . the prince, but . . . we have the opportunity to know his daughter . . . the princess." Explained Dra'Ir. "Aquina," said the commander. "The emperor's orders were for me to convey these to your father . . . because of circumstances . . . they are now rightfully yours." The belt translator operated quite well.

"Th . . . . thank you commander." Accepting the pouch, she opened it and took out two old style parchments and a small elegant crystal box. "Would you help me commander?" Aquina whispered, a tear from each eye running down her cheeks.

Dra'Ir bowed, and reached for one of the two envelopes. He paused to look at the assembled crew, at Aquina . . . . then began reading. Doing so slowly with emphasis the commander read the "Citation of Family Status," and was about to read the short proclamation:

> "We, Roak-eo-Tywr, Emperor Tucanan Empire acknowledge and know our nephew, one Roak Tywr, or his heir, duly and recognized member of the Tywr royal family. From this point and for the empire . . . be known as crown prince, and shall be entitled to all status, position and benefits as befitting that rank!"

Finished, Dra'lr put the two parchments back into the pouch, and reached for the ornate crystal box. Opening it he removed a diamond-like studded brooch, (set with other stones not known to her) which could be worn by either gender, and pinned it to her pant suit above the left breast . . . saying at the same time . . . . "Aquina Tywr . . . princess among our people, and princess of the empire!"

Her eyes began to fog and brim over, and more tears ran down her cheeks. "I'm both happy and confused, So much has happened so fast . . . and I . . . (gathering control, she dabbed at wet eyes) thank you, I still have to get accustomed to this."

Smiling, the assembled crew and officers applauded in their own fashion, but all showed pleasure and acceptance. And with the small impromptu ceremony concluded, Dra'lr convened a meeting of all senior officers. It was a chance for her to visit Dien, and Aquina seized upon the opportunity.

Aquina found Dien sharing a medium size cabin with three other bio-techs and knocked on the door. Two voices said to enter, and she did when the door whooshed open. She was immediately greeted by one of the ship's bio-techs, who bowed to her and Dien who was sitting up with cushions behind her.

Aquina sat on the edge of the molded bed, and touched Dien's arm. "I feel responsible. If I had been at the compound instead of chasing a dream that now, sigh, seems so frivolous, perhaps this would not have happened."

"An accident only. It could have happened at any time, and please do not worry. I am recovering thanks to my guildsman," and nodded towards the bio-tech sitting opposite them. Aquina turned to the woman. "Thank you for the care given to Dien." "It is our pleasure, my princess. Dien is important to our guild, as you are to us and the empire." The bio-tech said. Aquina smiled at the woman and touched her shoulder. "Thank you."

"Dien, these raiders . . . could they be the same ones who crippled my father's ship?" "It is quite possible . . . in fact . . . highly probable." Dien remarked with concern. Dien and the bio-tech watched as Aquina's face turned to a mask of sheer malevolence, and the right hand become a fist. Both women felt cold fear sweep over them and as if Aquina's mind was elsewhere . . . she said. "I will see you later." The two women watched Aquina get up to leave. Dien looked at her friend and . . . spoke. "I've seen her like this before during the great global war that raged on the planet below us, and the cruel-brutal enemy paid very dearly." "Then she is a great warrior?" Asked the bio-tech. "Her foster people below considered her that and much more. Too many of them the star shined on her alone."

While they talked, Aquina, the anger cooling a little, made her way to the control deck . . . waited, until Dra'Ir had concluded the meeting with his officers. In a few minutes the meeting was adjourned giving each ship's commander his appropriate orders. Turning he noticed Aquina, the seething anger, her eyes flashing with seeming blue-fire . . . arms crossed occasionally looking in the direction of the ship's main and secondary guns. "Commander, from the meeting, it is my understanding somewhere along our route we will probably be attacked." "Yes princess, we will." Aquina smiled slightly . . . a cold menacing smile. "Commander, may I ask a small indulgence?" "Of course princess."

"In the field of war and guns . . . I'm not without experience in such things, and you will need the best gunners." "Very true princess, as I have read your biography compiled with respect to your past life up to this point. All that is very well." The commander said. "But you must be kept safe at all costs." "Ohhh poo with being safe!" "Poo." Dra'lr thought . . . "What is poo?" But then she wasn't finished. The anger still seethed under the surface, under the fascade of politeness that threatened to slip any second.

"I simply require a gunner to instruct me. There exists not very far away from here a massive belt of asteroids. If . . . I'm unable to hit them, I'll bow to your wisdom." "Very well," he said, trying to appear stern, but not pulling it off very well.

The other two ships were signaled and the three did the hop to the asteroids, whereupon Dra'lr selected a gunner to act as instructor. Too be sure, it is a very self-concious gunner instructing Aquina in a crash course. He covered the basics first, such as the controls, targeting, melding oneself to the gun, nuances of aiming, short bursts as versus long bursts and ranging . . . leading the target during different gyro-manuevers.

She is still in the midst of the first lesson when all three ships arrived on station. Though he and the others waited patiently, Dra'lr knew the time would be put to good use. As if to reinforce his thoughts, the comm. officer spoke up relaying the message. "The other two ships are holding drills, and exercises, Sir." "Good . . . very good."

By intercom the gunner acting as instructor was told of the drills and exercises, and to continue with the princess until she is satisfied. Almost immediately a drill is called, and soon thereafter she asked the instructor to repeat the entire lesson. During which she asked for the fine points be explained again. During this period the entire schedule of drills had been performed. Soon she motioned to the gunner. "I'm ready, and thank you." "My pleasure, my princess." The gunner remarked and stood down in the second position.

Meanwhile, during the drills Dra'lr had visited Dien in an effort to understand Aquina's behavior. And not until Dien had explained about "her" and Kurt, the pain during the global war, the war years spent in Korea after the temple, and the short talk about Aquina's father, and the attack by the raiders. "Commander, during the war she was physically wounded many times, but all that is nothing compared to the mental anquish and the psychological pain that was suffered. And I am positive much of it is still with her." "Thank you Dien. I see now . . . why Aquina feels as she does. Rest now, and I will do what I can." Dra'lr said. Dien smiled. "She is everything to me." She said drifting off to sleep. He let out a sigh, and left the cabin, walking the corridor . . . trying to think.

It is something so new, she schooled . . . and calmed jumpy nerves. She quieted the involuntary first reactions to the seering bolts of pure energy erupting from the guns. Rolling, spinning chunks of rock and planetary debris came fast, some at blinding speed. Trying a number of short controlled bursts, she missed virtually every one. She paused for a moment to marshall thoughts and the super-concious part of the mind, and tried again.

With the instructor standing behind and to one side . . . he was able to see immediately the problem, and was about to speak . . . when Aquina began firing another series. Laying out a pattern, she began scoring hits some consecutively. She occasionally missed, but the instructor was tabulating the results, and is laughing and trying to clap his hands while making needed notations. His antics and the resulting commotion drew at first only a few crew. But as it continued the group watching became steadily bigger. The fact she is hitting anything surprised them. But when the gunner began telling the crowd . . . the gun targeting C'pter was disengaged . . . the crowd watched with intense interest. The gunner called the control deck and once the commander is listening, explained how the princess is doing and under what circumstances.

After completing her first go at it, the gunner leaned in and touched her left shoulder. "My princess . . . the C'pter is not engaged." "Huh?" She looked down . . . "Ohhh!" Immediately, she pushed the activate button. The results are startling, the action slowed and became simplified. Aquina had no problem sensing the motion and squeezed off another pattern . . . each . . . bolt hit its intended target, everytime. Those not coming so close, but further away were hit as well, and this time the ship was going through gyro-manuevers.

She impressed even the hard nosed gunners who quickly warmed to the situation. After speaking to the gunner via intercom, the commander called a halt. Obvious to everyone the princess is very good, and indeed probably one of the best on all three ships. She climbed out of the small gun compartment, and stood in the passageway seconds before the commander walked up behind her. Dra'lr bowed. "You have proven your point." And then not able to keep the stern visage, relaxed a-bit and chuckled . . .

"Our warrior princess." Unbeknowst to any of them, part of Dra'lr's quip would remain with her always.

"Commander, it is my desire to fight, and to be as much help as possible." "All is well princess." Dra'lr remarked. "The crew and officers all understand." Aquina smiled. Dra'lr turned to his crew. "Let us be on our way home." And he turned walking back to the control deck. Aquina followed a bit later after thanking the gunner for acting as instructor. Walking to the control area, she passed crew people who are familiar, and said hello, and received the same plus smiles and many salutes. It felt good, and she felt much more at ease. Stepping up to the control deck, Aquina retrieved her purse where she left it only a short time ago.

CHAP. 69

There wasn't any joviality here, it is all business. She stayed where she is, in a partial corner, looking and listening . . . learning. Orders are given and received by subordinates, communications from within the ship, and with the other two ships, and a series of small maneuvers designed to take them back to the emerald planet's satellite. Quickly it loomed into view occupying most of the main screen and her heart ached a little.

In those fleeting seconds before new co-ordinates would take them away . . . Aquina prayed . . . and made a vow to return. With eyes moist . . . holding in check the rising emotion, and in a flash saw the planet receed to be followed by the star and system.

She slowly looked around, and finally moved back to rest on Dra'lr. He looked here and there . . . then over to the comm. officer, and back to the main forward screen. Thinking to herself. "The ship is part of him," she thought, standing to one side watching Dra'lr give orders. One of those orders was for warp speed, and she watched the stars of normal space change, and become a sea of shimmering clouds of light in which waves upon waves of color moved and danced. She continued to watch the shimmering clouds and occasionally looked at Dra'lr. She waited for an opportunity to speak with him. A bit later he began to relax as certain things fell into a routine of sorts.

Dra'lr was thinking of her when she interrupted his reverie. "Commander?" "Yes princess." He said flashing a smile. Aquina asked about the possibility of visiting the wounded and the crew of each ship, and inquired about a compartment or cabin. "Certainly princess, aux. two will show you the cabin that has been prepared, and help with the ships and crews." "Thank you commander." He watched her shapely back as she followed aux. two down the steps and disappear around the corner. And continued to watch and think, savoring the scent of her perfume. Dra'lr thought . . . if he was from a noble family then there would be hope; but none existed for those outside of their circle.

Aquina sensed the reserve and self-conciousness of the young aux. officer, and when having reached the cabin, she decided it was time to do something about it . . . if she could. Aux. two Eio'br opened the door and bowed a little as Aquina entered pleasantly surprised at the size and the opulence of the cabin. It being much larger than anything she expected. Even her jewelry box was there on the wall counter, and all her cosmetics, some perfume and colognes. In the small attached bio-compartment, she found the mirror and some of the things arranged much as she had in the house. Most of her clothes are hanging up, boots, hats and coats, and jackets. Aux.

two Eio'br respectively showed Aquina the hideaway drawers and another closet holding the rifle, and the hunting bows with several quivers of broad-tip arrows. Plus she found her collection of swords, knives and daggers all with scabbards and sheaths, and the wooden weapon's box. One of the swords and the heirloom, had been hers for a very long time.

"Did you do all this?" "Yes princess," said aux. two. "Myself and aux. three. Aquina walked over to her lightly touched the aux.'s shoulder and asked . . . "Why are you frightened of me?" "You are something, she shrugged . . . more than a woman." "Why do you feel this way?" Aquina asked. "I was in the quaint ground vehicle when the four brutes attacked, and well . . . ? And when touching this ship . . . you felt something and communed with it." Aquina did not know how to explain it to her.

"It is alright, Eio'br, here sit with me." After the aux. officer sat, Aquina began to explain, but then stopped and partially shrugged, finding herself unable. "I don't know how to explain this to you.

But, we are shipmates now, and I need your help . . . you and aux. three. First, I think you and the others should call me Aquina." "Yes . . . Aquina." "Good. You can help me by teaching about all the little things that go on aboard these ships. But most especially . . . tell me of the officers and crew, while I fix my make-up." "Yes Aquina." The aux. two replied.

Eio'br began explaining about the officers onboard and what she knew of them. They sat well over an hour, and Aquina learned a good deal about the officers and some of the crew. She urged Eio'br to tell her what she knew of the commander. The aux. officer smiled. "Many of us have noticed you have feelings for him." "Yes I do." Aquina answered also with a smile.

The aux. officer related how the commander came to get the assignment for this rescue mission. "It started with him and a small crew beating overwhelming odds, his ship virtually destroyed, and still battled the raiders . . . and prevailed. Whereupon with only auxiliary power he brought his ship a considerable distance to a star system repair dock almost by himself. The one other officer, aux. commander Gri'ry, his close friend, is with him now. That effort had resulted in the saving of a large fully loaded passenger ship . . . many hundreds of people. He and the aux. commander were to be decorated, but were assigned this trip before he could receive it."

Eio'br related other information about the commander and listening avidly, Aquina absorbed all she could. Another fourty-five minutes and she mentioned how she would like to see all the wounded. That in itself was no problem, only the desire to visit the other two ships, and do the same. Eio'br explained how during warp phase, one could not go inbetween ships. Therefore, Aquina contented herself with visiting those on the command ship.

Again aux. two acted as guide, and they soon came upon aux. three, and after a brief explaination about Aquina's wishes . . . she smiled and became less nervous and self-concious. Aux. three resumed her schedule while aux. two continued to act as guide. One of the many things Aquina learned concerned the pattern of small passageways branching off the main corridor. And with exception of the engineroom, she visited every nook and cranny of the vessel. The bio-deck, or hospital, was reserved for last.

Aquina's visit is totally unexpected, as some are in various stages of undress, and all were dumbfounded and completely unprepared. Waiting patiently, while some put on clothes or otherwise covered themselves, she talked with the on duty bio-techs. Chiefly noticing only their wounds, whether they had two arms or more, three fingers, four or more made no difference whatsoever. Speaking with each and every one, she tried to bring levity with her, and thanked them for coming for her . . . even if indirectly. Aquina's attitude and body language indicated much as she helped feed both men and women, gave them drink and more . . . caring.

Aux. two helped Aquina where possible, and looked on as the princess pampered the wounded. Several were captivated by her hair, and so she flipped her head bringing the waves of blonde hair down around the face and leaned over giving them the opportunity to touch or smell it as they wished. Aquina thought how many variations there were, one or two really alien, but looking into their eyes, she knew each as a comrade.

While on the control deck . . . "Commander!" "Yes Tha'." "Warp drive is beginning to overheat." Stated aux. commander Gri'ry. "Very well, inform the other ships of our condition, and arrange for all three of us to re-enter normal space as a unit." Gri'ry nodded and walked over to the comm. officer.

Less than four minutes later all three ships had re-entered normal space, and continued on at best possible speed using full system drive. Aquina had only a moment ago finished visiting the wounded, followed by aux. two, and was exiting that area when both felt a subtle change in the ship. Eio'br commented, they had re-entered normal space. "Eio'br, let us go and speak to the commander." Aquina remarked. Already walking in that direction.

She found the commander standing alone, apart from the others and immediately broached the subject. He agreed, but insisted the shuttle be staffed by an experienced pilot. Though he smiled inwardly . . . pleased to see a smile brighten her child-like face.

With Eio'br again as guide, and an officer at the controls, she went from ship-to-ship by shuttle. First the second then the third doing virtually the identical things in each case. It amounted to giving food and drink, talking to each and thanking them. As on the command ship her caring made the difference. Probably the feeling, the emotion . . . but every person responded to her warmth. She also went around thanking the crews, and asked questions trying to relate to each as best she could. Her insatiable desire to learn . . . to know made asking questions easy of each crew person; and very often asked what they were doing, and why it had to be done a certain way.

Several times the young aux. officer felt privileged to be in the company of the princess, and knew she deserved the title . . . certainly more than some others she could name.

In all, not quite five hours and she is back aboard the command ship. Soon afterwards Gri'ry relieved the commander and almost immediately Dra'lr nonchalantly began a tour of the ship. He began on the opposite side from his cabin, the very area where the princess's cabin is located. And it appeared as if fate was cooperating . . . rounding the corner of the passageway and main corridor, Dra'lr virtually bumped into Aquina. Eio'br left to assume her duty schedule, leaving Aquina free to chat with the commander. They talked about many things, only one of which referred to the raiders and the expected trouble areas.

As a result of their "talk," Aquina altered her schedule accordingly. With Dra'lr repeating the lesson in ship's time, and only a little over a day . . . two at the very most before reaching the trouble areas, Aquina increased her activity. Chiefly it involved more visits to the decreasing number of wounded, and her own preparations for the expected attacks.

Thinking about what she should use, decided to snack while considering which weapons to use. Inasmuch as the crew normally took their main meal in the middle of the day, while she was off visiting the wounded. Aquina asked Eio'br to prepare food for both of them. And while the aux. officer was off on that errand, Aquina made her selection. Remembering the crew wore side-arms and dagger, when on her foster planet . . . well, she didn't own a blaster, but definitely did own swords and daggers. She selected her best sword, not the heirloom, but her favorite . . . fully three quarters the length of a normal rapier. A blade two inches wide, a quarter measure thick, and made of an alloy comprised of metals for toughness and ability to hold an edge. Smiling, she chose a well balanced dagger with a particularly vicious blade, fully eleven inches long to accompany the sword.

Gently she touched the sword and dagger testing the sharpness of the blades with a thumb. They were good, but Aquina knew the edges could be better and started rummaging in the closet for the special stone she kept for that purpose. It was a task she didn't relish, but always in the back of her mind was Kurt's warning about using a dull, or anything but a sharp slick blade.

Eio'br announced herself at the door and entered when she was bidden. Setting the tray down next to the two free standing chairs, Eio'br separated the food onto small dishes. While eating the aux. officer referred to the weapons laying on the bed. Aquina explained the weapons in the other closet and Eio'br began shaking her head and became increasingly nervous, until . . . "excuse . . . excuse . . . my princess." She virtually ran from the cabin. Aquina stood, at a loss to fathom . . . why, or what had she said to frighten the young woman.

The morning of the second day, after finishing a type of hot broth which she found invigorating, Aquina went to the control deck sought out the commander. Aquina stood several paces behind him until he finished with a subordinate. "Yes princess?" "Commander, I've no suitable clothes in which to fight." Looking down at herself . . . "I don't think this appropriate." "True princess, but the female officers are . . . ah . . . more slender and ummmm . . . smaller, and well??" "Commander, if I may have a large male officer's uniform, I will alter its form and make it fit." "An excellent thought princess. I believe we can do that." Dra'lr replied with a smile. Two officers happily complied, with slacks from one and tunic from the second.

She examined the glossy black material, and found it light, but incredibly tough. The scissors from her sewing kit did cut the material but only after repeated attempts, and using considerable hand strength. And then she was forced to pause frequently to sharpen the eight inch mini shears. It was the only pair that would cut the material, and that required almost two hours just to cut it along the proper lines.

Gradually with hours more in labor the alterations were almost completed making a very provocative and stylish uniform. Unbeknownst to her the slacks and tunic-like jacket were to snug, but didn't discover the mistake until all the seams et-cetera had been sewn. That's when she tried to put it on and found the tunic more than an inch to small in the bosom, and almost the same in the "seat." Annoyed with herself, Aquina took them off and began cutting the new seams. Happy and relieved she had left a decent margin of material, proceeded to let out the tunic two inches across the bosom, and an inch and a half in the slacks.

Well over an hour later she finished and tried the uniform again, but it did fit still though a bit snug in some places . . . such as the waist and crotch, but it is useable, and that was the only criteria. She knew her skills with a needle weren't sufficient to do more . . . so . . . Aquina was content with the uniform. And selecting her black chiffon blouse from the closet, stripped down putting the blouse on . . . refastened the high waist slacks, and then the tunic. At the last second, she left the tunic open from the waist up, and selecting a pair of sixteen inch patent leather boots with two inch heels to match. The last item to be included . . . a three inch wide glossy black leather belt, and she approved of the reflection looking back at her.

Other than for her ring, all she wore for jewelry was the sparkling brooch.

Aquina is all in black. Black everything except face and hands and of course the blonde-red highlited hair flowing around the fresh young face like waves in motion. She fixed the miniscule amount of make-up and left the weapons in the cabin within easy reach in case of need.

The door kind of "whooshed" open when her hand interrupted a lighted oval on the wall, and turned after stepping through, almost bumping into two female officers coming in the opposite direction. Both introduced themselves and Aquina did remember them. They asked respectively, if the princess would help them to look as stunning as she . . . herself. "Of course," she replied, flattered they should come to her. Turning she re-entered the cabin and bid the two lieutenants to come in and sit down.

"Now, how can I help you? First though call me Aquina." Both officers nodded and smiled. "Thank you, Aquina." They explained how both desperately wished to learn and use make-up. That started Aquina's tutorage amongst the women. Whether they are officers or regular crew it didn't matter. As things developed, it was a good habit she had keeping plenty of extras of brands, i.e. jars, lipsticks, powders, foundation, blush and all the other necessity's including refills. She then made a point of putting aside, to be analyzed at a later time, one of each type, brands et-cetera of make-up with a sly grin and an entreprenorial thought in her mind.

The gathering more or less broke up for most of the crew ate at that time in the ship's lounge. Both officers and crew ate at varying intervals depending on their schedule. Dra'lr announced himself and entered, after Aquina gave permission, and invited her to join him for the meal. She accepted, quickly put the tunic back on and walked up to the commander exiting the cabin together.

Though filled to capacity, it is effectively organized so that everyone has ample room irrespective of what race within the empire they might represent. The commander approached the door first and gave a nod. A chime sounded . . . and Dra'lr led Aquina in with everyone standing. As she said, "thank you." Dra'lr was helping her to sit down. Everyone sat expectantly smiling a little wondering how this person would act. He started a conversation with Aquina almost immediately, and nodded when he offered to make selections for her. She found it all very tasty, most tastes were new, but pleasant and tried some beitra. It is the first level of soft beitra, and watched everyone else drink including Dra'lr. She tried a mouthful. Aquina's eyes got bigger, and holding her lower throat coughed several times. "Wow! That's good." The whole lounge broke into laughter, but it was the good natured kind.

About fourty minutes later as they were leaving the lounge, she remarked to Dra'lr how she enjoyed the meal, and especially the beitra. Eio'br smiled, and went about her errand.

CHAP. 70

While walking they chatted about a variety of things including each other. Soon both arrived at Aquina's door, but continued on past, only to arrive at the control deck a moment later. Up the steps and while he conferred with Gri'ry, she was entranced with the main view screen. There filling the screen is an entire planetary system, although visually she could see only the star. The system is faithfully reproduced within the spatial cube. Nevertheless, it was the first time for Aquina to actually observe a planetary system from the outside . . . other than the brief glimlse of her foster planet's system after departing.

The commander walked up standing close to her back. "Is this the system Dra'lr?" "Yes princess. That is Arbus Ceti." Dra'lr said with a nod and a cold impassionate voice. His body was very close to her back and lowered his head. "I will not allow you to be harmed, my princess." Instead of answering, she turned slowly and gently moved against him looking up into his eyes. "I do not fear," and she smiled.

Aquina turned once again to the main view screen, backing until she felt his body. Slowly, she took his right hand in hers, and after some seconds brought it around her waist, holding it there. Dra'lr's mind is churning with emotion. He dare not, but the princess's signal is unmistakeable. His mind yelled caution repeatedly, and decided to wait . . . bide his time. After-all they would soon no doubt be in battle, and now was not the proper opportunity. Besides, he reminded himself, she may only be showing gratitude and not true affection.

The control deck crew nodded and smiled knowingly at each other. This is another episode adding to the fuel, the story, the accounts of things she had done.

Before leaving the control deck for her cabin, Aquina looked up at him. "It will be sometime tomorrow princess." She smiled and walked from the deck back to the comparative quiet of her cabin. Dra'lr watched her. Then turning around let out a quiet sigh and looked at the screen.

Entering the cabin, she noticed two bottles of beitra and two exquisite goblets sitting on an equally beautiful tray. She loved the goblets and spent a few minutes examining the artful workmanship, and then poured a liberal amount of beitra, sealed the bottle and sipped slowly. Taking the belt off with the translator, she put it on the counter continuing to get undressed. Changing into one of her black lace teddies, she slipped into the simple but elegant bed. About thirty inches high, it is molded into the bulkhead as a single form. Shaped like an elongated obloid, pleasing to the eye, the soft white covering was a single soft wrap. The two cushion-like pillows did not slide or move unless physically picked up and moved.

Once the common material touched itself it wouldn't slide or move unless with gentle pressure . . . it was picked up by a person's hand.

She layed under the sheet-like material finding it like silk, but warm with its own pleasing fragrance. The pillows molded themselves gently around her head with soft pressure. Aquina was asleep almost immediately and dreamt of Dra'lr.

Nine hours, ship's time, into the new day, Eio'br announced herself, but received no answer. She then knocked on the door . . . and a second time. Awakening, Aquina called out. "Come in!" The aux. officer entered carrying a tray of delicious smelling goodies. As Eio'br sat down, she quickly separated the food putting some small dishes on the table, and began to leave . . . bowed to her. "Don't leave, stay and eat with me." "Yes my princess and smiled. Eio'br began taking the other small dishes off the tray, while Aquina hurriedly dressed. Visiting the bio-compartment, she came out and finishing getting dressed, boots, belt and then sat down to eat.

Not only because of her rank, but the happenings witnessed by various crewmembers during the past few days, not to mention the biographical material, caused Aquina to be accorded a good deal of respect. Given by a people who do not impress easily, nor did they normally allow outsiders into their confidence, or the feeling of esprit-de-corps shared by the crew. Each ship's crew is a close knit family. They knew each other well and are thus able to work and live together. But above all . . . they are able to fight as a unit when the situation demanded, and or die if it is necessary to save the ship.

So it was, when the crew saw the simple but deadly weapons and the way she moved with them . . . they followed the commander's quip made earlier, and referred to her as the "warrior princess."

Aquina went forward to see the commander, but Dra'lr saw her coming first, and his blood quickened just a trifle. "What do you think?" His eyes went first down and then back up resting on her face. "I think, . . ." Dra'lr let out a small sigh. "our people will be distracted." With a half indignant look . . . "hmmmph." She turned and walked back toward her cabin smiling. And again that little area is filled with her bewitching cologne . . . Dra'lr watched her hips undulate as she walked.

Dra'lr enjoyed an enviable reputation, and was known for his risqué amorous laisons and past conquests . . . was accustomed to beautiful and exciting women. But he never had encountered anyone remotely like Aquina. Not even a close facsimile, and was not able to deal effectively with the feelings she invoked in him. More, and more he found himself thinking of her, wanting to be around her, and often fought for self control.

Going aft she found the two female lieutenants. They saluted and spent most of the day fixing and adjusting uniforms, and other such help as she could provide. The work was set aside for the meal, which she attended with the commander. But instead of their walk after the meal, she went back to her cabin, and helped other women. And for the small meal several aux. officers and a few ranks went to carry trays laden with tasty dishes back to her cabin.

Many hours later the substantial gathering began to dissolve, it being rather late, and well into their evening period. However, Dien who is feeling much stronger, arrived helped by two bio-techs and began an examination. Dien explained about the nutrient and bio-supplements that Aquina had been forced to do without . . . for too long. Therefore, she is given the one familier pill and a second with instructions they must be taken each and every day. Aquina was told the second unfamiliar tablet would stabilize her erratic "bio-clock" and slowly increase the natural genetic longevity. They departed soon afterward, and she prepared for bed.

However, Aquina slept fully clothed with the exception of her boots and weapon's belt and tunic. The tunic layed on the bed on top of her belt and weapons. She dreamt about many beautiful things and settings, but most of all . . . being in the arms of the commander.

Some hours later she awoke to the sound of an alarm. Realizing instantly what was happening, she swung shapely legs off the bed slipping on the boots at the same time. Once in the corridor, she clasped the belt on tight and ran for the control deck. She was just in time to hear . . . "Helm, how many do you count?" "So far . . . eight commander!" "Put them on the cube plot!" "Yes sir . . . closing fast commander!"

Directing an order at communications. "Send a complete record of all that has transpired, include our finding a legal and duly noted descendant of the crown prince. A princess who is aboard and all her biographical data. Also . . . about to be attacked by a force more than twice our strength!" "At once commander!" "Helm, activate all recording equipment, so that this may be recorded for future use."

Immediately she turned and ran for the first gun position. The regular gunner snapped off a salute. "Good luck my princess." "Thank you." She smiled getting into the seat and began quickly flipping switches and turned on the C'pter and master energy switches. Everything was warming nicely, and Aquina forced mental control, and relaxed measureably. This of course is duly noted in the fire control area. "Commander, first gun is occupied and battle ready, sir!" "Noted lieutenant, ahhh . . . who is operating that gun?"

Surprised the lieutenant answered . . . the princess, commander!" Dra'lr laughed. "Ha! It is the raiders who are out numbered!" The crew smiled. "Everyone to their positions and prepare to engage the enemy!"

Almost simultaneously the other two ships reported battle ready, along with the command ship, their spirits unusually high. Their own princess first of the nobility to ever fill a gun position. All that transpired is relayed to the empire, though seven hours time delay to Homeworld; the majority of the empire was watching the princess, and the ships actually engage in battle . . . almost as it happened.

The regular gunner stood just behind her a-bit . . . in goggles, with things ready for the princess. He is wound up itching, ready and privileged to be second gunner. The normal attendants, or second gunners, are in position and they shared in the overall pride felt by the entire ship.

Aquina sat with goggles on and felt the smooth even beating of her heart. She is calm, only the expectation of dealing out revenge stirred any adrenalin and to combat it . . . she began to hum. The intercom link to the "gun tub" was open and soon it filled the line to the comm. officer. Comm. reported it to the commander, who came over and listened. Aquina went from humming to singing in a soft lilting voice. She provided the voice the translator provided the words, a soldier's ballad.

"Comm., open link and ship-to-ship." "Yes commander." Instantly the song and her voice filled the three ships, and comm. recorded it securing the song permanently into the ship's C'pter. The various crews began trying to emulate the tone and words. Dra'lr smiled. He knew the fear in the ships was broken, now it would be a hard esprit-de-corp feeling . . . the three ships would fight like one crew. In a way Dra'lr felt sorry for the raiders, because they were already defeated. Normally areas of the ship are automatically monitored and filch recorded, for use by the military at a later date.

The battle had started. She melded with the gun using her mind, the super-concious, making the gun follow the motion and squeezed-off a hit. And while the raider suddenly turned, wobbling . . . fired again quickly scoring a direct hit. Her excitement and concentration increased, and the power emanating from her increased geometrically. Behind her and to one side, the opposite point or field of concentration, the gunner winced and the attendant blanched from the ever increasing pressure. They both moved out of the doorway . . . around the corner, and it is less intense. From there the gunner set up a visor-mirror to watch and record. It dawned on both of them where the psychic pressure was emanating from . . . and could only guess at its strength in front toward the raiders.

An enemy ship exploded into a ball of fiery energy. More came and Aquina scored hits enabling other gunners to destroy them. Her gunner assistant and attendant were keeping accurate records and are laughing. Still they kept coming as some medium hits had been inflicted on the empire ships, as well as one serious hit, but everyone kept firing, and so did she with devastating results. And all the while her mind pumped ever increasing energy, in front . . . out toward the enemy, it became palpable.

One ship came in wide firing at number three empire ship, and Aquina smiled and fired . . . scoring a direct hit marked by an incandescent ball of energy. Another ship came directly for her position . . . firing heavily . . . seemingly on target. The regular gunner watched in the mirror knowing they will be hit and let out an involuntary groan. But it didn't happen the energy pulses encountered something which deflected all of them but one, and it had been deflected enough to hit the top most part of the ship above Aquina's position. She did nothing . . .

Meanwhile, on the control deck a lieutenant called to Dra'lr, and Gri'ry. "Sirs, for a little while I have detected an unusual energy, which has been increasing geometrically. Only seconds ago it jumped enormously, and sensors close aboard register the energy pulses from an enemy ship have been deflected by this "field." It has enveloped almost the whole port side." The lieutenant explained. "Where does it emanate from?" Asked the commander excitedly. "From inside the ship, sir . . . ah . . . ah the area of first gun position." They went over to comm . . . "Turn all monitors on and link for first gun position!" Comm. reacted quickly not used to the commander being so excited.

What they saw caused the comm. officer to cover her mouth with a hand letting out an involuntary cry . . . for on the comm. screens was a sight to scare any normal person. Aquina sat slightly forward eyes closed, then open . . . hair billowing up undulating as if in a good breeze. When her eyes opened they flashed with blue fire, and the left arm and hand caressed the gun, while the right was on the firing stud. On the monitors, the inside anbient energy indicators, used to show escaping energy from a damaged gun were off the scales . . . all of them. But above all, it is her chant . . . first in one language then another, then still another and each time the translators coped. She then lapsed into one which defied their instruments . . . but cut through their minds, memories to that time when all tucanan youth hear and learn the temple prayers. It is the mother of all languages.

Aquina was calling to her father for guidance and help . . . to kill their enemies.

The enemy ship was coming closer. "Wait . . . wait . . . now you bastard!" He is very close, and she fired two quick bursts scoring with both . . . answered by a brilliant explosion. The gunner and attendant are laughing and yelping keeping an accurate tally. She had thus far scored three destroyed and four other hits. Another raider came from the opposite side underneath and up. Aquina tracked two quick bursts across the top of the enemy ship. It rolled and turned . . . and she squeezed off a quick third burst scoring a direct hit announced by another brilliant explosion.

Time and again number one gun scored direct and secondary hits . . . ultimately inflicting considerable damage on the attacking force; while the other guns and those of the other empire ships were also accounting for destroyed and or crippled ships.

Both Dra'lr and Gri'ry told the appropriate lieutenant to continue monitoring the first gun position and area.

The official count reported to the control deck by all three crews amounted to five raiders destroyed, two crippled and one fled the scene. Hits inflicted on the empire ships were mostly of medium damage, only one serious hit occurred. Repair personnel already on the scene in numerous areas, followed their procedures effectively according to the drills.

A lieutenant called to Gri'ry . . . and told him the energy readings are dropping very quickly in that area they discussed earlier. Gri'ry nodded, he informed Dra'lr. He attributed it to the lull in the action. Aquina sat up, moved the hair from around her face and forced herself to relax. She called to the gunner and attendant and asked for a goblet of beitra. The lieutenant answered. "A pleasure my princess." He handed her the goblet, while the gunner came into the doorway, and she drank a full mouthful . . . and she vented a deep sigh. "Hmmmmm, I do like this. Thank you second gunner." He bowed, beaming ear-to-ear. "Fantastic shooting my princess." "Ah, but then I had an excellent instructor." "Thank you my princess." But both men knew there was much more involved than mere luck. As the awesome steady pulsation of psychic energy proved they knew it had to have originated from the princess. She turned in the special seat. "Both of you . . . pour yourselves some beitra, and we'll toast." With a bow from each they filled a goblet, each and began toasting their comrades.

"Ran out of targets," quipped aux. commander Gri'ry. "I hope so." Dra'lr remarked solemnly. Dra'lr called for all crews to maintain their positions. "Stand to level two." The comm. officer instantly flashed the order. About twelve minutes later. "Commander!" "Yes helm."

"Sir! Seven more ships approaching, very fast. At least half are cruiser class, sir!" Dra'lr looked at Gri'ry then gave gyro maneuvering orders. Internal ship's comm. line carried the information. And everyone assumed their positions seconds before the order. "Battle ready, first level!" Aquina is back in her seat before the order, and readied herself . . . began concentragting. She is already part of the gun.

Immediately apparent as the battle was re-engaged, was the enemy's tactics. Instead of attacking singularly as before, they winged in two abreast; plus when disengaging a run, the raiders escaped by going inbetween the ships. They believed the imperial gunners not willing to risk shooting in the direction of their own ships.

One raider came straight for her position firing as he came without effect, then broke to Aquina's left. And just as the ship broke going inbetween the empire ships . . . she fired two quick bursts destroying him utterly. Two raiders started a run from a distance. Her C'pter picked them up and she fired two short bursts which bracketed them . . . her first misses, and fired two short bursts hitting one raider destroying it instantly. She fired three more short bursts crippling the other-or-second raider. The number two empire ship scored a direct hit plus numerous secondary hits. This meant a raider force of three remained.

Of the remaining three, one was crippled by gunners from the number three ship. But a raider somewhat larger then the others went inbetween the ships, securing itself to the main air-lock of the command ship. A good ploy, for the remaining raider did a faint . . . not actually shooting effectively drawing attention from the move of the other ship. Aquina had seen the ship sneak in and correctly guessed their purpose.

Calling to the regular gunner, "take over!" Aquina rolled out of the seat on the run. In her mind, she saw the ship come up and secure to the air-lock. And then she heard the alarm. "Repel enemy boarders!!"

She was thankful for the impulse, the thought which caused her earlier to pull the thirty inch two handed black temple sword . . . out to use. Aquina felt better with the master's sword securely strapped to her back. A short run to the main corridor, hair streaming out behind her with sword and dagger flapping against hip and leg. The woman in black had no way of knowing the action is being recorded and instantly sent out to the empire . . . Where tens of billions upon tens of billions were watching the battle first hand, and now the awesome apparition in black. What made it so unusual . . . . she is royalty.

Turning the corner, just as the commander went down wounded from enemy blaster fire, Aquina dove to the floor . . . grabbed his blaster and burned down the first two of the advanced group. Taking a grazing hit across the shoulder from one of the raiders . . . she didn't seem to notice, but grabbed Dra'lr, pulling him dragging him out of the way . . . . safely around the corner. Aquina rushed back adding her fire to the three crewmen already firing . . . . and accounted for many of the enemy in front. But their blasters are running down. Two crewmen went down wounded, the other caught by one in the leg. Her blaster ran out of charge, reinforcements were almost there, or so she supposed, but she kept going. Letting voice to a blood chilling scream of challenge, an ear splitting sound and thrice somersaulted down the corridor toward the advancing enemy. Her concentration fixed upon the hapless raiders. A malevolent mask of fury covered her face as she came out of the last vault kicking . . . . instantly killing one of the enemy. Recovering, she scooped up a blaster and fired point blank. Soon it gave out . . . and in a flash of movement the thirty inch sword came out with a ring, like a tiny bell; and the pressure continued to leap geometrically each second . . . but largely in front.

The monitors, impassionate and impersonal mounted in various locations caught all the action, made her look like an angel of death. For the deck, walls and her awesome blade . . . . covered everything in blood. She waded through the enemy leaving torn and cut . . . dismembered bodies in her wake.

More blasters ran out as an aux. two came out a side doorway firing valiantly until wounded and slumped against the wall. Aquina pushed the raiders hard killing many with her sword . . . but some were gripping their heads screaming only to see the bodies ripped apart by an unseen agent. Her hair and eyes reacted as before. She passed the black handled sword to her left hand, while the right grabbed the heavier sword. And with both swinging . . . . she cut the enemy literally to pieces.

Raiders still came through the air-lock trying to push forward, while those in front were being slaughtered. And all the while the energy pulsed and kept increasing . . .

She moved lightning fast leaping up into a split kick catching the front two simultaneously with a killing foot, on each side meeting an enemy throat. While they are falling a thin razor-like blade removed the head of the raider directly behind them. Diving to one side as she came down . . . the heavier sword swung catching the fourth across the midriff. A faint with the other blade and she lunged with the other sword, resulting in death. Slash . . . parry and riposte, again and again. Slashing, jabbed and swung with the other sword . . . . and another raider lay in pieces. Wounding one she side-stepped . . . turned out and a power kick to the sternum area killing another.

A step to the right side disarmed one raider by cutting his hand off then a slash . . . and more death. Death, the corridor is piled with it . . . bodies and pieces of bodies began yards behind her. Yet not once did she tire or slacken . . . but continued to push and kill.

It wasn't a battle . . . every citizen watching was rooted . . . stunned, the carnage so terrible . . . so gruesome. The raiders . . .

filled with horror, trying to stay alive; but fruitless, for Aquina continued to cut and slash her way through them.

A faint down on one knee thrusting around and up with both swords, and more death. After one particularly daring riposte again resulting in death, she parried-hook faint, lunge and kill. Thrusting again and more death. Another raider with a blaster, found himself on the receiving end when she threw the heavier sword burying itself in his chest. With her dagger she threw that . . . hitting a raider in the throat. Side-stepping a blow to the head, she caught the wrist and rolled breaking the arm at the shoulder, while delivering a kick to another . . . ending the one with a slash from her one remaining blade.

It is stained and covered, as she is top to bottom, with three different colors of blood. With a quick block and cut she disarmed one while slash and killing another, while delivering a knee to the side and an open hand crashing down behind the ear, causing a distinctive "crack" to be heard. She parried and half-hearted blow and thrust . . . more death. A thrust to one side . . . death. She quickly spun about . . . turn in an slashed as a raider literally lost his head. Turning she finished a cut and slash while delivering a power kick to a head cracking it like a ripe melon.

Those of the crew behind her kept their distance, terrified at the guttural sounds from her and the flashing sword . . . as a lieutenant's voice is heard above the melee. "The newab, the ancient one's newab, and her wand of death." It is said with unmistakable awe, as Aquina continued to wade through the enemy leaving shards and pieces of bodies to the sides and behind her. She seemed to gain strength and moved forward killing, disrupting their bodies . . . . like a maelstrom.

Picking up a fallen ax . . . she threw it burying itself to the hilt in a raider's chest. Spinning on her blood coated heel, her sword already coming down met more enemy bone and tissue. She continued allowing the force of the stroke to take her to the right, where with a faint . . . two power kicks . . . delivered a hand to the throat of another. But with the quick move to pick-up her heavier sword from a body . . . took a bolt from an enemy blaster . . . a grazing hit in the left side.

She screamed. A sound full of rage, not pain, and hate, and defiance. Dra'lr heard and saw with his own eyes, and still found it mystifying. There are perhaps nine or ten raiders remaining. She stood sword raised and spoke several words in that special temple language . . . and the air-lock door slammed shut, interlocks engaging.

Now in a crouch she slowly passed the black sword, now dripping with blood, from hand-to-hand . . . back-an-forth. The raiders stepped back . . . without warning she leaped into them. Being thoroughly demoralized and the air-lock door locked behind them . . . could do nothing but fight and die. She hacked to death the first four brutally, savagely cutting, stabbing . . . her sword, and now retrieved the dagger. Two died almost instantly because of loosing their heads.

Three are left and she dispatched one by sword . . . broke an arm and knee of the second, and finally . . . the leader, by the look of his uniform. With sword in hand, she smiled . . . and though he tried to defend himself . . . she toyed and played. Each stroke, or so, she cut him. The face she cut, an ear off, fingers off, chest and numerous other places were cut and gouged. Finally she tired of the sport and disarmed him, and lightning quick grasped him by the neck. And with sword in right hand held him up against the bulkhead. Slowly Aquina sank very strong, well manicured nails into his throat. He gurgled and tried to scream, eyes stark white saw only death's mask before him. Ripping her hand away, she caught him before sinking to the deck, and chopped with palm edge hard on the left side of the head.

Aquina brought her hand up slowly, then it came up quickly, and was about to bring it crashing down when two hands tried to stop her. Pumped up with adrenalin . . . the hand came down, albeit not as hard as it normally would have because aux. three was with all her strength trying to hold Aquina back.

"Stop princess, stop princess please, ugghhh . . . please!" Still in a daze, Aquina turned on the other raider . . . who wailed and screamed.

"Aquina . . . . Aquina stop!!! It is over, they are defeated!!" Ilea'nz was crying holding a hand on Aquina's arm, slick with blood, and gore. With chest rising and falling, Aquina stood still somewhat dazed covered in blood, black, red, and green all over everything.

Still with sword in hand . . . she half turned. "We won?" She asked blinking several times. Other crewmembers walked up cautiously. She turned to face them, an apparition right out of hell. Hair matted with blood, face splattered, wounded in the shoulder and a nasty wound in the side bleeding profusely. The uniform is cut, ripped and cut some more almost to shreds, entirely slick with blood and gore. The sword in her right hand is still dripping blood, the brooch hanging by a ribbon of material . . . still proclaiming-shouting her status and rank.

She still stood, though wobbly, and in a rasping tired voice. "The crews and ships?" "We are alright my princess." But Ilea'nz couldn't stop her tears. She could feel the scabbard still on her back, and with one quick sure move wiped off her sword with two fingers, one on each side of the blade, and swish . . . up over the head and deftly into the scabbard and shoved it down closed. Aquina reached for the other sword, but belt and scabbard were gone. Picking up her wet hand . . . saw the bright red blood and suddenly realized, she had been wounded . . . and her blood mingling with the rest.

"Oh, damn," and the corridor slowly tilted. She was only dimly aware of hitting the blood-gore covered floor.

Dra'lr quickly motioned to several aux. officers already in slick repair uniforms, with anxiety and concern gently picked up the princess and carried the still limp form to her cabin. Each of them had tears running down their faces, as they removed what remained of the blood soaked uniform. The brooch is affixed to the pillow and proceeded to carefully and gently cleanse their princess of blood and gore. The black sword and scabbard was laid on the wall counter. It rested there only seconds . . . when Eio'br came in . . . knelt bowing to the reclining unconscious princess, and walked softly to the sword. She picked it up with care as if expecting it to disappear and turned carried it to the two waiting soldiers . . . waiting out in the corridor.

Three bio-techs arrived and without flurry or fanfare, but moves born of countless repetition began tending to her wounds. The room is full of female officers including the three aux. officers who were with the commander on the search mission. Aux. commander Gri'ry stood in the doorway and had watched the soldiers take the sword. "It has started . . ." The senior bio-tech, and others, noticed the many faint scars on various parts of the body, as well as a larger one on the lower back toward the hip. "It seems our young princess has been wounded many times before in battle." The senior bio-tech said with respect. Immediately those inside and out in the corridor began talking and whispering about what the senior bio-tech had observed.

The senior brushed strands of hair from her face with paternal care shaking his head muttering. "Hardly more than a child . . . it isn't right for one so young . . . to have fought and seen such horror." With the nasty wound in her side tended too, they switched their attention to the superficial wound on the right shoulder. It required only a few minutes and they are almost finished.

Dra'lr entered and waved for them to stand easy, and inquired. Using low tones . . . the bio-tech explained. "If any person had come to me and asked . . . if any person with such a wound as this, could carry on a sword battle, regardless of its scope . . . no! I would say no . . . it is not possible. The fact of her not being a normal being, is more than obvious. But, the princess has been wounded in the past . . . . many times and survived." He sighed heavily. "All right, I have said what I had too. The princess has lost much blood, but it is very thick and clots quickly. Be assured commander . . . our princess will be walking soon. But how she could do all that fighting having lost so much blood . . ." The technic shook his head gathered his equipment and assistants and departed the cabin. Dra'lr nodded, his arm housed in a bio wrap looked fondly at the princess, and closed the door. He smiled and in spite of his shoulder felt good and very happy. Her breathing even, several female officers took turns watching . . . keeping their vigil, periodically alternating with others when they assumed duty schedules. The women sat and watched . . . occasionally whispering.

Gri'ry was right . . . a legend had been born.

CHAP. 71

The empire experienced a mixture of reactions. Everyone is ecstatic but there were other feelings coming to the surface. Many that had been buried for more than just generations, began to surface. Feelings such as pride, tremendous pride for the royal family, the military and themselves, and patriotism stirred, flourished and burning hot. And the more times the battle scenes were viewed, which was considerable, the hotter the flames became. Gradually it is mixed with a sense of duty culminating in part with a push, an urgency . . . to enter the military. First, perhaps a few hundred arrived at each office and building, and the military has many thousands throughout the tucanan empire and system. But, very quickly the number swelled to thousands at each locality. They brought their papers, their bodies, minds and above all . . . they have a single purpose.

But they all . . . every citizen who watched and observed, and then those who saw it later . . . she would never again be alone. No matter where she might venture throughout the empire, Aquina would have people around her, caring people for she entered their hearts with an emotional "bang." All at once she is their princess, their champion and in a shining moment showed them youthful fury, strength and valor . . . things the citizens needed to see, too be, too act. She is in their minds and on their lips, and for those working in the shipbuilding facilities, and supportive industries and complexes . . . to the orbiting yards . . . who saw, she became everything.

In one stroke, she turned the vary mundane required sword and dagger required classes in training centers, to an art form. The change, the metamorphisis was extroadinary. Students became ardent followers eager to learn and practice.

The empire down to Tucana itself, the city, the palace, court and council and especially the emperor talked of little else, but the battle. For hours and hours spatial information guild kept releasing more and more data about the princess, until all material had been released in the various mediums. Every shred of information had been given out, and the citizenry devoured all of it . . . beyond . . . buying filch recordings, reading page form plus others.

The emperor convened a meeting of all palace staff officers and began planning the festivities.

Once administrational reports were given, Dra'Ir began with his battle report.

"Met two separate attacks totaling fifteen enemy ships. All, but one which fled the scene, were destroyed or hopelessly crippled. We at one time were boarded by a total of twenty-two enemy raiders heavily armed, in which action our newly found princess effectively saved the command ship and crew, killing twenty of the enemy, and wounding two. Both survivors are in such condition as they are not expected to live. My three ships suffered several hits, many superficial hits and only one serious hit. Including the princess the number of wounded are surprisingly light, with the princess wounded twice during the above described action, and all are resting gently."

"Too date we have met and destroyed or crippled twenty-three enemy ships, twenty enemy killed personal combat, two prisoners, and one enemy ship escaping."

Finishing his report, Dra'lr mentioned to Tha' to keep an eye on the warp drive condition and went aft to inquire, and see the princess. He arrived to see a fair crowd in line outside the princess's door. Some wounded stood waiting their turn talking and gesturing discussing the battle. Those in the line began to make room deferring to the commander. "No-no, stay where you are. Rank has no privilege in this line." Dra'lr said smiling. With that he talked to some, touching a shoulder . . . patting an arm, talking working his way to the end of the line. He is amazed at how long it actually stretched. Passing many officers he exchanged knowing looks. Gazing down the line found smiling faces, heads and grins . . . releasing a small sigh. He walked back to the control deck.

"Tha'." "Yes commander." "Make up your list of all those for citations, promotions and the like." "At once commander." Tha' replied smiling. Dra'lr gazed at the main view screen only half watching the exquisite waves of color. He thought very hard about the princess and just exactly . . . how did he feel?

While he was occupied, Aquina is awake propped-up by extra cushions. Eio'br used one of the hair brushes and made Aquina's hair presentable. While aux. one Abn'te stood a pace away from the cushions and Eio'br positioned herself at the end of the bed. Ilea'nz stood by the door opening and closing it when necessary. The line swelled as more off duty crew stood waiting to see their warrior princess, and came in sometimes singularly, occasionally in pairs. Each knelt on one knee and bowed, then walked to the bed as Aquina held up her right hand. A replacement translator laying on the bed helped, as she addressed each person by name. Second and third ship's crews came first and they switched duty with the on duty personnel, so they might visit. The soldiers and gunners formed their own little groups, so for a brief period only members of each little "fraternity" visited. But each group had adopted the princess, and their greetings are filled with unaccustomed emotion and sentiment.

CHAP. 72

Meanwhile, most of the crew belonging to the command ship began the gruesome, grisly job of cleaning the main corridor of blood and gore. Dispensing of the bodies, and pieces, proved to be as difficult as it was unpleasant. The raiders had to be identified as far as group, because in many instances personal identification was not possible. An accurate count of bodies was taken and then disposed of as custom dictated in such cases. When the corridor had been thoroughly cleaned and sanitized by rad. light, all the weapons that had been saved were then cleaned and sanitized using much the same apparatus. An aux. two and three sorted through all the weapons and discarded equipment, until they found the princess's heavier sword, dagger and belt with scabbard and sheath.

These they cleaned again, sharpened the striking edges, polished the grips, and brought them to the commander for suggestions. Dra'lr decided after several minutes to present them to the emperor.

Aquina had perhaps twenty minutes to rest, be helped into the bio-compartment, and back to bed, and several decent sips of beitra before members of the crew started lining up outside. And as in the other two ships, the wounded that could walk entered first. As before she called each by name speaking with each person. More of the crew came in then relieved counterparts so they could visit. The gunners and soldiers hung back . . . until last, and gunners went in first. Her instructor was last and kneeling next to the bed . . . kissed her right hand.

Abn'te quickly looked away trying to blink back a tear, then looked back again. It is the soldiers turn next. The four of them came in together and knelt, bowed . . . the first soldier carried her sword wrapped in black cloth, and with care returned it to the counter. Each then did the same as the gunners. Two bio-techs entered and received permission to examine the principle wound. It required only a few minutes and the senior bio-tech renewed the salve wrap and asked Aquina to swallow some nutrient . . . about a shot glass size amount of green liquid. Two pills followed, and moments after the bio-techs took their leave . . . she began to get sleepy. In bare minutes, Aquina is sound asleep . . . dreaming. Abn'te and Eio'br sat down to watch the sleeping princess. Ilea'nz returned to her duty schedule, and is asked repeatedly about the princess.

When Aquina awoke, it is one hour past mid-day . . . she had slept for nine hours and some odd minutes. Immediately the aux. officers were on the side of the bed asking how she felt. "Much better . . . and hungry." Abn'te asked what selection of dishes she would prefer? Aquina smiled, and said simply, she wanted something hot; and for each of them to eat with her. The three bowed and left the cabin.

Impatient and tired of being in bed, she tried to move and found her side sore and smarted a-bit when she touched the "wrap" with only the slightest pressure. But, it wasn't painful and she was happy for that. Aquina thought now was a good time . . . and took a deep breath, air which held a slightly higher percentage of oxygen, and began to slowly move both legs off the side of the bed. She felt it is important to try this on her own. Afterall, if she were going to fall on her face . . . she didn't want witnesses.

Wearing nothing more than the bottom part of a cut-off teddy, she gingerly put more weight on her feet. It wasn't to bad . . . and a-bit more . . . and slowly holding onto the bed, she stood erect. Taking several breaths until the momentary dizziness faded, she moved carefully along, one foot in front of the other holding onto various things including the wall. With the soreness becoming more manageable, she practiced walking heading for the drawers over by the counter. Feeling her left side throb, and wincing occasionally, Aquina finally reached the proper drawer. Slowly she pulled out a black teddy and slowly pushed off the flimsy remnant remaining from the one cut away by the bio-techs. Made of silk, it slipped on easy though some arm movement caused her to wince . . . it still wasn't to bad.

Aquina had moved away from the drawer to the counter when her three friends announced themselves. "Come in." The three entered, aghast at finding her standing and walking. Setting down the trays . . . Abn'te was first to pour a liberal amount of beitra into the princess's goblet. While the other two busied themselves separating dishes. She took one healthy sip . . . then another and felt a little better. While Aquina sipped the beitra, Abn'te opened the closet holding most of the hangable items of clothing. Abn'te asked which will she wear? Aquina, on the other hand asked all three of them what colors would they choose, and the feeling was unanimous. "Okay then, the long turquoise blouse and the black glossy satin slacks. A wee bit painful, but that soon passed as they helped her dress. Leaving the blouse out, Aquina selected a narrow black leather belt, buckled it large and left the thing to ride loosely on her hips. With that finished, she sat down slowly and as Abn'te brushed out the long tresses . . . she quickly applied a certain degree of make-up, paying special attention to her eyes. Aquina did it in such a way as to draw attention to their size . . . the depth was already there.

Immediately afterwards they, all four sat down and ate. Aquina again watched and learned more about etiquette, and tried some new foods and a sauce. She first finished a fair sized bowl of broth that has a hint of something close to cinnamon. That was followed with warm cakes, small medium green things which the officers explained was made from a grain and a number of vegetables. The sauce used on the cakes was not unlike honey just as thick, but this was spicy and its flavor hinted of almonds, and it is hot.

It fairly steamed when she applied some to a cake and waited a moment for it to cool. By the time they finished eating almost another hour passed.

Just as aux. two and three exited carrying the trays back to the lounge, the commander was leaving the control deck; but not before nodding to crew members, and issueing some special orders. He spoke to other crew while on his way to the princess's cabin, and smiled. Dra'lr spoke into the intercom device next to her door, grateful for normal corridor traffic. His heart rate increased "a hair" at the sweet melodic voice, "enter." He is surprised to see her standing and dressed. "Are you well enough to be standing princess?" "Yes, I think so, but may I use your arm . . . ?"

"My pleasure princess."

"Commander, . . . what were our casualties?" "None. Though we do have wounded . . . but are recovering." "Wonderful, I should like to see them, if you will help me." "My honor and pleasure." Dra'lr remarked bowing his head brightened with a large smile. Her side throbbed and she winced occasionally on the way to the door. At the last moment, Aquina turned. "Do I look alright?" "You will always look alright, princess." "Thank you Dra'lr." And though sore she managed a smile. Walking out on the arm of the commander into the corridor filled with crew . . . to cheers, and a goblet handed to her . . . filled with beitra. Before she could say anything . . . "We honor our own," was the unanimous chant. "Thank you." She said.

"The crew and I honor you . . . for stopping the raiders and giving us time to rally . . . all would have been lost and you taken prisoner." Dra'lr said with a smile. "But all of you fought . . . it wasn't just me. I honor you for fighting with me, for I came a stranger to you." Dra'lr kissed her hand lightly. "It is that special quality that marks you for what you are."

"Princess. I believe I can speak for all three ships . . . you ceased being a stranger long ago." She looked up at him and smiled, "thank you." Aquina drank some of the soft beitra and swayed a little. Dra'lr caught her and . . . "are you alright?" "Yes, just a little dizzy. Oh . . . that is good." And everyone laughed. "May I have a little more please?" "Princess, you can have anything your heart desires."

As everyone looked-on and grinned knowingly, Aquina looking up into the commander's eyes, "careful commander, I may one day hold you to that."

Turning again to the crew. "Thank you. You all make me feel warm and welcome." Dra'lr then helped Aquina to walk, and though forced to limp she insisted on visiting the wounded. Though plainly sore, she talked to them calling each by name. Each wanted to see her and touch her . . . just not daring to believe the recorded scenes. They, each and together, were incredulous . . . she had done the fighting and still lived.

Aquina talked to each, and sometimes in pain . . . she fed them, and let them touch her hair . . . but each one kissed her right hand. Aquina is sore and it hurt to bend over, but these are her people, and when she looked at Dra'lr . . . she felt many things. Above all, she is going home, and although it is a bad time for her people, she is happy.

A whole new beginning for her and the empire. And she is excited . . . there is a war to fight . . .

To be continued . . . .

